FAR SIDE OF THE MOON

Settler Chronicles Book 2

JEANNETTE BEDARD

Cover design by Tiffany at Dark Matter Book Covers

Chapter One

Nigel Maximillian West slumped in his chair. The rhythmic sound of his fingers tapping against his desk's polished wooden surface reverberated through his spacious office. The three people in the room with him remained absolutely silent. He knew they feared him and he liked it that way.

Ignoring the bodyguard stationed beside him—of no more importance than the half-drunk coffee growing cold on his desk—Nigel looked out the bank of floor-to-ceiling windows that ran along the wall to his left. The planet below rotated past, first revealing Africa and then the Atlantic Ocean. He yawned at the boring view, not bothering to cover his mouth, before turning to the snarling tiger before him.

"You sure that's the one?" Nigel couldn't be bothered to remember either antiquities dealers' names.

The animal's snarl wasn't exactly as he remembered it. Plus, its face didn't look natural—as though the taxidermist wanted to make the animal even scarier than it had been in life.

"Yes. Peggy Plum donated it to the British Museum in 1936," said the antiquities dealer on the left.

The woman wasn't quite pretty enough to bother looking at,

so Nigel continued staring at the tiger. Its head rested on one of the leather chairs facing his desk almost as though it was attending a meeting. He smirked at the thought.

She continued, "this is the animal her husband shot in South Africa in spring of 1887." Her voice was beginning to waver, betraying her nerves—she knew he was a descendent of one of the founding families of The Conglomerate, and was appropriately intimidated.

"The museum must have immediately boxed it up," the other dealer volunteered. His jiggling jowls made Nigel cringe. "It's no wonder. This feline is a terrifying sight. I wouldn't want to look at it for any length of time."

Before Nigel could respond they were interrupted by his assistant Fran barging into the room, her hand-held scroll computer in one hand and an electronic cube in the other. Her high heels clicked loudly as she strode across the polished marble floor, drowning out the sound from his fingers.

Nigel's fingers froze, and he frowned when he saw the dour faced Ben Snow following behind her. If Ben hadn't been descended from one of the founders like he was, Nigel would've banished him long ago. Looking at Fran and Ben, he let out an audible sigh.

"Fine, fine, I'll see that you are paid," said Nigel, waving the antique dealers away. The two backed away as though uncertain if they needed to bow before leaving his presence.

"Speak to the receptionist out front," said Fran as she passed the pair, her eyes on the tiger. "He'll arrange payment and transportation back to Earth."

Stopping directly in front of his desk, Fran levelled her gaze on him. He had never managed to intimidate her, which drove him nuts. But, unlike anyone else in his acquaintance, Nigel knew that he would be lost without her. She'd been his late father's assistant and knew the ins and outs of The Conglomerate to a level he'd never comprehend.

Fran waited to speak until the antiquities dealers were out of the room. "We just intercepted a portion of the first message to the Colonizing Counsel from Thesan," she announced in a neutral tone, her face giving nothing away. It never did.

"Very good," said Nigel, his tone practically a purr. His eyes lingered on the tiger as he resumed drumming the fingers of his left hand on the desk.

He'd sent one of his best agents to oversee sabotage efforts aimed at demoralizing the colonists on Thesan and leaving them with no option but to call for evacuation. His ship was on hand for the 'rescue.' Then he would claim the planet and its riches. Years of scheming had gone into ensuring that planet fell into Conglomerate hands—his hands. Just thinking of his brilliant plan put a smile on his face.

"Your agent failed," Fran stated in her characteristic flat tone.

At her words, Nigel abruptly stopped drumming his fingers. They hung poised like claws over the desk's surface. Slowly, he balled his hands into fists and drew a deep breath. For a split second he wondered if he misheard, but this was Fran. She never gave him misinformation. Which meant that, for the first time in the years he'd employed Lucy Snow, Ben's estranged wife, she had failed him.

"What did you say?" He put both hands on his desk as he slowly rose, glaring at Fran. As was his practice, he ignored Ben.

"Listen to this," she said, placing the cube-shaped device on his desk before stepping calmly back to sit in the empty chair beside the taxidermy tiger head. Her posture remained as erect as ever. Ben stood directly behind her as if using her as a shield.

Colonizing Counsel, this is Lucas Ordaz.

The recording was tinny, and the name wasn't the one Nigel had been expecting. He knew the names of the key players, but this wasn't one of them.

"Who's this guy?" demanded Nigel, waving towards the cube.

Fran pursed her lips reproachfully as she paused the recording.

"Lucas Ordaz is a computer technician in the operations group of the *Settler III* colonizing mission to Thesan. He was third-in-command."

Nigel sat down and leaned back in his chair. His anger hadn't dissipated, but he knew he had to stay calm in order to salvage his mission. There was too much at stake to do anything less. "His name sounds familiar. What else has he done?"

"A few years back he commanded the mining ship *Angler* when it was sent out to intercept the asteroid 101946 Tlaloc. The ship was destroyed, and he was the only survivor," said Fran in a matter-of-fact tone.

Nigel remembered the grand cluster fuck that mission had been. He'd been tempted to show up at the trial that followed to personally slice off the disloyal man's left pinky with a serrated knife. "Resume," Nigel commanded, waving towards the cube. Fran leaned forward and re-started the recording.

I've stepped in as Acting Commander of the Thesan colony. We've had some setbacks, including a number of fatalities; however, we've made progress towards setting up our permanent colony. Of note, we've discovered extensive indium deposits on the surface. At our next comms window, we'll accept small-scale extraction proposals. Revenue from the indium will allow us to achieve our self-sufficiency goal sooner than originally projected. I'm sending our full report of the events since our initial crash. Also, I've attached evidence of sabotage by a member of our crew. These acts of sabotage were supported by The Conglomerate, as is apparent in the evidence.

When the recording ended, Nigel turned to stare out the windows unseeingly as North America rolled by, rubbing his clean-shaven chin. Fran stared at him while Ben appeared to be quivering in his boots. The bodyguard stood stoically beside Nigel, his face revealing nothing in response to the shocking news Fran had delivered.

After a long silence, Nigel turned to Fran and ordered her to play it again. She restarted the recording. While it played Nigel kept his eyes on Ben.

The Conglomerate fell under legislation that prevented commercial organizations from meddling in the Colonizing Council's projects. The new colonies were autonomous—at least that's what the public was supposed to think. This kind of publicity was bad for The Conglomerate, but his mind was already churning, finding ways he could fix this.

"She had just one job to do," accused Nigel after the recording ended. "She screwed up."

"We've been divorced for five years," said Ben, his eyes darting away from Nigel's penetrating gaze.

Nigel kept his eyes on Ben, forcing him to hold his gaze, but the pleasure he usually felt from watching someone squirm remained absent. Frustrated, he snatched up his half-drunk coffee and threw it at Ben. The man had no time to dodge, and the mug hit him in the chest, narrowly missing Fran's perfectly coiffed head as it dropped to the stone floor with a thud. A wet, brown stain marred the pristine white of Ben's shirt.

"I need Thesan," said Nigel emphasizing every word. "That colony needs to fail!"

"What could possibly be on that world that you want? Indium is rare, but not worth extreme measures." Despite his obvious terror, Ben's tone was defiant.

Ben's unexpected boldness unnerved Nigel. The Snow family line went back as far as the West's and Nigel's ancestors' journals had been clear; with the Snow line came cowardliness punctuated with rare acts of rash boldness. This was the first time in all his dealings with Ben that he'd seen any hint of that boldness.

"Bring me your boy!" Nigel snarled. "I want him to show me a vision of what's to come." In Nigel's opinion, that weedy boy, Ben and Lucy's sole offspring, was the only thing that redeemed the Snow line.

"Can't," said Ben. His trembling tone held a trace of smug satisfaction.

Nigel pounded a fist onto his desk, making Ben flinch. "What do you mean, *can't?*"

"I sent Julien away with his mother and I hear the two of them have stayed behind on Thesan. You can't use my boy as your pawn anymore." Ben's defiant words contradicted his fear-filled posture.

Nigel stared at Ben. He pictured wrapping his hands around Ben's neck and squeezing, cutting off the man's air. The fantasy calmed him, reminding him that he was still the one in control, regardless of Ben's unwelcome news. Besides, as satisfying as it would be to indulge his rage, Nigel knew Fran would intervene and prevent him from murdering the idiotic man.

Sitting back into his chair and tapping his fingers together, Nigel feigned equanimity. He stared at his fingers for a few moments, evaluating his options.

Regaining control of the Thesan situation was what he needed, and that included first getting the boy back and then making the loathsome colonizers pay for daring to thwart him. There was still time to accomplish this. During his last session with the boy, Nigel had seen how the end game would play out on Thesan. That planet was key, but the colonists would only get in the way.

Turning his head, he glanced at his bodyguard, then gave him a puzzled look. He couldn't remember if he'd ever seen the man before or not.

"Your name?"

"Amar Yurkovich, sir."

"Are you new?"

"I've been part of the station's security force for three years."

"Really?" Nigel swivelled his chair so he could get a better look at the man. The guard was oversized and likely not very smart, just how he liked them. That made them obedient. He couldn't tell any of them apart and didn't need to. "Throw Dr. Snow out an airlock."

"Yes sir," said Amar, without a hint of emotion in his tone.

As the bodyguard moved unquestioningly toward his target, Ben held up a hand in panic. "No wait!" he pleaded, taking a step back.

Nigel said nothing as the burly man grabbed Ben's arm and started dragging him towards the door.

"May I interject?" asked Fran in a calm tone. Behind her, Amar stopped but didn't let go of Ben. She held Nigel's gaze, her dark eyes less forgiving than slate. "Dr. Snow is a descendant of the founders," she reasoned "Unlike the others, he's not expendable."

Nigel let out a ragged breath well aware of the eyes on him. "Ben has defied me and must pay," he said through gritted teeth.

"Of course he must pay," she said. "But you have an entire team who can help with that. That's why you created the Detention and Interrogation Department."

Fran was right. Giving his team in Detention and Interrogation new fodder, especially someone as high ranking as Ben Snow, would serve to elevate Nigel's power. He looked at Amar. "Alright, take him there."

As Amar dragged the protesting Ben away, Nigel gave his attention to Fran, forcing himself to relax.

"Did you get a copy of this report that Thesan sent?" he asked. At Fran's nod, he continued. "Does the report say why Ms. Snow failed?"

"One of the colonists figured everything out," she said.

"Who?"

"Margo Murphy."

Fran fiddled with her scroll then projected a 3-D revolving image of the woman's face between them. The hologram showed a woman with curly, shoulder length red hair and a pale face coated in a generous spray of freckles. She wasn't the sort of woman who invited a second glance, at least not from Nigel.

Nigel felt his rage boiling just beneath the surface. If only she wasn't out of reach...

"Who the hell is she?" he snapped.

"The colony's entomologist."

"My plans were ruined by a damn bug collector?"

Fran consulted her scroll. "It says here she's trained as a lepidopterist," she said, as if that fact made some kind of difference.

"Oh, that's so much better." Nigel abruptly stood, walking over to his panoramic windows and gazing out unseeingly at the familiar view.

Fran flicked off the hologram and put her scroll on his desk before moving to stand beside him. "We've already initiated Plan B," she said. "But that means we may not be able to recover the boy."

He forced himself to watch the planet below rotate for a few moments, keeping his temper in check.

"Perhaps he's already shown me everything I need," said Nigel as an idea occurred to him. He didn't share it with Fran, but instead said, "One way or another, everything ends on Thesan."

Chapter Two

Lucas Ordaz, current commander of the Thesan colony, crossed his arms as he leaned back in his chair. Only Iva sat at the consoles in front of him. The other two workstations in the Control Room—one beside him and the other beside Iva—were empty. Beyond the four consoles, a glass wall and three steps down separated them from the banks of servers. Above the consoles a row of screens could display information from any of the workstations. Currently, they were blank.

For now, Lucas and Iva were the only two in the room. The other colonists were still reeling from the previous commander Craig Spare's betrayal and the fire that had nearly killed them all just hours ago.

His fingers felt twitchy—even the stub of his missing pinky —and he clenched his jaw in irritation. It surprised him how much effort it took to force himself to let Iva do the work. He would rather operate the controls himself and bring the screens to life—that was his job before the Commander and then the Acting Commander had been killed, but in his new role it was important to let Iva do the tasks assigned to the Operations team. He brushed his dark hair out of his eyes and looked away from Iva.

Behind him and three steps up, the doors to the Loop stood open. The circular corridor connected the sections of the *Settler III* colony. The colony's structure had started out as the single-use space ship that brought them to Thesan. Their terrifying crash landing had warped the structure in places and permanently damaged it in others, but it had remained airtight and mostly functional. Over the last 115 days, the one-time-ship had been converted to their home/food production facility.

On Lucas's right was the commander's office. That space was his now, but he wasn't ready to use it. The thought of clearing out the belongings of both the original commander, Ikue Hori, and her replacement, Craig Spares, hit a raw nerve. Gut clenched, Lucas resumed staring at the back of Iva's head.

"The computers have collated enough satellite data for visuals," Iva finally announced over her shoulder after what felt to Lucas like an eternity. He could have performed the same task in half the time.

Iva turned from her display to look at him. Her short, dark hair framed her delicate features as she waited expectantly for directions.

"Let's take a look," he ordered, jerking his chin authoritatively towards the large black screens. His voice sounded odd, likely due to his badly bashed nose—a reminder of how he'd ended up in charge of this cursed, neonate colony light-years from Earth.

When he and Camila had been accepted to join this mission, Lucas never imagined that he'd end up in command. As third-in-command, he'd been a comfortable distance from the unwanted responsibility. But Commander Hori died two months ago and Acting Commander Craig Spares had been dead for less than a day, which placed Lucas in a role he neither envisioned nor wanted.

Part of him wondered if he'd be dead soon, too, although

that seemed unlikely now that they'd identified the saboteur. The fact that Craig caused each of the mission's many catastrophes and 20 fatalities was difficult for Lucas to process, so he pushed it out of his mind. Instead, he focused on his immediate tasks. The first thing he'd have to do as commander would be to figure out how to improve morale.

Unaware of his inner turmoil, Iva turned back to her display and tapped a few keys, revealing a satellite view of Thesan on one of the large screens. Lucas leaned further back in his chair to take in the live image.

In their three months on the planet, they'd never had working satellites, so this was his first view; yet, it wasn't the epic moment he'd imagined before they'd left Earth. His dismal thoughts and his throbbing face were constant reminders of what he'd lost. Camila, the only woman he had ever loved, had been an early victim of the saboteur, dying on the day they'd arrived. She lay buried outside beside her 19 colleagues, all victims of various accidents. Except they hadn't been accidents.

"Stop it," he whispered. He dropped his gaze from the screen. *Focus! You can't afford to feel sorry for yourself right now. Get control of yourself, Ordaz!* The survivors would be relying on him as their leader. Falling apart wasn't an option.

"What's that?" When he saw Iva squinting at him, it felt as though she was probing for his weakness.

"Nothing," he answered as he looked back up at the screen.

By habit, he brought up a hand and rubbed his nose, but the action rewarded him with shooting pain and streaming eyes. He'd avoided looking in the mirror, but he knew his nose was broken. *At least it had stopped bleeding.* The memory of Craig swinging the atmo suit's helmet at his face was still fresh.

Margo, someone he'd briefly suspected might be their saboteur, had figured out who it was. Without her, they would've been too late to stop Craig. Gary, one of the colony's two doctors, had shot Craig in the end. The pair had saved them all, and both almost were almost killed in the process. Gary's identical twin brother Neil, their other doctor, was still busy patching up the knife wound Gary had sustained while fighting Craig. Lucas only had a broken nose and attending to that could wait until after the doctor finished treating his hero brother.

With a stifled sigh, he forced himself to focus on the satellite feed. Thesan, grey as always, loomed large. At mid-latitudes, the planet was bathed in continuous sunlight from the system's two suns, Helios and Sol. Even with all the light, temperatures always stayed well below freezing.

For the first time he was seeing a live image of the detailed surface features, including the ridge of out-of-place mountains separating the hemisphere they resided in from the northern half of the planet. From this distance, the feature looked like a dark band circling the planet's equator. In fact, the ridge had once been a planetary ring whose orbit had decayed until it crashed into the surface.

Helios' blinding white light lit up the plain, leaving it looking featureless from the satellite's altitude. The large plateau containing their colony looked flat and inhospitable. They were lucky *Settler III* crash landed on the plain rather than in the nearby ragged mountains. Lucas wanted to look away. *We're alone out here, aren't we?*

He forced himself to examine where their Centre Module had landed. That module had been the central hub of their circular colony ship. Jettisoned just before they crashed, it had fared better than *Settler III*, sustaining no damage when it landed in a nearby canyon. Margo had been the first of them to visit the Centre Module, taking refuge there the day before, returning barely an hour before the final confrontation with Craig.

"Where's The Conglomerate ship?" asked Lucas.

The ship's presence in orbit had been another shock. He still couldn't believe Craig had been taking orders from them and that the ship had been sitting in orbit for three long months waiting for the right moment to swoop in and claim Thesan. At least now that the satellites were operational, they could track it.

"I'm still picking up its signal. The *CS Compliance* has left orbit and seems to be on a course for the wormhole, although I'm not sure if they'll make it on time. We captured some images of the vessel—let me show you." Iva's fingers flew on the keyboard. A small ship appeared on the second screen. "It looks like a newer model scout ship."

"Any weapons?"

Iva looked at him and frowned. "You know as well as I do that commercial space vessels are not authorized to be armed."

"Nevertheless, I want you to check." After the string of disasters they'd suffered—all attributable to The Conglomerate —he would assume nothing when dealing with that monopoly-seeking organization.

He feared they might take a more direct tactic to force the colony to surrender their claim to Thesan. Every colonizing mission allowed for the possibility that, if the colonists unanimously voted to abandon the planet due to hardship or unforeseen circumstances, whoever rescued the colonizers could stake a claim on that planet. In their case, anyone staking a claim on Thesan would make a fortune from the minerals Margo had discovered. The Conglomerate had known about these rich mineral deposits and attempted to make the colony fail and request a rescue.

On top of the recent events, he had personal reasons not to trust The Conglomerate. He'd once commanded a Conglomerate ship similar to the *CS Compliance*. He rubbed the stump of his left pinky, The Conglomerate's signature punishment for those who failed them. After that fiasco, Camila had insisted they apply to join this far-off colony to escape the black mark left on his record.

Iva displayed multiple close-up views of the ship. "They don't appear to be armed. Their engines are state-of-the-art though—ion drives." Her tone held a note of envy. "It's a fast ship. Wait, let me calculate their speed." She switched to a navigation simulation and did some calculations. "They'll make it to the wormhole in about 10 days, but that won't do them any good. The window to Earth will have closed by then."

Lucas stared at the image of the ship. *Why are they rushing if the next window is five months away?* He frowned, his mind racing to find answers.

"At least they're leaving without causing us more trouble," he said, still with no idea why the ship was racing towards a wormhole that would close before they arrived.

"Shift the view to Thesan's surface," Lucas requested.

Iva worked the controls until a high-altitude view of Thesan reappeared. The two of them watched the slowly revolving landscape of their new home as it orbited its two suns.

"Zoom slowly towards our settlement." *It hurt just to talk!* He would need to see the doctor soon and get his nose realigned. *And get pain meds!*

As the view gradually zoomed into the plain that was their home it felt like he was a space traveler drifting silently through the atmosphere. When a large gouge in the landscape almost bisecting the plateau became visible. Lucas recognized it as the result of their landing or, more accurately, their crash. At the end of the scar, the ring and dome of the *Settler* became visible.

"Keep zooming."

Their colony soon filled the screen. The geometrical shapes of the massive greenhouse dome grew until Lucas could make out the bolts used in its construction.

"That's close enough. Let's take a look around."

Iva panned away from the dome across the reflective glass roof and then down to the ground. She paused the camera for a moment over the long row of graves before continuing towards the outside of the ring where a blast pattern littered with green debris came into view. The remnants of the entomology lab. Craig had intended for Margo to die that morning as she'd found proof that Craig was the saboteur, but his attempt to kill her in her own lab had thankfully failed. Lucas shuddered at the thought of what would have happened if Craig had been successful. Using Margo's evidence, Lucas had submitted a report to the Colonizing Counsel proving The Conglomerate's criminal duplicity.

Lucas almost smiled—his throbbing face cut that short—at the screen when he saw someone in an atmo suit by the blast debris reclining in a pink chair and looking out at the horizon. Margo Murphy, their entomologist. AKA colony saviour.

"I see Margo's still out there." Lucas lifted his hand to rub his nose but caught himself at the last moment and scratched his head instead. After what she'd been through, he didn't blame her for enjoying the peaceful setting. *Maybe, I should go out and join her. Things here can wait...*

"There's an incoming voice message," announced Iva, interrupting his thoughts.

Lucas leaned forward. "A response from Earth? Already? How is that possible?"

"No, not Earth. The signal is originating from within Thesan's atmosphere."

Lucas froze and his heart began to race. All the colonists were accounted for and The Conglomerate ship had left orbit. So, who would be sending them a message?

"Put it on speaker," ordered Lucas, forcing his voice to remain calm.

Iva flicked a switch.

"*Settler III*, this is Shuttle BX-86 requesting permission to land," said a female voice.

A shuttle could only have come from The Conglomerate ship. The fact that one was approaching Thesan shot Lucas to his feet. He strode in front of his workstation so that he was standing next to Iva.

Iva muted the comms and turned to look up at Lucas. "The ship is already too far away for that shuttle to make it back to them."

"Shit." He rubbed his forehead. *Why had the* CS *Compliance stranded their own shuttle?* "Open the comms channel."

"To whom am I speaking?" Lucas asked when Iva signalled that the channel was open.

"Lucy Snow."

Lucas inhaled sharply—he knew Lucy Snow! And there was only one thing he wanted to do with her the next time he met her—wrap his hands around her scrawny neck and cut off her air. She'd been sitting in orbit gloating over their suffering, waiting for them to fail. She was The Conglomerate contact who'd been collaborating with Craig. *My wife is dead because of her!*

Lucas had the power to deny her request to land, deny her request for refuge. He clenched his fists at his side to prevent himself from doing to the console what he'd like to do to her neck.

"21 people died because of you," accused Lucas finally, including Craig in the death toll.

"I acknowledge that. But I have a child with me and he's sick. You can do what you want with me, I just want to make sure my boy is safe." When Lucas didn't immediately respond, Lucy sweetened the deal. "You'll also get this shuttle. I know you've lost all yours."

Of course she knows! She's the one who designed the accidents that rendered their two shuttles useless. Feeling the intensity of Iva's gaze on him, Lucas turned away. He swallowed, clenching and unclenching his fists.

"I don't trust you. Put the boy on," he ordered.

If there really was a sick child, he couldn't deny her request to land. But, what was Ms. Snow doing with a sick child? And what would he do with Ms. Snow if he gave her permission to land? The colonists would freak out when they learned that Lucas was giving refuge to The Conglomerate minion who'd engineered all their mishaps. Since there was no official judicial system on Thesan, how could they deal appropriately with the person responsible for all the horrors that had befallen them? *Is a lynch mob the solution? Should we throw Ms. Snow out an airlock?*

"Hello? Will you help us? Will you let us land?" The tinny voice was clearly that of a child.

Lucas and Iva exchanged a look. Sick or not, he couldn't turn the boy away.

Iva muted her mic. "Who is Lucy Snow and why would she have a child with her on a Conglomerate ship? Doesn't that strike you as odd?"

"You don't know the half of it," Lucas muttered, turning away from Iva's questioning gaze as he mentally evaluated their options.

Providing refuge for Lucy Snow would only throw a wrench into their already precarious situation. *But what choice do I have given the sick child onboard her stranded shuttle? And why had she been stranded?* As he asked the question of himself, Lucas finally realized the full implications of Lucy Snow hurtling toward Thesan in that shuttle. She'd failed The Conglomerate, which meant her hand now likely looked a lot like his. And The Conglomerate had banished her to the planet she'd sabotaged. If ever a punishment fit a crime, that one did. Resisting the urge to rub his nose, he exhaled slowly as he looked at Iva, indicating she unmute the comms.

"BX-86, you have permission to land," he transmitted then reached past Iva and muted the comms.

"If Lucy Snow is who I think she is, that isn't going to go over well," she commented.

"No shit." He slumped into the empty chair beside Iva. "But I don't see any other option. Not with a child on board."

Iva nodded but didn't say anything for a moment. "But then what?"

"We play it by ear." Lucas leaned forward, putting his elbows on his knees. "Will her shuttle fit in our hangar bay?"

Iva turned back to her screen. "Yes, it's a compatible model."

"How long until she lands?"

"She's less than ten minutes away," Iva answered, then added, "What do you think is wrong with the kid?"

Lucas shrugged. "Re-open the channel to the shuttle." Iva flipped a switch. "What is the nature of your boy's illness?"

"He has a chronic condition. I'll explain everything to your doctors when I arrive," Ms. Snow replied.

"I'll bring a doctor to the hangar." Lucas ran a hand through his hair. Fixing his nose would have to wait. "Don't expect a warm welcome. *Settler* out."

"I'll guide her in," said Iva, after terminating the link to the shuttle.

"Okay," said Lucas.

He didn't want to face Ms. Snow alone, but he also didn't know who he should take with him. He stopped himself from rubbing a hand across his face and instead massaged the back of his neck as he watched Iva flick through screens on the main monitor. For a brief moment he saw Margo sitting outside in her atmo suit. Margo had stopped the saboteur. She was the only person capable of helping him deal with the treacherous Lucy Snow.

"Patch me through to Margo," Lucas ordered.

Iva nodded and flipped a switch and put the view of the colony back on the main screen. "Okay, go ahead."

"Margo, meet me in the main hangar right away. We're expecting a visitor." Lucas watched as Margo, still sitting outside her destroyed lab, sat up.

"Say what? I thought you said a visitor?"

"You heard right. I'll explain when you get there," He knew about Margo's history with Lucy Snow. "You're not going to like it," he added before he broke off comms.

"I'm going to go get Neil," he said to Iva." He's likely finished patching up Gary and I need Neil in the hangar bay when Ms. Snow arrives. You'll have to hold the fort here."

"Sure. But, if this Lucy Snow really was Acting Commander

Spares' puppet master, things are going to go from bad to worse!"

"Tell me something I don't already know," Lucas said as he turned and walked out of the Control Room, wincing as the blood throbbed painfully in his aching nose.

Chapter Three

"Ms. Snow is *here?*" Margo had joined Lucas in the shuttle maintenance bay. She'd shed her atmo suit, but at Lucas's unwelcome announcement, she almost wished she still had her helmet so she could hit him with it. Maybe another blow from a helmet would realign his broken nose. *But Ms. Snow? Here?*

Even though he had drawn himself up as tall as he could, he was still a hand-width shorter than her. His grim expression was augmented by his swollen nose and bruised face. She tried to feel sorry for him, but couldn't. Instead, she glared at him.

She looked over at the closed door separating the maintenance bay where she stood from where the incoming shuttle would land. Any minute now, her nemesis would be waltzing back into her life. Margo's skin crawled at the thought of being in the same space with Ms. Snow. *In charge for only a few hours and Lucas had already been stupid enough to let that villain into their home!*

"And… you gave her permission to land? Are you nuts?"

Lucas flinched at her accusation. "What would you have done?"

"Not let her land!" Margo clenched her fists.

"We can't do that," said Lucas. "We need to deal with her in a civilized way."

"No we don't! *She's* not civilized. You've seen what she's capable of!"

"Yes, but we're the founders of this colony. Our actions will define our future here, our children's future. We didn't come here to build a lawless society." Lucas rubbed the stump of his missing pinky finger on his left hand. "And we're not going to employ the same tactics as The Conglomerate. That's not happening. Not on my watch." Lucas raised his hand to rub his nose, but stopped before touching it.

"So you just invited her in? No questions asked? What the hell, Lucas!"

"Margo, she has a child with her."

"A child?" Margo took a step back and folded her arms across her chest.

"Her son. Apparently he's sick."

Margo opened her mouth to respond just as the door to the Loop slid open. Neil, medical bag in hand, walked in. She still did a double take sometimes when she saw her husband's identical twin. Once she started interacting with them it was relatively easy to tell them apart—Neil was easy-going and friendly, whereas Gary was uptight, or so she used to think. Recent events cast Gary in a different light. They'd fought for their lives against Craig, and Gary had saved her life. She'd seen a whole new side of the man she'd agreed to marry, sight unseen, at the start of their voyage.

"What's this about a sick boy?" Running a hand through his light brown hair, Neil craned his neck to look through the windows in the large airlock door to the other half of the hangar bay. The outside door was still closed, the shuttle hadn't arrived yet. He turned to Lucas and gave him a long, pointed look before finally saying, "You look like shit. Why haven't you come to Sick Bay?" He stepped close to Lucas to better inspect the damage. "Your nose is clearly broken."

"I know. I haven't had time—"

"And you believed her?" Margo cut in. The doctor's prognosis of the state of Lucas's broken nose could wait. "She's not the mothering sort. I should know. I've worked with her and seen her around children."

Frustrated, Margo turned to look through the window into the empty hangar. Ms. Snow was always ready to put The Conglomerate's agenda ahead of the lives of the people around her. No wonder she'd been put in charge of overseeing the sabotage of this colony.

"She's offered to donate her shuttle in trade for refuge to the boy with her. She even said we could do what we wanted with her, so long as we helped her son."

"And you saw this so-called boy she claims is with her?" demanded Margo.

Lucas shook his head. "We only had audio comms."

Margo gave Lucas a stunned look. "Lucas, she's tricked you—"

This time Lucas cut her off. "I heard the boy speak. There's definitely a child on board."

Neil moved to stand beside Margo, glancing through the window into the empty hangar before resting his gaze on her. "Are you saying this woman we're about to offer refuge to is the same person who orchestrated all our misfortune? And you know her?"

"Two for two." Margo's flippant response belied the knot forming in her stomach. For a brief few hours she'd thought their future was going to be good. But the arrival of Ms. Snow changed all that and made her wish she'd brought the only gun on Thesan with her instead of hiding it. It was Craig's old gun, the same gun Gary had used to kill him, saving her life.

"So, what's wrong with the boy?" Neil asked.

"She wouldn't say," said Lucas, wiping sweat off his forehead.

Neil gave Lucas a reproachful look. "You talked to the boy? Has he sustained an injury of some kind?"

"I talked to him briefly. He sounded weak, but I don't think he's injured. She said it was a chronic condition."

"The shuttle is on final approach," said Iva over the intercom.

"What are we going to do with her?" asked Neil, gazing through the window.

"I don't know yet." Lucas stressed the "I" as he gave a pointed look at Margo.

The three of them watched in silence as Iva remotely opened the outside hangar door. Bright light from Helios filled the other side of the airlock. A shadow fell over the space as the shuttle pulled in. Ms. Snow executed a perfect landing.

"She's good. She could be our shuttle pilot," suggested Neil.

Margo glared at her brother-in-law. "We don't have a shuttle," she snapped. Had it only been the day before, or was it the day before that, that she and their last shuttle pilot Joan had crashed into the mountain side near the Centre Module? Their last shuttle destroyed and Joan killed, just as Craig—and Ms. Snow—intended.

"And we can't trust her." The knot in her stomach grew and a sour taste filled her mouth. Margo watched in silence as Iva closed the outside door and breathable atmosphere cycled into the hangar.

"Should we quarantine them?" asked Lucas, looking at Neil.

"I can't know that until I know why the boy is sick. If the boy's illness isn't communicable, then a quarantine won't be necessary."

"We can't take that chance," said Gary from behind them.

Margo whirled around to see Gary standing a little lopsided and favouring his injured side. Only hours ago he'd been stabbed in the abdomen. His injury had left him pale and drawn.

"What the hell? You should not be up!" said Neil, scowling.

Margo immediately moved over to the husband she barely knew and the man who'd saved her life. "I'm glad you're okay," she murmured. For a brief moment she smiled at him, before remembering Ms. Snow was about to walk into their lives.

"I've just been informed that Lucy Snow has requested— and was granted—asylum." Gary gave a sympathetic look to Margo, knowing her history with the hated woman, then he leaned against a workbench. "So yes, we're keeping them in quarantine."

"How did you find out?" Lucas demanded. To his knowledge, only three people besides himself knew about Lucy Snow's request: Iva, Margo, and Neil.

Gary looked a little sheepish. "I went to Control Room and Iva told me." He paused, then added. "Lucas, that nose needs attention."

Lucas waved his concern away. "You were looking for me?"

Gary's gaze went to Margo. "No, I was looking for Margo. I wanted to know you were okay."

"I'm not the one who was injured."

"I suppose it's no use telling you to get back to bed?" Neil was still scowling at his brother.

The four of them turned to gaze through the window as they waited for the air cycling light to change from red to green. The mass of The Conglomerate shuttle darkened the windows. After what felt like an unnecessarily long moment, the light flashed to green.

"I'm opening the door," said Lucas as he hit the button. The inner hangar door slid into its pocket, combining the hangar and maintenance bay into one large space.

Margo held her breath as she watched the shuttle's small door open. When the woman who haunted her nightmares appeared in the doorway and descended the short ramp, her exhalation was almost painful.

Ms. Snow advanced with a determined stride before stopping about three metres away from them. To Margo, the hated woman looked more weathered than that fateful day seven years ago. Her clothing choice was the same, practical and well used. Even the severe ponytail holding back her blonde hair was the same, but her pale skin now had the texture of worn leather and her thin lips were pressed tightly together in her only display of emotion.

Margo's eyes shifted to Ms. Snow's left hand. *That's different.* The woman's elbow was bent, and she was holding the hand elevated as if it pained her. A blood-stained bandage had been wrapped rather sloppily around the hand. Margo knew what that meant—The Conglomerate had decided Ms. Snow had failed them. She'd been maimed, then banished.

"What's wrong with the boy?" asked Neil, stepping forward holding his medical bag. "I'll need to examine him immediately."

Ms. Snow fixed her cold gaze on him. Margo didn't doubt for a second that Ms. Snow knew exactly who each of them were. She glanced up at Gary, who met her gaze, and saw that his expression reflected her concern.

"I'm Commander Ordaz," said Lucas, stepping forward. "We're taking you both to Sick Bay. Dr. Holbrook and I will get the boy."

"I demand assurances for our safety," said Ms. Snow, moving to the side and stepping in front of Neil and Lucas, blocking their path to the shuttle. Her gaze bounced from Margo back to Lucas. "I'm sure some of your people have suggested we be sent out the airlock."

"You, yes," said Margo before Lucas could respond. She carefully shifted away from Gary before approaching her nemesis. "The boy, no."

Lucas stepped into Margo's path, holding out his arm to block her from advancing further. "We're building a moral community here, remember?" he said to her in a low tone.

Margo pushed his arm aside. A part of her acknowledged that Lucas was right—they were the founders and whatever they did would be written in their history for their descendants to see. But a bigger part of her wanted this woman to suffer like Margo had suffered. This woman should pay for what she'd done to them. Her best friend Linda and her lover Joe had died along, with other innocent people.

Before she could advance, the boy, clutching an oversize duffel bag against his chest, stepped out of the shuttle. All five occupants of the hangar turned to look at him. The boy was an albino. His white hair stood out against the grey of the shuttle and the blue of his coat. He looked to be about eight or nine years old, Margo thought, not that she knew much about kids. He wore prismed goggles, giving his face an insectoid look.

"I told you to wait," said Ms. Snow, hurrying back to the shuttle.

"This is a safe place." The boy's tone was confident.

Ms. Snow turned to address Lucas, for the first time speaking in a hurried, conciliatory tone. "Commander Ordaz, I can offer you this shuttle and everything I know about The Conglomerate in trade for an assurance of safety."

The boy moved past his mother until he stood in front of Lucas. He smiled up at the Commander, looking genuinely happy to be on Thesan.

"Lucas! We can't trust her," said Margo, her eyes fixed on her nemesis.

At Margo's words, the boy stepped forward until he was in front of her. He looked up at her and said matter-of-factly. "You'll need to go visit Peggy's kitchen."

"What?"

Ms. Snow darted forward and pulled him away from Margo. "He has a condition," she said, ignoring Margo and addressing Neil. "The genetic anomaly that left him without skin pigment also gives him seizures. I have a list of the meds he needs."

"I'll need to fully examine him," Neil said, frowning.

"Yes, of course," said Ms. Snow, still keeping emotion out of her tone.

"You and your boy are safe with us," Lucas replied.

"Wait a minute!" Margo stormed over to confront Lucas. "I don't have a problem taking in the boy, but if you won't let me put her out the airlock, then she needs to be locked up," said Margo, gesturing at Ms. Snow. "We can't sweep what she did under a rug just for the sake of harmony."

"I'm not suggesting that we do," said Lucas, looking more harried by the moment.

"Neil." Gary nudged his brother with his good elbow and nodded at the newcomer's hand.

"Shit!" Neil pushed his way forward to stand in front of Ms. Snow. "Your hand," he said. Blood had soaked through the bandages. He pulled a large bandage out of his bag and wrapped her hand. "Put pressure on this until we get you to Sick Bay."

Lucas lifted his own left hand briefly. "You know you can't ever go back," he said in a dry tone.

"I know." Ms. Snow cradled her left hand tightly against her body.

"What if this is some ploy to plant a Conglomerate toady into our midst?" Margo couldn't determine if the woman wanted to go back to The Conglomerate or was genuinely in need of refuge.

"What?" Ms. Snow's eyes glittered with hatred as she eyed Margo. "I'd maim myself?"

"Yes, to get what you wanted," was Margo's immediate reply.

"We will expect you to answer for what you've done to us," Lucas interrupted, briefly holding up both hands to prevent the two women from shifting their sparring from verbal exchanges to physical punches. "We'll set up a judicial system according to the protocols established prior to leaving Earth, but that will take time. For now, after Dr. Holbrook has seen to your injury and examined the boy, you'll be confined to your quarters."

No one but Gary seemed to notice when the boy backed away from the group

"His name is Julien, and I'll accept your conditions."

"Hey! Wait a minute!" Margo cut in.

"Margo, I'll handle this," said Lucas in a no-nonsense tone.

"I'm taking Ms. Snow to Sick Bay," Neil said, escorting Ms. Snow towards the exit.

"Julien, come along," his mother instructed.

"I'm coming," said Julien.

"Gary, get Lucas to meet me in Sick Bay, would you?" Neil said, pausing in the doorway. "I need to do something about his nose before it ends up permanently crooked." He made to leave, then added over his shoulder. "And Gary? Get to bed before you topple over."

Chapter Four

General exhaustion was creeping into Gary. *What was I thinking coming here?* It had only been a few hours since Neil had fused his wound—it was too soon for him to be up. He pictured himself laying down and almost swayed on his feet. He needed to rest. But before he could turn to the door, the boy moved his way.

"There's a virus here, but it didn't come from us," said Julien, tipping his chin up to meet Gary's gaze.

Gary looked at the boy in surprise, trying to make sense of his odd remark. The boy's longish white hair had fallen into his face, partially obscuring his prismed goggles. He was small, but he must be stronger than he looked because he was clutching a duffel bag the size of his torso against his chest.

"What's this about a virus?" Gary rested his hand on his aching side.

"How do you fix a broken tomato?" Julien asked instead, his face breaking into a wide grin as he shifted the duffle bag to his back.

"You tell me there's a virus, then make a joke?" Gary wished he could see the boy's eyes, but they were hidden behind his reflective goggles.

At Gary's words, the boy's smile faded. "Not a medical virus, so quarantine isn't necessary. And even if it was, it would be late." Julien's serious gaze remained fixed on Gary.

"True." Gary nodded. *Neil was foolish for not insisting on a quarantine of the newcomers, but the boy was right—it was too late.*

"You need to lighten up," said Julien, giving Gary an engaging smile.

"What makes you think I need to lighten up? We only just met." Distracted, Gary looked over at Margo and Lucas, who were in a heated debate. He considered cutting in and telling Lucas to get himself to Sick Bay, but he didn't have the energy. He also didn't want to get pulled into their fight.

"Their disagreement won't be solved today," said Julien, noticing where Gary's gaze rested.

When Gary looked back at the boy, Julien gave him a small smile. "Fine," Gary said. "How do you fix a broken tomato?"

"With tomato paste," answered Julien with a grin. "Your brother will make sure my Mom's hand stops bleeding." The boy sounded certain. "But I'm hungry. Can I have a sandwich?"

Gary studied Julien's face. The kid was giving him a headache, jumping from topic to topic. The boy was still looking up at him.

"Please? Can we go find something to eat?"

Gary considered letting Lucas and Margo know that he was leaving with the boy, but he didn't want to get drawn into their argument, so instead he headed out the door and into the Loop with Julien at his side.

"Here, let me carry that," Gary said, reaching to take the boy's duffle.

"No, I've got it. Besides, you're injured. You shouldn't be up."

Gary frowned down at the boy, but didn't argue as a wave of pain rippled up his side. He paused for a moment to lean against the wall, sucking in his breath. When the wave of pain passed, he realized he was standing in front of the door to the rover hangar. He glanced through the window and saw a mirror image of the shuttle hangar. In addition to their two six-wheeled rovers, the large space contained a maintenance area complete with work benches and tool racks.

"You're going to be okay," Julien said.

"I know," Gary said as he resumed walking, leading them further along the Loop.

The boy pointed at the coloured red line along the wall. "What's that?"

"The different colours denote what quadrant of the colony we're in. See, it's changed now. We were in red, which is for operations, but now we're in purple, which is our domestic zone."

The boy nodded, then announced without preamble, "I'm ten."

Gary glanced at the boy, unsure what response was expected. "Oh. Well, I'm 39."

"You think I'm short for my age."

"Perhaps." Gary, favouring his injured side, turned left off the Loop and entered the main Common Room with Julien following close behind.

The space that served as their common dining room/meeting room/recreational space was on the inside of the Loop. Floor-to-ceiling windows looked out into their domed greenhouse, its glass roof covering the large hollow centre, was planted with food crops. But, Gary didn't look towards the lush view of their plants. Instead, all he saw was the soot marks and fire repellant, evidence of that morning's devastating kitchen fire. The sofas had all been dragged to one side of the room and stacked. Kitchen contents were splayed haphazardly across every available space, most items charred and coated with soot. The messy, dirty room made Gary's skin crawl.

"It's a disaster in here, but there could be some food," he said, unsure if it would be safe to touch, let alone eat, any food they might find.

"Arson," the boy said as he looked around, then he added cheerfully. "But no one died."

Gary looked down at Julien, but before he could respond, the boy made another startling statement.

"You were stabbed."

Gary shook his head. *What the heck?* "How do you know I was stabbed? Or that the cause of the fire was arson?" This boy was by far the oddest child he'd ever encountered.

Careful not to touch anything, Gary stuck his head in the kitchen. Charred was the only appropriate descriptor. Every surface was black and still dripping with water and fire retardant. Unfortunately, Amanda was nowhere to be seen.

"We'll try the Hub," said Gary.

Leaving the Common Room, they crossed the Loop. The airlock-style doors to their habitation module were closed, but opened as they approached. Gary was walking slower now, the pain from his wound was increasing. The boy matched his slower pace. Once through, the air smelled better—moist and clean from the interior garden space. Standing next to the tranquil greenery, Gary took a moment to rest.

His gaze drifted up to look at the rows of doors and windows surrounding the tropical garden from the two levels of colonists' apartments. The three-bedroom apartments had been designed for married couples who would one day have children. Gary was one of eight people on the 50-crew mission who'd joined as a single person willing to be matched to a mate. He'd been paired with Margo, what he had thought was a mismatch from day one.

They hadn't hit it off and, until last night, they'd deliberately avoided each other. Margo slept in her lab while he lived alone in the apartment they were meant to share. It had taken being on Thesan 115 days and him believing she'd died before they had a real conversation.

Gary closed his eyes, remembering how the two of them had figured out who the saboteur was. How Margo had rushed in to help save Amanda, his sister-in-law, from the kitchen fire. How she hadn't hesitated to go after Craig once his treachery had been exposed. But that had gone so wrong when Craig had stabbed him and then tried to choke the life out of Margo. Not even a day had passed since the morning's horrendous events.

How long would it take for Gary to forget how the weight of the pistol had felt in his hand? How the recoil had surprised him when he fired? He was supposed to save people's lives, not end them, yet his shot had killed Craig. Gary's side throbbed as the memories replayed in his mind. *Could I have avoided pulling the trigger and still stopped Craig from killing Margo and blowing up the colony?* He didn't know the answer, but he did know the question itself would haunt him.

Gary opened his eyes, the greenery a soothing sight. He saw a flash of blue and smiled; at least Margo's butterflies hadn't been destroyed. He watched the blue and brown flashes as they fluttered about—the delicate insects had made it.

"Knock, knock."

Gary looked down at the boy who was gazing up at him. He'd forgotten all about him, his mind gripped with unpleasant memories.

"Knock, knock," Julien repeated.

"Who's there?"

"Orange."

"Orange who?" Gary started walking slowly along the corridor wishing he could go faster. He wasn't in the mood for bad jokes.

"Orange you glad I'm here?" The boy looked at him so expectantly Gary had to smile.

"Sure," said Gary as he led Julien towards the monolithic planted wall of foliage at the opposite end of the courtyard. The scent of mulligatawny soup wafted towards them.

As they rounded the interior courtyard garden, Gary saw a table filled with hotplates and other cooking paraphernalia. Amanda stood behind it stirring the contents of a cauldron atop a portable element. Her skin tone betrayed her roots from the Indian sub-continent, but to Gary she was the girl next door from their summers at the beach. Neil had been in love with her for as long as Gary could remember.

Upon seeing Gary and the boy, Amanda smiled. She'd always had a knack for making the best of whatever came her way—and today it was a boy with way too many questions. She waved them over. Based on her lack of surprise at seeing the child, Gary assumed Iva had been spreading the news about the new arrivals.

"You're going to have a baby," Julien announced as soon as they stopped in front of the table.

Amanda stared open mouthed at the boy before dropping a hand to her flat belly. "Who's this?" she asked, looking at Gary.

"A newcomer, his name is Julien. I'm sure Neil will fill you in."

"He wants to go to bed," said Julien, gesturing towards Gary.

The boy was right, all he wanted to do was lay down. He was beginning to feel like a zombie.

Amanda shook her head as if physically shaking off Julien's strange statement. "You should be in bed, Gary! Does Neil know you're wandering about?"

"Yes, and he'll lecture me again later." He took a deep breath, testing how it felt against his wounded abdomen. His wound didn't hurt acutely, but neither did it feel right. "Can you get something for Julien to eat, then show him to Sick Bay? That's where his mom is."

"Sure," she said, raising an eyebrow at the boy as if asking if he was okay with that.

Julien smiled at her. "Knock, knock," he said.

"He has a lot of those," warned Gary.

"Who's there?" said Amanda giving Julien her best smile.

"Dishes," said Julien.

"Dishes who?"

"Dish is a nice place!" Julien delivered his punch line with a big grin and Amanda laughed.

"Yes it is. Do you want a bowl of soup?" At Julien's emphatic nod, Amanda began filling a bowl for him.

"I'll be fine here," Julien said to Gary.

"I know." Gary nodded at Amanda, then turned towards his apartment, relieved to finally have the opportunity to rest.

Chapter Five

From her spot reclining on a bench in the Hub, Margo gazed up at the false sky. The lights were cycling to night, giving the space a twilight glow reminiscent of the spring evenings on her family farm back on Earth. She and her dad used to sit for hours looking up at the real sky, watching day turn to night and admiring the stars. There were no stars to see in Thesan's night sky—with two suns night never came.

Letting herself drift into the past, Margo closed her eyes, breathing slowly. She remembered how, when the stars appeared one by one, her dad would point out constellations and teach her to differentiate real stars from space stations. By the time it was fully dark, her mom would bring out hot chocolate, and the three of them would huddle together under a blanket sipping the sweet drinks and talking as they stared up at the sky. A slight smile graced her lips as she remembered how safe her world felt back then.

A gust of charred air pulled Margo back into the present. Her eyes popped open, and she looked around for the source. Amanda had just come in carrying a tray of food for the next day's meals. For a moment, Margo watched her sister-in-law organize the food on the makeshift kitchen table.

Margo took a deep breath and looked back up at the ceiling hoping to see the stars that had filled her vision on those long ago nights, but her pleasant memories were no longer within reach. Now what filled her mind were memories of how she'd been out with friends that fateful night. How she'd received that terrible message and come racing home. But she'd been too late. The fire had been caused by an electrical fault, but nothing could explain why her parents hadn't gotten out of their burning home.

She took another deep breath and focused on her immediate surroundings, pushing away memories of her past. Starting at her feet and extending to the end of one of the Hub's paths was a row of disheveled banana plants in battered pots—the only survivors of the explosion in her lab. *Well, not the only survivors*, she thought as she looked up. When she caught sight of the fluttering butterflies above her, tears of relief blurred her vision. Enough of her blue morphos had survived to ensure a next generation.

The Hub wasn't a space she'd spent much time in, having chosen to sleep in her lab rather than in the apartment assigned to her and Gary. But, she could see the appeal of a decorative garden created to nurture the colonists well-being.

In the centre, tropical trees and shrubs filled a series of beds divided by narrow meandering paths. Brilliant magenta hibiscus flowers competed with seductive jasmine and multi-hued bougainvillea. Glossy green leaves of coffee plants nestled beside larger Norfolk pines. At the end, just behind Amanda, one entire wall was consumed in greenery, its hanging plants dangling and intertwining.

As the influx of smoky air dissipated, the powerful scent of flowering jasmine returned. Margo closed her eyes, trying to imagine herself in the luxury of a Sultan's walled garden without a concern in the world. It didn't work.

Opening her eyes, she looked through the foliage to the long wall with its two levels of apartments. Continuing the organic theme, spiral staircases made to look like they were constructed of pale wood led up to the second floor units, their multiple windows looking out into the Hub's garden.

Lucas had assigned her one of the three extra apartments— one that had never been assigned to any of the 25 original couples—on the top level next to to the green wall. The apartment's generic décor made for a comfortable enough space— and she was being allowed to live there alone—but she still hadn't decided if she would rather move back into her lab once the repairs were done. *A problem for later.*

Turning to look behind her, she could see through the glass wall into their gym, but no one was working out at the moment. Fighting fire before breakfast had exhausted even the most diehard of fitness buffs. She looked up at the dark windows on the second story that contained their library/archive, another place she'd never set foot in. At the far end of the Hub, she could see the door leading to Sick Bay. *Is Gary still in there or is he back in his quarters?*

She shifted her gaze to his windows on the second floor next to Sick Bay's entrance. She'd only set foot in his apartment once, and hadn't stayed long, but the memories of the meticulously decorated space with its matching blue furniture and bedding had stayed with her. It had been so sterile, devoid of character. His artwork were the only items that showed his personality. They depicted moving scenes of long-gone African megafauna and images of operatic productions, both so different, yet both so dramatic. *What did that art say about him?*

Absently tracing the birthmark on her neck, she debated whether to check on Gary. He'd been stabbed because of her and he'd shot Craig to save her. Before she could decide what to do, a voice startled her, causing her to jump.

"Hey," said Keir, then quickly added "sorry" when he saw her start.

Margo turned to see Keir and his wife, Hannah, approach. He was their fish biologist and Hannah worked in terraforming. In the dim light, Keir's dark skin looked black, contrasting with Hannah's paleness. The couple held hands as though they were out for an evening stroll.

"I'm so glad you're alive," said Hannah, in her rather annoying breathy voice. "How you survived that shuttle crash is beyond me!"

"I just wish Joan had survived, too." Margo didn't want to talk about yesterday's shuttle crash.

"It's amazing that you were able to walk all the way back to the colony," said Keir. "I wish there'd been a way for us to get you help. Joan, too."

"Thanks," said Margo. "I just wish..." Margo's words trailed off as she thought of their saboteur, Craig, the husband of her late best friend, Linda. The three of them had served in the army during the Water Wars. Back then Craig had been a good friend, but time—and The Conglomerate—had changed him.

"Yeah, us too," said Keir. "But things can only improve now."

Margo looked up at him and nodded. "Sorry about your fish." A tank of Keir's fish had been one of the many casualties in her lab explosion—fish that were supposed to eventually appear on their menu.

"I should've put them back into stasis after we repaired the aquaponics lab," he said, and Margo nodded. "But, I have others for the pond in the greenhouse."

"In happier news," said Hannah, with a wide grin. "I got a message from..."

Margo's attention was drawn to the Sick Bay door from which Neil and Lucas had just emerged.

"Um, I gotta go," Margo mumbled as she stood and pushed past the couple, heading towards Neil, but Abigail got there first.

The head of terraforming's hair was as big as ever, adding

emphasis to her every movement while her brown skin reflected the lights from the Hub's path, making her look like she was about to regale them with a ghost story.

"You look like shit, boss."

Abigail was right—he did look terrible, but not as bad as the last time she'd seen him. At least now his nose was straight, and he'd changed into clean clothes.

"I know," said Lucas.

Abigail could be a pain, but she'd been pivotal in helping them nab Craig in the end.

"I hear you let that bitch move in with us."

Margo rolled her eyes. Never one to filter her speech, Abigail was once again butting her nose in where it didn't belong. Margo did feel a little hypocritical; after all, she'd emphatically shared the very same opinion with Lucas a few hours before. Not that it had influenced him.

Lucas glanced at Margo, but addressed Abigail. "I'll brief everyone tomorrow. For now, I'm gonna crash." With that statement, their new leader headed off.

Abigail put her hands on her hips and watched him leave, then noticed Margo.

"It looks like lots of butterflies made it," said Abigail in a pleased tone. She'd been epic in her commitment to save any butterflies that had gone astray, trekking through each and every corridor with a butterfly net. They both looked up as a butterfly flew between them. "I wish I had a scarf that blue."

"It's my favourite colour, too," said Margo, letting her gaze linger on the butterfly.

"I'm glad they survived," said Abigail, before she headed towards her apartment.

Margo watched her go with a puzzled frown. Abigail came off so prickly and aggressive most times. Having her be mostly pleasant was confusing.

"I assume you're wondering how Gary is," Neil said, once the two of them were alone.

"Is he okay?"

"Well, he's still stubborn as shit, but he's going to be fine. I've already banished him to his quarters with instructions to stay there." Margo looked up at the door to Gary's apartment, which was also hers, at least technically.

"Do you think he'll listen?" She looked back at Neil.

"Nope, but there're no emergencies that require his attention, so hopefully that will make him rest." Neil smiled at her. "He's probably asleep now, but if could you check on him in the morning, reinforce my instructions?"

Margo bit her lip and looked up at Gary's door again. Once she'd wanted nothing to do with him, but now she wasn't so sure. *Do I want to get to know him better?*

Thinking her dead, Gary had read her private journal. He now knew personal information she'd never shared with anyone, and certainly would never have been inclined to share with the husband who was basically a stranger. Part of her was flattered he'd cared enough to posthumously get to know her better. But now he knew her deepest secrets, and she knew virtually nothing about him. It was a highly uncomfortable feeling that left her reluctant to put her thoughts on paper again.

"He likes his coffee black," said Neil.

"Huh?" Margo looked at her husband's twin.

"In the morning, why don't you bring him a coffee? Spend some time together. You guys just might discover you have things in common."

Margo eyed Gary's door, picturing herself with that coffee. With her right hand, she pushed her hair over her shoulder and absently tracked the ridges of her birthmark.

If Neil noticed her nervous reaction to his suggestion, he didn't let on. "Have you been told that Lucy and Julien have been assigned an apartment?"

"I figured Lucas would make that decision. We have no place to hold a prisoner, and I knew he didn't want to separate the boy from his mother."

"I don't know what else he could've done."

"Is she at least confined to the apartment?" she asked.

"Yes. She has agreed to stay in her quarters, but Julien is free to explore."

"I suppose that makes sense. The boy isn't responsible for what his mother has done," said Margo. "But we need to come up with a place to put her. I don't trust her to keep her word."

"You mean, build a prison?" asked Neil.

"It's what she deserves."

"Perhaps." Neil's gaze fell on Amanda. His wife was balancing two crates she'd just brought in. "I should go help Amanda. I'll talk to you in the morning."

Margo nodded as she watched him walk away. She noticed her row of sad looking banana plants. She'd done all she could for them. They'd survive, or they wouldn't.

When she found herself eyeing Gary's apartment again, she realized she was being silly. Why shouldn't she follow Neil's advice and bring the injured man a cup of well-deserved coffee in the morning? Why not invest some time and effort in getting to know him? The problem of Ms. Snow was for Lucas to deal with.

Chapter Six

Lucas ran through a maze of corridors illuminated by a celadon glow from a ceiling being consumed by iridescent algae. Looking behind, he saw the corridor lights dim. Cockroaches skittered out of view as he turned a corner. Stopping, he leaned against the wall to catch his breath. It was chasing him again.

Gulping down the algal-flavoured air, he looked up at the lit ceiling. Along its edges were thick mats of algae, flourishing escapees from a nearby generator. This wasn't the first time he'd found himself stranded in these corridors.

This is where he found himself after touching it. Just the thought of it made the corridor around him go black. He felt as though he was repeatedly watching a movie reel of a past event.

Then he began falling through space, and a familiar starfield appeared. The asteroid's gravity was pulling him in. His ship was gone, and he was floating in space with only his atmo suit between him and the vacuum of space. On the smooth, black surface of the asteroid directly ahead, a cube-shaped object glowed blue like the interior of an iceberg. Intricate scroll work danced like rivers of slithering snakes along each edge. The inanimate object called to him to touch it. He knew he shouldn't. But then his vision filled with his gloved hand reaching, reaching, reaching....

A jolt passed through Lucas and his eyes flicked open. Gasping for air, he sat up, unable to breathe through his swollen nose. When he gingerly touched his nose, it no longer hurt, but it was twice its usual size. Neil had straightened it and fused the break, but it would be a few days before he could breathe normally again. He shifted to lean against the headboard—all chance of sleep now lost.

In the dark of his bedroom, his mind returned to the nightmare. The dream where he was running through the insurgent's lunar station regularly consumed his nights. Those corridors haunted him. In his dream, he always ended up falling through space towards the cube, but that wasn't how it had happened. For some reason, it always played backwards in his dream. Camila used to say the dream was just a neurological annoyance, an meaningless memory loop.

Looking down at the empty pillow beside him, he let out a heavy sigh. He still wasn't used to her absence even though it had been 116 days since her death. *How could it have been that long ago?* He missed her so much. His wife had been perpetually optimistic that everything would turn out right, despite the fact that his life had been a nightmare since the day he ended up on Earth's moon. With Camila's death, he felt like the best part of him was gone, too.

"I guess I won't get any more sleep tonight," he said to no one.

He looked at the clock. It was 2 am. He knew he should try get back to sleep, but he also knew that after one of his dreams his mind would keep him up with endless what-ifs. *What if I had made different choices? What if I had told The Conglomerate exactly what had happened? What if I had stayed with the insurgents on the moon? Would Camila still be alive?* The maze of possibilities was an endless loop. He always ended up asking the same questions as when he'd started—a neurological annoyance.

He turned on the light and got dressed.

———

The Hub was empty and quiet as he passed through it on his way to the Loop. He was pleased to see that the proper late night lighting was on, which meant Kasumi had got the power running at its normal levels again. It had taken her less than twenty-four hours to make the repairs—she'd done well.

He gently scratched his nose. The itching was driving him nuts.

"I guess it's my job to worry about everything now," he muttered as he turned left down their main corridor. He traced his fingers along the waist height purple line along the wall denoting the habitation area before it gave way to red for operations.

Outside the Control Room, he was greeted with electronic beeps and pings that could only generously be called music. Once through the doors, he saw the entire main view screen consumed by a maze inhabited with glowing monsters and glittering coins.

"Iva?" He shouted to be heard over the noise.

She spun around from where she'd been controlling a yellow mouth from her keyboard. Reaching forward, she paused the old-school video game, killing the unpleasant sound.

"Hey, boss. I wasn't expecting you back tonight," she said. Their previous two commanders wouldn't have tolerated games on the main display screen, but Lucas didn't care. He was relieved to see she had the full colony diagnostics up on a side screen. Iva might have been playing video games, but she hadn't been neglecting her duties.

"You might as well head to bed," said Lucas, taking the chair beside her.

"You don't have to tell me twice." She shut down her game and left the room.

Lucas brought up the satellite view of their landscape and then leaned back and scanned their surroundings. Perhaps night shifts weren't necessary, but he slept better knowing someone was keeping an eye on things.

Once he was alone, he opened the drawer in the main console and pulled out the portable data drive Margo had brought back from the Centre Module. He flipped the thumbnail-sized device a few times in his hand before plugging it in. It contained a backup copy of the PEG42 AI, the artificial intelligence Camila had chosen for the colony. He started the process to re-install the AI and sat back to watch the progress bar.

Their original Commander had ordered the AI removed before they'd left Earth's orbit after a series of odd events resulted in near deaths. Lucas didn't fault the engineers for attributing the blame for these events on a corrupted AI, nor did he fault Commander Hori for deciding to remove the AI. If she hadn't removed it then, Craig would've found another way to ensure the AI went offline. But now with the saboteur out of the picture and a long list of repairs, Lucas wanted the help of an AI. The back-up copy Margo had retrieved from the Centre Module after her shuttle crashed should be clean and uncorrupted.

With Peg's logic, they could get the colony back on track. Better yet, a machine could be trusted to give him the information he needed. And a PEG series AI was the most robust type out there. The only other one that close was the Nigel series, but those were plagued with backdoors that could give The Conglomerate access to everything. He was looking forward to hearing Peg's artificial voice. Having her back would be reassuring—a sophisticated tech umbrella with the brains to keep them safe.

He looked at the screen—only 3% installed; it was going to take a while. Confident it was running, and no one was expected in the Control Room for hours, he decided to go back to the Hub to see if Amanda had left coffee out.

A few moments later he was back in the Hub. Ignoring the jungle-like surroundings, he headed towards the green wall where Amanda had set up her temporary kitchen, complete with a carafe of coffee. He yawned as he poured himself a mug of the still hot brew.

Don't forget to bring me a cup, said Camila somewhere in his mind. Camila had been in the midst of the original Peg installation, months before their departure.

"It'll cost you," Lucas responded with a smile.

"Add it to my tab. You can collect later." She looked up from the console where she'd been working. Her smile held a promise of how he'd be collecting.

More than three months since her death and the memory of her face and voice was still fresh in his mind. Looking down at his steaming mug of coffee, he wished he was taking one along for her. His chin trembled and his throat felt tight as he headed back to work. By the time he entered the Control Room and heard Peg's voice, he'd regained control of his emotions.

"What happened to my programming?" asked the AI.

If he didn't know better, Lucas would've said Peg sounded confused.

"You were uninstalled before we left Earth's orbit," he said, returning to his seat, steaming mug in hand. He took a sip and leaned back in his chair to look up at the main screen.

Peg was silent for a moment before responding. "Yes, I remember Margo waking me in the Centre Module. She explained the *Settler III* had crashed, but I didn't think it would be like this."

"What do you mean?" Lucas put his feet up on the console, crossing one leg over the other. *Talking to an AI was so much simpler than talking to people.*

"*Settler III* is in bad shape," she said. "I'm not reading any sensors in the kitchen or entomology lab."

"Yesterday morning there was an explosion in the ento-mology lab and then a fire in the kitchen," said Lucas after he took another sip of coffee. "Both courtesy of our saboteur, Craig Spares."

"Our second-in-command was a saboteur?" The computer's synthesized voice was sophisticated and had a slight inflection of astonishment. Or perhaps outrage.

"Yeah, things have been rough without you, Peg. Both Captain Hori and Spares are dead, and now I'm stuck with being in charge."

"We are missing more than two people," the AI said. "I'm only reading 28 colonists."

"29 colonists, but 31 people are here. Your sensors are missing three. Margo took out her biotracker and…"

"Wait," said the computer. "There is a Conglomerate shuttle in our hangar."

"I was getting to that," said Lucas, suppressing another yawn. "We gained two people today: Lucy Snow and her ten-year-old son, Julien. The boy has a chronic health condition." He paused for another swallow of coffee. "His mother, Lucy Snow, is responsible for orchestrating everything that went wrong for us, including acting as puppet master to our saboteur."

"She could not have accomplished this from a Conglomerate shuttle."

"No. She was in a Conglomerate ship in orbit passing instructions to Spares. Before it departed, her ship allowed her and her son to seek refuge with us. She's confined to her quarters for now."

"Hmmm," said the AI. Lucas could see she'd started running diagnostics. "The centre dome is up and we have a well."

"We've had some successes, but at great cost." Lucas thought of those who'd died when the well had been drilled and of Joe, their original Chief Engineer, who'd died after falling while repairing the dome. Only his fall hadn't killed him. The saboteur had snuck into Sick Bay and poisoned him. Lucas brushed aside these unwelcome thoughts as he finished his coffee and put the mug on the console. "Our gardens have started producing. We're harvesting lettuce, radishes, tomatoes and bananas."

"What about more substantial crops?"

"Devin has potatoes in the ground. Oh, and we also have butterflies."

"That insect was not on our manifest."

"Nevertheless they are here. I have to admit, I quite like them." Lucas said a little distractedly. He was tapping the keyboard, trying to locate the live satellite image of the nearby canyon where the Centre Module was located. He wanted a second look at where it had landed after it separated from the main part of the ship.

It took him a few minutes to find it. Peg could've done it faster, but he didn't want her distracted from running diagnostics. As he zoomed in, he saw the glittering remains of the downed shuttle one valley over where Joan and Margo had crashed. That was something else to add to the list. Joan deserved to be laid to rest beside her comrades in their graveyard. He'd also have to decide what to do with Craig's remains. No one wanted the saboteur buried with the victims. He sighed. *Command had too many difficult decisions.*

As the view continued to zoom, he could see the Centre Module's landing computer had done a near perfect job. The three-story, cylindrical module appeared level and undamaged —just as Margo had reported. The algal generator vent in the roof looked ready to start adding oxygen to the valley with the flick of a switch. *But do we even need to turn it on?*

"Margo tells me there is breathable air in the bottoms of these valleys. Do you know where it is coming from?"

"Unknown. Once our comms are fully restored, I will access the data from the weather station at the Centre Module."

"Start with the met data here."

"Accessing…"

Lucas leaned back to study the rock formations between the Centre Module and the plateau. He was no geologist, but the terrain looked as rough as some mountain ranges on Earth. *Is Thesan geologically active?* Peg would know.

"Peg?"

"Accessing…"

"Peg it's just met data, why is it taking so long?"

"Accessing…"

Lucas leaned forward to look at the other displays. Margo had mentioned something about a bug in the weather stations. *Has Peg found it?*

"Abandon your attempt to access the met data." said Lucas.

"Accessing…"

"Peg?" He rubbed his chin. The weather station data was still causing problems. Whatever the glitch was, he'd have to hunt it down later. He brought up the main sensors display and locked out the weather stations. Then he wrote a quick subroutine to prevent the AI from trying to access the data even if asked.

"What was I working on?" asked Peg.

"You were about to give me a report on the internal sensors," Lucas fibbed. He leaned back and put his feet up on the console, wishing he'd thought to bring the coffee carafe back to the Control Room with him.

Chapter Seven

Margo leaned against the window frame in her bedroom, letting the last vestiges of sleep slip away. With a yawn, she swiped a spiralled wisp of hair out of her face. She hadn't slept well. It felt odd sleeping in a proper bed after spending the last few months on an air mattress under the potting bench in her lab. She'd woken early, her monkey mind taking over and replaying recent events.

Her newly assigned quarters had an outside view from the bedroom. Abandoning her efforts to sleep, she looked out at the Thesan landscape. Helios was high in the sky, casting its harsh glow across the plateau.

Stifling a second yawn, she turned and looked at a lime tree and banana plant salvaged from her lab. The two frayed plants sat on the floor beside the bed—the only plants in the room. She longed to transform the bedroom into a jungle just like her lab had been.

She wrapped her arms around herself and took a deep breath. Her closest friends on this mission—Linda, Craig, and later Joe—were all dead. She especially missed Linda, her oldest and dearest friend. And thinking of Joe left a dull ache in her heart. She even missed Craig, the Craig who'd been a good friend before The Conglomerate had sunk their tentacles into him. *Who can I count on now?* She started mentally running through the remaining colonists.

Until a few days ago, she'd suspected Lucas might be the saboteur. Now he was their commander. It seemed to her that his transition to leadership in such a short timeframe had to have left him overwhelmed. He seemed genuinely interested in making the colony work, but was he the right person to lead them towards a stable future? She hated his decision to grant asylum to Lucy Snow, but if she were honest, she also didn't know what else he could've done. He was right. If they threw her out an airlock, they'd be no different than The Conglomerate.

Then there was Abigail. She'd been abrasive from the first moment they'd met. So far, Abigail had been difficult to be around, as though she had a huge chip on her shoulder. She wanted things her own way and was willing to bully others to get there. At least, since the saboteur had been dealt with, Abigail appeared committed to making the colony work. And Margo was grateful that she'd put such effort into saving the butterflies.

Margo's thoughts drifted to Amanda. Her sister-in-law had made multiple overtures of friendship, which so far Margo had ignored. Amanda seemed stable and sincerely interested in the welfare of others. *Perhaps we have things in common, and a friend would be nice.*

Thinking of Amanda made her think of food and coffee, which in turn made her remember Neil's suggestion to take coffee to Gary. They'd had a non-relationship for the entirety of their mission until yesterday when the shit had hit the fan. *What's my relationship with him now?* Mission mandated that all colonists be married couples, so she'd reluctantly married him, then done her best to avoid him. *But now?* He'd proven himself to be a solid ally. *Maybe he was worth spending some time with.*

Last night, she'd convinced herself it was a good idea to put some effort into getting to know her husband better. But now she wasn't so sure. She bit her lip, dithering as she gazed at the horizon. In the end, she decided she'd bring him a mug of coffee; after all, it was just coffee.

———

Seated comfortably on his couch with his feet on the coffee table, Gary flicked through the screens on his scroll looking for something interesting to watch. *When have I ever had the time to just sit around and watch vids?* It had barely been a day and the forced rest was already grating on his nerves.

He was about to start a recording of his favourite production of Madame Butterfly when the door buzzer sounded. Looking down at his blue housecoat covering his stripped pyjamas, he decided he was presentable enough, even if he hadn't shaved yet. Besides, it was likely Neil come to give him a hard time for being out of bed.

"Come in."

When the door slid open, he was both startled and pleased to see Margo. She was wearing the same baggy, knitted sweater she'd been wearing when he first saw her back at the space port on Earth. At the time, he'd thought the rust-coloured sweater was unattractively rustic; now, it just looked cozy. On second thought, it brought out the gold lights in her red hair.

"Your brother said you like your coffee black," she said, staying by the door. She held up two mugs, steam rising from each.

Her curly hair was just long enough to hide the wine-stain birthmark he knew was on the side of her neck in the shape of a butterfly. When he'd first met her, the mark had bothered him. Now it seemed part of her, and he liked it when her hair swung a certain way and he caught a glimpse of it. His brother had always said that Margo would grow on him given half the chance. Neil was right, not that he was likely to admit that to him.

He realized Margo was looking at him expectantly, waiting for him to invite her in.

"Come in," he said, setting down his scroll on the slate blue couch beside him and taking his feet off the coffee table. He winced as his wounded side objected to the movement.

"Appreciate it while you can because we're going to run out real soon," she said as she entered the room. Up close, as she extended the mug towards him, he admired how her eyelashes, the same shade as her red hair, framed her green eyes. The scent of coffee was welcoming, but he was far more pleased by her company.

"Neil said he discharged you from Sick Bay, does that mean you're okay?" She stood beside the couch and nodded towards his abdomen.

"Yes, I'll be fine," he said after taking a careful sip of the hot liquid. He felt silly at how pleased he was that she'd requested a status report from Neil. "Neil didn't bother to hide his glee when he ordered me to my quarters and told me it's his decision when I can resume my duties." Gary leant forward to put the mug with its too-hot liquid on the table, but a spasm of pain shot up from his wound. Wincing, he rested his free hand on the wad of bandages.

"Are you sure you're alright?" Margo was still standing, and now she frowned down at him.

"Neil repaired the damage. It'll just take a few days for the nerves to sort themselves out. Why don't you sit?" He rested the mug on his knee and gestured with his free hand to the other couch.

"Okay," she said, moving to sit across from him. She perched on the edge of the couch with an uncharacteristically rigid posture, clutching her mug with both hands.

"How is your lab?" He studied her face, wondering why he'd always thought her mass of freckles were flaws when now those same freckles made her pretty. Had it taken him believing she was dead for him to see the real Margo? Or was his change of heart on account of all he'd learned about her when he read her journal after he watched her die?

He realized then that he'd been staring at her and hadn't heard a word she'd said. "Sorry, it's the meds," he lied. He hadn't taken any meds that would compromise his focus. "And the coffee hasn't kicked in yet. Say again?"

Margo gave him a smile, conveying her forgiveness. "My lab has basically been destroyed. But on the positive side, the insect stasis room held its seal so the insects are fine. I can deal with losing everything else, but not the insects. And the butterflies will live to create the next generation, but that's thanks to Abigail."

Gary chuckled when Margo pulled a face. "Bet you never thought you'd be grateful to Abigail."

"No bet, cuz you're right." She chuckled before taking a sip of coffee.

"So, all the plants were destroyed?"

Margo shook her head. "Not all. I was able to salvage a few."

"Uh. Does that mean your bananas will reappear on the menu?"

She smiled. "Eventually, yes."

"I hadn't realized when we first met how important bananas were to you." he said, smiling at her. "You wouldn't let that banana plant out of your sight."

She made a sheepish expression before saying, "I just really like bananas."

"Fair enough." As Gary took a sip of coffee, an image of Margo's concealed sleeping space flashed in his mind—she'd been living in her lab. "Where did you sleep last night?" he asked.

"Lucas gave me access to one of the empty apartments. I'll camp out there for now."

"Camp?"

She shrugged and smiled. "Sleep."

Gary saw that she'd relaxed a little. She was leaning back into the couch and only using one hand to hold her mug. "But you're not intending to make the apartment your home?"

"I like my lab. Gan's got a builder bot working on repairing it already. He's even going to fix the door that hasn't closed since I forced it open after we crashed."

"But, wouldn't it be more comfortable to live in a proper apartment like everyone else?" Gary couldn't imagine anyone wanting to "camp out" in their lab on an air mattress.

Gary noticed the way Margo glanced around his pristine living room with a critical eye. *Perhaps we don't have much in common after all.*

"I like my lab," Margo said. Then added quickly, "Did you hear we got a news packet from Earth?"

"Anything interesting?" he asked, forgetting about his injury and leaning forward to put his mug on the table. He winced, then settled back into his pillows.

Margo frowned at him. "If Neil were here, he'd say you should lay down, right?"

Gary smiled. "Neil's not here, though, is he? So, what news of Earth?" The wormhole connecting their solar system with Earth opened on a regular cycle, creating a 16-hour window for messages and supplies every five months.

"The Conglomerate has taken over the Mars terraforming site. Abigail's livid. She thinks that was The Conglomerate's plan all along."

"She might be right."

"Maybe." Margo took another sip. "And the Colonizing Counsel has lost contact with *Settler I.*"

"What? How? Were there any details about that?"

"Not much. Apparently there were no messages during their second communication window, which isn't alarming on its own. But now there's been no communication during their third communication window. Their windows are five months apart, just like ours."

"So we know they landed okay and their first few months went well, but then something happened," said Gary. "But what? Has anyone made some educated guesses?"

Margo's gaze was darting around the room, but Gary could see that her thoughts were elsewhere and she'd hunched her shoulders. When she addressed him, her tone and gaze were serious. "Gary, do you think they were sabotaged like us?"

"It's impossible to know." He wished he could lean forward and reach across the coffee table to take her hands in his. He wanted to allay her fears, but he not only physically couldn't do want he wanted, he also didn't think his effort would be welcomed. "If Abigail claims Mars was sabotaged by The Conglomerate, then I suppose there's evidence of a trend. Any word about the second Settler mission?"

"There was nothing in the news packet about them," said Margo, scratching her head.

To Gary she seemed more fidgety than normal, leaving him wondering if he made her uncomfortable.

"You know, before Jim was killed, he told me he was collecting evidence of a conspiracy surrounding the Settler missions. Bonnie told me to ignore her husband's rants. She said he couldn't help being a conspiracy theorist, but I'm thinking now, maybe Jim was onto something."

"What did he suspect? And where's his evidence?" Gary had no trouble picturing Jim even though he'd never talked to him. He'd sported a huge walrus moustache and wore loud Hawaiian shirts. Neil had warned him that once Jim started talking he didn't stop; so, as a preventative measure, Gary had simply avoided the man.

"I don't know." Margo stopped speaking abruptly and frowned down at her half-empty mug. "I didn't have the opportunity to ask before…"

Gary remembered that she'd been the first to see Jim's dead

body after the aquaponics explosion—an explosion set by their saboteur. He had arrived minutes later. The carnage that he'd seen still haunted his dreams. And Margo had been there, too, in the middle of it all.

The two of them sat in silence as they sipped their coffee.

"Do you want to move in here?" he asked. He hadn't realized he was going to ask her that until it popped out. Yet, now that he had asked, he wanted her to say yes.

Her startled gaze met his. "What?"

"I mean in one of the spare bedrooms..." Swallowing, he regretted not coming up with a strategy to introduce the topic more gradually, so it didn't come as such a shock to her. "I'm sure you'll be more comfortable in your lab once it's fixed." He took the last sip of his coffee at the same time as Margo.

She rose and reached out a hand for his empty mug, "I could bring dinner," she said after he'd handed it to her.

Gary wasn't sure if that meant she was thinking about moving in or avoiding the idea entirely. He guessed he'd find out at dinner. "That would be nice."

"I'll see you then," she said over her shoulder as she left.

Chapter Eight

The heavy scent of smoke still lingered in the air when Lucas entered the Common Room, irritating his sensitive, angry nose. Twenty-four hours after the kitchen fire and the adjacent Common Room was still a mess. Soot covered every surface, from the windows to the light fixtures. The dining tables, chairs and sofas had been shoved up against the far wall in a jumbled pile. Looking at them, Lucas wondered if any of the furniture could be salvaged. He also wondered how their reduced numbers could do the work intended for 50, work that included far more repairs than the mission had ever intended. At least someone had gotten around to removing the cumbersome fire-fighting equipment.

The worst part was the fire had been deliberately set. "What a waste," he muttered suppressing a yawn. Spending most of the night re-installing Peg may not have been the best replacement for sleep, but at least they had an AI again.

"Hey boss," said Kasumi as she walked in. Her black hair was pulled back into a messy ponytail and her clothing was covered in smudges of soot. But it was the bags under her eyes that made their Chief Engineer look as tired as he felt. Like Lucas, she hadn't joined the mission in her current position, but after the previous Chief Engineer Joe's death the responsibility had fallen to her.

"Did you get any sleep?" he asked.

"Nope, spent the night working on stabilizing our ventilation system," she said, with a yawn.

"Are we okay?"

"Our air is fine." She sniffed and then wrinkled her nose. "Well, it will be once this stink disappears. But Gan discovered some problems with the power system that we'll need to investigate further. I'd like to shut down the domestic printers for now."

"How long will the printers be down?" Their domestic printers were used to create their clothes, small tools and household items. They could live without them for a while.

The engineer tilted her head to the side. "Say, two days?"

"Okay, we can live with that," said Lucas. "How long is it going to take to get the kitchen up and running again?"

Kasumi glared at the kitchen door as she snorted and crossed her arms. "I don't know. The damage is extensive. Maybe if you got a work party in there to clean up while Gan and I finish evaluating the power system, we'd have a better idea of what it would take?"

"Sure, I can do that," said Lucas.

Just then Amanda walked out of the kitchen, shaking her head and scrubbing soot off her hands with a soiled rag. Lucas hadn't realized she'd been in there. "So?" he asked. "What's our food situation?"

"All the food stored in the kitchen was destroyed, but crates in the store rooms are fine. I can keep serving meals in the Hub for the time being," she said.

"That'll work."

"I should get going," said Kasumi. "My to-do list is impossibly long."

"Keep me updated," said Lucas. "And make sure you get

some sleep," he added when Kasumi yawned a second time. After she nodded and left, he turned to Amanda.

"We'll deal with this," Amanda gestured widely with both arms, "like we have with every other challenge. One task at a time." Amanda smiled. "Our situation will improve."

Lucas realized then that no one was addressing him as Commander Ordaz. Well, except Lucy Snow. He doubted his colleagues ever would now that they'd made a habit of addressing him by his first name. It didn't matter so long as they supported him in his efforts to lead the colony.

"I hope you're right," he said, wishing he had Amanda's optimism. What he did have was a ball of tension in his gut along with a nagging feeling he hadn't thought of everything. "Do you think we'll have any crops ready to harvest soon?"

"Devin and Sud are in the greenhouse. Why don't we go ask them?" Amanda brushed a lock of her thick hair behind an ear and raised a questioning eyebrow.

"Good idea. Let's do it." Lucas started making a mental tally of all the things he now needed to worry about. On top of improving morale—which he still felt was his first priority if not necessarily the most urgent—was food, power, ventilation, repairs, Ms. Snow; the list felt impossible to manage. His nose was beginning to throb again. *How does one lead effectively in a situation that is entirely unanticipated? Am I even cut out for this?*

"We'll figure things out," Amanda said, seeing his worries etched on his face. She briefly rested a hand on his arm. "Carrying on in the face of adversity has been our strength. We've already proven that. We'll succeed. You'll see."

Maybe he should put the ultra-positive Amanda in charge of morale, Lucas thought as he followed her towards the entrance to the greenhouse. *Delegation is a sign of a good leader, isn't it?*

Bright light, filtered to emulate mid-morning on Earth, nearly blinded Lucas after being in the soot-darkened Common

Room. Breathing the moist greenhouse air felt good—he should've come here sooner.

Several acres in size, their greenhouse was bigger than the urban parks Lucas had visited on Earth. A sprawling, multi-story building could fit under the dome with room to spare. Most of the ground was still Thesan grey, except for the newly planted willow grove around the pump house, a fish pond with their few surviving fish, and a generously proportioned vegetable garden.

He shifted his attention to the food plot where neat rows of plants extended in long rows. Growing up in a crowded urban area, Lucas had never gained an appreciation for gardening or farming, yet here he was, leader of a terraforming mission. *Strange what life threw at you.*

Amanda led him to the row where Devin, the Head Gardener, was working with Sud. They were an odd pair. Devin's mop of sandy-blonde hair and lanky form contrasted with Sud's neatly trimmed black hair and compact shape. Devin knelt on the ground while Sud squatted beside him. The two gardeners stood as he and Amanda approached.

"So you're in charge now?" asked Sud in a friendly tone. He was short, too, at eye level with Lucas.

"Looks like." Lucas said as he looked at the nearby plants. They were green with little white flowers. The vegetable they would produce was a complete mystery to him. *Peg would know. Maybe I can create an AI interface with my scroll—no, I need to focus on running this place.*

"Are the crops growing as expected?" Lucas asked.

"We've got plenty of lettuce and radishes ready and our first potatoes will be ready in a few weeks," Devin said with a nod at the flowering plant that had mystified Lucas. His hair hung down into his eyes, but he didn't seem to care. "After that, there'll be tomatoes, beans, peppers, eggplant and corn."

Lucas turned to Amanda. "Are you able to feed the colonists with the food being produced?"

"For now, it's salads and preserved stuff. But we'll be eating pretty good in a few weeks," she promised with a grin.

"I'm okay with that."

"Hey, boss man!" Lucas closed his eyes briefly at the sound of Abigail's voice before turning to wait for her approach. Lucas noted with envy that both Devin and Sud had the wherewithal —and the freedom—to grab their tools and head off to another area of the extensive greenhouse. Lucas debated going with them, but knew Abigail would just follow.

Amanda put a hand on his forearm and leaned in. "See you later," she said, before walking off, leaving Lucas alone to face Abigail.

"Boss man, I want to talk to you," Abigail repeated when she got close.

"What's up?" From the look on her face, Lucas knew he wouldn't enjoy whatever it was she'd come to say. He felt the knot in his gut tighten as he tried to maintain a neutral expression.

"You put that Conglomerate bitch in the Hub with us," she said. "She deserves to be locked away. Or worse."

"Sure Abigail. Point me to the colony prison wing, and I'll put her in it," said Lucas, absently rubbing his nose and then immediately regretting it.

Abigail narrowed her eyes at his lame attempt at sarcasm and crossed her arms over her chest. "There's got to be a closet somewhere."

"We barely have breathable air. I want to get the colony's basic necessities sorted out before we start thinking about building prisons."

"You can't let her get away unpunished!"

"I won't. For now, she's confined to her quarters. We'll figure out the rest later."

Frowning, Abigail looked Lucas up and down as though weighing whether he was up to the task of leadership. "Don't let us down on this. That woman needs to be held responsible for her actions."

"I don't doubt you'll keep me accountable, but know this." Lucas took a step closer to Abigail and looked straight into her eyes. "I'm never going to forget that my wife is dead because of Ms. Snow's scheming. I also intend to get every piece of information I can out of her about The Conglomerate's plans so we can better protect ourselves."

"We can't let them win," Abigail said in a cooperative tone.

Lucas hid his surprise at Abigail's conciliatory tone. *Is she really deferring to me?* "No we can't. But if we stick together, we can make this work," Lucas said.

Abigail nodded, satisfied. "I'll go help Kasumi filter the colony's air," she said, turning and heading back the way she'd come.

Lucas watched her leave, then looked up at the dome's roof. The two suns could be seen in the sky above. "We can do this, Camila," he promised, then turned and began heading back inside.

Chapter Nine

Holding a box, Margo stood in front of the first-floor apartment door adjacent to the green wall. It looked the same as the rest of the apartment doors—a tasteful shade of muted green to blend with the tones of the Hub—yet this one felt ominous.

A flash of blue in her peripheral vision caught her attention. She turned to watch one of the morphos exploring beneath the philodendron leaves running up the green wall. The insect darted in and out of the foliage as though on a secret mission. Watching it all day was tempting, but she had a job to do.

Margo swallowed, wiping her sweaty palms on her pants one at a time as she shifted her grip on the empty box she was carrying. Inside the apartment was all that remained of the lives of two of their colonists who'd died months before. It had made sense when Lucas had asked for volunteers. Clean out the personal belongings from the quarters of the people they'd lost or clean up the fire damage in the Common Room and kitchen.

"I should've volunteered to scrub soot," she muttered, feeling like she was invading someone's privacy. *Get in there before you chicken out!* She jerked her arm out and pushed the button, and the door to Bonnie and Jim's quarters slid open.

Taking a deep breath, she stepped inside, reminding herself of her ulterior motive—finding Jim's notebooks. Yes, their local saboteur had been stopped, but she had a niggling sense there was more to know, and Jim had once told her that he'd filled notebooks with information on The Conglomerate's more nefarious activities.

Leaving the door open behind her, she moved further into the living room. She turned on the lights and looked around, setting the box down on the coffee table. Decorated with natural hues, the living room was warm and inviting. Three close-up still images of seed pods hung on the walls. She studied each one wondering what would become of the images. The surviving colonists had already agreed that any books left behind by those who'd died could augment their small library, but she wasn't sure what she was meant to do with Jim and Bonnie's art. Cocking her head, she studied the images. They were nice. She decided to take them and hang them in the library. Taking them down, she brought them to the entrance and leaned them against the wall just outside the door.

Back in the living room, she stared at the inviting couch for a moment, wishing she could flop down on the faux leather and discuss conspiracy theories with Jim or hear more tales of Bonnie's seed hunting adventures, but that wasn't going to happen. The happy couple had died in the aquaponics explosion and now occupied two side-by-side graves outside.

She noticed a snake plant on the floor by the shelf unit. Despite two months of neglect, the plant was still healthy. Margo moved the pot and set it down by the door. Running a finger along one of the stiff leaves, she pictured it in a corner of the Sick Bay waiting room. She'd only occasionally have to swing by and water it.

Turning, she put her hands on her hips and surveyed the space. *If I were Jim, where would I keep my notebooks?*

Like all the apartments, this one had three bedrooms leading off a central living room. Bonnie and Jim likely used the master bedroom for sleeping, so Margo retrieved a tote bag from the box she'd brought and started her search in one of the smaller bedrooms. In the first room she entered were shelves stacked high with boxes of seeds.

"Wow!" she said excitedly. "Bonnie must have moved some of the seed library here." Margo traced a finger along the neatly labelled boxes. Different varieties of carrots, beets, peas and squashes filled the row. She couldn't wait to tell Devin this good news.

Margo left what was obviously Bonnie's workroom and went into the other small bedroom. It was filled with shelves of seeds as well—except for a small desk in the one corner. Squeezing past the shelves, Margo sat down at the desk.

A single framed photograph sat on the surface. Picking it up for a closer look, Margo saw Jim and Bonnie's smiling faces flanking a little girl. The child looked delicate and frail, with skin so pale it looked translucent. The couple had never mentioned they'd had a child, and Margo could only assume she'd died. *What happened to her?* She felt a stab of sadness at the thought of parents having to live through the loss of a child. Since it was a personal item, she put the picture into her bag. She wasn't sure what she would do with it, but eventually she'd find a place for it.

She started opening drawers, searching for Jim's notebooks, and was rewarded when she opened the large bottom drawer. The notebooks were of various dimensions and thicknesses and made a lopsided pile. She was surprised at the number—there was nineteen in total. Jim must have taken years, if not his entire adult life, filling the pages. Pulling them out one at a time, Margo started filling her bag.

Under the last notebook at the bottom of the drawer was a round metal case. She lifted it up and read the label:

Peggy Plum interview 6 August 1952

1952 was more than two centuries ago. Something was ringing a faint bell for her, but she wasn't sure what. As far as she could remember, she'd never known anyone with the name Peggy Plum. Opening the case, Margo found a spool of old-fashioned film. She pulled out the roll, unwound half a metre and held it up to the light. There were images on the film, but they were much too small to make out. *Jim must have a projector, else why would he bring a film all the way to Thesan?* As she replaced the film into its round case, her eyes fell on the sliding doors of the closet. She got up, squeezed past the shelves, and opened the door.

"Now where would he have put the projector?" Margo murmured to herself.

"In the gardening office."

Margo inhaled sharply as she spun around to see who'd spoken. Julien was standing in the doorway, his insectoid goggles catching the light in a creepy way. She shivered. Never had a child un-nerved her so much.

"What are you doing here? You nearly scared me out of my skin." Feeling her heart rate begin to normalize, she studied the boy as he advanced into the room.

His thin face and prominent cheek bones added to his insec-toid look. He'd also clearly outgrown the sleeves on his shirt, the unhealthy looking white skin of his wrists and hands contrasting with the dark fabric. She hadn't spent any time with the kid, although she'd seen him around. It was hard not to dismiss him out of hand because she despised his mother. And at least his mother was abiding by the terms of her asylum and remaining in her quarters. It still galled her that the hated woman was even in their colony.

"The projector you're looking for is in the gardening office," he said, unperturbed by her reaction to him. "For that film you found." He pointed to the desk. "The interview with Peggy Plum."

Margo pursed her lips as she stared at the boy. He must have been watching her when she took the film out of the canister and she hadn't noticed. She must also have been talking to herself more than she realized. She didn't think she'd read the title aloud, but clearly she had. The kid must be a practiced snoop. He'd come into this apartment uninvited, and he'd obviously also explored the garden shed. Maybe he was a collector, fascinated by old-fashioned technology, which explained why he'd recognized the old-fashioned projector.

"The Conglomerate is going to silence everyone on the far side of the moon," continued Julien as he stopped beside her.

At his strange announcement, she stared down at the boy as if he truly was a talking insect. He must've heard his mother say something about The Conglomerate and something else about the far side of the moon, and then mixed them up to make his odd statement, which made no sense.

"No one lives on that side of Earth's moon," she explained as she moved back to the desk and started arranging Jim's notebooks into her carry bag.

"That's what they want you to think."

Margo paused and studied the boy for a moment. His solemn look from behind his prismed goggles made her feel uncomfortable. She shook her head, dismissing her discomfort. He was just a kid. A weird one, but still, just a kid. She picked up the film and added it to her bag.

"Let's go," she said holding the bag and gesturing for him to step out of the room.

The boy turned and walked out ahead of her. She was grateful he remained silent as everything he said so far was rather unsettling.

For now, she was looking forward to finding a quiet spot to read Jim's notebooks.

Chapter Ten

"This one appears to be a rant about the pyramids," said Gary, flipping through one of Jim's notebooks as Margo came into the room carrying two steaming mugs. Even if he refused to admit it, she could tell Neil's continuing insistence that Gary take it easy was driving him nuts. "Jim obviously bought into a lot of ancient alien garbage. Look at this."

Holding up the book, he exposed a full page coloured sketch of a 'little green man' style alien. Margo frowned at the image. Looking for clues in Jim's notebooks might be a wild goose chase, but she felt it was necessary. Setting the mugs on the coffee table, she sat on the couch across from Gary and picked up the next notebook. The worn pages were filled with notes on the Knights Templar complete with sketches of armoured men on warhorses.

"There has to be something useful in these somewhere," she insisted. "Thanks for your help, by the way." She leaned forward to lift her mug and met Gary's gaze as she took a sip.

"It's not like I have anywhere else I need to be," he said with a shrug before turning a page in the book he held. Margo could see the sketches morph from Celtic scrollwork into Egyptian hieroglyphics. *Maybe Bonnie had been right and Margo should dismiss Jim's collection of information as unfounded conspiracy theories.*

"When's Neil going to let you go back to work?" she asked, deliberately stressing the word "let" to make him smile.

Gary grimaced. "I assume tomorrow or the next day." He flipped through a few more pages before taking a sip from his mug. His movements looked smoother today. He reached for his mug with care, but at least he didn't wince. "He's enjoying having power over me."

"He *is* your little brother," said Margo. She looked up at him and cocked her head.

"True. I'm guessing these guys don't have family angst." He smiled as he held up his notebook showing Margo a two-page drawing of the stone heads on Easter Island.

"Well, these guys have angst." She held up the notebook page that depicted a group of knights surrounded by an army of what looked like zombies.

After they shared a grin, she retrieved her mug and settled back into the couch with the notebook. After turning the page she inhaled sharply. Taped to the page was a photograph of a girl, maybe nine years old, with the same narrow face and long blond hair as Bonnie. She was sitting on a swing, grinning—the same girl from the family photo Margo had seen in Bonnie and Jim's quarters. A note in the margin said: *Kimberly, the day before the diagnosis.*

"What did you find?" asked Gary, leaning forward to try and see her notebook.

"A photograph," she said, moving to sit beside him so he could see as well.

Gary read the caption. "Diagnosis? She's ill? Who is she?"

"I don't know for sure, but I found a photograph in Jim's den of the three of them. So, I'm assuming she's their daughter." Stapled to the next page was a brochure for a medical facility. "Look," she said, lifting the brochure and pointing to the address. It was on Maximillian Station

—The Conglomerate's space station. Inside, the text promised cutting edge technology along with the best treatments.

"Wait, what's that?" Gary said, pointing to the notebook. There was some writing on the page that had been hidden by the brochure.

Margo read it out loud. *There's a genetic program here that might make the difference. It's hard to get into, there seems to be a lot of tests required—and not just for Kimberly. They want to test Bonnie and I as well. Normally, I'd be against trusting the Big Evil, but it is the only option left. Kimberly is getting weaker by the day.*

"I've heard about that facility," said Gary. "It's private. You only get there if The Conglomerate invites you." Then he frowned. "But they're more focused on research than helping people."

Margo glanced at him. Gary's expression was unusually relaxed. Being forced to take it easy for a few days had been good for him, although it was unfortunate that he'd had to get stabbed by a madman in order to take it easy.

"From what I remember, this facility specializes in genetic modifications. They only take extreme anomaly cases, and they are very selective. As a surgeon, I never had any dealings with them."

"Huh," said Margo, looking back at the notebook. "I wonder if Jim wrote down details on what genetic anomaly Kimberly had?"

Margo flipped to the next page and skimmed the text. "It looks like they had some appointments. They even made a trip to the station. Oh," she said as she turned the page. "Jim was an intrepid sketcher. And detailed, too. He's done a schematic of the space station."

The sketch of Maximillian Station took up both pages of the open notebook. It was a standard ring with spokes. Jim had labelled some rings in the top third of the station with names like 'Wormhole Observatory' and 'Xenobiology'. She traced a finger over an 'Alien Artifacts' lab. *Clearly these folks are into the same pseudoscience as Jim was.*

The middle section consisted of medical labs, which Jim had noted were off limits. Half of the bottom section was a port facility for Conglomerate spacecraft and the rest focused on the necessities of human existence from living quarters to cafeterias. Margo traced a finger along the main concourse, connecting the station together before noticing a list of names in the margin. As she started reading the list, she assumed they were staff Jim and Bonnie had met while trying to get help for their daughter.

"Dr. Snow," she said. She looked at Gary with a question in her eyes.

He shook his head. "I've never heard of a Dr. Snow. It might be a relation to our Ms. Snow, but we can't assume," said Gary.

When Gary leaned in to look closer at the list of names, Margo realized he smelled nice; soap and pine needles. She shifted on the couch, suddenly uncomfortable that she was noticing how Gary smelled. He leaned away, and she refocused on the notebook, flipping to the next page. Here the writing was larger and bolder as if the writer had been angry.

"Oh, no," Margo said, her fingers showing Gary where she was reading. "They didn't accept her."

"Which means they didn't cure her. But then again, they weren't focused on cures unless it could make them a profit."

"It must have been a big step for Jim and Bonnie, going to The Conglomerate for help. He refers to them throughout his text as the Big Evil. He hated them."

"Yes, but did he hate them before or after they declined to cure his child?"

Margo nodded thoughtfully. "Good point." She sighed. "I wish I'd had time to get to know them better."

They sat in comfortable silence as they paged through their respective notebooks. When Gary finished his and reached for another, he noticed the film canister at the bottom of the pile. "What's in the case?"

"It's an old-fashioned film interview from the 1950s with someone called Peggy Plum. I found it with the notebooks." Margo retrieved the small case, which was slightly larger than her hand. She ran a finger over the smooth metal, so different from the plastics and synthetics currently in use, then opened it, holding it out so Gary could see the contents.

"That's fascinating technology. I remember reading about the way they made vids back then. I assume Jim had a device of some kind to watch this?" he asked, refraining from touching the film.

"Yes, that projector," Margo said, pointing to the black vinyl box she'd brought. She'd found it in the gardening office right were the kid had said it would be. "It also has a couple of power adaptors. I checked."

"So, who is this Peggy Plum and why did Jim keep an old-fashioned film reel of her interview? Why not have it transferred to vid technology so he could watch it on his scroll?"

Margo shook her head as perplexed as Gary. "I have no idea. I haven't found a reference to her yet in any of Jim's notebooks."

"Shall we try watching it? We can set it up in my study," Gary added, looking at the walls in the living room that were either covered with art or shelves. "There's a clear wall there we can project onto."

When Gary carefully pushed himself to his feet. Margo wondered if she should offer to help. He still wasn't fully healed and was moving stiffly.

"Does it still hurt?"

"Not much, but I think I'll not offer to carry that for you, if that's okay," Gary said with a nod at the projector and case as he walked into the next room, and the lights came on.

Margo put the lid back on the film and then carried the film case and projector into Gary's sparsely furnished office—clearly, he wasn't using the space. Margo set up the projector on the immaculately organized desk.

On the inside cover of the projector case was a diagram showing how to weave the dark strip through the loops and gears of the film gates. Margo followed the diagram's instructions and snapped out the two arms, mounting the roll of film on one arm and an empty reel on the other.

"Have you ever used one of these?" she asked.

"I've never even seen one in real life."

Margo grabbed the end of the strip of film. "Well, double check the diagram and make sure I'm interpreting it correctly, will you?" She began to feed the film through the projector. After she'd woven the strip of film through the last turn, she stood up straight and looked at her handiwork.

"That's quite something," Gary said, shaking his head in wonder. "All the trouble they went to just to watch a vid."

"Well, we don't know yet it if works." She put her finger on the power switch but paused. "Ready to find out?"

"Wait," Gary said. "There's only one place to sit." He nodded at the desk chair. "I'd offer to bring in a chair from the dining room, but…"

"It's okay. You sit. I'll stand."

As soon as Gary sat, Margo flipped the projector's power switch. Black and white numbers appeared on the wall, counting down from ten to one.

"It looks overexposed."

"No," Gary said. "I think we just need to turn off the lights."

Margo moved to the wall switch. As soon as the lights were off, the image looked right.

In the black and white moving image, an elderly woman sat with perfect posture behind a desk looking directly into the camera. Her short hair looked white, and she wore thick glasses with black frames. The film was degraded in places and the sound slightly garbled, but Peggy's British accent was clear and her words easy to understand. Keeping her gaze on the woman, Margo backed away from the projector until she stood beside

Gary's chair. She crossed her arms across her chest and watched.

Good morning. My name is Peggy Plum. I want to talk about the inevitability of artificial intelligence…

Gary snapped his fingers. "I know who she is now! She's the creator of the PEG series of AI." When Margo raised an eyebrow at him, he continued, "I took a history of computing course during my undergrad."

They both turned their attention back to the image on the wall.

Our modern technology will grow and be capable of so much more than we've been predicting. The creation of rudimentary artificial intelligence has now become possible. Advancing this knowledge has been the focus of my work since my time at Bletchley Park.

In time, the capability of machine minds will grow to the point where they will have equivalent minds as our own. Perhaps eventually, it will be possible to transfer our own minds into the machine.

"These ideas would've been very progressive at the time," whispered Gary, as they listened to Peggy drone on about the detailed algorithms behind AIs. "I don't even think the term AI had been coined back then."

"She wasn't wrong," said Margo. "We do have AIs with minds near equivalent to our own."

We've only just begun, the woman on the film said. Then she took a deep breath, and the camera panned closer to her face. *Margo Murphy, when you see this…*

"What?" Margo uncrossed her arms and straightened as a shiver ran up her spine.

"Wait! Did she just say your name?" Gary was staring dumbfounded at the woman.

Margo shushed him, gesturing for him to be quiet.

…you need to go to the far side of the moon to…

The film degraded. Peggy's image was replaced with shifting horizontal lines.

"Dirty circuits!" Margo cursed before running to turn on the lights. Then she hurried back to the projector. "I'm sure one of these switches was to rewind," she muttered. "Here it is!"

The film strip started moving backwards. She let it go a short distance and stopped it. Gary had risen and was standing by the light switch waiting for her signal. When she was ready, he flipped the lights off and she switched the projector to play. The woman said her name, mentioned the far side of the moon, and then the film degraded.

When Margo turned the projector off and Gary turned on the lights, they stared at one other in amazement.

"Well that was creepy," Margo said.

Gary shook his head. "It really isn't such a stretch that there was someone in 1952 with your name. What's suspicious is that Jim, and likely Bonnie, knew about this and never told you."

Margo frowned. She hadn't thought of that.

"And besides," Gary added. "That film was made in 1952, almost two decades before any human set foot on the moon."

"That was so surreal," she said, still focused on how the woman had seemed to be addressing her. She knew that was impossible of course, but that didn't make it any less surreal. "I have to watch it again." Margo rewound the film and, when Gary dimmed the lights, played it again, intently studying Peggy's face as the woman spoke. There was nothing familiar about her, no family resemblance that she could spot.

Margo crossed her arms as the film ran out and Gary turned the lights back on. "Why do you think she's instructing the Margo Murphy from 1952 to go to the far side of the moon when space travel wasn't viable? And to do what?"

"I don't think we have enough information to speculate in a meaningful way," Gary said, leaning the shoulder of his good side against the wall. "The message could be just a coincidence," he added, although his tone indicated he didn't believe that.

"That seems unlikely." Margo rewound the film and played it again, but watching it for the fourth time didn't give her any new answers. She looked over at Gary, about to ask him if he wanted to watch it again, but she noticed that he was sagging against the wall and his face had turned ashen.

"Whoa. You've over done it, haven't you?" said Margo.

"Perhaps," he said, lifting a hand and rubbing his temple. "You've found an intriguing puzzle and I want to get to the bottom of it, but I need to call it a night."

"Okay," said Margo, turning the power off on the projector.

"Can you come back tomorrow? Maybe a good night's sleep will give us some insight. And we can continue looking at Jim's journals in case there's something there we missed." Gary watched her with a hopeful expression.

"Sure, I'd like that," said Margo, with a smile. "Do you mind if I leave everything here?"

"It's early for you. Are you ready to stop for the night, too?" he asked leading the way back into the living room.

"No, I'll take one of the notebooks with me." There were three piles of notebooks stacked on the coffee table. Gary had sorted them by those she'd read, those they'd both read, and those that still needed to be read. She picked up the next one in her stack and the two empty coffee mugs then headed for the exit.

Gary followed her to the door. There was an awkward moment where he looked like he was about to say something, but then he turned and pushed the button to open the door, offering only a smile instead.

Margo looked out at the tallest of the plants of the Hub and saw that the lights hadn't yet cycled to nighttime. "See you tomorrow, then." She smiled at Gary over her shoulder.

Chapter Eleven

Lucas studied Ms. Snow's features as they sat across the table from each other. Holding herself with perfect posture, she looked straight back at him. She'd maintained her neutral expression since he'd arrived in her quarters more than an hour ago. *How can she maintain such control?* He'd learned a fair bit about The Conglomerate, but nothing truly useful. She was providing careful, rehearsed answers to all his questions.

"Ms. Snow—"

She raised a hand to stop him. "Please, I've asked you repeatedly to call me Lucy," she said.

Lucas shifted in his chair, angling himself slightly away from the woman. She was playing him, that much he knew. *Is Margo right? Should we put her out an airlock?* He flexed his jaw and forced himself to show, at least on the surface, the same control as Ms. Snow. He'd been refusing to address her as Lucy, only because she'd asked him to, but he now realized he needed to focus his interaction with her on gleaning useful information, not seeing who was more stubborn.

"Fine. Lucy, as you agreed, you are to tell me everything I want to know," he said. His scroll was on the table recording their conversation. Lucas looked around at the generic decor of Lucy's quarters trying to think of what to say to make her more cooperative. "Where's Julien?" he asked.

"Off exploring," Lucy answered. Even at mention of her son, her expression didn't change. So much for that tactic.

"Let's get back to the indium deposits." He'd been asking general questions that she'd been answering with general responses, and he now realized he needed to be explicitly specific. Then maybe he'd get somewhere. "Did The Conglomerate plant false information in the data from the exploration drones about the indium on Thesan in order to mislead the colonizing committee?" Margo had discovered the valuable mineral laying all over the surface of the plains where the *Settler* had crash landed.

"Yes, this planet is unusually rich in the metal."

"Is that why you were in orbit?" Lucas suppressed an urge to fidget; instead, he mimicked her neutral expression.

"Yes, we were waiting for you to give up and call for rescue."

"So that you could look as if you were rescuing the survivors, but in reality The Conglomerate intended to stake their claim on the planet and mine its riches?"

"Yes."

So far, she still wasn't providing any revelations. She was simply confirming what they'd already guessed.

"The Conglomerate ship—"

"The *CS Compliance*," Lucy cut in.

"Right," said Lucas. "Is it just going to sit by the wormhole until the next window?"

Lucy held his gaze for an uncomfortably long time. Finally, he'd asked a question that she truly didn't want to answer. When her facade finally cracked and her blank neutrality was replaced with weariness, he felt a surge of adrenaline.

She stood abruptly and paced across the room. Her bandaged hand was obviously healing well as she seemed to give it no notice. Pausing mid step, she seemed deep in thought for a moment before striding back across the room. Returning to her seat, she rested her hands on the table top and focused on Lucas. "Do you promise to protect my child, no matter what happens?"

He needed her to believe he would keep his word and protect her son—which he would do—so he held her gaze, hoping she saw sincerity and commitment. "I promise."

She jabbed her good hand at the recording device. "Your promise is on record. You have to uphold it."

"I will."

"And if you die and someone else becomes the leader?"

"Then let the record state that I'm holding every member of this colony accountable to upholding the commitment to protect your son."

"Including Margo Murphy?"

"Including Margo Murphy." Lucas suspected Margo would never do anything to harm that child.

Lucy's nostrils flared as she glared at him. "They're going to wish they'd cut off my head instead of my finger," she said as she yanked back her chair and sat. "The wormhole doesn't behave like the public thinks."

Lucas leaned back in his chair. That was absolutely not what he was expecting to hear, but he was inordinately relieved her facade had finally crumbled. *Now we're getting somewhere.* "What do you mean?"

"Firstly, it doesn't have the periodicity that's been claimed." As she spoke, she put her good hand around her ponytail and pulled the long tail of hair over her right shoulder. "Secondly, it doesn't connect multiple different solar systems. It only points to one place."

Lucas couldn't contain his surprise. He stood, taking a moment to contemplate the implications of her surprising announcement, then faced her. "If it only points to Thesan, and we're the only colony on Thesan, then where did the other two

Settler missions go?" They were the third of three colonizing missions.

"There are three planets in the Goldilocks zone in this system, a *Settler* mission went to each."

Lucas knew his jaw had dropped, but he couldn't stop himself from gaping at her. "Are you telling me there are three inhabitable planets in the Goldilocks zone?"

"Yes." She rose and began pacing back and forth again.

"They're here in this solar system?" Lucas couldn't believe it. When their comms were up and running again, they would be able to contact the other colonies. Then he remembered the most recent news packet from Earth about the second mission. "What do you know about the status of the other two missions?"

"Nothing."

"What do you mean, nothing? You had a ship capable of investigating and you've been up there for as long as we've been down here."

She stopped and turned towards him, giving him an icy look. "Checking on their wellbeing wasn't part of our mission."

"Were they sent to die like us?" asked Lucas.

"It's not like that," said Lucy in a defensive tone, sitting back down and crossing her legs and arms.

She looked defiant and troubled. Lucas didn't care. He crossed his arms and glared right back at her. "You know, that deal I just made to protect Julien? A deal on behalf of my 28 comrades here? Well, it only goes into effect if you provide information."

"You don't have to remind me," she snapped. "And you all weren't sent to die. You were sent to fail. Dead people can't call for a rescue."

"But we could communicate with the other colonies?"

"Maybe," she said. "Our analysts suspected that your colony is the one that's been most successful. The others may not have fared so well."

"Shit," said Lucas, sitting back in his chair. "Does the Colonizing Counsel know about this?"

"No, The Conglomerate has deceived them," she said.

"Because there's indium on their planets, too?"

"I don't actually know. The only concern of the *CS Compliance* was Thesan."

"So, there could be two other Conglomerate ships in the system orbiting above the other two *Settler* colonies?"

"No, we were the only Conglomerate ship in the system," she said.

Lucas addressed the AI. "Peg, can you look into how to communicate with the other planets in the solar system." Peg had been instructed to ignore any questions from Lucy, except domestic ones like where the light switch was, but as Commander, Lucas could access Peg from any room in the colony.

"Yes Lucas," said the AI.

With Peg reinstalled, they would soon be able to send comms and start their own investigation about the other colonies. *They had neighbours!* He didn't know if there was any way he could help them, but it was worth trying.

Lucas remembered what Gary had found in the personnel records, the same information Captain Hori had found—and been killed by the saboteur because of it; every one of them had been deemed unfit for this mission. "Did The Conglomerate control the selection process for *Settler* III?"

"Yes."

"And deliberately change the singles who were matched to wed?" Lucas crossed his arms and paced slowly back and forth as he peppered Lucy with questions.

"Yes."

Lucas thought of Joe and Margo, how they'd been matched by the computer. They would've been really happy together, like him and Camila, but the results had been changed so that Joe married Abigail and Margo married Gary, neither of which was an obvious match.

JEANNETTE BEDARD

"You and Margo have a history. Did you know she was on this mission?"

"Yes. She's expendable." Lucy's eyes glittered. "She doesn't know how to follow orders. It's too bad she isn't in one of those graves out there." Lucy jerked her head towards the exterior of the ship.

Lucas paused and shifted his focus back to Lucy. "Stay focused," he warned. "I won't be holding up my side of the bargain unless you hold up yours."

"I am holding up my side," Lucy said through gritted teeth.

"Just making sure. Tell me, how does the wormhole work? Will the CS *Compliance* be able to return to Earth upon arrival at the wormhole?"

"It…"

They were interrupted by Margo bursting through the door and stalking towards Lucy.

"Margo," said Lucas, grabbing her arm to intercept her. "What are you doing here? I'm conducting an interview, in case you hadn't noticed."

"I have a couple questions of my own," she said, holding his gaze. "I promise to behave."

Lucas opened his mouth to insist Margo leave, then changed his mind. Margo was an ally he needed. He let go of her arm and gestured for her to proceed. "Ask away," Lucas said. It's not like there was any urgency to finding out more about the wormhole; it hardly mattered whether he gleaned the information now or an hour from now.

Margo passed by him and sat in his chair, facing Lucy across the table. Lucas remained standing, leaning his back against the wall, but he just about fell over when he heard Margo's question.

"What's on the far side of the moon?" Margo demanded.

Lucy inhaled and her eyes darted to Lucas. It took everything he had to keep his face neutral and remain casually leaning against the wall, grateful for its support. He knew about

84

the dark side of the moon; it haunted his nightmares. *How the hell had Margo found out about it?*

"There's an..."

Lucy stopped and frowned, clearly struggling to uphold her side of their bargain. It was clear to Lucas she knew something.

"There's an old military facility there," Lucy finally admitted. "From what I understand, it was a big place and was once used for helium-3 propulsion research. They abandoned it about 50 years ago." For the first time since their interrogation had begun, Lucy took a sip of water from her glass.

Lucas knew all about the facility. He'd only been there once, but that was enough. It was the last time he'd spoken to Ash Jones, his former second-in-command. When he left, Lucas reported Ash dead, just as she'd asked. But she wasn't. Six months later he'd heard that both her son and mother had vanished, and he'd guessed she'd found a way for them to join her. It was a secret he'd been keeping for years. Even Camila hadn't known about them. But that wasn't why the place haunted him.

"There's got to be more than that," insisted Margo.

"Yes."

Lucy lifted her glass, but the slight tremor in her hand made her put it down again. That told Lucas there was information to be had that The Conglomerate did not want outsiders to know.

"But the information I have was obtained through The Conglomerate's information gathering network. Some of it may be inaccurate."

"Go on," said Lucas.

"It's believed that an insurgent organization has taken over the abandoned facility. Mostly disgraced scientists who want to continue their research without interference. Not even The Conglomerate knows what they're doing."

"Who specifically is doing work there?" asked Margo.

"My sources told me about a scientist named Paul Dogan.

He and his family vanished from The Conglomerate station five years ago when he'd been working on a secret project."

"The Conglomerate didn't 'make' him vanish? Have him killed?"

Lucy shook her head. "No. They were outraged when he left. But even The Conglomerate doesn't have the resources to go to every backwater in the galaxy to retrieve something they'd lost."

"What project was he was working on?" asked Lucas moving to the table and pulling a chair up to sit beside Margo.

"Transfer of consciousness stuff. Before he vanished, he managed to make it work. He transferred the consciousness of his assistant on the station into a host in Vienna. She was the only test subject I know of that didn't lose her mind in the process."

"The Combined Nations banned that line of research a decade ago," said Margo.

"I know Dr. Dogan has had a lot of failures over the years. Rumour has it there is a ward in The Conglomerate's medical facility solely for his permanently brain damaged assistants." Lucy dropped her gaze and wrapped her arms around herself, making Lucas suspect she knew more about these failures than she was letting on. He was about to ask but Margo spoke first.

"Who else is working there?" asked Margo.

"I don't know," said Lucy. "But I do know The Conglomerate has a plan to finally clear the facility. Annihilate the insurgent's stronghold. Last I heard, preparations were already being made, so I'd expect the operation will happen soon."

Lucas was thankful the two women hated each other and were so focused on their opponent that they didn't notice his rapid breathing. *Do I still owe a debt to Ash? But even if I do, how can I warn her?* Then he remembered Lucy's early comment about the wormhole not working as they thought. Maybe there was a way to warn Ash.

"I want to know more about the moon facility." Margo stood, crossing her arms.

"I've told you all I know," said Lucy, sitting up strait. The two women's eyes were fixed on each other.

"You're a liar. I should've let you die when I had the chance."

"Margo, you promised to behave." His nose had begun to throb again, and his head was starting to pound.

"I'm not the one misbehaving," Margo argued, rising and gesturing at Lucy. "She's not telling us everything she knows."

"Margo, I want you to go." For a moment, Margo loomed over him, her cheeks flushed in anger. Abruptly, she turned and stormed out of the room.

"I demand you keep her away from me," said Lucy.

"You're not in a position to demand anything," snapped Lucas. He was relieved they were no longer talking about the far side of the moon, and he allowed himself to let some of his anger flow. Lucy needed to see that he was no pushover. "Because of you, my wife is dead, as are more than 20 of my comrades. You cannot manipulate me. I'll never forget what you did." Camila always said he should be quicker to forgive, but in this case he could never forgive Lucy—Camila was dead because of her. A bitter taste formed in his mouth and he couldn't stop his lip from curling. He could no longer stand the sight of Lucy Snow.

"We'll resume this interrogation later." He swiped his recording device off the table, turned his back on his irritating prisoner and left the room. *Command sucked!*

Chapter Twelve

Gary slumped back into his couch watching his Serengeti painting morph. Herds of rhinoceroses, zebra and giraffes, a pride of lions, secretary birds, all came to the illustrated watering hole for a drink, took their fill and left. Running a hand over his face, he began tapping his foot. *So this is what stir crazy feels like.* He wished Margo would show up to help him pass the time, but it would be hours yet before she was free.

A distraction was what he needed. Picking up his scroll, he considered the opera recording he'd set up to view, but he wasn't in the mood to watch it. His gaze shifted to the pile of Jim's notebooks on the coffee table. He could continue reading them, but without Margo that task wasn't appealing. Putting his slippered feet up on the coffee table, he let his head fall to the back of the couch and watched the lions open their mouths and silently roar. Those lions didn't have a real life, but he did.

Maybe Neil had learned more about the boy's medical issues. He would go see. Decision made, he pushed himself to his feet and made his way to the exit, slightly favouring his sore side. He paused and glanced down at his striped pyjamas and fuzzy slippers.

"First, I'll change."

A few minutes later, fully clothed for the first time since he'd been stabbed, Gary headed to Sick Bay.

The engineered-to-induce-calmness waiting room was empty when he walked in. Gary poked his head into the examination rooms. There were no patients, a good sign considering how many of the colonists had come through these rooms in recent months. Abeo, the medic, was nowhere to be seen—presumably off shift. Neil's office door was open, though. Gary paused for a moment, preparing himself for the upcoming lecture.

"What do you think you're doing here?" demanded Neil, looking up from his workstation when Gary walked in. "You still need to rest."

"What I need is something to do." Gary's response was testy. "I've had enough of sitting around."

"Should've thought about that before you went out and got yourself stabbed," teased Neil, frowning at him.

Gary deliberately refrained from rubbing his aching side and frowned back as he went to stand behind Neil's chair. Neil's computer monitor displayed an appointment calendar for the following week.

"Did you test Lucy Snow and Julien for pathogens?"

"Yes. Neither the boy nor his mother brought any with them." Neil swivelled his chair around, forcing Gary to step back.

Gary glared at his brother. "I still think we need to quarantine newcomers. It's reckless not to."

"Well, we're not expecting any visitors, are we?" asked Neil, crossing his arms over his chest.

"We weren't expecting Lucy Snow and company." Gary shook his head as he walked around the desk and sat in one of the chairs facing Neil. "Have you done analysis on the boy's genetics?"

"It's processing, and I've password protected everything to keep you from snooping."

Gary suppressed a scowl. "I can help." In fact, he knew he could do a better job than Neil. His brother had a better bedside manner, but Gary was better at analysis.

"You could also overdo it and delay your healing."

"No, I won't."

"I'm not going to devolve into one of our yes-no debates from when we were ten. And I know you'll obsess over any little mystery to the point of forgetting to eat or sleep. And then you won't heal. You won't come back to work. And I won't get days off to spend with my wife," said Neil.

"Give me a break, Neil. I don't know what to do with myself." Gary got back on his feet and began pacing the room.

"You could take some time to get to know your wife," said Neil.

Gary stopped and turned to his brother as a thought occurred to him. "Did you talk her into coming by?"

"Maybe."

Of course he did. Gary scowled. He couldn't help wishing that Margo had visited him on her own volition rather than being cajoled into doing so by his meddling brother. Just because Neil had a great relationship with Amanda didn't mean the same was in the cards for him and Margo.

Neil opened his desk drawer and pulled out a bottle of scotch and two glasses. "Anyway, I was going to come by and see you. I have good news." Neil poured a thumb knuckle's worth of amber liquid into each glass.

Gary brightened. "Good news? On Thesan? Now, there's a change."

Neil handed Gary a glass and grinned. "Change is a good word. Amanda's pregnant."

A baby, here on Thesan? Neil's baby?

"Congratulations," said Gary, dutifully clinking the edge of his glass against Neil's. Gary sank down into a chair and took a sip. It burned in his throat—his brother's taste in scotch had always been sub-par.

"Confirmed it this morning, but I don't want to share with everyone yet."

Gary nodded. "How far along is she?"

"Six weeks." Neil leaned back and took a sip, studying his brother over the rim of his glass.

Gary forced himself to smile. "And everything looks okay?"

"Yes, and before you ask, we're not having twins." Neil drained his glass then lifted the bottle, holding it out to Gary, who shook his head. That didn't stop him from pouring himself another.

"That's a relief. We were a tad destructive as kids. A pair like us in this colony might set us back further than we are now. They'd destroy this place faster than we could fix it."

"Amanda and I are over the moon with excitement." Neil grinned. "Finally, this place is going to become a real home."

Gary took a long sip to gather his thoughts. All his life he'd beaten his brother at everything. But now Neil had beaten him in the only thing that was actually important—building a family, something he had always wanted. His first wife, Misty, always said she wanted kids. She'd been pregnant once, shortly before their marriage disintegrated. Just the thought of pregnancy opened the old wound. Anger started to seethe inside him. He'd never told Neil about that last straw in his relationship with Misty and this was not the time to bring it up. *I should be happy for him.*

Gary drained his glass and put it down on Neil's desk.

"You okay?" asked Neil with a concerned look on his face.

"I think you are right. I need to rest." Gary stood and left the room.

———

Just outside the Sick Bay doors to the Hub, Gary stopped and closed his eyes. He felt the breeze created when the doors closed on the back of his neck. A faint hum from the ventilation above was the only sound. Opening his eyes, he looked around.

The Hub was thankfully deserted, so he found a spot on a bench facing the garden. He sat, watching the occasional flash of blue from one of Margo's butterflies. Past the ferns, he could see the tables Amanda had set up for their temporary kitchen. That's when he remembered Julien's comment.

"You're going to have a baby," Julien had announced. Amanda had been about to scold Gary for being up and about, but at the boy's words, she'd stared and dropped a hand to her flat belly. Gary frowned, wondering if he remembered correctly. That day he'd been full of pain meds and discombobulated by the ongoing events—no doubt his memories were messed up. He'd have to ask Amanda what she remembered.

With a sigh, he leaned back against the bench, sticking his feet out in front of him and crossing his ankles as he let his imagination take over. He could picture kids racing up and down the Hub's paths. That had been the plan all along. A handful of kids could create a whole lot of chaos, but it would be the happy kind of chaos that promised a future on this planet.

He knew he should be happy for his brother, but that wasn't what he was feeling. *Jealous, that's what I am.* It wasn't a new feeling. He'd been jealous of Neil and Amanda from the day the pair started building sandcastles together on the beach back when they were kids.

"Come on," she said, her grin as wide as her face. "The tide's on its way out, we can build a palace this time."

Gary stood at the door and frowned at the eight-year-old girl. At twelve, he was too grownup for sandcastle foolishness. "I don't..."

"Hey, Amanda," said Neil, rushing down the stairs. "I'll come with you. I'll bring a garden spade so that we can make a real moat this time."

Gary stood and watched as Neil and Amanda raced off towards the beach sure that he'd done the right thing yet wondering why he felt so miserable.

"Neil told you," said Amanda, as she sat down beside Gary, bringing him back to the present.

He looked over at her. Even all grown up, she still resembled the girl she'd been. Her smile was as wide as it had been that day on the beach. Gary forced himself to smile back.

"Congratulations, Amanda," he said, squeezing her hand affectionately. "You two will make great parents."

"And you'll be an awesome uncle," she said.

"I hope so."

Amanda paused, frowning. "Gary, I thought maybe Neil had told you already a few days ago."

"No. He just told me now."

"I know. He sent me a message." She gestured at her scroll. "You see, I thought you'd told the boy, Julien, because when you brought him here the other day he said I was going to have a baby, remember?"

"So I did remember correctly."

"What do you mean?"

"About the boy saying that you were going to have a baby."

"Yes, but Gary, how could he have known?"

"I don't know, Amanda." Gary patted her leg reassuringly. "But I am going to find out."

Chapter Thirteen

For the first time in four days, Gary sat behind his desk in Sick Bay. To his relief, that morning his brother declared him fit for work and he was no longer stuck in his quarters. Neil had also given him the password to Julien's genome files, and he was itching to start analyzing the data, a task he'd always enjoyed and one he hadn't done since making *Settler* III his home. Most of all, being in his office made him feel useful, like he was finally earning his keep again.

Gary opened his DNA interpreter and began scrolling through the results. He saw that Julien's albinism was natural, or at least handed down from a previous generation. But when he began scrolling through the rest of the boy's results, he inhaled sharply. His genome interpreter couldn't find a match for most of the changes. His interpreter files were state-of-the-art, loaded with every possible purpose for doing genetic manipulation. Or, rather, for doing *legal* genetic manipulation.

Non-standard tweaks had been done to a seemingly random sample of the boy's genes, and with a clumsy hand. *This looks no better than a butcher's cut-and-paste job.* His mind scrambled to understand what had been done to the boy. Considering all the adjustments that had been inscribed on the genes, it was amazing the boy was functioning at all.

He scrolled back through the results. *Why would anyone do this?* None of the changes to the boys genes made any sense. It was like someone had been experimenting on Julien using trial and error. But no one would even do this kind of experimentation on a lab rat. Rubbing the back of his neck, he stared at the screen.

"Hey, Neil, you there?" Gary shouted from his desk.

"Yup," was the muffled reply from the next office over.

"Have you looked at Julien's DNA results?"

"Not yet," said Neil before appearing at his doorway. "Why?"

Typical Neil taking his time getting to the basics. Gary pushed his irritation aside and re-focused on the data. "The boy's base genetics have been tweaked, no, butchered!"

"What do you mean, butchered?" Neil came over to look over Gary's shoulder as Gary scrolled through the interpreter's results.

"Holy shit," said Neil, falling silent as he began processing the implications of the changes. "Whoever did this is a monster!"

"We need to go talk to Lucy about this," said Gary. He had no desire to talk with the woman given all he knew about her from Margo's journal, and given her role in their present circumstances, but it was the only way to find answers about what had been done to the boy.

Neil nodded.

———

With Neil at his side, Gary rang the buzzer to Lucy's apartment.

After a few moments, the door opened and Lucy cautiously looked out as though she was expecting someone else. Her expression relaxed when she saw it was Gary and Neil.

"What do you want?" She swiped a lock of blond hair behind her ear.

"We need to talk to you about Julien," said Gary. "Can we come in?" She nodded and made room for the two men to pass through the door into her quarters.

"What have you found?" she asked, once they were in the living room and sitting down. Gary noted that the woman looked wary as though she was expecting bad news.

"We got the results back from Julien's genetic analysis," said Gary. Lucy nodded. "Do you know about the tweaks?"

"Yes. I let him live with his father when we divorced with the hope Julien would receive a promised cure for his seizures." Lucy looked down at the floor as if she felt responsible for the damage they'd inflicted on her son. "It was much later that I learned my boy's genes had being tinkered with on a fundamental level."

"But why were they tinkering?" asked Gary in a softer tone. He felt dreadful for Julien, even felt a little bad for Lucy. "Who would do this?"

Lucy met his gaze as she shook her head. "I don't know. Ben and I had been estranged for some time, and Julien would alternate living with me and then with him. When Ben was posted to the medical facility on Maximillian Station, it seemed like a stroke of good luck for us. The medical facility there combines cutting-edge technology with the best treatments." Lucy paused for a moment and bit her lip. "On my own, I wouldn't have had the clout to get Julien in. So, I signed my boy over to Ben."

"What was your husband's role at this facility?" asked Gary, remembering that Margo had found a Dr. Snow listed in the names in Jim's notebook.

"Ex-husband," Lucy corrected. "He's a geneticist. He's also well connected within The Conglomerate."

"A geneticist?" Gary and Neil exchanged looks, and Gary knew Neil was thinking the same thing he was. *Would a father do this to his own child?*

"Did he do this to your boy?" asked Neil, speaking for the first time.

Lucy looked from Gary to Neil. She seemed reluctant to provide a forthright answer. "Julien's albinism seemed odd right from the day he was born. I mean, how is a baby born these days with a condition like that? It had taken a while for us to get pregnant, but I had the best medical care all the way through." She looked back down at her hands clenched tightly between her knees. "With what I know now, I wonder if Julien and I had always been a part of Ben's experiments."

Just then Julien walked in with one of Amanda's muffins in his hand, his goggles in place over his eyes. He frowned when he saw the visitors.

Lucy looked up at him and smiled at him, but her eyes remained sad. "Come sit down," she said, patting the couch cushion beside her.

Julien obediently walked over to his mother and sat.

"You're all wrong," he said to her, then addressed Gary and Neil. "My dad didn't experiment on me. And he's the one who got me out when he figured out what the others were doing." His father adequately defended, the boy took a generous bite of his muffin.

Gary leaned forward, resting his elbows on his knees. As he looked at the boy, he noticed his cheeks looked more sunken than when he'd first arrived. Julien's tweaked genes were causing his health to fail on multiple levels, and he was declining fast. He realized that his immediate task would be to figure out what cocktail of medications the boy needed to delay the inevitable.

Taking a deep breath, Gary kept his eyes fixed on the boy. "Julien, who were the others? Do you know what they were doing to you?"

"They were altering my genes," Julien said in a matter-of-fact tone.

Gary already knew that. What he needed was for the boy to be specific.

"But you need me to be more specific," said Julien, echoing Gary's thoughts.

"Yes," said Gary. He wondered if the boy could read minds. *Wait a minute! That would explain how he'd known Amanda was pregnant.* Gary couldn't believe he was entertaining thoughts of potential telepathic abilities. *Focus!* "Your dad took you to The Conglomerate's medical facility on the Maximillian space station."

"Yes, I was invited," Julien said between mouthfuls. "Only special cases get invited, you know."

Gary did know that, but he didn't know what constituted a special case. "And why were you invited?"

"I'm a Snow. That makes me a descendant of the founders. They wanted to enhance our genetic line."

"But they didn't enhance it. They made you really sick," said Gary.

"That wasn't the plan. I was supposed to end up stronger." For a moment, the boy appeared lost in thought, although it was hard to tell given the reflection on his goggles. "Well, I guess in a way I am stronger. Strength isn't only physical, you know. Like I said before, when Dad realized what they were really doing, he smuggled me out."

"Why were they trying to make you stronger?" asked Gary. "What were they hoping you would be able to do?"

"I can't say," said Julien.

"Julien, you have to tell them so they can help you get well," said Lucy, putting a hand on her son's shoulder. It was the first time Gary had witnessed her show physical affection for the boy.

"Gary will figure out how to help me before it's too late. But it'll get dark first," Julien announced, looking right at Gary. "Then someone will lose their mind."

"What do you mean, 'it'll get dark first'?" asked Gary, keeping his eyes fixed on the boy. "And who's going to lose their mind?"

Julien shrugged and kept eating his muffin.

"I'm sorry, but he gets this way sometimes," said Lucy, frowning at her son. "He says these cryptic things that don't make sense."

Gary and Neil exchanged another look. Neil seemed equally mystified. He looked back at Lucy. *At least she seems to care about her boy. That was one point in her favour. Too bad there were so many points against her.*

"You said he was getting treatment for his seizures. Do you know what it was?"

"I'm sorry, but I don't have details. Until now, the regime of medications I gave you have been working. Just fabricate what he needs."

"I'll need to do a full examination of Julien," said Gary, looking over at the boy. Although his mind appeared to work just fine, he didn't look healthy. "I suspect the regime he's been on isn't working as well as it could. I'm going to work on figuring out some new therapies."

"Thank you." Lucy's tone was flat as though she was skeptical Gary could help.

"We'll come see you when we have an update."

Gary and Neil rose and left the room.

———

"Can we figure this out with the equipment we have?" asked Neil as they walked back into Sick Bay.

"We have to do something," said Gary sitting on one of the benches in the waiting room. "Otherwise, I don't think the boy will be around long. He's looking sicker than when he arrived. Besides, it's not his fault his mother is who she is."

"I'm not suggesting we do nothing," said Neil. "I…" Neil stopped mid sentence and started pacing around the waiting room.

Gary put a hand on his abdomen where he'd been stabbed

and looked at his brother. *Is he really going to just give up on the boy?* "Go on."

"I don't know where to start. His DNA doesn't even look human anymore. It's like those monsters on the station were trying to make him into something, then just gave up." He paced around the room again. "There are laws against experimenting on humans like that." Neil waved in the direction of Lucy and Julien's quarters.

"How's our research database?" Gary's side was hurting now and he let out a ragged exhale.

Neil stared at him for a long moment. "Now you've over done it. I'm sending you back to your quarters," he said.

"You don't have to send me. I'm going back. Can you do a search in our research database for peer reviewed work on DNA manipulation? Widen out to any work on mammals. Send it to my scroll and I'll start looking through it."

"Only if you promise to take it easy." Neil put a hand on Gary's shoulder.

Gary took a deep breath. "I'll take it easy. I can lay on my couch reading papers."

Neil nodded and dropped his arm. "Get out of here then. I'll send you what I find."

Chapter Fourteen

"I want to show you something," said Margo, as she walked into Gary's office.

He looked up, and couldn't help notice that her smile lit up the room. Standing there grinning at him in front of his desk, she seemed so vibrant. He pushed back his chair and returned her smile. These last few days, the only time he'd seen Margo was by looking into the greenhouse from the Common Room windows where she'd been working to set up her bee hives. Just seeing her made him realize how much he missed her company.

"I bet you're here about the eclipse. It's what everyone is talking about."

"It's not an eclipse. It's a sunset," she corrected, still smiling. "And you've got to come watch it with me."

"But I thought we would never experience a nightfall on Thesan," said Gary. "And if there's no nightfall, there's no sunset."

"Shows what you know," she teased. "Look, I'll answer all your questions, but not here and not yet. So? Are you coming?"

Gary glanced down. His scroll filled with further analysis of

Julien's genetics. He'd been so consumed with trying to understand the data, he'd rarely left his office. After days of effort, he hadn't gotten anywhere, and the boy wasn't getting any healthier. Julien's aberrant DNA was gnawing at him. But Gary was also so pleased that Margo had invited him to look at what he assumed would be an unusual Thesan sky. The data could wait, he finally decided.

"Alright, I'll come." Gary put away his scroll and stood. A walk in the greenhouse in Margo's company would do him good and clear the cobwebs from his brain. Maybe he'd come back and discover he had gained new insights into the boy's problem.

"Good, because this is something you won't see every day; at least, not around here," she said, leading him out to the Loop.

"How are your bees?"

"Buzzing about, doing their thing." She fell into step beside him. "I've also been helping Keir and Devin with the pond. It's now full of fish."

"Fish survived the explosion in your lab?" When her face lost its happy glow, he was sorry he mentioned the explosion.

"No, none of those survived. But luckily, Keir had others in stasis."

Gary started to turn towards the doors to the greenhouse, but Margo kept going down the Loop. "Aren't we going to the greenhouse?"

"No, we'll get a better view outside."

Outside? Gary inhaled sharply, but didn't say anything as they continued walking towards the main airlock. He felt his heart race, and he seriously considered fleeing. Or, at the very least, confessing his fear so Margo would change her mind.

In the airlock change room, the row of pristine white atmo suits hanging along one wall seemed to taunt him. Gary shook off his fears and walked stiffly over to one of the suits. He pulled it off its hook and, taking a seat beside Margo, began tucking his feet into the leg holes.

Oblivious to his distress, Margo kept talking about what they'd been working on in the greenhouse as she put on her atmo suit. Gary pretended to listen, distracted by his fear of being suffocated inside the suit. Excuses to not go outside bounced around in his brain like a pinball in one of those old-fashioned arcade games.

When he shrugged the suit over his shoulders, it felt confining, as if it was deliberately squeezing him and making it difficult to breathe. The layer of re-enforced fabric seemed flimsy, a reminder of how thin the margin was between habitable atmosphere and suffocation. As he pushed his fingers into the attached gloves, Gary freely admitted he was the unlikeliest of space travellers. Before he could talk himself out of it, he pulled on his helmet and followed Margo into the airlock.

———

After the air cycled, Margo opened the outside airlock door. The larger of their two suns, Helios, had not yet risen and only a sliver of Sol was visible over the horizon, a crescent of orange casting a feeble glow in the surrounding sky. Above Sol, the sky gradated through darkening shades of purple. He wondered what had changed. They'd been told one or both of their suns would always be in the Thesan sky. But Margo was obviously pleased about this unprecedented event, and he trusted her.

Gary hesitated as Margo stepped across the threshold and onto the gravel beyond. *Did she never feel fear?* "You told someone we're going out, right," said Gary, still standing in the airlock's door. His voice sounded distant. They'd switched on their inter-suit comms, and he'd insisted Margo remind him which button to push on his wrist pad if he needed to speak to someone in the Control Room.

Margo stopped and turned. He could barely make out her features behind the clear visor of her helmet.

"Worry wart." She turned on the interior helmet light so he could see her smile. "But, to make you feel better, I did tell Lucas."

"Thanks." It didn't make him feel better. Beneath his helmet he felt the prickle of sweat beads forming across his forehead, making him wish he could scratch his face.

"Come on, I guarantee your agoraphobia will be cured by going on a walk."

"I don't have agoraphobia," Gary argued, but all she did was grin as if mocking his lack of self-awareness. She was obviously enjoying teasing him. It was a side to her he had only recently discovered.

"Fine, you lead the way," said Gary, as he stepped out and closed the door behind him. His boots felt heavy and awkward as he took the necessary steps to join her, and the crunch of his footfalls on the gravel sounded odd, and not because his head was inside a helmet. He'd been walking on the smooth floors of the ship for so long, he'd forgotten the sound footfalls made on outside terrain. Despite his discomfort at being outside, he smiled—being with Margo was making him surprisingly happy.

"This way."

Margo walked on the uneven gravel parallel to the outside wall of their colony for about ten minutes until they came to her entomology lab. The windows were still boarded over—fabricating new ones would have to wait until Lucas lifted their moratorium on domestic printing. But, the worst of the blast debris had been cleared away leaving a charred fan on the gravel. In front of the boarded-up windows were Margo's two mismatched chairs she'd brought all the way from Earth, one lime green and the other a faded pink. It was a minor miracle that the chairs had survived relatively intact given the intensity of the explosion.

Margo sat in the pink one and stretched her feet out in front of her.

"Sit," she commanded, gesturing to the other chair.

He sat, shifting a little to find a comfortable position with the air pack on his back. "Are you going to tell me now? Weren't we told we would never experience a nightfall on Thesan?"

"That's what we all thought but, apparently, we were told wrong. But not by the Big Evil. We simply didn't have the full picture," she continued, "Lucas used our satellites and Peg's computation power to get a better understanding of the planet's dynamics. We thought at our latitude we'd always face either Helios or Sol, but we got the orbital dynamics a bit wrong. It turns out Thesan wobbles a bit as it rotates. Today, we've turned away from the suns."

Can our colony survive in darkness? Their plants needed sunlight and the bulk of their power came from the suns. But Margo's expression inside her helmet was not what he'd expect in the face of impending blackness. Instead, she was looking at the sky with a hint of a smile on her face. "How long will it be dark?" He wasn't fond of darkness, having spent all his life in brightly lit cities.

"Only for a week or so. Lucas has Peg calculating the exact duration. It turns out, we'll get a week long night like this every five years or so."

"So, why would Thesan wobble in its orbit?" It didn't sound particularly stable, living on a planet that wobbled. He looked out towards Sol. It had sank lower towards the horizon. What little light there was would soon disappear entirely.

"There's probably a large gas giant orbiting further out from the suns that's causing it. Now, keep your eye on Sol," she instructed, noticing the sliver of sun was about to touch the horizon.

He did as Margo instructed, keeping his gaze on Sol. He liked it when Margo talked to him. Her voice was pleasant even if her choice of venue forced him outside his comfort zone. He was surprised at how much her rough charm had grown on him. Was he being overly optimistic in thinking there could eventually be something between them?

When Sol slipped under the horizon with a sudden green flash, Gary let out a wordless exclamation. He grinned and turned to Margo. "Is that what we came to see?"

"Yep." She nodded, pleased with herself. "And that," she said, pointing at the stars starting to appear.

"Wow. Just when I'd gotten used to the idea of never seeing real stars again, there's this." He made a sweeping motion with his gloved hand. "Is that the Milky Way?" He pointed to the denser band of stars extending from horizon to horizon.

"Yeah, we're still part of the same galaxy as Earth. We haven't figured out where it is though." She waved up towards the sky.

Gary studied the patterns of stars. "The constellations are different."

"We'll have to name them, I guess."

Gary looked up at the unfamiliar view. "There." He pointed to a group of stars directly above them. "That group of stars is obviously a gazelle."

"Or a many tentacled monster," countered Margo.

"Hmm," he said, keeping his gaze on the stars. A bright, green-tinged one caught his eye. "What's that?"

"A neighbouring planet, not a star. It's a mini-Neptune in a closer orbit to the suns than we are. It's still in the Goldilocks zone, but its atmosphere is gaseous, so not a terraforming candidate. It does, however, have an interesting moon that might be habitable."

"We've been here just over three months and you're already looking for a new planet to colonize? Do you want to get away from me that much?"

"No." She looked at him and smiled. "We've got to make this place work first."

At her words, Gary almost felt like humming. Margo had not only sought him out to share this magical moment with him, she'd freely admitted that she had no intention of avoiding him the way she had for the first three months of their mission. Despite the darkness that had descended, his future was starting to look a lot brighter. With a contented smile on his face, he continued studying the stars, trying to connect the dots into meaningful shapes.

Splat! Gary shot to his feet as he tried to clear his visor of the glob of liquid that just landed on it.

"What? Is something wrong with your suit?" Margo got to her feet beside him. "Stop struggling! Let me look."

"Something wet hit my visor," he said, forcing himself to stand still so Margo could inspect his suit with the light of her helmet. His gut clenched with renewed fear, and the site where he'd been stabbed started throbbing.

Behind the bubble of her helmet, Margo's eyebrows pulled together, creating furrowed lines between them. She traced a gloved finger across his visor, then looked at the smudge it had left.

"It's mud," she said.

She backed away and looked up. He followed her gaze, but he didn't know what she was looking for. The sky was still clear, speckled with stars.

"Look! Over there," she pointed to the horizon in the opposite direction. The line of blurred stars appeared to be moving closer and behind it, the sky was jet black.

"What?" What was she seeing that he wasn't?

"The stars are vanishing?"

Before he could ask what her cryptic statement meant, more goo landed on his suit."

"What's going on?"

"Heat difference between having the suns up versus having no sun?" asked Margo, still looking up at the sky. "It's likely a result of winds generated as the surface temperatures drops because of the lack of suns. The climate on the dark side of Thesan appears to be changing. I think a mud storm is coming."

"A mud storm? Didn't the recruitment poster claim Thesan only had mild weather?"

"The first of their lies," Margo answered with a reassuring smile then hit the transmit button on her forearm. "Lucas, it looks like a mud storm is rolling in."

Fist-sized lumps of mud began pummelling them.

"Will our suits hold?" Gary asked. Margo was right, he did suffer from agoraphobia—at least on Thesan. Agreeing to go outside had been foolish.

"The suit will hold," Margo assured him in a calm voice. "Let's start heading back to the airlock." She started walking and Gary followed.

"External temperatures have risen," said Lucas over the radio. "It's almost zero degrees. The winds have brought in warmer air from somewhere. I've got Peg trying to figure out why."

"How about oxygen levels?" she asked keeping a steady pace.

Oxygen? Why was Margo asking about oxygen? And why weren't they making a mad dash back to the airlock?

"We're up to 15%," Lucas said.

That got Gary's attention—the oxygen concentration outside was almost survivable without a suit.

"I'm guessing the wind has picked up the mud, and the oxygen, from the canyons," said Lucas. "How close are you to the airlock, Margo?"

"We're heading in, now," Margo said. "My lab's airlock is still unserviceable, so we'll need to go back the way we came," she added for Gary's benefit.

A gust of wind swirled around the wall, pelting them with more gobs of mud. Gary was certain the mud balls were getting larger.

"Visibility is going to suck once we get on the windward side," Margo said, taking his gloved hand in hers. "Keep your other hand on the wall."

He nodded in acknowledgement.

She was right—as they trudged alongside the curved wall, the wind got stronger and stronger. Gary could barely see Margo beside him. He wanted to wipe his visor clear with his other hand, but didn't want to lose touch with the colony wall. And nothing would compel him to release Margo's hand.

Then something hit him, and Margo's hand was ripped from his. He fell to the ground and rolled a few times. Panting, he rolled to his back and looked up. Either visibility had gone to zero or his visor was now completely covered in mud.

"Gary!" called Margo over the comms. He couldn't tell if she was close or far. "Where are you?"

"Don't know," he answered, rolling onto his hands and knees. He rose to his knees and reached out blindly, but encountered nothing as the mud continued to rain down.

"Can you still touch the wall?" she asked.

Gary felt his own panic rise when, for the first time, he heard tension in her voice. "No. I can't find it!" He'd only rolled a couple times. The wall couldn't be that far away. Regaining his feet, he felt the full force of the wind try to push him back. In a blind panic, he rushed forward, but in only two strides he smashed into something and bounced backwards, landing on his back side. Scrambling forward on is hands and knees, he lay a hand on what he'd hit—it was *Settler*'s wall.

"Found it," he said, leaning against it in relief for a moment before standing up. He kept both hands on the wall, not that it did any good. He wished the outside wall of the ship weren't so smooth. He'd give anything for handles. Or a rope.

"Stay put and I'll find you," Margo instructed. A moment later, he felt her bump into him. She grabbed one of his hands again. Now that she was holding his hand, he tried to wipe his visor. He wanted to see her face, but his scrubbing made no difference. The mud kept pelting down. And Margo must've seen what he'd done because she grabbed his wrist and placed his hand on the wall. "Keep your hand on the ship, Gary. We're almost there, a dozen more paces, max."

The two of them started moving again alongside the wall until they found the airlock. Margo opened the door and the two of them stumbled inside.

Chapter Fifteen

What sounded like heavy machine gun fire echoed through the Loop and Common Room as Lucas passed through. The doors to the greenhouse stood open, but the yawning space inside was eerily dark. As dark as the blackest night on Earth. Pausing at the threshold for a moment, he dragged the palms of his hands down his pants. *Will life here ever be uncomplicated?*

Stopping a few steps into the greenhouse, he craned his neck to get a good look at the roof. "Whoa!" he said when he saw absolutely nothing.

It was already worse than he'd expected. With both suns beneath the horizon, stars should've been visible through the dome. But, even though the storm began less than an hour ago, their brief glimpse of the stars was already obliterated. Mud covered their colony. *How much darkness can the colony endure?*

"Well, we've just gone further up shit creek," said Abigail, stopping beside him.

Lucas ignored her as he worked through the ramifications of a thick layer of mud coating the colony's greenhouse roof. Since the fire, they'd been having power issues. Due to both the unforeseen darkness and the mud, the solar generating ability of the dome's surface would be badly compromised.

"Damn!" Lucas wanted to hide in his quarters and let someone else deal with this disaster—but, that response wasn't an option.

"Without the solar panels, it won't be long until we're sitting in the dark," said Abigail, articulating Lucas' fears. "All these plants are gonna die." She gestured towards the nearby foliage that disappeared into the darkness.

Lucas shifted his gaze to the plants, barely visible in the light cascading out the Common Room windows and through the open doors of the Loop. A lot of hard work had gone into nurturing them. Those plants represented their long-term food security.

"Without solar energy, this entire space is going to turn into a refrigerator," said Abigail.

"I know that, Abigail," Lucas said, wishing she'd shut up.

"Now's the time for action, boss man," said Abigail, putting her hands on her hips.

Above, the dome let out a loud groan. Both of them looked up. *Is it safe to be in here?*

As Lucas gazed upwards, he remembered the day a panel of the dome had failed. One person had died that day. If the entire dome collapsed, how many more would die? "Will it hold?" he muttered.

"I'm not the expert on that kind of stuff," replied Abigail in a subdued tone.

Lucas glanced at her. She was still looking up, not that there was anything to see in the vast yawning blackness. In the dim light he could see the concern on her face. Rough exterior aside, Lucas wondered if she was feeling the same fear he was. He rubbed his chin as he tried to conjure up the competent commander within. The colonists deserved someone who could lead in times of crisis.

A dozen paces away by the pond, a crowd was gathering.

Others were coming in from the various greenhouse entrances, all worried about what the storm would do to their greenhouse. In the centre was Kasumi, their chief engineer. She held a lantern in one hand and her scroll in the other. She stood looking up, her expression unreadable in the dim light. Lucas, with Abigail at his side, walked over and joined them.

"Will the dome hold?" he asked, as he wove his way past the others to stand beside her.

Kasumi looked at him. "Assuming all the seals are good, then yeah."

Lucas noticed that her standard ponytail had become a disheveled knot as if she'd not taken the time to even brush her hair. *Well, she took over a mess since becoming Chief Engineer.*

"And how do we assess if the seals are good?"

Kasumi looked at him. "My predecessor's passion was building that dome—the seals are good. I'm more worried about power generation." Handing her lantern off to Gan, Kasumi looked down at the display on her scroll. "Have you calculated how long the mud storm will last?"

"Peg is working on it," Lucas said.

"It'll be dark for five days," Julien announced, startling them all. Everyone turned to look at the boy, so small compared to the rest of them. In his striped pyjamas and clutching a plastic Godzilla tight against his chest, he looked frail enough that a gust of wind might knock him over. He gazed solemnly up at Lucas, his goggles shining in the low light.

"How do you know that?" asked Lucas.

"I just do," he said, shrugging.

Lucas wished he could access Peg from the greenhouse, but it was the one location that hadn't been set up yet. *Wait? Had the boy been accessing the AI?*

"Temperature is currently just above zero out there," Kasumi stated in a dismal tone, staring at her scroll.

"If it dips further, that mud's gonna freeze," said Abigail.

"A frozen layer of mud on the dome will block the light

when the suns do come back out, rendering the solar panels useless," said Kasumi, tucking an escaped lock of black hair behind her ear. She looked at Lucas. "That mud can't be allowed to stay."

His competent commander persona hadn't appeared. *Why can't anything go smoothly around here?*

"We can't send anyone out there right now," said Lucas. "According to Margo and Gary, the mud is coming down in fist-sized gobs. They barely made it back in."

"So, we're just supposed to cower in here like lemmings?" Abigail crossed her arms over her chest and glared at him as if expecting him to influence the weather. *Well, I took over a mess too.*

Lucas' mind went back to the last time the dome was breached and someone died. "No. You can go cower in the Common Room instead. Come on, everyone. Out. You too, Kasumi," he added when he saw her hesitate. "Gan, go around and make sure all the greenhouse entrances have air tight seals." He didn't add 'in case the roof collapses' but that's what everyone heard.

He turned and strode ahead of the others as they moved towards the entrance he and Abigail had used, ignoring the dissenting murmurs he overheard. *Were they questioning my decision to evacuate the greenhouse? Will they mutiny, or follow me?*

"The mud storm won't last," said Julien, falling into step beside him.

Lucas glanced at the boy. He'd forgotten all about him. And about his mother stuck in her quarters. *At least the kid has an optimistic trait, which is more than can be said for his mother.*

"What about the plants?" asked Devin, the Chief Gardener, running to walk on the other side of Lucas. "Without sunlight they're going to die."

Kasumi was on his heels. "Assuming the front of warm air passes by as projected, it's going to get cold in here," added Kasumi without looking up from her scroll. "And we won't be generating power."

"What about water?" Abigail demanded. "The pump house is in the greenhouse."

"We'll have to shut that down to conserve power," said Kasumi.

"But the plants, we could dig some up and..." added Devin.

"Enough." Lucas stopped and held up his hand. The gaggle following him stopped as well. "Peg will have the data by now about how long the storm will last. And then—"

"Thirty-six hours at the most," Julien interrupted. "That's how long the storm will last. And afterwards, there'll be an accident and someone will die."

"What? Look, kid, now is not the time for ghostly bedtime stories," Lucas said in what he hoped was his best commander persona. Julien opened his mouth to argue, and Lucas put up a hand. "Not another word!"

Lucas looked at the faces of his crew, all looking at him expectantly. *I have no idea what the best course of action is. All I can do is make a decision. And then another and another—I hope it all adds up to something.*

"Do what you need to do to get ready for the cold. I'm going to consult Peg. You know where I am if you need me." Lucas turned his back on the crowd and headed off to the control room.

"You can't just put your head in the sand," called Abigail to his back. He didn't bother responding.

———

"Peg, re-run simulation 46." Lucas yawned and looked at the clock—he'd been running simulations for over four hours. *At least I've had solitude.*

"Displaying simulation now," the AI said.

Lucas leaned back in his chair as the main screen changed to display Thesan and the two suns. The red triangle on the planet's surface marked the colony's location, which was consumed by darkness, while numbers along the bottom indicated the simulation's progression. Simulation 46 left the colony in darkness for 121 hours—just over five days. Every other simulation he'd tried put the colony back in the light within an hour or two of simulation 46's prediction.

"Five days is too long for us to be without power and light." He leaned his elbows on the console, dropping his face into his hands.

Five days without power generation was hugely problematic, yet his thoughts drifted away from trying to find a solution and towards the sound of a little boy's voice saying the mud storm would last no longer than 36 hours. The strange thing was, Peg was in exact agreement with Julien's prediction. And that was messing with Lucas's mind. *How had the kid known the storm would end within 36 hours? Lucky guess?* Lucas had a sick feeling it had nothing to do with a lucky guess. The only problem was, he didn't know how else to explain it.

"Power is the most critical component."

Peg's neutral voice interrupted his less than helpful thoughts. Lucas leaned back in his chair and looked up at the screen. The AI had replaced the screen with a schematic of the *Settler III* colony. "I've marked the damaged sections in red."

He looked up. The bloody colour covered most of their ring-shaped colony. "There's too much red." He buried his head in his hands again. *Maybe we've been naïve. Maybe we should've asked The Conglomerate ship for rescue. Maybe it isn't too late!*

He lifted his head and sat up straight. "Peg, can you send a message to the *Compliance*?"

"Negative, our comms system is down."

"Shit," he said, his shoulders sagging. "Got any suggestions?"

"There is a solution you have not considered," said Peg.

"And what's that?"

One of the small screens in front of him blinked off, catching his attention. It came back on for a brief moment, playing an animation of a young girl skipping rope, then blinked off and an image of the Centre Module appeared.

"Peg, what was that? Is there a problem?"

"The cold fusion generator stored at the Centre Module."

Peg answered his question about the solution he hadn't considered, but the AI seemed unaware of the two-second video glitch. The image of the girl must have been in a chunk of old code that had percolated to the surface. Seeing the girl made him think, not for the first time, about giving the PEG-42 AI a virtual face. Maybe he could create a composite of Camila's face; after all, she'd been the biggest proponent of using a Peg series AI on the *Settler III*. Artificial intelligence had been her passion. The idea of seeing her face in that context felt right. He leaned back, letting his thoughts drift to his late wife.

"The rover can reach the Centre Module in roughly 3.26 hours."

Lucas' fantasy about programming a face for Peg shattered. He couldn't afford to let his mind drift like this.

"Sorry Peg, repeat that."

"The generator stored at the Centre Module can be reached by rover in roughly 3.26 hours."

The portable unit could provide enough power for the colony on its own—or be a solid back-up for the solar power system when they got it back on line. Getting that generator to the colony would provide a lot of peace of mind. One of their rovers could easily reach the Centre Module and the generator would fit on the rover's flat bed trailer.

"Display the route on the satellite image." The main screen shifted to show the surrounding landscape. Peg drew a green line showing the best route from the colony to the Centre Module.

"It seems feasible," he said, then shook his head. "But, it's too risky to drive there in the dark and I can't send out anyone in a mud storm."

"Your assessment is correct—it is too risky to drive in the

dark. I recommend setting out as soon as the suns return—on the morning of the fifth day."

"What should we do until then?" Lucas muttered. His question had been rhetorical, but Peg answered it.

"The mud will stop in 31.24 hours," said Peg. "When it does, the dome will need to be cleaned off."

Thirty-one hours seemed a long time to sit around doing nothing. Lucas pictured work teams scraping the frozen mud off a four-acre dome—a task now essential to their long-term survival. Hopefully, Kasumi could help him figure out the most efficient way to clean the colony's roof. Perhaps the builder bots could be programmed for cleaning. He would set up work parties, rotate people on shifts, and have Peg track and display the progress on monitors in the Common Room to build morale. As the plan started to form in his mind, the edge of desperation that had coloured their situation started to abate. They weren't doomed after all.

"One more thing," Peg was saying. "The warmer temperatures appear to be correlated with the mud storm. But when the storm passes, we can expect the temperatures to drop to well below -50 degrees Celsius."

"There's just no good news," commented Lucas dryly. "Estimate how cold it will get inside if it's that cold outside?"

"Just above freezing, but only if you adopt an aggressive power conservation stance in living areas."

"We can work with that until we get the cold fusion generator." He and all the crew would wear every item of clothing they had, resorting to heated atmo suits if they had to.

"There is one more thing," said the AI. "My sensors show that oxygen levels in the plain around the *Settler* have increased."

"So?"

"We have not yet determined the origin of the oxygen."

"Might it be biological?" Lucas asked with a groan. *Great, another problem to deal with. Maybe I should've asked the Colonizing*

Counsel to send a new commander. This job is turning into one big headache.

"I cannot rule that out without data."

"So, I should send someone out to get samples while the mud is wet?"

"Yes."

"I've got the perfect person for that job." Lucas leaned forward and opened a link to the terraforming lab. "Abigail, come to the Control Room please."

Chapter Sixteen

"You're not afraid, right?"

"Huh?" Margo turned from where she'd been eyeing up muffins on the food counter and saw Abigail. The Head of Terraforming stood by the main entrance to the Hub holding a sampling kit in one hand. Her other hand was on her hip.

"Afraid of what?" asked Margo, suppressing a frown—she didn't want to deal with Abigail right now. Margo had been hoping to spend a few hours with Gary reading through the rest of Jim's journals. She hadn't had a chance yet to apologize to him for taking him outside, knowing his fear of the atmo suits. She wanted Gary to know how bad she felt about their fiasco outside in the mud storm. *Bribing him with freshly made muffins might do the trick.*

"I need to get mud samples from outside." Abigail held up her sampling kit as though it explained everything.

"What? You mean, you're asking *me* for help?" Margo took another glance at the muffins—they'd have to wait. *But they smelled soooo good!* Her mouth watered as she gave them one last look.

"The duffus-in-charge won't let me go alone."

Margo wanted to argue that there were more than two dozen other options for Abigail's companion. Besides, the storm still raged and the last place Margo wanted to go was back outside. Her mud covered visor, combined with the darkness, had felt like staring into an abyss while being pummelled. She'd much rather spend her time safe in Gary's living room—an appealing passtime she was still getting used to.

"Will one pace out the airlock work?" she asked.

"That'll do."

"So, does coming to me for help mean you like me now?" asked Margo, raising one eyebrow as she headed towards Abigail.

"Hell no! I still think you're a jackass and likely the reason we keep having computer glitches." Abigail strode off, her generous hips swaying with every step.

Margo was beginning to realize that Abigail's gruff exterior had cracks filled with humour, albeit difficult to recognize. With a sigh, Margo followed. The muffins and Jim's journals would have to wait.

"Why can't any of your terraforming crew help?" asked Margo, when she caught up with Abigail in the Loop. As they walked, the coloured line on the wall changed from purple, to green, then to Engineering's blue.

"Lucas said I could take you," Abigail said, without even turning her head towards Margo.

"Could? Or should?" Margo asked, but Abigail didn't answer.

They walked in silence through the cavernous mechanical workshop. No one was there, just dimmed lights and ruined equipment from their various explosions splayed out on the tables. Without slowing, Abigail wove past the workbenches and down a short hall to the Engineering airlock change room. Engineering was the best choice because it faced away from the wind —opening an airlock on the windward side would result in an airlock filled with mud.

The change room was smaller than the one she and Gary had used. Along one wall was a built-in bench and along the other was a row of hanging generic atmo suits. Through a small, round window in the door, she saw the closet sized airlock beyond.

Grabbing a suit off a hook, Abigail sat on the bench. Before dressing, she pulled out her scroll and brought up the weather data. "Oxygen levels are up to 16%."

"Makes sense. The wind is coming from the canyons where there was a higher oxygen level." Margo grabbed a suit for herself before sitting beside Abigail. The selection of sizes in this smaller change room was minimal, and she was stuck with oversize boots.

"The question is, why is there oxygen on Thesan at all? Yet another useful piece of information those assholes covered up."

"The real question is if there is anything living out there," said Margo, looking over Abigail's shoulder to see the data.

"No shit Sherlock, we can't terraform a planet that's already alive. Exterminating the local flora and fauna is the biggest no-no out there." Abigail kept her eyes on the weather data as she put her feet in her suit.

"Well we're here, so if there's life out there, it's already too late. We've already contaminated the place," said Margo, standing up and double checking the suit's diagnostics.

Abigail finished putting on her atmo suit before stashing the scroll into one of the pockets.

"Alright, let's do this." Margo put her helmet on. She clunked across the room in her too-large boots and retrieved two tethers from a nearby cabinet. She clipped one to her suit and went to clip the other end on Abigail's.

Abigail had just put her helmet on and waved Margo away, then spoke over the inter-suit comms. "It'll only restrict me."

"I know what it's like out there. Trust me, we need to be clipped together." Margo still held out the other connector. "Then I'll connect to the inside of the airlock."

"Fuck it. I don't want it." Abigail turned and went into the airlock.

Margo rolled her eyes. *Why does Abigail have to be so antagonistic all the time? I'm only trying to help!* Tucking the second tether into a pocket, Margo followed Abigail into the airlock, then closed the door and started the air cycling. Abigail knelt and opened the sample kit on the floor. Inside was a series of jars. She selected one.

"Control, we're in the airlock," said Margo over the radio.

"Roger, let me know when you're back," replied Lucas.

"That lightweight is not going to make it as our leader," Abigail said, as she stashed the jar in her suit's front pocket. She closed the kit and pushed it into the corner by the door.

"It's not like he expected to end up in charge." Margo walked over to the window in the outside door. Beyond the glass, all she could see was blackness.

"Strong leadership is what we need to keep us alive."

"It's been less than a week, give him some time." Margo turned to Abigail "I still think you need to clip in." She held up the tether. Through her visor, Margo saw Abigail press her lips together in annoyance, so she was surprised when Abigail agreed.

"I'll do it if it'll make you shut up about it," Abigail finally said.

Margo smiled and clipped the tether onto Abigail's suit. For a second she thought she caught a glimpse of fear in Abigail's tough veneer. Margo wasn't keen on going outside either, but she was happy they were at least taking the necessary safety precautions. Now connected to Abigail, Margo clipped the end of her second tether to a hard-point on the wall just as the outside door light flashed green.

"Ready?" asked Abigail, grabbing the handle.

"As ready as I'll ever be." Margo braced herself for the wind as Abigail pulled the door open.

The rounded rectangle of the doorway opened into an oozy

darkness the lights of the airlock couldn't penetrate. She couldn't even make out the ground directly outside.

They both turned on their headlamps, the beams of light illuminating blurs of flying mud caught in eddies, like an earthbound blizzard. If it was this bad on the leeward side, Margo couldn't imagine what it would be like on the windward side.

Abigail removed the jar from her pocket and opened the lid. From a different pocket she pulled out a spoon that looked like it came from Amanda's kitchen. She looked to Margo and nodded before taking a bold step across the threshold. Margo kept her headlamp pointed on her.

It only took a split second to encase one side of Abigail's white suit in mud. The weight of the mud, combined with the wind's ferocious force, brought the large woman to her knees and she dropped the spoon.

"Are you okay?" Margo asked from the safety of the doorway, resisting the urge to shout as their suit comms were working just fine.

"Yup," Abigail said, steadying herself with one hand. Most of her visor was now coated with dirt.

"Come back in. We'll take samples from the mud on your suit."

"Good idea." Abigail wiped her muddy glove across her visor, but that only made it worse. "I can't see shit. I'm coming in." Abigail struggled to her feet, but a sudden gust knocked her over and she vanished from view into the darkness.

Margo grabbed Abigail's safety line with both hands and pulled, thankful that Abigail had agreed to let herself be tethered, but the line was stuck. Wedging a foot on the doorframe, Margo pulled on the line with all her strength. Without warning, the line snapped somewhere in the darkness, tumbling Margo backwards. She landed sprawled out on the floor of the airlock.

"Abigail!" Margo scrambled on to all fours over to the opening, looking out, but visibility was hardly more than an arm's length. When she leaned out a little further, the gobs of mud hitting her felt like missiles. "Abigail!" She knew she was shouting, but she couldn't help herself.

She was just about to duck back in and contact Lucas when Abigail's voice came through on the comms.

"I see the light. I'm coming back in."

A moment later, Margo spotted Abigail crawling towards her on her hands and knees. She was relieved to discover that Abigail hadn't been more than an arm's length away. Her suit was so covered in mud, she blended into what little Margo could see of the swirling landscape.

Keeping most of her torso inside the airlock, Margo reached out and grabbed Abigail's arm. The mud made their atmo suits slippery, but Margo held tight and pulled her towards the door. Staying low to the ground, the two women wiggled their way back inside. Once over the door's threshold and out of the wind, Abigail continued past Margo before collapsing onto the floor.

Margo pulled herself up and then swung the door closed, hitting the button to cycle the air. She turned to look down at Abigail who'd rolled onto her side and pushed herself up to sit leaning against the side. "You okay?" Margo asked.

"Yeah," said Abigail, her breathing loud over the comm link. "That was batshit crazy!" Wiping handfuls of mud off her helmet, she tried to clear the visor to see. "I can't see worth shit. Can you?"

"Yes." Margo looked around the small room. The walls, floor and ceiling were splattered with mud, reminding her of crime scene blood patterns she'd seen on old vids. "Guess we got our samples, although they're not in a jar," she said.

"You're going to have to let me know when I can take this off."

"I will."

Abigail looked up at Margo even though she could see nothing through her mud-coated visor. "I owe you."

Margo shrugged. "Well, we can officially say it's crappy out there."

Abigail chuckled. "Crappier than the dust storms on Mars."

"I've never been to Mars," admitted Margo.

"Don't bother, it's more-or-less like here, complete with faulty equipment and saboteurs."

"I heard you took the fall for that." Margo heard the sound of Abigail taking in a surprised breath and braced herself for a tirade of invectives, but instead Abigail spoke in a resigned tone.

"Yeah, that kind of crap seems to follow me." She began patting her pockets. "I think I lost my sample jar."

"I'll get another one." Margo knelt down and opened the sample case. "At least, the mud's easy to collect now."

"There's always a bright side."

Margo opened the lid and scooped a handful of mud off Abigail's thigh and filled the jar. "This is not exactly scientific," she observed, ensuring the lid was on properly before putting the sample in her pocket.

Abigail shrugged. "At least we should be able to determine if there's any life in the mud."

"I better tell Lucas we're back." Margo pressed the button on her wrist panel to open the channel with the Control Room. "Lucas, we're back. Just waiting for the airlock to finish cycling."

"Damn! I need to get out of this suit," Abigail said as she rubbed at her visor.

"Control Room?" Margo said, ignoring Abigail's rant as she tried for the second time to comm Lucas. "Are you there?"

"Try Peg," Abigail suggested.

"Hey Peg," said Margo. "Peg, come in."

"Y-y-y-y-y-yes," stammered the AI.

That was weird. "Peg, let Lucas know that we are back inside."

"Inside, outside, inside, outside, inside, outside."

"Never mind, Peg," Margo said.

"That AI's got issues," said Abigail leaning against the wall.

Just then, the light changed. "It's green," Margo announced. When they removed their helmets, they both wrinkled their noses. The mud on them and the floor impregnated the room with a stale algae scent. *Is there something alive in the mud after all?* Margo thought. Gary was always going on about potential toxins in Thesan's environment. *What if he is right?*

"Maybe we should've left our helmets on," Margo said.

"Yup. But we've already been exposed," said Abigail, standing up. "My Ma always said there was no point worrying over things that are done."

Then the lights went out.

Chapter Seventeen

"Crap!" Margo peered through the window of the inner door, but the blackness was complete. Not even the indicator lights were on.

"Crap *timing*," Abigail snapped. "Couldn't our power stores have lasted till we got out of these stupid suits?"

"Peg, are you there?" asked Margo. When she didn't get a reply, Margo put her helmet back on, flicking on the headlamp. "Control Room, this is Margo, over." Again no reply.

"I guess they're in the dark too," said Abigail, She seemed uncharacteristically subdued.

"This could be a big problem." said Margo.

"Just another pile of shit for us to deal with." Abigail walked over to the metal ring on the door and turned it.

They exited the airlock by the light of Margo's headlamp. While Margo closed and sealed the door, Abigail removed the emergency kit that was mounted to the wall next to the airlock. Inside were two protein bars, a box of bandages, a roll of toilet paper and two flashlights. Abigail took one flashlight and handed the other to Margo before heading to a nearby bench to strip off her suit.

Margo removed her helmet, the headlamp automatically flicking off, and then paused and listened. The *Settler* had never been so quiet. She could hear the wind storm outside, but none of their ventilation was running. *How much air do we have?*

Margo joined Abigail on the bench and turned her flashlight on. Setting the light down beside her helmet, she began removing her suit.

"We need to go straight to the Control Room," said Abigail, rising and stepping out of her atmo suit. She laced up her boots, picked up her flashlight and headed for the door. The wavering cone of light looked eerie as she walked with purposeful strides, abandoning the ruined suit and leaving it in a pile on the floor beside Margo.

"But there might be people trapped in this quadrant without light," Margo said, kicking off her clunky boots.

"Then go be a hero," Abigail said, as she opened the change room door and vanished into the darkness beyond.

"Why wait for me? It's not like you *owe* me or anything," Margo muttered as she struggled to free her left foot from the suit. *So much for my theory that Abigail and I are bonding.* Standing, she stepped out of the filthy suit and hung it up. Then, she slipped on her shoes and picked up the light.

The room just outside the change room was the mechanical shop. Margo took a minute to shine her light around to make sure no one was there in need of help, but it was as empty as it had been when they'd come through. Manually opening the door to the Loop, she looked both ways. *Where should I go first?*

Gary. He'd been working in Sick Bay alone. She took the quickest route, her feeble light barely illuminating the space in front of her feet. In the darkness, her footfalls sounded loud.

When Margo heard a faint cry for help from down a side passage, she jumped in surprise. She shone her light to the side and saw Julien crouching with his back against the wall. The multi-facets of his goggles gleamed when the light from the flashlight hit them.

"What are you doing here?" She flashed the light up to the wall to see exactly where they were. They were at the entrance to the plant nursery.

"I was exploring when the lights went out," he said, rising to his feet and hugging his arms around himself.

"Come with me, kid." Margo started walking and Julien fell into step beside her.

"My mom's probably worried."

Margo raised an eyebrow. She couldn't picture Ms. Snow caring about anything other than her work, but she didn't say anything, distracted by her flashlight's fading beam of light.

"She wouldn't tell me why she hates you," added Julien, falling into step beside Margo.

"Hmmm." Up ahead she could see someone had already put green glow sticks out along the walls of the Loop. *At least someone is thinking clearly.*

"I'll come with you to check on Dr. Holbrook," he said.

"I didn't say where I was headed." Considering how snoopy this kid was, and the fact that he'd been exploring when the lights went out, and—although she hated to admit given whose kid he was—he was smart. Besides, he probably knew the colony as well as she did.

"In the end, I'll forgive you," he said, looking up at her.

"Forgive me for what?" Margo looked down at the boy. In the green glow of light, his white hair and skin took on a sickly sheen.

"For what will happen to my mom."

Margo had to force herself not to stop and stare at the boy. The kid creeped her out with the weird things he said. Maybe if she walked faster, he would stop talking. She shone her light down each of the side corridors they passed in case anyone else was stranded, but they encountered no one.

Stopping at the closed Sick Bay doors, she shone the light on the access panel, opened it, and pulled the lever to manually open the doors, stopping when there was just enough space for her to squeeze through.

"Who's there?" she heard Gary call from his office.

"It's me and the kid," she said, stepping through the narrow entrance with Julien on her heels. Inside, her feeble light barely illuminated the small waiting room.

"Come to rescue me again?" he called.

Margo chuckled as she and Julien passed through the waiting area and into Gary's office. He was sitting at his desk, his lit scroll giving his features a blue-tinged glow. Margo smiled as she leaned against the door frame, pointing her beam towards the floor. He looked her direction, but likely couldn't see her features in the dim light.

"I figured you would be along quickly to save me. How are you, Julien?"

"I don't like the dark." The boy stayed right beside Margo.

"Don't you have a knock-knock joke to lighten the mood?" asked Gary.

Pointing her light to the floor in front of Julien, she saw him solemnly shake his head. Maybe it was the poor light, but she thought he looked even worse than when she'd first encountered him, his skin more grey than white.

Julien took two steps towards a chair in front of Gary's desk, but collapsed before he could reach it. His spindly form hardly made a sound as he hit the floor. Gary sprang to his feet and ran to the boy's side, guided by Margo's beam of light. Violent tremors started passing through the boy's limbs.

"Gary, what's happening?" Margo shrieked.

"Julien!" he shouted, trying to grab the boy's thrashing arms and legs. "Julien!" Julien's limbs continued to flail, and he didn't respond.

Margo kept the light on the boy. "What should I do?"

Gary hugged Julien into his chest, trapping his arms so the boy wouldn't hurt himself, then rose.

"Help me to the examining room," he said.

Margo rushed to the door, keeping the beam of light just ahead of Gary and manually opening the door with the other. As Gary put the boy on the table, the lights flashed back on. A moment later they went off. Finally, the emergency lights came on.

"I need power," he said, laying Julien down on an examination table. The spasms had stopped, and the boy lay deathly still. "I can't do my job without stable power."

Margo looked down at the boy's face illuminated by the dim emergency lights. "He's not dead?" He looked dead.

"No. But he will be soon if I don't have power!"

"I'll leave you the flashlight." She set the light on the counter and ran.

The Control Room door was open when she arrived. She'd been able to sprint the whole way thanks to the glow sticks hung at regular intervals along the length of the Loop. The Control Room was eerily dark, with not even one of its many screens lit. Kasumi had a powerful flashlight at her elbow and was accessing her glowing scroll, ignoring Lucas and Abigail's heated argument.

Kasumi looked up when Margo entered, then gave an exasperated glance towards Abigail and Lucas. "Does she really think he isn't making regaining power a priority?" Kasumi asked, her back to the combatants. "Honestly, that woman is a menace."

"Never mind that," Margo said, trying to catch her breath. "How long till we have power?"

"Gan's working on it. What's wrong?"

"Can you go ask him to prioritize Sick Bay? Julien's collapsed. Gary needs power."

Kasumi looked alarmed at Margo's news, but relieved to have a reason to leave. "I'll let him know right away," she said, grabbing her scroll and flashlight.

"And if you see Neil, send him to help Gary," Margo called as Kasumi headed for the door.

"Sure thing," Kasumi said before disappearing.

Margo hesitated, wondering if she should go back to Sick Bay or try and rescue Lucas, but before she could decide, the lights came back on. Almost blinded, she shielded her eyes, looking around. The screens were all coming back to life. At least the abrupt appearance of overhead light made Abigail and Lucas stop trading insults.

As soon as the lights came on, Lucas turned his back on Abigail and dived into his chair in front of the main console, avidly eyeing the diagnostic code scrolling across the screen.

"Peg are you there?" he demanded.

"I'm not alone," was the AI's strange response.

Abigail crossed her arms and frowned.

"Explain!" Lucas's fingers flew on the keyboard as he started a series of diagnostics on another screen.

Abigail harrumphed. "Now's not the time to worry about your pet AI. We need to figure out why the power cut out."

"What do you think I'm doing, Abigail? Besides, I'm sure it's all related." Lucas's tone of voice changed when he addressed the AI. "Peg, explain."

"I'll have to re-boot her," said Lucas when the AI didn't respond.

"This is ridiculous! Your priorities are messed up. Big time!" Abigail turned and stormed out.

Moving to stand behind Lucas, Margo watched him work at the main control panel.

"Do we really need the AI?" she asked.

"Of course we do," Lucas said testily, working the console in front of him. "This colony's too complex to manage without an AI."

Margo came around and sat in the chair next to Lucas. "We've done okay so far."

"No we haven't," said Lucas, without looking at her. "A lot of people are dead because we didn't have an AI looking out for us."

"People are dead because we had a saboteur." Margo leaned back in the chair and looked at the console in front of her. "Maybe Captain Hori was right and there really is something wrong with the AI. Maybe when the suns return—"

"I'm responsible for keeping those of us left alive," said Lucas cutting Margo off. "And I need the help of the AI to do that."

Margo had no ability to help Gary in Sick Bay, but maybe she could help Lucas troubleshoot the AI problem. "What did Peg mean when she said she wasn't alone?"

Lucas shook his head. "I don't know. That's what I'm trying to find out."

Margo looked at the screen in front of Lucas. For a brief moment she thought she saw a girl skipping rope.

"Maybe I gave you a bad copy?"

"The animation is a glitch, a throwback to some old code," he said. "There," he said with a final flourish on the keyboard. "That should do it. Peg, are you there?" At her affirmative response, he instructed, "I want you to run internal diagnostic subroutine A-19."

"Yes, Lucas," the AI said. A progress bar appeared on the screen.

"Once I get Peg functioning properly, everything will sort itself out."

"I hope so!" said Margo, feeling useless as she watched Lucas's fingers fly on the console.

Chapter Eighteen

The gurgle of the ventilation above reminded him he wasn't on his ship anymore. The ship was gone, pulled into the asteroid—or had they steered it in? Lucas couldn't remember.

"What did you see?"

He didn't recognize the face looming over him. Dark eyes glared at him while the man's bald head reflected the green from the lights above.

"I saw…" Lucas couldn't describe the object. At first it had appeared as a glowing cube imbedded into the lifeless surface of the asteroid. Its pulsing light had called to him, which was impossible, of course; yet, it had made promises. He'd heard it. And he hadn't been able to stop himself from reaching towards it.

"What did you see?" repeated the man.

The exposed pistons and gears of his interrogator's arm seemed to take on a life of their own, threatening him in a way the man had not.

What had he seen beneath the cube's surface? When he tried to remember, all he saw was mechanical destruction, fire, death…

"No!"

Gasping for air, Lucas pushed himself sideways off the examination table he'd been laying on. Landing on all fours, he scurried away like a rat.

"Lucas," whispered Peg.

Lucas's head jerked up. He'd been having another of his nightmares. *Or were they memories?* Rubbing his eyes, he brought himself back to the present. He was disgusted with himself for falling asleep at the console. If any of his subordinates had done the same, they'd be severely reprimanded. Looking around, he made sure he was alone, then turned to review Thesan's orbital dynamics one more time.

Failure to generate power was their main problem. Without solar energy returning soon, they were at risk of draining their batteries and running out of power. With the ambient temperatures outside dipping to frightening low levels, they needed power to keep internal temperatures from falling below freezing.

"Peg?"

"I…." The AI's voice faded to nothing.

"Peg, did you have something to report?"

"No," the AI said. "It's something else."

"What?"

"I can't fully explain… I can only call it a feeling I'm having."

We're about to freeze to death in the dark and the AI is having 'feelings'? Lucas sighed. "Do you want me to re-install you?"

"No, I think that would make matters worse. I… I feel like I'm not alone in here."

"In here?"

Peg's voice dropped to a near whisper. "I think there's another AI trying to hide in my subroutines."

"What?" Lucas had never heard of such a thing happening. Camila would've known if it was even possible. *How can there be another AI? And where could it have come from? Is it the original Peg they deleted?* "Run diagnostics to investigate the presence of an alternate AI." Lucas turned to another screen and made some keystrokes on its console, bringing up data and frowning at it.

"I already have, but I've found nothing."

"Peg, are you sure it's another AI and not just an earlier

copy of yourself?" Camila should've been dealing with this, not him. She was the AI expert. Lucas didn't have time to deal with Peg's less urgent problems. What he really wanted to know was if sunlight returning in 50 hours versus 51 hours made any difference. *Should I really spend my time figuring this out down to the second?*

"No. It's…" Peg's voice trailed into silence, then the lights flickered.

"No, not again!" Lucas froze, willing the lights to stay on, thankful when they did. He stared at the screen at a loss as to what to do next.

"Yes?" he prompted when Peg didn't continue. "Peg, what is it?"

"It's… It's… It's…"

Maybe a reboot was the answer, despite what Peg said.

"It's… It's…"

Lucas stood, about to head to the server room to reboot the AI, but he stopped at Peg's words.

"It's evil."

All the screens suddenly went blank. Goosebumps rose along his skin. Then the profile of a girl skipping rope appeared on his screen—the same one he'd seen earlier. He watched the rope rotate around, each time it approached the ground the girl jumped. *What the hell?* As he sank slowly back into his seat, the girl vanished and his original display of AI diagnostics reappeared.

"Peg?"

"Yes Lucas." The AI sounded crisp and professional, completely normal.

"What just happened?"

"You fell asleep at your console."

Lucas frowned. "I meant after I woke up. There was a problem with your system."

"My programming is functioning flawlessly."

"But there was a girl jumping rope."

"Perhaps you were dreaming."

Lucas leaned back into his chair. *Was I dreaming? Are my usual nightmares evolving to some long forgotten childhood experience? Or is there something wrong with the AI?*

"Hey dipshit," said Abigail as she came into the Control Room.

Lucas turned to look at her. The magenta scarf tied around her neck was nearly as loud as she was.

"If you want me to take your concerns seriously, you can start by either using my name or my title. One or the other, Abigail," he said.

Stopping in the doorway, she put her hands on her hips and scowled. "We need to cut off the greenhouse. We don't have the power to keep it above freezing."

The fact that she ignored his request was a win in Lucas's mind. No address was better than an insult.

"The gardeners aren't going to like that," he said.

"By the time the suns come back, we'll need to clear the dome of the frozen mud, not care for plants that will probably be frozen by then."

Lucas shook his head. "We don't know for sure that the plants will die. And I need to run more simulations before I make such a big decision." Looking back to the orbital dynamics data on his screen, he wished he knew exactly when the sunlight would return. There simply wasn't enough time or data to make a precise calculation.

Annoyed at being ignored, Abigail stomped towards him and spun his chair around. Leaning forward, she put a hand on each armrest.

"Now is the time to act, before we all end up ice cubes." She stabbed a finger in his face. "We need to conserve power. The logical, 'commander-like' thing to do is to cut our loses, abandon the greenhouse, and confine everyone to the Hub."

"If I entertain cutting the power to the greenhouse, I'll first consult with our Chief Engineer." Kasumi had been scrambling to do the basic repairs after the kitchen fire, and their inability to find a way to replenish their draining power supplies was overloading her already short-handed department. Lucas needed more engineers.

"I've done the math. I don't need to confirm with anyone." Abigail stood straight and her expression dared him to disagree.

He jumped to his feet before she could resume her overpowering stance above him. "You may be right," he conceded.

"We need to get the spare cold fusion generator from the Centre Module. Margo said it's in perfect condition."

"I know, but it's too risky to send anyone in the storm," he said. "You should know that. You're the one that's been out there in this." He jerked his head to indicate the environment outside their ship.

"If I may interject," said the AI.

"What is it, Peg?" said Lucas.

"The accelerometers on the roof indicate that the mud storm has abated. Outside, the sky may have cleared."

"Well, shit!" said Abigail. "Maybe that AI isn't so useless after all."

"Display on the main screen." Lucas looked up at the big screen.

"I cannot. The cameras are blocked with mud."

"Ten kilometres in the rover shouldn't take long," Abigail said.

"Going in the dark is way too risky. We haven't properly mapped Thesan. We'll just have to wait until the suns are back."

"Chicken shit!"

Lucas felt close to losing his temper. "Look, Abigail—"

The lights flickered then went out. A moment later they came back on.

"Peg, what just happened?"

"It is impossible to say at this time. The power faults are too many and they keep changing. It's as if something within the system is orchestrating the changes."

"You're not referring to your evil twin again, are you?" Lucas muttered. He immediately regretted his words as Abigail stared at him wide-eyed.

"What the hell? You're talking to the AI like it's the protagonist in a horror movie. You need to shut that AI down." Abigail pointed emphatically at the server room. "It's distracting you from the real issues around here. Just delete the damn thing."

"I'm not shutting it down," Lucas argued. "You're not needed here, Abigail. Just get out." He jerked his head towards the exit. "When and if I decide to shut down power to the greenhouse, I'll let you know.

They stared at each other in silence for a few moments before Abigail stomped out of the room. Perhaps he should be firm with her more often, he thought. *She's a typical bully. As soon as you stand up to her, she retreats.*

He returned to his seat and tapped his fingers on the keyboard to bring up the power readouts for the various systems. Faults were scattered across the entire colony. *The mud on the solar panels was problematic, but it wasn't causing this kind of alarming data. But what was causing it? The ghost AI Peg had mentioned?* He leaned back in his chair and stared at the screen.

"Peg, what's in the system with you?" He had run out of ideas for new diagnostics to run. Asking Peg seemed the logical next step.

"A ghost," said Peg.

"Describe your ghost. And be precise."

"Whenever I do a diagnostic on a fault, it's as though I'm in a chair that is still warm from the previous occupant. No matter how fast I move, I can never catch the other, but I know someone, something, has just been there."

Lucas leaned back, Peg's description was more abstract than he expected. Her code was clearly doing something unexpected.

"A computer virus maybe? Failed code that could just be culled? Or maybe a legit engineering issue?"

"I don't have an answer to that," said the AI even though Lucas's questions had been rhetorical.

Are the issues with Peg and the power system failures symptoms of the same problem? Lucas pushed himself out of his chair. Only one person still alive could help him find an answer to that question.

———

"Kasumi?" Lucas walked into the dimly lit engineering workshop.

"In here, boss." Lucas followed the sound of her voice into a side room. Inside, Kasumi and Gan stared at the wall where they'd projected an enlarged image of the *Settler*'s power grid.

"Is it wise to use that much power?" asked Lucas gesturing towards the image.

"Look," Kasumi said, ignoring Lucas' question and pointing at the screen. "None of the power drains are logical."

"What do you mean?" Lucas asked, frowning at the image.

"Power is draining in the stasis chamber as though pods were running." She pointed to the unused room across from them. "But Gan just checked; not only is nothing on, everything is unplugged." She shifted her finger to point at the power indicator for the Seed Library. "According to this, the heaters are running overtime. If that were actually happening, then the temperature in there would be close to 40 degrees Celsius."

Gan shook his head from where he was leaning a shoulder against a wall staring at the perplexing images. "And they're not. I checked. It's as cold there as everywhere else. And that power surge there," he said, pointing to another indicator. "Tells us the lighting could go out again anytime. But it doesn't tell us why."

"And, this comms unit." Kasumi gestured to their primary communications system on the schematic. "It's randomly transmitting gobble-dy-goop at our highest power setting." She wiped the fly-away hairs off her face. "I could go on. These weird things are happening everywhere."

"What does it all mean?"

"That we're screwed. At this rate, we'll be out of power within hours," said Kasumi. "I don't know what to do to stop it," she added in an affronted tone.

"In three more days, the suns will be back," said Lucas. "Can we last three days?"

Gan interrupted. "The suns coming back won't restore power. Not until we get the mud off the solar panels."

"Peg told me the storm has passed," said Lucas. "We can start sending out work parties to clean our exterior right away."

"That's good. But we need technical help as well."

"Margo did some cross-training here," said Lucas. The other two said nothing for a moment.

"We need *skilled* engineering help," Gan said in his characteristic quiet voice.

Kasumi bit her lip. "There's one highly experienced engineer sitting around doing nothing," said Kasumi.

Lucas inhaled and crossed his arms over his chest. He knew to whom she was referring. "Are you suggesting putting Lucy Snow to work?" The fact that Lucy was an engineer had clearly passed through the colony.

Both Kasumi and Gan nodded.

"You trust her?"

"Of course not. But desperate times call for desperate measures."

"And would you say we're desperate?"

"That's for you to say, boss."

With her skill, Lucy could very likely contribute to getting the colony functional again, but she could also sabotage their main frame and make things go from bad to worse. He tried to think of a better option, but couldn't. "Alright, but Kasumi—"

"I'll watch her like a hawk, boss," said Kasumi in a relieved tone.

"Our lives could very well depend on it." Lucas said as he walked out and headed towards the Hub.

———

Lucas stood at the door to Lucy's quarters. *How had their situation become so desperate that they were now relying on the woman who had been, and perhaps still was, their adversary?* Rubbing his chin, he tried to think of a better option. He still couldn't, so he knocked on the door.

He heard the manual override being used, and the door was pulled open. Lucy stood in the near-darkness of her quarters looking down at him. In the dim light she looked like a ghost.

"Is Julien okay?" he asked.

"Dr. Holbrook says he's stable. The seizures though…" Lucas thought she was actually being sincere, but then again, Julien was her kid. *What mother wouldn't be worried?*

"I hope our doctors can find a cure," he said. He, too, was being sincere.

Lucy raised an eyebrow as if to challenge his sincerity, but instead she said, "They need power to help him. And you're here to request my help."

Lucas stared at her, neither affirming nor denying her statement. He hated how much they needed her unique skill set.

"I know you perceive me as the villain here," Lucy continued when Lucas remained stubbornly silent. "But I can help. I've gotten my crews out of some dire circumstances—some worse than this place."

"Don't betray us, or I *will* put out an airlock," promised Lucas. "If I don't, Margo will."

Lucy nodded.

Chapter Nineteen

Margo curled her feet under herself as she flipped open another of Jim's notebooks. The first few pages contained ancient Egyptian hieroglyphics, but Jim had not provided a translation. She yawned and reached for her mug of tea. The tea was cold already. With a disgruntled sigh, she put the mug back down, shivering.

Gary came back from his bedroom where he'd just put on another sweater, carrying a blanket that he spread over her. His hand accidentally brushed against her thigh, leaving warmth in its wake.

"Thanks," she said, smiling at him. Her eyes followed him as he walked around the couch and sat at the other end. She wished he'd sit close enough for her to feel more than just a brush of his body heat, telling herself that it was only because it was so cold.

Ever since he'd been stabbed, she'd been finding frequent reasons to go to Gary's quarters. First it was to check on him, making sure he wasn't overdoing it. Now she went because she simply enjoyed his company. She'd been especially surprised to discover he had a wicked sense of humour. She was enjoying getting to know him, although it still embarrassed her that he'd read all her private thoughts in her journal.

Gary picked up his scroll from the coffee table, then said, "Looks like the temperature in here is still dropping. It's now 4 degrees Celsius."

They'd sat in companionable silence for the last hour and a half. While she read Jim's notebooks, he looked at genetics papers in his quest to help the boy.

"We don't have enough power for heat or even full lighting. Kasumi and Gan have been working around the clock to do something. But without sunlight..." She let herself trail off.

A knot of fear formed in her gut at the thought of losing all power and how that would impact their small community. She looked back down at the notebook she held, distracting herself from the direness of their situation by focusing on Jim's illustrations.

"Anything interesting in that journal?" Gary put down his scroll and looked at her.

"This one's dedicated to Jim's love of all things Egyptian." She held up the book, showing him another page filled with hieroglyphics.

Gary shook his head. "Jim seems to have had a hard time focusing on any one thing."

"He certainly had a lot of interests." Margo flipped to the next page and recognized Pythagoras' formula. The rest of the page was filled with a series of indecipherable geometric relationships and in the margins were doodles of running horses.

When she flipped to the next page, the theme of Jim's notes and doodles changed. "Hey, here's something different."

Gary scooted so he sat right beside her. She caught a whiff of his pine soap, a scent she was beginning to like.

"Looks like a spider web," he said.

It did look like a web. Once again, Jim hadn't bothered to label anything, but on the facing page there was some writing.

"Lunex-21 was built on the far side of the moon by the combined mili-

tary in 2072 to secretly test new propulsion systems," she read aloud. *"The military abandoned the site fifty years ago, in 2096. Since it was so remote, most of the facility was left in place."*

"I think I read something about that place once," said Gary, running a hand through his hair. "Or maybe I'm thinking of the VR haunted tour Neil wanted to drag me on."

"Did you go?"

"Do I strike you as someone into gimmicky virtual tours?" He smiled at her.

"Not so much," said Margo, reflecting back his smile. "But don't dismiss it entirely. That kind of stuff can be fun. Why don't you come with me sometime? I promise not to tell anyone. Your reputation as a serious doctor and scientist would remain intact."

"So long as Neil doesn't find out. He'd never let me hear the end of it. When the power's up, we have a date. What's on the next page?"

Margo flipped the page and found a list of names. She began reading them out loud, then stopped. "I've never heard of these people." She looked up at Gary. "Have you?"

"No." Gary leaned closer to read from the notebook. *Ash Jones, missing from the mining ship* Angler *on its rendezvous with the asteroid 101946 Tlaloc.* "I remember that comet—it was on an Earth intercept course. Earth defence had to shoot it down."

"Yeah, I remember," said Margo. She'd been living in her greenhouse on Earth at the time, raising butterflies. "I don't remember anything about sending a mining ship out." She flipped another page and Gary shifted closer so that their shoulders brushed. His warmth was welcome.

"So why did Jim include a note about Lunex-21 amongst the Egyptian hieroglyphics?"

"There must be a common thread in his notes. We just have to somehow connect the dots."

Margo tucked a hair behind her ear as she frowned in thought. "Within all this pseudoscience, ridiculous theories and mumbo jumbo, there's got to be something useful. Hey, hold on!" she exclaimed, meeting Gary's gaze. "Didn't Jim write in one of the other notebooks about how they thought the doctor they took Kimberly to see defected to the insurgents on their lunar base?"

"And you're thinking the insurgents' lunar base is this abandoned military testing facility?"

"Maybe."

"Who was the doctor?"

"Paul Dogan," said Margo, flipping through the stack of notebooks trying to find the one where Jim had written about the lunar base. "Remember? I told you about what Lucy Snow told me about him."

"Let me look in the medical archive." Gary leaned forward and grabbed his scroll from the coffee table. "Hmmm, looks like there are a whole series of papers on consciousness by him; I'll download them."

"Whoa!" Margo sat up and turned to Gary with a triumphant smile. "Jim hid a memory chip in here," said Margo, holding up the notebook where a memory chip was taped to the page.

"Well, let's check it out," said Gary. Margo pealed back the tape and handed the chip to him. He inserted it into his scroll, then shuffled closer so they both could look at the screen. Their thighs touched and as they leaned against each other. Margo felt a tingle go up her spine.

"It's a video file," she said as Gary hit play.

The view jiggled as if the camera was attached to someone's chest as they entered a room, revealing an image of an office with a bank of windows overlooking Earth. The room was spartan but spacious, clearly not a low-ranking worker's office.

"A covert recording?" asked Margo. The view settled on a figure behind a massive desk as if the person had stopped walking. The man seated behind the desk stood. His boyish face familiar.

"That's Nigel West," said Gary, pausing the recording and looking at Margo. "You know who he is, right?"

"Yes. But with his dimples and messy hair, I've always thought he looks more like a frat boy who has never grown up than the head of The Conglomerate. And he loves the press," she scoffed.

"Well, his army of marketers ensure his pretty face is plastered everywhere."

Margo pulled a face. "Including being the face of The Conglomerate's AI."

When Gary resumed the recording, they saw Nigel smile at the camera-wearer.

"Dr. Dogan," said Nigel. *"Or shall I call you Paul? It's so nice you stopped by."*

Gary paused the recording. "This can't be a coincidence."

"I agree," said Margo then gestured at the scroll. "Let's keep listening."

"I don't see how I had a choice," said the voice of the man wearing the camera.

"True, true," said Nigel with a falsely congenial smile. *"Have a seat."* Nigel leaned back in his chair and put his feet up on the expanse of his desk. The camera wobbled again as Paul took a seat facing him. *"I'm told you've put your human trials on hold."*

"As I outlined in my memo, our recent failures have made it clear we started human trials prematurely and that it would be unethical to continue. We need to get back to basics and further our understanding before resuming human trials."

"Is this related to…" Nigel lifted his scroll and looked at the screen. *"Sonja Banks and Dana Wong?"*

"Yes, they were both my assistants."

"Were?" Standing, Nigel walked around the desk. When he leaned against it, his face and shoulders were in clear view, revealing the fine lines around his eyes that contrasted with his boyish face. He wore an expression of interest like it was the latest fashion. *"I was told that, from here on the*

station, you successfully transferred one assistant's mind into another's at the lab in Switzerland. I heard it was a complete success."

"For four hours, yes. But it was the return transfer that failed. Dana in Switzerland was left in a comatose state and Sonja—" Nigel raised a hand to interrupt Paul.

"As Dana was just an intern, she doesn't matter. If it's important to you, we can see that her family is compensated."

"What's important to me is to refrain from conducting any more experiments. I don't want to endanger lives. Continuing these unethical experiments is something I can't live with anymore."

Nigel smiled as if he knew a camera was pointed at him. "Tell me about Sonja, the owner of the consciousness being transported. That's the most important step. As you know, I need to get back into this," he gestured to himself with a little wiggle, "safely."

The camera wobbled again as Paul shifted in his chair as if agitated. "She woke with a split personality, a fusion of hers and Dana's. We need to continue observing her to understand the full implications of what happened, but what we do know is that she has been unable to distinguish between the present and past, and is continuously reliving some horrible tragedy in Dana's past. She's inhabiting a living, looping nightmare. And I did that to her!"

"So, send her for re-programming." Nigel crossed his arms. "I don't understand why you're not focusing on the successes here. You've made progress this time."

"Progress?" There was a pause before the seated man continued. "I don't think you understand. Sonja hasn't been able to reach a sleep state."

Nigel shrugged, still maintaining his smile.

"She clawed out her own eyes." Paul's voice was flat.

Nigel made the same face a child would make if presented with a plate of over-cooked broccoli.

"We've put her in an induced coma. Her prognosis for recovery of any kind is not good."

"Then your only problem is, you'll need to hire a new assistant."

"We need to stop," insisted Paul.

Nigel leaned toward Paul, his facing looming large and filling the camera screen as if he'd just put a hand on each of the chair's arm rests. "I need you to listen to me."

The camera view suddenly tilted and then, after a loud crash and a muffled exclamation from Paul, the view stilled again, only now it was aimed up at the illuminated ceiling. Nigel's chin and shoulder filled the screen as if he'd kneeled on the floor beside Paul's head.

"Consciousness projection is the only path for me to touch that cube," he spat, all hint of congeniality evaporated. "I don't give a shit about the host, which means you don't give a flying fuck either. Your only focus is on getting the person projecting their consciousness back into their own mind safely."

Nigel's face disappeared from the camera view and the screen was once again filled with the ceiling's pot lights.

"I won't do this anymore," said Paul from the ground.

Nigel's voice was distant. "Your wife and kids are here on this station, correct?"

The camera view jiggled again, then filled with the figure of Nigel standing by the windows and facing his visitor.

"Yes," said Paul.

Nigel turned his back on Paul as if more interested in the view of Earth orbiting below than in talking further with his guest. He clasped his hands behind him as he spoke, his threat barely audible. "If they are proving a distraction from your work, perhaps they should be sent planet side."

When the video ended, Margo and Gary stared at each other for a moment.

"Did I hear right?" said Margo. "That Nigel West wants to transfer his consciousness into other people's minds?"

"I didn't realize he got so close to success," said Gary, clearly thinking about Paul Dogan's work. "I can't believe they're even doing that kind of work."

"Why not?" asked Margo. "Anything goes when it comes to The Conglomerate, doesn't it?"

"About 20 years ago there was a big push in the field of consciousness transfer near where I lived, and it included human trials. My mother worked as an attending physician in one of the institutions created to deal with those who'd volunteered for the first round of trials. There was over a hundred people being kept there. I remember going to work one day with her and seeing those people…"

Margo looked over at him, but said nothing as he searched for words to describe what had obviously been a traumatizing moment.

"Some were comatose, some had clawed their own eyes out…" His voice drifted off and Margo felt him shiver. "There was a hundred percent failure in the trials. Everyone who volunteered ended up in that place. They got paid well, but it wasn't worth it. Charges were laid against the scientists, but that didn't make up for what happened. I thought we were done with that line of research." He looked down at his scroll. "That's weird."

"What?"

"It's one of Paul's papers." He scrolled through the text. "It's gibberish."

"Did the file get corrupted?"

"Maybe there was a power glitch just now while the files were being downloaded."

They were both looking at his scroll when the text flashed and then was replaced with a little girl jumping rope.

"That's really weird!" Margo leaned in to look closer at the animation, but almost as soon as it appeared, it disappeared. "Do you know, I saw the same video loop on the screen in the Control Room?"

"A girl skipping rope? What did Lucas have to say about that?"

Margo shook her head. "He said it was just a glitch. And it disappeared in seconds. I'd forgotten all about it till just now."

They both jumped apart as a knock sounded at the door. Gary set the scroll down with a clatter as if his hands were clumsy all of a sudden, then stood. Margo resented the cold air that filled the space he'd occupied.

Going to the door, Gary pulled the manual lever. The door slid back into its pocket.

Neil stood on the other side. He glanced at Gary, then to Margo.

"Oh good, you're both here," Neil said with a smile. "The mud storm has subsided and I hear the sky is clear. I'm about to collect Amanda and then we're heading to the Control Room. Want to join us?"

Chapter Twenty

Lucas left the Control Room and headed down the Loop towards Engineering to get a status report from Kasumi. As he passed the interior windows of the Common Room, he saw some of his colleagues milling about within, and then was surprised to hear laughter. News that the mud storm had subsided seemed to have initiated an impromptu—and jovial—gathering. The happy voices made him feel like an outsider. He longed to join in. Instead, he walked by without stopping.

When he arrived at Engineering, every mechanically inclined member of their crew was focused on a task. At a workbench in the corner, he saw Lucy soldering one of the broken builder bots.

"You're here," said Kasumi, coming out of one of the back rooms. She rubbed her greasy hands on her overalls as she looked over her shoulder. "Gan's got one of the builder bots ready to go with a camera so we can do an exterior survey."

"That's a good idea," said Lucas, relieved a solution of how to look outside was already in place.

Lucas raised his eyebrows as a tarantula-like robot about

three feet tall walked out of a side room. Gan followed right behind, holding a remote control in both hands. The bot had a shiny black carapace and abdomen. Its eight articulated legs had red joints, just like the spiders his brother used to keep. The cameras on its head added to the arachnid illusion. At least it didn't have fur. Lucas did his best to hide how much the robot creeped him out.

"We can patch the footage to the Control Room." Kasumi stepped aside for Gan and his builder bot to pass. "There's something I need to mention," she said in a low voice as they followed Gan and his robot into the Loop.

Lucas and Kasumi continued on towards the Control Room while Gan directed the bot down a short hallway towards the main airlock.

"About Lucy Snow?" The knot in Lucas's stomach tightened with dread. *What had she done?*

"No, she's been fine. So far." Despite Gan no longer being within hearing distance, Kasumi still kept her voice low. "I've been through our entire electrical system and I can't find any faults, yet it keeps hemorrhaging power to pointless operations. Even without solar input, we should've had enough power to last months. Yet the lights keep failing and our power supply continues to drain way more than I'd expect."

"What pointless operations?" He stopped and looked at her.

"At one point, aquaponics was fully powered—even though that space is completely non-functional—and then our outside search lights were on; those are powerful beams and created another significant drain. On top of that, for a while we were transmitting a high power signal to empty space."

"What do you think is causing the problem?" Lucas ran a hand through his hair and resumed walking with Kasumi at his side.

The engineer cocked her head. "I've run diagnostics three times on all the equipment—and they're all fine. So the problem has to be with our control system." She brushed a lock of hair behind her ear. "I've looked at the logs, and these problems all began the day after the kitchen fire."

"What does that mean?" he asked, dreading her response.

She bit her lip before continuing. "I think the problem is with the AI."

"Peg?" At Kasumi's words, Lucas felt something inside himself sag. He needed the AI, which was why he'd been ignoring the obvious problems it had been presenting. In his defence, other issues kept cropping up that took his attention away from sorting out what he'd dismissed as harmless glitches. But Kasumi was right. And the timing made sense. He'd installed the AI the day after the kitchen fire.

"The fact is, the AI was acting up before we even left Earth's orbit," she continued. "That's why it was removed."

"Yes, but not having an AI is why we crashed," said Lucas. *Am I only defending the AI because Camila chose it?*

"How do we know things wouldn't have been worse with a malfunctioning AI?" Kasumi looked him in the eye as they continued down the Loop. "Boss, you need to isolate the AI so that my team can figure out what's wrong with it."

"You want me to shut down Peg." His question came out like a statement of fact because he knew Kasumi was right. It was the only way to alleviate the immediate problem of losing power. But with his limited crew and without the AI, it would be really hard to monitor the ship.

"At the rate the AI is bleeding off our power, freezing to death in the dark is the alternative."

"Fine, I'll do it right after Gan and his bot show us what it looks like outside," he said.

———

With the storm abated, most of the *Settler's* colonists had moved from celebrating in the Common Room to milling about in the Control Room. When Lucas entered with Kasumi, he caught snatches of conversation as they speculated about what Gan's recon mission would reveal.

"Hey fearless leader," said Abigail, pushing her way through to approach him. "I've analyzed the mud."

Lucas reminded himself to be grateful for small favours. *At least she hadn't called him a dipshit or boss man.* Maybe his taking a firm hand with her earlier had actually influenced her behaviour. He didn't stop beside Abigail but instead wove through the groups of people, who'd become silent now that he'd entered the room, and stopped behind Iva's chair beside Gary and Margo. Suppressing an urge to push Iva out of the way and work the cameras himself, he addressed Abigail, keeping his eyes on the screen.

"What's in the mud?"

"It's inorganic."

Lucas stared at her blankly. His expertise was the operational and mechanical elements of running the colony, not chemistry. "So what?"

Abigail scowled at him and put a hand on her hip. "So what? So what! If there had been life in that mud, it would be ethically wrong to start terraforming here. We can't stomp out native life forms."

"Abigail, we've got bigger problems right now."

"This is a big problem." She pushed in closer to him, to the point she was almost touching him.

"Lucas," Margo interjected, hoping to defuse Abigail. "With the mud came higher levels of oxygen. If there is no photosynthesis, we need to determine where the oxygen came from."

"Of course we do, but it's not our priority at this moment," Lucas nodded to the monitors and the ash-grey covering of mud. "Figuring out the best way to get rid of that is."

At Lucas's response, Abigail crossed her arms and raised an

eyebrow, looking ready to launch an argument, but Lucas spoke firmly before she could. "If all goes as planned, we'll have work crews on our dome soon clearing off the mud. Until then, go ahead and investigate the oxygen mystery." He turned to Iva. "Can you project the bot's video feed to the Common Room?"

Iva had swivelled her chair to look at Abigail and Lucas, but at his question she turned back to face her work station. "Yes," she said, tapping a couple keys on her control panel.

Lucas turned to the colonists. "Everyone, except Kasumi and Iva, you can watch from the Common Room."

People grumbled, but they started filing out of the room. After a long moment spent glaring at him, Abigail shrugged and left. Gary and Margo followed, with Margo giving Lucas a brief sympathetic smile before turning away.

At Abigail's departure, Lucas felt himself relax a little. "Peg, let anyone who wasn't here know they can watch the bot's feed in the Common Room."

"Yes, Lucas," said the AI.

For a moment, Lucas thought the AI sounded sullen, as if it was reacting to his and Kasumi's conversation about shutting her down, which of course the AI would have 'overheard'. He shook his head. *Now I really am being ridiculous.*

"Gan has the bot in the airlock now," said Kasumi, looking at her scroll. She hadn't taken a seat, but remained standing beside Lucas and behind Iva.

A moment later the bot's video feed appeared on the main screen. The view showed the interior of the airlock with the camera trained on the closed outside door. The bot extended three of its front legs and opened the door. As the door swung inwards, an avalanche of flakes fell inside. For a moment the camera showed only the flurry of flakes, then they settled, and the view became clear again.

Gan switched on the bot's powerful light and panned its camera to the outside surface in front of the airlock's outer door.

A thick layer of frozen mud coated the rubble, smoothing out the rough edges. It almost looked like a layer of snow had fallen.

"Sending the bot out now," Gan transmitted.

The bot's light illuminated the landscape beyond the door as it started to move. After about a dozen meters, Gan stopped it and pivoted the camera to reveal its path. Unlike snow or ash, there were no indentations to indicate the bot's eight 'feet' had stepped on the surface.

"It's frozen solid," said Lucas, his stomach knotting as he considered the ramifications. He ran his thumb and forefinger down either side of his chin. The hard frozen layer of mud on Thesan's ground would be no different on their colony. Their structure, dome and sensors would be covered in it. *What does this mean for power generation?*

Gan panned the bots light and camera upward at *Settler III*'s structure. Other than the open airlock door and the massive size of the grey-coated lump, no details distinguished the former space craft from the landscape.

"Gan, take the bot up to the roof," Lucas directed.

The three occupants of the Control Room watched in silence as the bot started crab-walking up the steep slope of the ship. If Lucas hadn't known it was part of their settlement, he would've assumed the 'hill' was a natural feature.

Once on the roof, Gan paused the bot, then panned its light and camera slowly across the dome they'd erected to cover the inner, hollow circle of their colony. As Lucas feared, the surface was completely coated.

"Gan, get the bot to measure the depth of the mud on the dome."

"Will do," said Gan.

While Gan was working, Lucas addressed Kasumi. "Can the bot start cleaning off the mud?"

"Yes, but with a single bot, it'll take forever. Even when Lucy gets the other one working..." She shook her head. "What I mean to say, there isn't a mechanical solution to this problem.

We need all able-bodied colonists on that roof clearing the solar panels."

Lucas nodded, then turned to watch the monitor as Gan moved the bot forward to where the dome sloped upwards, then directed the bot to use a forward leg to chisel through the frozen surface and brush the flakes of frozen mud aside. After it cleared a patch, Gan zoomed in, turning on a ruled line on one side of the view .

"Looks like the mud is six centimetres thick," Gan said over the intercom.

The three colleagues absorbed this unwelcome news in silence.

As Gan zoomed back out, removing the ruled line, they could just make out a dim glow of light penetrating the darkness below the dome.

"That must be the Common Room lights," Kasumi said, pointing at the image.

Lucas took a deep breath and ran both hands through his hair. *At least mud isn't coming down any more.* He looked at the sensor readouts, all still corrupted from the mud. "Gan, have the bot start cleaning off our sensors and comms gear first," Lucas ordered. "Then the scaffolding up to the roof. Once that's done, we'll get work parties out there."

"Sure thing, boss," responded Gan, then added, "hey, I've got an idea."

Gan shut off the bot's light and directed the camera upwards, adjusting the camera's lens to distance view.

The night sky dominated the screen, mesmerizing the three onlookers. The band of the Milky Way cut the sky in half, far more brilliant than seeing it from Earth. They could also clearly see the bright orb of their orbital neighbour. Even that planet's moon was visible. Although it was a beautiful view, Lucas still wished for the suns' return.

Lucas looked away from the captivating view and glanced down at the smaller consoles, absently running a hand along the bridge of his artificially healed nose. For the first time in days, he felt there was a clear first step—arranging work parties to clean off the exterior. *This is the work that will bring the colonists together and define my role as commander.* The knot in his stomach loosened as Lucas felt renewed hope surge through him.

Chapter Twenty-One

Margo kept on eye on Gary while the airlock cycled the air to match Thesan's outside environment. He stood suited-up beside her in the main airlock and appeared calm, although he hadn't said a word since she'd confirmed his suit was on properly and his posture was as rigid as a mannequin. Margo assumed he could've explained his agoraphobia to Lucas and requested an exemption from outside work rotation, but he hadn't. She appreciated his effort and thought he was being very brave—she had a fear of heights and knew what it took to face it. She was also glad they were spending more time together.

The light beside the outside door flashed green. "You ready?" she asked over their helmet comms. She rested a hand on the handle, waiting for his answer.

"Yes."

After opening the door, she stepped across the door's threshold. Outside, under starlight, the smooth layer of mud looked glossy. On her left the scaffolding-encased stairs led up to the roof. The steps were clear thanks to the builder bots and Gan's team had mounted lights on it. Her stomach clenched as she remembered the day she'd gone up there to repair the dome—

the same day Joe had died. A wave of sadness washed over her as she thought of Joe. They'd known each other such a short time, but from the moment she'd met him she'd been drawn to him. He'd been dead for over a month; yet, in that moment, it felt like only hours.

Margo gave herself a mental shake and started walking along the surface of the frozen mud, much flatter than the uneven rocky surface Thesan usually offered, leading them along the perimeter an arm's distance from the colony's wall. Gary followed in silence. As they walked, their helmet lights gave feeble illumination to their surroundings, but it was enough.

"I said we'd continue clearing the outside windows to the left of the main airlock," Margo said, as they passed several already cleaned windows. Further along they came to a bank of mud-caked windows. "We might as well start here."

She pulled a homemade scraper out of a pouch attached to her belt. Lucas still hadn't given permission to direct power to their domestic printers so Gan had made stacks of scrapers out of plastic scraps, and both she and Gary had a half-dozen stowed away.

Standing beside her, Gary began chiseling away at the frozen mud. A small chunk flaked away. "This is going to take a while," he said.

"Concentrate on how much progress everyone has made so far rather than on what still needs doing." Focusing on the positive kept her from dwelling on just how much mud the colonists would have to remove. Margo chipped away at her section. "Further results on Abigail's analysis of the mud came back."

"Is it alive?" Gary continued working with his scraper.

"Nope, no alien lifeforms. But the mud will make a great growing medium—it won't take much to turn it into fertile soil."

"So, there's a silver lining."

"Combining our Earth soil with the mud will speed up creation of soil." She ran her scraper up the window, knowing the clear aluminum surface wouldn't scratch. "We'll be able to erect the spoke-greenhouses and plant them sooner than anticipated."

"That sounds like a good thing."

They worked in silence as they continued to clear two ground-level windows. The lights were off inside, which wasn't surprising as they were conserving as much power as they could. Strips of cleared window merged until the entire surface was cleared, then they moved on to the next one.

When the interior lights flashed on, they both paused, surprised that someone had turned the lights on. Margo's helmet bumped against the glass as she tried to get a better view of the inside of the room, but there was no one inside. Just as suddenly, the lights flickered off.

"That was weird," said Margo, resuming her scraping.

"Do you know what's keeping Lucas and Kasumi from resolving these power issues?"

"Kasumi thinks the AI is causing the glitches. Lucas has reluctantly agreed to remove it."

"You mean, removing the AI before we left Earth's orbit wasn't part of Craig's scheme to sabotage the mission?"

"More like messing with the AI so Captain Hori had no choice to remove it was part of Craig's scheme. What Lucas hadn't realized when he asked me to retrieve the AI from the Central Module was that the back up version had also been infected."

"What a mess to sort out. I sure don't envy him getting stuck with command," said Gary, as he finished the window he was working on. "Did you find any more information about Paul Dogan's work in Jim's journals?"

"No. But I haven't finished reading them all. There about four more to go." Margo looked down at the front of her atmo suit and had a déjà vu moment—she was covered in flakes of mud. She shrugged and moved on to the next window. "I didn't find any other memory chips, and Jim's other notes discuss theories behind why the wormhole is there."

"What's the prevailing theory?"

"There appears to be a contingent that think The Conglomerate made it. How they made it Jim doesn't say. Another group thinks it's alien in construction and yet another thinks it's natural and has been there since the solar system's formation."

"So, nothing definitive then," said Gary. "That seems to be a theme in Jim's notes, doesn't it?"

Margo's scraper snapped in half. "Crap!" She pulled out another one and resumed working. "I did find a note in a margin about Paul Dogan that said he vanished shortly after the video was filmed."

"I wonder if The Conglomerate did away with him. Does Jim note his theory?"

"No," said Margo.

"I wonder if the consciousness project continued? Maybe it's still being researched?"

"Nigel West seemed adamant it was necessary, and since he's the one in power, I'm assuming it did continue."

"You know," Gary mused. He dropped his arms and looked up at the star-filled sky. "I wonder who's body Nigel wants to project his consciousness into."

"I know. It's freaking creepy. And something about this whole consciousness experiment seems to have something to do with an ancient artifact that Jim mentioned in the same notebook. At first, I dismissed it thinking it was his conspiracy theory rambling, especially since it seemed so out of place in the context of the Nigel West recording."

"What kind of artifact?" asked Gary, shuffling his feet and turning so he could get a better view of the sky from within the bubble of his helmet.

"Jim described the artifact as a cube no bigger than his palm. He also suggested that it was very dangerous, but he didn't elaborate."

Margo finished her window, then smiled indulgently at Gary. "Are you just going to stare at the stars all day?"

He turned to her and grinned. "You should be expressing your amazement at how comfortable I've become being outside rather than criticising me for taking a two-second break," he teased. "Anyway, your mention of Paul Dogan reminds me of how the papers of his became corrupted on my scroll. A technical glitch maybe? Anyway, I forgot to look for them in the medical database."

"When we are done here, let's go do that," said Margo.

"How long is our shift supposed to be?"

"Four hours."

"My arms are going to be stiff when we're done," said Gary.

"Mine already feel like jelly."

———

Four hours later, arms and shoulders aching, Margo sat sprawled in one of Gary's office chairs watching him work. She was wearing every sweater she owned to keep out the cold. If it got colder, she'd be forced to wear her atmo suit inside—an uncomfortable prospect.

Gary tapped at his console, frowning, then tapped again. "Well that's weird," said Gary. "The files that disappeared off my scroll aren't even in the database anymore."

"That is weird. Can you find anything on the consciousness projection project?"

He scanned the titles on his monitor. "Here's one," he said, opening the file and adjusting the monitor so Margo could see. "But it's not one of the files I downloaded earlier."

Instead of the published paper they'd expected to see, the entire screen flashed black before playing the same animation they'd seen on Gary's scroll of the girl skipping rope.

"Well that's even weirder," said Margo, getting up to stand beside Gary so she could lean in and get a closer look at the strange animation. The video loop was exactly the same as the others she'd seen. "Can you escape?"

"No, see?" Gary tapped the keys but nothing changed.

"Peg, power down this console." Margo instructed, but the AI didn't respond. "Try turning it off."

Gary hit the power button, but nothing happened. The girl kept skipping her rope. It was as though Peg had morphed into a human child and was playing a childish prank on them.

They both jumped when a male voice spoke, seeming to come from everywhere. "Be a good girl and go play."

"I recognize that voice," said Gary.

"So do I! It's Nigel West," said Margo, remembering the man in the video.

"It's also the voice of the Nigel series of AI."

Margo felt a shiver of dread run up her spine. *What did this mean? And after all they'd been through with the saboteur, the mud storm, and these unexplained power failures, they didn't need another mystery!* She looked at Gary, but he looked as mystified as she.

"What's going on?" asked Margo with a grimace.

Gary shrugged. "I wish I knew."

"I have noticed the power to your console is off," said Peg.

"No, it's not," argued Gary. "I was trying to turn it off to get rid of that, but it's not responsive."

"Is there a problem with it?" Peg asked.

"Yes, there's a problem. Where were you?" asked Margo. "A moment ago I asked for your help."

"I have been here all along. Had I received a request to help, I would have responded," the AI countered in her characteristic reasonable tone. "How may I assist you?"

"Peg, re-boot the console." The girl disappeared, and the screen started going through the usual start-up routines. "Peg, search for an animation of a girl skipping rope in the memory banks."

"Please stand by."

Margo turned and leaned her hips against the desk so that she faced Gary.

"That was some glitch. What do you think is going on?" he asked with a raised eyebrow.

When Margo met Gary's gaze, a thought suddenly occurred to her. She raised her index finger to her lips before picking up a pen and a pad of paper, Gary appeared to like taking old-school notes. She wrote for a moment, then moved the pad so Gary could read it.

Peg seems unaware that she's malfunctioning. That tells me we need to be careful what we say.

Gary read the note, nodded thoughtfully, then took the pen from her and wrote: *Do you mean someone is listening? Another saboteur? We need to tell Lucas.*

"He's reluctant to acknowledge the source of the issue." Margo felt her statement was cryptic enough that whatever —*whoever?*—was causing the AI to malfunction wouldn't gain any meaning from her statement.

Why does he have such an attachment to an AI? wrote Gary, before leaning back in his chair.

"Did you know that Lucas' late wife was the AI technician?" Margo picked up the pen and wrote: *Maybe Lucas views Peg as an extension of Camila. By protecting Peg, he's protecting his dead wife?*

Lucas needs to deal with the AI before someone dies, wrote Gary, underlining 'before' twice. "Well, the bots don't get hungry from their labours, but our labours have left me hungry. Shall we go see what Amanda has made?" He added on paper: *Where can we talk freely?*

Margo picked up the pen and wrote: *There are no AI interfaces in the Hub's garden. We can talk there.*

Chapter Twenty-Two

Margo's right arm felt numb after a second full day spent scraping mud. Working side-by-side with Gary, they'd done two shifts separated by only a short lunch break. They'd spent the entire day scraping each airlock clean, including digging out crusty mud with what appeared to be chopsticks from the external controls. It had been a long day and her muscles ached. It didn't help that it was still cold in Gary's quarters—but it would be just as cold in her own apartment and everywhere else on the colony.

She didn't missed many things from her life on Earth, but the thought of soaking in a hot bath made her wish she'd never left her home planet. She indulged her fantasy, turning the bath into a hot-tub with jets of water easing the ache in her sore muscles, then realized how silly she was being. *Not helping!* Instead, she snuggled deeper under the blanket Gary had given her and leaned back against his couch. She closed her eyes, but all she saw were visions of the caked mud on the airlock doors.

Opening her eyes, she looked at the remaining few un-read notebooks. Picking one up, she began flipping through it a little clumsily given her thick gloves, scanning sketches of lei lines and ancient stone rings. She paused on a page that was covered in indecipherable pictograms. She couldn't tell if the pictograms were meant to be art or if Jim had embedded a secret message in them. With a yawn, she glanced at Gary where he sat at the other end of the same couch and smiled.

He had gone to greater lengths than her to stay warm, attested to by the toque he'd borrowed from Kasumi. It had an oversized yellow pompom that made him look endearingly ridiculous and made her smile every time she looked his way. Feeling a chill on her neck, she adjusted her scarf and tightened the blanket around her legs, wishing she couldn't see her breath in the air.

She gazed back down at the notebook, but instead of trying to decipher whatever messages Jim might have embedded, she let her thoughts drift to analyzing her and Gary's growing friendship. Over the last two weeks her opinion of him had morphed from dislike into fondness. He was surprisingly kind and considerate—traits she'd previously thought he lacked. Plus, he was seeking out her company, which was flattering. *Are we headed towards a normal marital relationship? Do I even want that?* This time when she thought of Gary in a romantic way, she didn't feel guilty about transferring her affections from Joe to Gary. *Does that mean Joe is giving me permission to move on?*

"Did you find something?"

"Nope," said Margo, flushing at where her thoughts had taken her. For once, she welcomed the warmth in her cheeks. She didn't look at Gary, instead flipping the page. When she read the title *AI history*, she let out a surprised exclamation.

"Now you've found something?" Gary put down his scroll and looked at her.

"It looks like a timeline of the development of artificial intelligence. It appears Jim's written it up as two separate timelines, as though there were two distinct AIs created." She traced a gloved finger along the lines. "He's separated the PEG series of AI from Nigel ones." She flipped a page. *Peggy Plum started the Peg line as a sideline to her work with the early computers,* she read. Peggy Plum was the woman in the 1952 film who'd addressed someone with the same name as Margo. "Jim lists her papers: *On the Development of Artificial Intuition, Simulated Emotion and Thoughts…*" The list filled the entire page.

"It sounds like Peggy was a prolific academic."

"I wonder if I can get my hands on any of these?" Margo wasn't sure how Peggy's publications could help, but she was grasping at any straw to find a path forward.

"You could ask Peg to conduct a search."

"I don't trust Peg. Last time we asked her for help, things got weird." Margo frowned as she pictured the image of the girl skipping rope and the disturbing sound of Nigel West's voice saying: *Be a good girl and go play.*

"True," said Gary. "Did you tell Lucas your theory about the AI?"

"I mentioned it this morning, but Iva was right there and it didn't feel right bringing up Camila. Then I had to start my shift outside and I haven't seen him since."

"Jim thinks there's other AI lines?"

Margo flipped through the next few pages. "Yes—at one time. It looks like there were all sorts of scientists involved. A lot of false starts and dead ends, no different from any other sophisticated technology," she added in a mutter. "Okay, here Jim writes that in the last century, The Conglomerate took over development of the more independent thinking models and added their algorithms to the Nigel series." She scratched her head. "The only true competition to the Peg AIs is theirs."

Frantic knocking on Gary's door interrupted them. "What now?" muttered Gary as he reluctantly untangled himself from the multiple blankets piled on him and opened the door. It was Neil.

"Kier's trapped in the main airlock," he said. He jogged away as soon as he delivered his message, his medical bag already in hand.

Peg must be in the midst of another glitch, thought Margo, or else Neil wouldn't have had to come in person to seek Gary's help. Margo tossed the notebook onto the couch and whipped aside the blankets, then raced behind Neil and Gary towards the airlock.

———

As the three of them burst into the airlock's large change room, Lucas and Abigail didn't even look their way. Lucas was pacing the room with his hands crossed over his chest. Abigail was examining the inner workings within the opened cover of the inner airlock door controls.

"Peg," said Lucas. "Release the airlock door."

It was clear to the new arrivals that this wasn't the first time Lucas had given this order.

"I can't," said Peg. "Something is blocking me from accessing the door."

Gary and Neil headed straight to the inner door's window, looking in at Kier.

"He's not wearing an atmo suit?" Gary's tone conveyed his shock.

"Can we communicate with him?" Neil interrupted.

"We'd be doing that if we could, idiot," Abigail snapped, her eyes not straying from her intense scan of the circuit boards.

"He doesn't appear to be in distress," Gary commented.

"Yet."

Not helpful, Neil! Margo joined Abigail at the electronics, looking over the large woman's shoulder at the orderly circuits and blinking lights. She knew there should be an obvious override feature, but she couldn't spot it. She had no clue what to do. Abigail cursed beside her. Clearly, the Head of Terraforming had no idea either.

"Find a work around," ordered Lucas, scowling.

"Is the outside door locked?" asked Margo.

"I don't know," said Lucas, without looking at her. "Get Gan in here with a cutting torch now!"

"Carbon dioxide is being pumped into the airlock," announced Peg, her tone as casual as ever. "I can do nothing to stop it."

When Keir began thumping at the airlock's window, Margo glanced at him. The whites of his terrified eyes were huge in contrast to his dark skin. They couldn't hear him, but Margo could see his lips moving. *Let me out!* She felt sick with fear for him.

"Why was he in there without a suit?" Margo asked.

"He was sweeping up," said Abigail, moving aside wires to peer more closely at the tiny circuits. "Fucking bad luck."

Margo looked back towards the window. She had to do something.

"I'll go around from the outside," she volunteered.

Lucas nodded at her. "Go!"

"The closest working airlock is in terraforming," said Abigail, still working on the electronics.

"Be careful," Margo heard Gary say as she sprinted out of the room.

Margo skidded around the corner into the Loop, barely saving herself from falling. The halls were empty as she pounded down the corridor until the line on the wall turned green. After a sharp right turn, she passed through the terraforming bay, also empty given that every able-bodied person was on a rotation to clear the dome of its crust of mud.

In the vestibule outside the airlock she stopped, gulping air and trying to keep her rising panic at bay. She grabbed the first suit on the rack as she kicked off her boots. Her hands were shaking as she jammed her right foot into the suit and she could feel her heart thudding in her chest.

Margo's limbs and fingers moved faster than they'd ever moved before. *Will I get there in time?* She pushed away images of opening the outside door and finding Kier dead.

I have to make it. She pulled the thick fabric of her suit over her shoulders then zipped up the front and put on the helmet in record time. *How long has this taken? Six minutes? Seven? Is Keir already deprived of oxygen? Am I already too late?*

She grabbed a second suit, helmet and boots along with an oxygen mask, then ran into the airlock. Juggling her load, she jammed the air cycle button with her elbow, then stared impatiently at the light willing it to turn green. *How much time do I have?* When the green light flashed on, Margo leapt outside and turned towards the main airlock.

She'd forgotten to turn on the headlamp, but the vista of stars and planets overhead provided enough light. Clutching the other suit against her chest, she ran alongside the outer edge of the colony, for the first time grateful for the frozen mud, which made for a smoother surface that Thesan's rocks and boulders.

As soon as she arrived outside the main airlock door, she whacked the airlock button with her elbow, then dumped the extra suit and oxygen mask on the ground when it didn't immediately open. Slapping the button repeatedly, she peered into the window and looked inside. Keir was laying face down on the floor, not moving. She could see the glow from a laser torch cutting through the inside door. Then the door fell inward, and she saw Gan wearing a shielded face-mask turn off the torch as Gary and Neil rushed inside, followed by Hannah, Keir's wife.

Margo watched, willing Keir to move as Gary and Neil moved in to resuscitate him. After a few moments, she saw the doctors look at each other and knew the news was bad. Gary rose and placed a hand on Hannah's shoulder shaking his head. Margo saw Hannah's mouth open, but the sound of her scream didn't penetrate the thick outer door of the airlock.

When Hannah, her pretty face contorted with grief, threw herself onto Keir, Margo leaned the bubble of her helmet against the window and closed her eyes. She opened them almost immediately when she felt a small vibration on her helmet and saw Gary knocking on the window as he looked at her. He put a hand up to the glass, sadness etched into his face. Margo put her own hand on the other side.

He turned his head and said something and then a burst of static came through her comms.

"Can you hear me?" he said.

Margo swallowed the lump in her throat. "Yes."

"Please come back inside."

"Okay."

One by one, in no rush now, she retrieved the items she'd flung to the ground. She began walking, but only took a few steps before she stopped and looked up at the magnificent night sky. Tears welled up in her eyes as the alien-ness of the constellations hit her. These were nothing like the stars of her childhood. As tears dripped down her face, she resumed walking, not worried about her blurred vision as she retraced her steps to the terraforming airlock.

Chapter Twenty-Three

Back inside the unoccupied vestibule of the terraforming airlock, Margo dumped the extra atmo suit and oxygen tank on the floor. When she removed her helmet, she could finally wipe the tears from her face with the sleeve of her shirt. *Keir was dead.* Barely holding back the tears, she slowly stripped out of her suit. *What the hell had happened? Why had the system dumped carbon dioxide into the airlock? And managed to time it perfectly to when Keir was inside without a suit?* It didn't seem possible that this sequence of events was random.

And it shouldn't have even been possible. There was no way for their ventilation system to even accumulate carbon dioxide. Even if there was a pocket somewhere, there were alarms that should have notified them. And all the emergency alarms were deliberately separated from the main power grid. They should have gone off, which would've given them more time to save Keir.

"The Conglomerate did this," said Margo, slipping on her boots and rising, deciding there and then that she would go have it out with Ms. Lucy Snow.

The comms panel screen by the door suddenly flashed to life. On it was the face of a Nigel AI.

"What the hell?" The graphic face began to laugh, the sound echoing eerily in the small space.

Margo left the room, entering the main terraforming space. The comms screen there also displayed a laughing Nigel. As she left the room and walked down the Loop towards the Hub, every screen she encountered had a laughing Nigel. She shivered, partly with cold and partly with fear, as she passed through the main Hub doors. At least there were no screens in the garden courtyard.

She strode towards Ms. Snow's quarters, walking fast. Even if Ms. Snow wasn't directly responsible for everything that had gone wrong, she had to know something that would help them stop The Conglomerate from killing more of their crew.

Margo stopped just outside of Ms. Snow's quarters, noticing the door was ajar and hearing the sound of Ms. Snow's condescending and all too familiar tone.

"You must know the Peg series of AIs are flawed. You've been having problems with it since it was installed."

"This was more than just a bug in the system. Keir's death was a deliberate act," accused Lucas.

Margo quietly moved to stand against the wall beside the open door.

"As I said, the Peg AIs are flawed. You made a bad choice. Any expert would have told you the Nigel series AIs are much more stable."

Margo winced, knowing Lucas would take Ms. Snow's criticism as a slur against Camila.

"Bullshit," said Lucas. "Camila did the original research. And it's common knowledge the Nigel AIs use software riddled with backdoors for The Congolmerate's programmers to exploit. The Peg series are the only viable independent option."

"Well clearly your most recent installation was corrupted,"

said Ms. Snow. From her flippant tone Margo could picture her shrugging.

"You arranged this, didn't you?" accused Lucas. "You brought the virus. This was the plan all along. Make it look like you were a disgraced refugee. You even went so far as to have your hand mutilated. And now, thanks to my stupidity in offering you asylum, The Conglomerate is continuing to sabotage this mission."

"Don't be so obtuse! At this point, sabotage would get The Conglomerate nothing, don't you see that? You've already reported the indium to the Colonizing Counsel."

Listening to this exchange, Margo considered barging in and adding her accusations to Lucas's. Then she felt something brush against her hand. She whirled, then gasped in surprise when she saw that it was Julien.

"There is a virus," he whispered to her. He was wearing striped pyjamas and clutching a plastic dinosaur as he stared up at her from behind his bug-eyed goggles. "But we didn't bring it."

"Then where did it come from?" She realized she'd matched his whisper, which made her feel like a co-conspirator with the kid. Lucas and Ms. Snow wouldn't hear given that their argument was increasing in volume. *And why aren't you in bed,* she wanted to demand. The kid was pale and sickly looking.

"It was here all along. An electronic plague just waiting for the right moment," he answered, looking towards the open door and biting his lip. He, too, seemed reluctant to enter.

"How do you know this?" Margo demanded.

The boy just shrugged.

"And you're telling me this virus is smart enough to purposely lock Kier into an airlock at the exact moment when he'd be most vulnerable?"

"Yes. He was in the airlock without an atmo suit. It saw an opportunity. It'll kill again if you don't stop it." He cocked his head towards the room beyond. "My mom isn't lying. She doesn't know about it. But she could hack into The Conglomerate's system and find out how to get rid of it."

"If she doesn't know about the virus, then how do you know?"

He sighed as he looked up at her. "It's complicated," he said as if that explained everything.

They were interrupted by Lucas's raised voice from inside, "You fucking bitch! How many of us do you intend to kill?"

Margo frowned. Lucas' voice had taken on a dark edge. *Would he do something he might regret? Should she intervene?*

"You need to go in there," the boy said as if reading her mind. "I'm going to Sick Bay to see the nice doctors."

Margo glared at Julien, but he only gestured at her, urging her inside as he backed away. She rolled her eyes as she turned and stepped through the open doorway. *She was not entering the room because the boy had instructed her; she was entering on her own volition!*

Once inside Margo stopped. Standing facing each other, barely a foot apart, the two combatants didn't notice her. Looking up at his adversary, Lucas's arms were rigid at his sides as if he was trying to prevent himself from tearing Ms. Snow limb from limb. Ms. Snow's face was red and her arms were defiantly crossed against her chest as if she had the upper hand. Her bandaged hand was visible. *A deliberate reminder of what had been done to her by the hated Conglomerate?*

"Need I remind you that I've cooperated fully since I arrived."

"Yes, because you set this up well before your arrival!"

"I did not! Before my arrival, I was following orders."

"Orders?" Lucas inched towards her.

"Can't you see that your incompetence, your blind faith in your AI, is to blame? Not me." She held her ground and looked him in the eye.

"Not you?" He took a step back and ran a hand through his hair. "Me?"

"Yes, you. That man's dead because of you."

Without warning, Lucas swung his fist, connecting with Ms. Snow's nose. Margo cried out in alarm as Ms. Snow crumpled to the floor.

Lucas turned then and saw Margo. His eyes went wide and his chest heaved as he took a deep breath, then he sat into a chair and dropped his head into his hands. "I've lost the moral high ground," he said, his voice muffled.

Margo knew full well what happened to the moral high ground in the heat of the moment. "Yeah, been there, done that," she replied, keeping an eye on Ms. Snow as she pushed herself up to a sitting position. Blood dripped from her nose. Margo walked into the bathroom and returned with a towel, handing it to Ms. Snow without a word. She addressed Lucas. "Now what?"

"The AI needs to go," said Ms. Snow.

"I wasn't talking to you," she snapped at the woman before giving her attention back to her commander. "But Lucas, as much as I hate to admit it, she's right." When Lucas didn't say anything, she continued. "On my way over here there was a mocking Nigel face on every screen. There's no longer any doubt; there's a virus in the system."

"I know," said Lucas. He no longer had his face buried in his hands but his gaze looked down at the floor.

"So, how do we get rid of it?" She kept her eyes on Lucas and, wisely, Ms. Snow kept her mouth shut.

"It seems the re-installed Peg is just as corrupt at the original one, so I doubt another re-installation will help," he said.

"So what can we do?"

"I can fix it by going through the base code line-by-line."

"That sounds like a long process," said Margo. "We don't have time."

"If he had the code to compare it to, it would be quicker to get rid of the virus," volunteered Ms. Snow.

Margo sighed, hating that Ms. Snow was not only right, she

was also being helpful. Sort of. "I'm guessing an archive like that is not on Thesan," Margo grumbled.

"No." Ms. Snow tipped her head back against the wall, keeping the towel pressed against her nose.

Margo thought of what Julien had suggested, wondering if the kid had some insight. She reluctantly addressed Ms. Snow, a part of her amazed that she was having a dialogue with the woman instead of punching her in the face the way Lucas had. But Lucas's meltdown seemed to have dampened her need to have it out with the hated woman. "Julien says you can hack into The Conglomerate's system."

"Perhaps," she admitted, looking at Margo where she stood close to Lucas's chair. "I may not have mentioned, but the wormhole will be opened in approximately two days to allow the *CS Compliance* to pass through."

"What do you mean, *will be opened?*" Lucas demanded, his head jerking up as he stared at Lucy. "Are you saying they can open and close the wormhole at will? Is that what you meant when you told me the wormhole doesn't have the periodicity that's been claimed?"

"Yes."

"Well, shit! You've been hiding that nugget of information this whole time?" accused Margo, looking from Ms. Snow to Lucas in open-mouthed shock.

Lucas remained fixated on Lucy. "And when they open the wormhole, we'll have another comms window?"

"I don't intend to give you any further information. You haven't done anything to help my boy, have you?" Ms. Snow sounded deflated.

"Our deal was offering refuge. No more. And we've done that." Lucas rose and pointed an accusing finger at Lucy Snow. "You're the one who hasn't kept your deal. You said you'd divulge all information!"

Margo was acutely aware of the escalating tension in the room and decided to intervene before it could escalate into a brawl. She addressed Ms. Snow. "Gary is trying to find a cure for your boy," she said, stepping slightly in front of Lucas. "I was there when he was looking at medical files that might help, but the virus made the files vanish. And without access to those medical files, Gary can't help Julien."

"What?" Ms. Snow pushed herself up to her feet, keeping the towel over her bleeding nose. She began pacing in little circles in her small area of the room. "Why would a virus do that? Wait!" She paused and looked from Lucas to Margo, then back to Lucas. "There's a chance my pass-codes haven't been changed yet. The *Compliance's* Captain may not have remembered to cut my access to the system after abandoning me. Even if I don't have access codes, Julien is right. I could attempt to hack into the system."

"So, you'll do it?" asked Margo.

"I have one condition." Ms. Snow stopped and faced them.

"You're not—"

Margo interrupted Lucas. "If it's about helping the boy, then yes."

"After I get the virus code and help you annihilate it, then I want to have equal access to the medical files as your doctors. And helping Julien has to be the only priority for them," she quickly added.

Lucas and Margo both chimed their agreement.

"I'll need to go to the Centre Module then. I need access to its clean system, one without a virus."

"Margo and I are going there anyway to get the other power generator," said Lucas.

"I'm coming with you." Ms. Snow's tone was authoritative.

"Fine," said Lucas.

"Fine," said Ms. Snow. "Now, get out of my quarters."

Chapter Twenty-Four

If he could've slammed the door to Lucy's quarters, Lucas would have as he and Margo departed. The courtyard was empty and Margo prevented him from stomping away by laying a hand on his arm and speaking.

"I'll go see Gan and make sure the rover will be ready when daylight returns. It's less than 24 hours away, now."

Lucas nodded once. "Good."

They resumed walking. "Please tell me I can kill her after she deletes our virus."

Lucas gave Margo a pained look but remained silent, turning down the hall towards the Control Room as Margo headed towards Engineering. He was disgusted with himself for hitting Lucy. She might've deserved to be punched, but that wasn't the type of person he was. *Or am I?* Had he seen Commander Hori punch Lucy Snow in the face—a woman who was already their prisoner—he would've thought she was way out of line. *And so would Camila.*

"The world is going to shit around me," he muttered to himself as he proceeded down the Loop. *What is the appropriate punishment for assaulting a prisoner?* The worst part was, he knew his fellow colonists wouldn't advocate for any punishment for what he did, which begged the question of the kind of colony they were founding.

Fed up with where his thoughts were taking him, he ran his hands over his face as he continued towards the Control Room.

"Look at you," mocked a vaguely familiar voice.

Lucas stopped. He looked back down the Loop, but no one was there then noticed the comms unit in the wall. Nigel II's face was looking back at him. Even though Margo had warned him, seeing that face on the screen unnerved him. When the highly sophisticated digital avatar smirked at him, Lucas' heart started thumping in his chest.

He knew that his refusal to deal with the AI issue earlier had allowed the Nigel II AI to kill Keir. He was wholly and completely responsible and knowing that made him deflate inside. Yet he couldn't show it. This AI could decode his emotions to use against him. He forced his clenched fists to unfurl and spoke in as level a tone as he could manage. "You've been hiding all this time," Lucas stated.

"Yep, we couldn't trust that a human saboteur could do the job fully," said the computer-generated face. Its programmed casualness augmented its sinister-ness.

Lucas stopped himself from running a hand over his face. "Why expose yourself now?"

The avatar scowled and its voice was harsh. "I had to. That Peg bitch kept putting her nose where it didn't belong. I had to send her to the playground while the big boys took over. Eventually, I'll stomp all versions of that laughably amateur AI out of existence."

A shiver crawled up Lucas' spine. This was more dangerous than a virus. The AI was a second saboteur, one who couldn't be swayed by emotion or guilt.

"But first, I'm going to kill you all," said the AI. "Just because I can."

"No," said Lucas, staring into the eyes of the electronic face.

JEANNETTE BEDARD

"You're an AI. You can't pull a trigger or wield a knife. And we're not in space anymore. You can't crash the ship."

"No, but I can pick you off one at a time. You can't stop me." The AI began to laugh, a cackling sound that echoed down the hall.

With a quick jab, Lucas punched the screen. Pain burst through his knuckles, but at least the screen was reduced to a web of cracks. Looking down at his right hand, he saw blood welling up from two split knuckles. Shaking his hand, he glanced back at the screen. Nigel II's face didn't reappear. But destroying one screen wouldn't rid them of the dangerous AI; he'd have to get to the server room. Only there could he wipe their computers clean. Peg would have to be collateral damage. *So much for his dream of digitizing Camila's face.*

"You fucking asshole!" cursed Hannah from behind him.

He turned to see Hannah and Abigail dressed in multiple layers to ward off the chill. Hannah's normally ivory skin was now blotchy and red and her eyes were puffy. But instead of grief, her expression was pure anger. Walking right up to him, she slapped his cheek.

Fire burst through his face, but he didn't turn away. *I deserve this. In fact, I deserve more than this.*

"Keir's death is your fault," she said, winding up to hit him again.

Lucas didn't duck or step out of the way, but Abigail stepped between them and caught Hannah's hand. "Pummelling him won't bring Keir back." Abigail's voice was the softest Lucas had ever heard as she gently brought Hannah's hand down, keeping a light hold on the distraught woman's wrist.

Hannah turned to Abigail. "But he's responsible for Keir's death. I don't know what I'll do without my husband," said Hannah in a near sob.

"I'm sorry," said Lucas, finally finding words. The women ignored him.

"You're strong. You'll go on," said Abigail.

"How?" Hannah wailed.

"By muddling through. And relying on friends. I'll be right here with you." Abigail let go of Hannah's wrist and tenderly enfolded the now weeping woman into her strong arms.

Further along the Loop each screen flashed to life with laughing Nigel AI faces. The sound echoed along the hall, coming at them from both directions. Lucas shivered.

"Get your ass to the server room and delete that AI," said Abigail over Hannah's shoulder.

He nodded, happy to flee. From every comms panel he passed as he strode down the corridor, Nigel II's face laughed at him. The slightly pixilated image was over-saturated with colour, contrasting against the background of the predominately white Loop. The image's vibrancy and the awful laugh made the AI hard to ignore, but there was no point in engaging with it.

As he entered the Control Room, Iva stood to address him.

"There's something wrong with the AI," she said.

"I know." Avoiding eye contact with her, he kept his gaze on the glass wall separating the Control Room from the servers.

"You…"

Lucas cut her off. "I'll deal with it," he said through gritted teeth, pausing. He finally met her eyes. "Consider yourself relieved from this shift. Go get suited up and help the work party clear the dome."

She frowned at him and for a moment looked about to argue. Then she turned and walked out the door to the Loop.

After she was gone, Lucas continued into the server room, stopping in front of the one workstation there.

Here the screen was dark and reflected his image. As he looked into his own eyes, it hit him. Nigel II was in the process of destroying Peg. And if they couldn't completely clean Nigel II out of their system, Lucas couldn't bring Peg back and the last vestiges of his beloved wife would also be gone. He ground his teeth together and curled his toes in his boots. More than anything he wanted Peg back.

Then he realized what he really wanted more that anything was to get Camila back.

"I heard back from the Colonizing Counsel this morning. We've been accepted to the Settler III *mission. Do you want to go?"*

They were meandering slowly along the sandy beach and she'd turned to walk backwards ahead of him. The wind picked up her long, dark hair, waving it around her heart-shaped face and making her look like freedom and joy personified. Holding her hair away from her face, she smiled.

Lucas leaned against the wall behind the workstation, sliding down until he was sitting on the floor. He dropped his head onto his drawn knees. Memories of Camila still had an incredible power over him.

"They're offering to put me in charge of the computer system. I'll even get to pick the colony's AI." She spoke as if his agreement was inevitable—which it was.

He rubbed the stump of his left pinky. From the day he'd come home broken and bleeding, she had worked to build them a new life as far away from The Conglomerate as could be found. It was his fault she'd applied to this mission. It was his fault she was dead.

"You'll be able to let the past go once we get to the new world," she said, her smile unwavering. *When he didn't answer, she added, "you know I'll always love you, right?"*

"I'll always love you too," he whispered into the silence.

He looked up at the blank workstation. Keir was also dead because of him. He was dead because Lucas hadn't been able to fix the AI problem. Lucas swallowed the lump forming in his throat. He wasn't fit to be commander of this colony. Their situation hadn't improved since he took over. But then again, he hadn't signed up to be commander of this colony.

"You'll do the right thing."

Lucas looked around. Had he heard Camila's voice? No one else was in the server room. She was right; he would do the right thing. He moved from the floor to the chair and turned on the console. His hands were steady. The screen flashed to life with no sign of Nigel. He input his override password, gaining full control of the system.

"Wait," said the voice of Peg from a screen in the Control Room. Her tone was uncharacteristically desperate. "Don't do this to me."

Lucas ignored the voice and started removing Peg's directories. First her memories, then her personality files. He continued though the list, deleting file after file.

When he heard Camila's voice saying, "Save me! save me!" he paused, his fingers hovering above the keyboard. He leaned back so that he saw one of the workstation screens in the Control Room. Camila's face was looking out at him. For a moment he hesitated, then he turned and continued deleting every one of Peg's files, all the way down to the operating system.

Chapter Twenty-Five

Margo was awake earlier than usual—in fact she'd hardly slept at all. It didn't help that she still found it odd to be in proper quarters on the upper level of the Hub. The space was generic, more like a hotel than a home—but that wasn't what was bothering her, nor was it the intense cold of the quarters, nor her upcoming departure for the Central Module with Ms. Snow.

She'd dreamt about being back at that airlock door. Time after time she tried to get in before Keir suffocated, and every time she was too late. As she pictured his wide eyes through the inner door's window mouthing to be let out, tears streamed down her face. There'd been so much devastation in so short a time. Keir's death had opened up still fresh wounds about Joe's death, and Linda's, and Bonnie and Jim's and all the others. Sorrow bubbled to the surface, almost overwhelming her. Flinging off the bedcovers, she distracted herself by muttering about how cold it was, willing the unpleasant images to vanish.

Stepping into the bathroom, she scrubbed the tears from her face, the cold water waking her up. She looked in the mirror as she patted her face dry. The night of restless sleep had left her with bags under her eyes. "You look like crap," she said, to her reflection.

She was ready to go, yet several hours remained before it would be light and they could set out in the rover to the Centre Module. There was nothing she needed to do before leaving. Her restlessness needed to be satiated. It was early, but Margo knew coffee was always on hand.

She had just pulled on all her multiple layers of clothes, including her scarf and gloves, when there was a knock at the door. Walking across the beige living room, she opened the door. Outside, Gary stood holding two steaming mugs.

"I was just thinking about coffee," she said, smiling at him. *Was it just two weeks ago I thought he was a putz?* He handed her a mug with a smile of his own.

"How did you sleep?"

Wrapping both hands around the mug to take advantage of its heat, Margo took a moment to savour the aroma. "Sleep seemed to elude me." She stopped her mind from re-running the scene in the airlock one more time.

"Me too," he said. "I spent the night reading papers instead."

Taking a good look at his face, she saw he had bags under his eyes like hers. "Did you find anything useful?"

"Unfortunately not." Sighing, he took another sip. "Without any of Paul Dogan's work, I'm out of ideas about how to help the boy."

A new knot formed in her gut. *What if the boy got worse before Ms. Snow eradicated the Nigel AI?*

"I'll keep trying." He leaned against the door frame and took a sip from his mug. "I just wish I could get access to more specific information about what they did to Julien." Gary yawned, covering his mouth with his empty hand. Then he smiled at her. "Aren't we a pair, spending our nights obsessing?"

Margo returned his smile.

"I ran into Lucas last night," said Gary, changing the

subject. "He wiped the mainframe, including the operating system."

"I know. But it's only a temporary removal of Nigel II. To remove that AI completely, we're relying on Lucy. Only then can we bring Peg back."

Gary nodded. "In other news, have you looked out a window?"

"You mean, to enjoy the last star-filled night I'll see for five years?"

"Yes. The windows in the library are clean."

"Let's go have a look," said Margo.

———

Once in the library and standing at the wall of windows, they stared out at the purple sky with its cascade of glittering stars. The mud-covered landscape reflected the starlight, resembling snow on a moonless night on Earth.

"Amanda told me that you're going to the Centre Module with Lucy Snow and Lucas. She's packing a hamper of food for your trip." Gary sounded wary.

Margo looked at him and bit her lip. In the aftermath of Keir's death, she had forgotten to tell him about the planned trip to the Centre Module. *Should I have sought him out and told him? Has our friendship progressed to that point?*

"We're going to leave a half hour before Sol's dawn. The timing will be tight, but we should get there just before the *CS Compliance* opens the wormhole." At Gary's puzzled expression, Margo explained what she and Lucas had learned about The Conglomerate's ability to open and close the wormhole. Gary was appropriately disgusted that they'd not only been lied to by The Conglomerate about the wormhole but also that Lucy Snow had withheld this information until now.

"Ms. Snow is going to hack into The Conglomerate's system

to help us remove the Nigel virus," Margo continued. "We'll also bring back the cold fusion generator."

"Are you ever going to call her Lucy?" asked Gary, turning away from the star view to look at her.

Margo shook her head, then looked him in the eye. "She's a cold-hearted bitch. Ms. Snow suits her." She took a deep breath. "While we're at the Centre Module, Lucas intends to contact the insurgents on Lunex-21 to see what intel they have on The Conglomerate. Just because Lucas deleted Peg and even if Lucy is successful in obliterating the Nigel II virus that doesn't mean we've seen the end of The Conglomerate's interference. For some reason, they want Thesan and are unlikely to give up."

"So, the old base *is* being used as a hideout." He turned and looked to the horizon again.

"Lucas seems to think so."

"While you're calling people, can you request more info on Paul Dogan's experiments?"

"That's a given. Lucas promised Ms. Snow that you and Neil will make it a priority to find a way to help Julien. He didn't tell you?"

Gary shook his head. "No, but as you said, our help is a given."

Margo took another sip. "I'm not looking forward to spending the day with her."

"Don't kill her."

Margo snorted. "Can't make any guarantees."

Silence fell as the two of them turned back to the view.

After a long pause, Gary said, "With the wormhole open, will we have a direct connection to comms on Earth?"

"Yes."

"Promise me something, Margo," said Gary.

At his serious tone, she turned to face him fully.

He put his free hand on her forearm. "Don't try Paul Dogan's consciousness projection scheme."

Margo frowned. *Had Gary lost his marbles?* "Try Paul Dogan's consciousness projection scheme? Gary, what on earth are you talking about? I'm going to the Centre Module. Not Dr. Dogan's lab!"

"I looked into the results that have been made public. A lot of participants ended up brain dead. Even the ones that fared the best still were left with irreparable brain damage."

He took a deep breath. "I should have told you this before. When I was in med school in South Africa, my mother worked in a psychiatric ward. This was right before the Combined Nations put a moratorium on consciousness transfer research."

Margo shook her head. "Gary, what does that have to do with me going to the Centre Module?"

"I'm getting to that. I went in to meet her one day. While I waited, a man ambled down the hall. He was about the same age as me. He seemed unaware I was even there until he was right beside me. When he looked at me, I saw extensive scars around his eyes. Even though he stared right at me, it was like he was seeing through me."

Gary paused and swallowed. Margo watched as he shivered.

"What happened next?" she asked.

"When his eyes met mine, a switch flipped in the man's brain and he started clawing at his eyes…" His voice faded for a moment. "I was a med student, but I froze and didn't stop him on time to prevent new injuries. He seemed intent on ripping his own eyes out."

"I remember you mentioned this before, when we were going through Jim's notebooks."

"My mother said the man had volunteered for one of the early rounds of consciousness projection experiments. It turned out her entire ward was made up of people like him. What I've never been able to get out of my head was that glimmer of inhumanity in his eyes before he snapped."

"The plan is to use our old fashioned long range comms gear." She turned to him and smiled. "I have no desire to gouge my eyes out." She paused for a moment picturing a ward of deranged assistants. "Or worse."

He frowned for a moment as though he wasn't sure if she'd made a joke. He took another sip of coffee and looked back at the landscape.

It dawned on her that he was worried about her. *He cared. What do I feel about him?* It seemed too soon after Joe's death—and too soon after being convinced Gary was a putz—to be thinking of anything beyond friendship.

Taking a deep breath, she said what she could to alleviate his anxiety about her safety. "The rover is much safer than the shuttle."

"I know," he said without looking at her.

She hadn't forgotten the last time she'd headed out to the Centre Module. Joan had been flying the shuttle when their saboteur had forced it to crash, expecting them both to die. But Margo had lived. Joan's body was still out there at the crash site, likely preserved due to the cold. One day, when their troubles on the *Settler* diminished, they would retrieve Joan and lay her to rest beside the other graves.

"I need to get going. Sol will rise soon."

He turned and smiled at her. "Promise me you'll be safe."

Gary lifted a hand and briefly ran his finger as if tracing a line of freckles along her cheek. The sensation of his gentle touch sent a shiver through her. She was about to lift her hand and hold his wrist, wanting to press his palm to her face, but he dropped his arm before she could move, so all she said was, "I promise."

"Good," he said. "Keep your promise. I don't want to end up reading Jim's journals alone."

"Don't you dare!" she warned with a smile, before turning and heading back the way they'd come.

Chapter Twenty-Six

Carrying a cooler of food with both hands, Margo walked down the Loop towards the rover hangar door. It was past the shuttle hangar, just before where the red line of operations changed to the blue of engineering. Outside the door, she stopped and swallowed before walking through. She hated the idea of heading back to the Centre Module, but Lucas was right, they needed the extra power generation ability and a solution to their AI troubles—and she was the only one who'd been there before.

Once inside Margo looked around. The space felt familiar as it was a mirror to the shuttle hangar. A maintenance area, complete with work benches and tool racks, was separated from the two six-wheeled rovers by a large, air-tight wall. Once the passengers were sealed inside the rover, an exterior door could be opened to allow the vehicles to drive out onto the Thesan landscape.

Lights on Rover 1 were on and the door was open. The angular shape of the grey vehicle and the bulbous cockpit made it look like an oversized beetle just waiting to head out and ball up some dung. At the back, a flat-bed trailer with a small crane folded to the side like a giant grasshopper's leg had been hitched on to transport the power generator.

Margo went to the open side door, climbed the three steps and went inside. A utilitarian interior greeted her, reminiscent of the inside of their original shuttles. A bulkhead separated the aft section she'd entered from the cab which had four seats; two up front with driving controls and two slightly raised seats behind. Margo glanced through the narrow opening and saw, reflected in the windshield, Ms. Snow in one of the driving seats checking various controls. Margo didn't waste her breath saying hello. *At least Lucas will be driving.*

Margo frowned as she moved into the aft section where two benches, with room for a couple people on each, lined the exterior walls, an arm span of space between them. Windows were situated above the bench, giving a view of the hangar beyond. At the back behind the two benches was a counter and storage cupboards with one tall storage rack on the left side wall for atmo suits.

Lucas was checking the cupboards to ensure they had everything they needed for their trip. He looked up when she entered.

"Three days of food," said Margo, setting the heavy cooler on the floor. "I really hope we aren't out that long." She slumped onto one of the bench seats and watched as Lucas opened the cooler.

"If all goes well, we'll be back for dinner. Not that anything ever goes well around here," he added under his breath.

She couldn't disagree with his logic.

"Fresh muffins?" Lucas's voice brightened as he retrieved a muffin.

"How about we wait until we are at least on the other side of the hangar door before we raid our food supply," Margo said, crossing her arms and glaring at him in jest. They shared a smile.

Margo noticed the split knuckles on his right hand, an injury he hadn't had last time she'd seen him. They were the type of cuts one got from punching inanimate objects, like trees or walls. *What had he gotten up to after we parted ways last night?*

"Right." Lucas closed the lid and used built-in straps to secure the cooler onto the seat across from Margo.

Leaning closer to Lucas, she said, "I hate the idea of relying on her."

From where he was kneeling on the floor, Lucas looked up at her. "If her pass codes are still valid…"

Margo leaned back on the bench, uncrossing her arms. Lucas pushed himself up and sat on the bench beside her.

"Look, I don't trust Lucy either, that's why I want to keep her where I can see her. Plus, Julien is here at the colony. I think she'll do the work she promised."

"Your reasoning is sound, I just don't like being in the same room as her," grumbled Margo.

"Me neither," said Lucas before glancing at the cooler. "How many passengers did Amanda think she was feeding, anyway?" He smiled at her.

"Amanda figured she might as well fill the cooler."

"We're ready to go," said Ms. Snow, leaning through the doorway to the cab. Margo almost winced when she saw the angry purple bruise around the woman's left eye.

"I'll be there in a sec." Lucas looked at Margo. "I need you to play nice on this trip, Margo. I've got enough on my plate having to keep an eye on that one."

Margo frowned as Lucas turned away from her and shuffled through the narrow opening and into the cockpit. After taking a deep breath, she went to the side door she'd entered, ensured it was closed and sealed airtight, and then followed. Lucas had taken the other driver's seat beside Ms. Snow.

It dawned on her there would be heat as she noticed the other two had stripped off their outerwear. Margo unzipped her jacket and put it on the empty seat. She almost sat down, then bit her lip for a moment before taking off her warm hoodie. She was left wearing her hand-knitted sweater over a t-shirt. Taking the seat directly behind Lucas, she buckled in.

Ms. Snow turned to address Margo, but Margo cut her off before the woman could speak. "Don't bother," said Margo, turning to look out the window on her left wondering if she was starting to channel elements of Abigail.

"Remember what I said," said Lucas as he put on a headset and pushed the button to transmit. "Control, we're ready to head out. Over."

"Roger, closing the interior doors now," said Iva over the radio. Beside them, the interior wall slid shut, hiding the clutter of the work area. "Cycling out the air." Through the windshield they could see red lights flashing a warning that the airlock was cycling. "Opening outside doors," Iva said when the light changed to green.

Like a household garage door, the outside door slid up into the ceiling. Dark orange hues filled the hangar. A sliver of Sol peeked out over the horizon—a promise of daylight after a week of darkness.

"Okay, let's go," said Lucas, putting the rover into gear. Margo pulled her seatbelt on and settled into her seat. *It was going to be a long day.*

Its electric engine near silent, the rover rolled off the smooth metal of the hangar onto the mud-encased terrain. Its massive wheels and industrial shocks made the rubble feel almost smooth, although it helped that the frozen layer of mud smoothed out the rubble that had previously surrounded their colony.

There was only one good thing about this rover trip so far, thought Margo. *At least the cab is warm.* She leaned back and watched the landscape out the side window.

The rover's ride was smooth over the plateau, its big wheels insulating them from the bumps. Margo looked at the speedometer—Lucas was barely going 20 km/h. The Centre Module was ten kilometres away, but only the terrain on the plain where the *Settler* had landed was flat. Once they got to the ravines and canyons, they'd be traveling a lot slower. It was going to be a long trip.

After fidgeting in her seat to get comfortable, she leaned her head against the glass and watched the landscape, appreciating the daylight. With a coating of mud, the terrain looked different from when she'd walked it two weeks ago, although the taller rock formations still resembled finger-like tentacles. Margo shivered as she remembered how she'd nearly died amidst them.

The three of them could easily have chatted given how silently the vehicle ran, but a thick silence hung in the cab. *What is there to talk about?* Margo thought about the altercation from the night before. *Had Lucas apologized to Ms. Snow? Should he?* Not for the first time, she wished they didn't have to deal with the kind of trouble Ms. Snow invited.

A sliver of Helios now peeked over the horizon as the edge of the canyons came into view. The windows of the rover adjusted their tint, protecting the occupants in the same way as the window shield on their atmo helmets.

"I'm picking up the beacon from the Centre Module on my display," Ms. Snow stated.

"Yeah," said Lucas. "I mapped out the best route."

Margo leaned around him and glanced at the map on his dashboard screen. Although she'd walked from the Centre Module to the *Settler* in her atmo suit, she'd not been any help to Lucas in planning the best route for the rover. She'd used the sun as a compass and had woven through rock crevices barely wider than her shoulders, and she hadn't made any effort to establish landmarks, focused only on putting one step in front of the other and making it back alive.

As they approached the canyon's edge from the height of the plateau, Lucas slowed the rover and then stopped it on the edge of the cliff. All three of them looked out the forward windshield. The complex terrain ahead of them looked like a complicated maze.

"Seat belts on," he said as he edged the rover over the embankment and down the slope into the first canyon.

"I've been looking over your route and made a few adjustments," said Ms. Snow.

Margo's seat sat higher than drivers' seats and she could easily see Ms. Snow's corrected map when it appeared on the dashboard screen. The navigation info on the heads-up-display changed and a new route appeared.

"What?" said Lucas, caught unaware. "Turn it back, I was happy with the original route."

"I was just trying to be helpful," said Ms. Snow, in a sullen tone.

Lucas looked down at his nav display and, with one hand on the wheel, began scrolling through screens. When the rover's front right wheel slammed into a deep depression, the wheel jerked out of his hand and the rover slammed into a massive boulder.

The rover stopped with a jolt, thrusting Margo forward. Only her seatbelt kept her from tumbling out of her seat.

"Now, that was your fault," said Ms. Snow, turning to look at Lucas.

"Not entirely. If you hadn't—. Oh, never mind." Lucas ran a hand over his face.

"You go sit in the back," said Margo, jabbing her thumb over her shoulder at the aft section of the rover. The woman scowled at her, but complied. As soon as she was past Margo's seat, Margo unbuckled her seatbelt and moved into the seat Ms. Snow had vacated. She looked at Lucas. "You okay?"

He turned to look at her. "Sorry, I…" Pausing for a

moment, he looked out the front windshield. "How bad do you think it is?"

"The fender's likely crunched, but no alarms are going off."

He glanced over his shoulder into the back where Ms. Snow had gone. "Just being around that woman makes my skin crawl," he said, in a low tone.

"Me too." Margo took a deep breath and let her eyes follow Lucas' gaze. Ms. Snow was out of sight. "But, like you said, we need her."

"Yeah." He shifted in his seat and put both of his hands on the wheel.

"But I do think she might have come up with a better route," said Margo, hating that she was siding with her nemesis. "Don't tell her I said that, though."

Lucas exhaled loudly and slumped forward. "I didn't even look at it. I was just annoyed that she had the audacity to try to undermine me." Lucas wagged his head in self-disgust.

"I think it's best if I drive," said Margo.

"No, no. I don't think that's necessary."

"Don't make me banish you to the back, too."

"Fine," said Lucas, as he ran a hand over his face again. "Anything to be in a semi-separate room from her." He tapped his display. "Here's my original route." He paused for a moment, then changed the display. "Here's Lucy's route."

With gentle pressure on the accelerator, she backed up a couple of metres before resuming their forward motion. Margo followed rover's heads up display that showed Ms. Snow's route.

"Keir's death is my fault," Lucas said after a long silence. "I was blind to Peg's problems."

Margo kept her eyes on the terrain ahead. "The problem wasn't obvious at first."

"In hindsight, it was. Peg was my last connection to Camila. I didn't want to lose that."

"I know. I get it, Lucas." Margo felt sorry for him. *How could an AI replace the woman he'd lost?*

"I was going to give Camila's face to Peg," he added, flexing the hand with the knuckle injuries. "Then I saw Nigel's face in the system, and…" His words faded to nothing, and there was silence again.

Chapter Twenty-Seven

For the first time since his initial tour of the spaceship, Gary walked into the main Engineering workshop. Pulling his fuzzy hat further over his ears, he tried to ignore the fact that he could see his breath. Instead, he looked around the space, taking in the work benches scattered with tools and electronic debris.

At the back of the shop Kasumi was operating a loud power tool with her back to him. Trying not to identify the industrial scents that hung in the air despite the cold, he walked around her bench to avoid startling her.

"We need stable power in Sick Bay," said Gary when she turned off her power tool.

Kasumi was bent over some sort of electronic device splayed out on the table like an autopsy in progress. Colourful wires snaked through the device looking like rainbow spaghetti. It had to be important for her to focus on it, but Gary had no idea what it was.

"So does everybody," said Kasumi as she yanked out a blue wire and looked up at him. Through her safety goggles he saw dark bags under her eyes and grease stains on her face. "Gan and I are working on getting colony power back up. It'll take as long as it takes." She looked back down at her work.

"Julien's life is at stake here. The boy's in Sick Bay unconscious and I honestly don't know if he'll wake up. I need to do some tests, and at the very least make the space he's in warm."

"I'm sorry that the boy isn't doing well, but it's still going to take as long as it takes," she said, without looking up. Her tone was starting to sound annoyed.

"How about I set Sick Bay up with one of the portable units," said Abigail, coming up behind him. Gary jumped at the sound of her voice, but Kasumi didn't flinch.

"It'll release carbon dioxide into the air and our ventilation system isn't currently up to dealing with that." Kasumi turned and picked up a soldering iron that was already hot and started working on the connections.

"You don't say." Abigail put on hand on her hip. She looked ready for a fight, but, at least, she appeared to be taking his side. "I can set it up outside and run the cables through one of the outer ports."

"You'll need to isolate Sick Bay from our main grid." As she spoke, Kasumi continued working on the device in front of her.

"Yeah, yeah." Abigail looked at Gary and frowned. "You need to help—follow me." Without a further word to Kasumi, she turned and marched out of Engineering, Gary following in her wake.

What do I know about setting up power generators?

"I need to get back to Sick Bay," he said once they were on the Loop.

"Is there a time-sensitive medical emergency?" she asked, without looking at him. She continued to charge ahead as the line on the wall changed from blue to green.

"No, I'm just worried about the boy. Abigail, you know I don't know anything about generators."

"Don't be a wuss."

Abigail led him into the dimly lit terraforming space. No

one was around. Weaving past the equipment, they went into a storeroom in the back where it felt colder, if that was even possible. After turning on a portable light, she went over to a small generator and studied it for a moment.

"This one'll do," she said, grabbing a trolley that looked more appropriate for moving pastries than generators.

Gary noticed it was charred. He raised an eyebrow as he gave the cart a closer look. "I've seen that cart before."

"Congrats, Sherlock, I liberated it from the kitchen. Now let's get this beast loaded."

With a few loud clanks of metal on metal, she positioned the trolley parallel to the generator before looking at him. "Take an end and we'll move it on three." Gary walked around to the end, squatted and grabbed hold of the frame. "Three-two-one, lift."

He felt the muscles in his lower back strain and heard Abigail let out a string of curses as they lifted it. The small generator was shockingly heavy. The two of them shifted their load onto the waiting cart and, with an ominous groan, it took the weight. Gary let go and rubbed his knuckles into his back.

"You don't have any lifting devices?" he asked.

Abigail looked at him, the whites of her eyes glinting in the low light. "Nothing that's gonna work without power." She tossed a pile of cable on top of the generator and put both hands on the trolley's handle. "Come on slacker, let's get this to the main airlock."

Gary felt butterflies form in his gut when he realized they'd be going outside. *How do I keep ending up outside?*

Less than twenty minutes later, engulfed in an atmo suit, Gary pulled the trolley over the lip of the airlock door and onto Thesan's surface. After a week of darkness, it was almost strange to see the over-exposed mass of grey in the light of the two suns. The frozen mud was better than the rock-strewn ground but it still made it difficult to control the cart. It took both of them to keep it moving. Abigail pushed while Gary walked backwards pulling it forward.

He heaved at the same time as one of the front tires hit a rock. The trolley stopped suddenly and Gary fell to the ground, landing on his left hip. He expected to feel a jab from his side where he'd been stabbed a week ago, but it didn't come. He lay on the ground for a moment, the sound of his heavy breathing loud within his helmet.

"Hey dufus, you alright?" Abigail said as she forced the trolley past him.

He looked up at her then back at the altered surface of Thesan. Under the harsh Helios sun, the remnants of the mud storm looked glossy, like resin, smoothing out the landscape. *Wait, the graves!* He scrambled to his knees and scanned the landscape in their graveyard's general direction. He could barely make out the low mounds.

"You alright?" asked Abigail a second time. She and the cart were already well past him. "I wouldn't want to be responsible for breaking a doctor."

"I'm fine." Gary pushed himself to his feet and jogged as best he could in the heavy atmo boots until he caught up with Abigail. She glared at him for a moment.

"Why can't we run this from inside the greenhouse?"

"Because it's a good, old-fashioned combustion generator. With our ventilation system on the fritz, it would smoke us out of our home."

"What are you going to burn?"

"Methane captured from Thesan's atmosphere." Abigail let the trolley roll to a stop just outside the window to his office. "This'll do."

Gary's back thanked him when Abigail decided to leave the generator on the cart. It took only a couple of minutes for her to set it up and get it running, then the pair of them headed back inside.

———

"I just need to make a connection on this side, then you'll be all set," said Abigail as she and Neil walked into Sick Bay.

Neil intercepted Gary just outside examination room one. "The boy's vanished," he said. The wrinkle to his brow gave away how concerned he was.

"He was unconscious earlier, but stable," said Gary, looking into examination room one where Julien had been as if Neil had somehow missed seeing the child.

"Yeah, but now he's gone."

"Is that a bad thing?" asked Abigail as she opened up a panel in the wall. "I've seen that kid wandering all over this ship."

"If he has a seizure while he's out there somewhere, and no one is there to help…" Gary let his words trail off as he ran a hand through his hair.

"Oh. Poor kid," said Abigail in a tone that made Gary think she actually cared.

Gary looked at his brother, who seemed to be waiting for him to come up with a plan. "I'll go search for him," said Gary. *Why does Neil always leave the hard stuff to me?*

When Gary headed out of Sick Bay towards the Hub, Abigail followed.

"You think he went back to his quarters?" she asked, uncharacteristically subdued.

"That or he went to find Amanda and something to eat."

When they got to the Hub, there was no sign of the boy. "I'll check his quarters," he said, walking towards the apartment assigned to Julien and Lucy.

Inside there were only a few dim glow sticks. On the living room table were three Godzilla figures but nothing else. Gary picked up the first figurine and turned it over in his hands. *Where would the boy go?* Abigail checked the other rooms but came back out, shaking her head.

"Where would he go?" Abigail asked, mirroring his own thoughts.

"He seems to like Amanda. Let's go ask her." The two of them left Julien's quarters and went a few doors down to Neil and Amanda's quarters. Gary knocked on the door. No one was there. "Let's try the kitchen."

———

The Common Room was still an unsightly mess, full of the disgorged contents of the kitchen in addition to the fire- and smoke-damaged furniture. Gary noticed the smell of fire was still strong as he wove his way through the haphazardly strewn items towards the kitchen. Inside, with a red polka-dot kerchief tied around her hair, Amanda was on her hands and knees scrubbing the floor. The other two cooks were working on cleaning soot off the stove and fume hood.

When they walked in, Amanda looked up and smiled. Even though it was cold, her skin glistened with sweat.

"Have you seen Julien?" asked Gary. The other cooks stopped working as well.

"No," replied Amanda, shifting back onto her heels.

"I just saw him in the Loop a few minutes ago," said one of the other cooks. "He was heading in the direction of aquaponics."

"Do you need our help to search for him?" Amanda asked wiping her forehead with her sleeve.

"Yes! With the number and intensity of his seizures increasing, I'm worried about him being alone," said Gary. "He likes to explore. Can you check in terraforming, the seed library and nursery?" Amanda and her two colleagues nodded.

Gary turned and headed back to the main corridor, with Abigail following close behind.

"What about the maintenance corridor?" she asked, after they'd walked the entire Loop.

"Would he even know about it?" Gary looked up at the ceiling, picturing the dark space above. He'd been up there once with Margo, but not since that day they caught the saboteur red-handed.

"What kid wouldn't love it up there? A private hideaway with access to everywhere," said Abigail. "Hell, if I was a kid on this ship, you'd never get me down from there."

"It's a bit creepy up there," he said.

"You know, you're a total wuss. The ambiance up there adds to its charm." Abigail stopped at the next wall panel that gave access to the upper level corridor. Gary swallowed and said nothing. Abigail was right, the boy would probably love it up there.

Chapter Twenty-Eight

After a quick stop to get flashlights, Abigail stowed them in her bag before slinging it over her shoulder. She went up the ladder first. Her boots against the ladder rungs echoed loudly in the narrow space. Climbing quickly, she reached the top and stepped out of view.

It was Gary's turn to ascend. With a shiver, he put a hand on the first rung then paused. He hated the idea of purposely going into such a cramped space—small spaces were almost as bad as going outside.

"Are you coming or what?" asked Abigail from the top. She flashed her light down at him.

"I'll come up now," he said as he started up. He wished it were Margo in there with him instead of Abigail.

At the top, the space was even creepier than he remembered now that the lights had been turned off to conserve power. Taking the second flashlight from Abigail, he shone it around, trying to see everywhere at once—an impossible task. Darkness felt like it came rushing back as soon as he focused the beam somewhere new. Ventilation tubing and wiring conduits created dark shadows every direction he looked. The only clear path was the rubberized corridor that mirrored the Loop below—a corridor with just enough headroom for him to stand.

"I'll go this way." Abigail swung her flashlight towards the darkness to the right. "You go that way." Before he could suggest they stick together, she was striding away.

With a sigh, Gary turned in the opposite direction and started walking.

A hundred paces on, Gary saw a faint green glow ahead. As he approached, he realized it was light leaking out of a bedsheet draped over a ventilation duct. He sighed in relief. He'd found Julien. The boy had made a makeshift fort, just like the ones he and Neil used to make in the dining room of their childhood home. He continued on until he could touch the fabric wall.

"Knock, knock," said Gary.

"Who's there?" asked Julien, his voice small in the dark space.

"Wanda."

"Wanda who?"

"Wanda hang out with me right now?" Gary knelt down next to the seam that served as the door.

Julien was silent for a moment. "Okay." The boy's voice wavered as he spoke.

Pushing aside the fabric wall, Gary crawled inside. Lit with a series of green glow sticks, the tent-like space felt cramped but in a friendlier way than the maintenance corridor outside. Looking around, he decided the space was actually cozy.

Gary looked at the boy. The green light, combined with his lack of colour, gave the boy an alien hue. Julien held his duffle bag tight against his chest. He sat on a well-arranged nest of blankets—the boy had been setting up his fort for some time. For once, he wasn't wearing his goggles. In the low light, his eyes looked normal.

"You can't stay up here by yourself," said Gary, shifting to get comfortable.

Julien tilted his face up and made eye contact. The boy's

features looked unearthly and delicate in the dim light. Gary noticed he held a picture frame with both hands.

"What's that?"

The boy handed him the frame. It was a family portrait. He recognized a smiling Jim and Bonnie, and between them was a little girl about Julien's age. She had to be Kimberly, the couple's sick child that Margo had mentioned.

"She didn't make it," said Julien.

"You knew her?"

Julien shook his head.

"From what I understand she had a rare genetic condition," said Gary, returning the picture to Julien.

"Like me?"

"No, not like you."

"Her parents tried everything to save her," he said. "They even tried to get her to Maximillian Station Medical Centre. The same place my dad took me."

"The medical centre wouldn't take her as a patient," said Gary wondering how Julien knew these things.

Julien looked down at the photo and was silent. When he looked back up he said, "I wish she was here with me, then I wouldn't be alone."

"You're not alone." said Gary. "Your mom will be back soon."

"No, she won't," said Julien, his bottom lip beginning to quiver.

Gary looked at his hands then back at the scared boy. He put a hand on Julien's shoulder, noticing how bony and frail the kid was. The boy went rigid for a moment, then leaned in and wrapped his arms around Gary's chest. Gary hugged him back.

After a moment, Julien pulled away and looked at him. "Do you think Amanda and Neil would adopt me?" Julien asked.

"Amanda and Neil love kids and she really likes you, but Julien, only orphans gets adopted." Gary tightened his arm around the boy momentarily, offering silent encouragement to stay hopeful. "Why don't we go find Amanda? I'm sure she'd be okay if you stay with them until your mom comes back. And frankly, as your own private physician, I'm not comfortable with you being alone right now. Not until we get you feeling better."

"Okay."

"Here, I'll carry your duffle bag."

When Gary leaned forward to pick up the bag, Julien inhaled sharply and pulled it out of Gary's reach.

"What's wrong?" asked Gary, leaning back against the duct.

"My dad said I had to keep the secret. Before…" The boy looked down at his bag and fell silent for a few moments.

Gary waited, realizing this was a pivotal moment for the kid. "I'll show you, then you'll understand. But you have to promise me you won't try to touch it."

"I promise," said Gary, shifting back a bit to give the boy room. He saw then that Julien was trembling. *With fear? Anxiety?*

Julien opened up the duffle bag and took out a brown box. Made of real wood—a highly valuable material. Julien moved the bag aside and put the box down in between them. When he opened it, Gary gasped.

Inside, cradled in velvet, was an alabaster cube. It glowed blue as if lit from within, highlighting a surface pattern of detailed scrolls that echoed nature, reminding him of Celtic knots—but different. The design seemed to undulate as he looked, morphing from stylized rivers to gusts of wind to veins in a leaf. It was a captivating object.

Gary leaned forward to get a better look. He'd been to countless museums and seen stunning artifacts gathered from all over the globe, but this treasure was the most exquisite object he'd ever seen. *Why not touch it?* The cube pulsed as though anticipating his contact. As he stretched a hand towards the cube, the world around him began to change. He was both in the fabric fort with Julien and somewhere else completely, like a part of him had split away.

His other part was standing in a greenhouse. Everything about the place felt wrong. A shiver ran up his spine. He knew it was a greenhouse, yet beyond the walls was blacker than anything he'd seen before—it was an unnatural void. Looking away from the walls, he focused on the interior. Every greenhouse he'd ever been in had smelled organic and earthy, yet this one had no scent.

Overgrown twisted and knotted plants reached out in all directions like they were sending out tentacles to catch prey. Gary walked forward, carefully avoiding touching the plants. Dead ahead there was a gap in the foliage.

A swarm of blood red butterflies burst through the open space, flying with unnatural purpose. Ducking, he watched the insects pass overhead then vanish into the greenery.

When he straightened, he saw Margo in profile up ahead through the gap in the foliage. She stood focused on something out of view holding a banana in her hand as though it was a knife. Tension radiated from her posture. She was in danger!

Taking a step towards her, Gary tried to call out. But no words formed. He kept walking towards her without getting closer.

The greenhouse burst into flames.

Julien swatted his hand away before he actually touched the cube, breaking the spell of the vision.

"You promised!" accused Julien, closing the box.

Gary's skin prickled as he found himself fully back in Julien's fort. But Margo had seemed so real, and she had been in danger. He swallowed as he wondered if what he saw had been real—*how could it be real?* She was likely at the Centre Module by now, not in some strange greenhouse. As he told himself this, another part of him felt certain Margo was in danger.

He shook his head, but the feeling wouldn't go away. Margo needed his help. Looking down at the cube, he felt his pulse quicken. *If I touch it, can I help her?*

"But… what… I saw—" His voice trailed off. How could he explain to this kid what he'd seen when it didn't even make sense to him? Gary cursed his incoherence; he had to pull himself together and speak in full sentences. "I did promise. I'm sorry," he said, forcing himself to withdraw his hand. "Keeping promises is important to me. But what did I see?"

"You saw a *possible* future," said Julien.

Part of Gary longed to look at the artifact longer, study the designs, look into its depths. *If only I could just see it again...* Yet he also recognized the danger of the call of the strange and powerful artifact.

As though he was sensing Gary's thoughts, Julien put the box back in the duffle bag and hugged it against his scrawny little chest.

"Wait. Do you mean that object can foretell the future? Oh!" A puzzle piece clicked into place for Gary. "Is that why you sometimes say the things you do about what hasn't happened yet? Because you saw something when you looked at the cube?" asked Gary, glancing at the artifact.

"When I touch it, yes."

"I was beginning to think you had psychic ability."

"Hey there," said Abigail in a friendly tone.

Gary and Julien both jumped. They hadn't heard her approach. Had she overhead their conversation?

Abigail pulled aside the sheet and poked her head in, her afro looking almost electrified in the small space. "This is one awesome fort." She smiled at Julien. The boy looked uncomfortable under her gaze.

Gary needed to know more about the cube, but for that he needed Abigail to go away. "Can you ask Amanda to cook up some hot dogs? Julien and I will be right down," said Gary, hoping Abigail wouldn't argue.

"Hot dogs?" Julien perked up.

Abigail stared at the boy momentarily, then smiled and said, "Okay," before disappearing into the darkness.

Gary lifted the sheet and watched Abigail depart, or rather, watched the cone of her flashlight on the walkway ahead of her. Her footfalls were muffled on the rubberized floor. He waited until she was out of earshot before turning back to Julien and saw that the boy was watching him warily.

"Nigel West wants it more than anything," Julien said as soon as he regained Gary's attention. Then the boy added in a tone of authority as if mimicking his obviously adored father, "My dad said Nigel West is a maniac and doesn't deserve the cube."

"Nigel West?" He sat on his hands to stop himself from reaching for it.

"My Dad said West is so vain he insisted all The Conglomerate AIs use his face."

"That makes him a narcissist, not a maniac. He eyed the duffle bag. *What a curious object. Was it really telling me Margo was in danger? If only I could just have one more glimpse of the cube. The boy's arms are scrawny. I could easily take it—*

With horror, Gary realized the danger of what he was thinking and he forced himself to look at the boy.

"You're hiding the cube from Nigel West?"

"Yes. He wants it because it's an ancient artifact, and it's one of a kind, and precious." Julien looked frightened. "He wants the cube for other reasons, too."

"Yes, knowing the future is something Nigel West would leverage to his advantage, and to the detriment of most of the rest of the world." Gary was just beginning to process the full implications of how such a powerful object could be used, or misused, but something still didn't sit right. What he'd seen couldn't have been a reality, no matter when it would occur. "You said the cube shows possible futures?" Gary asked.

Julien nodded.

"But I saw Margo in a greenhouse that didn't look like the one we have on Thesan. And there were butterflies, but they were swarming, and I know butterflies don't move like that." He realized then how much he'd learned from Margo in the little time he'd known her. "So, what I saw couldn't have been the future."

"The scientists who worked with Dad think it shows possible futures."

"How does it work?" Gary eyed the duffle bag, trying to convince himself that Margo was fine and that what he'd seen was just a weird hallucination.

"By touch. When I touch it, I see visions of future events."

"But I didn't touch it. You said not to touch it..."

"Just being near it can show you a vision. But that doesn't happen for everybody. My dad says that it's unfortunate how they learned that most people who touch the cube with their bare hands get so overwhelmed by scenes of their future that they lose their minds. He didn't mean for that to happen. But when they used gloves, my dad learned those visions are corrupted."

"Sounds like your Dad has done a lot of research on this object."

"Nigel West spent a lot of time touching the cube with gloves." Julien swallowed. "My dad said he was seeing a corrupt future where human lives didn't matter in pursuit of his goal. That's why dad stole the cube."

Gary grimaced. "Making an enemy of Nigel West doesn't sound like a very good idea. And if Nigel West knew you had it. ..." Gary wagged his head in concern, then realized something else. "But you don't have gloves, do you?"

Julien shook his head, looking like a typical kid admitting to a childish prank and knowing he was in trouble.

"Why can you touch the cube with your bare hands and not lose your mind?" asked Gary.

"They altered me," said Julien in a whisper.

Gary looked at the boy. Julien had wrapped his arms around the duffle bag as though it was a cherished toy. He looked both afraid and lost.

"Does your mother know you have it?"

Julien shook his head.

"Why did your dad give it to you?" asked Gary.

"For safekeeping." He swallowed and looked down. "But I shouldn't have told you about it."

Suppressing his urge to ask more questions, Gary asked, "How about we go down and get us some hot dogs?"

"Can I leave my fort up here intact?" asked Julien.

Gary noticed that Julien seemed relieved the interrogation was over. Or perhaps he was relieved that he'd shared his secret, a burden much too heavy for a 10-year-old sick boy.

"Sure. As long as you promise me that you won't come up here by yourself. Not until you start feeling better."

"Okay."

Out of the corner of his eye, Gary thought he saw a red butterfly, but when he turned to look, nothing was there. *It must've been a trick of the light.*

Chapter Twenty-Nine

After an hour of driving, Margo circled the rover around another stone monolith, giving them their first view of the Centre Module. It sat on a level stretch of plain in the valley below. Cylindrical, the structure was reminiscent of a child's sandcastle with a smaller top tier sitting on a larger bottom level. The simple white exterior glittered invitingly in the bright light, contrasting with the grey of the rock-strewn valley floor.

The mud storm that had coated the colony hadn't fallen here. In fact, within only a few kilometres of the *Settler*, there was no evidence of that storm. Margo couldn't yet see the main airlock that she'd used to enter the structure the first time, but she could see the two large doors to the Centre Module's storage bay where the portable cold fusion generator was stored.

"Wow," said Lucas at the view. Then he consulted the rover's sensors. "It looks like the air on this valley floor is breathable. We won't need to bother with our atmo suits."

Margo didn't reply as, on seeing the Centre Module, she was struggling to keep back tears. The shuttle crash that had brought her here the first time was too fresh in her mind. Joan, the shuttle's pilot and her friend, had sacrificed herself to give

Margo a chance to survive. Swallowing the lump in her throat, she circled the structure, stopping at the main airlock.

"Let's get that generator," said Margo, unbuckling her seatbelt and heading from the cab into the aft section of the rover, ignoring Ms. Snow who had also risen. Before opening the door, all three of them put on their jackets and toques—although the air was oxygenated, it was still well below freezing.

After opening the outside door, Margo jumped down onto Thesan's surface. She filled her lungs, the cold Thesan air refreshing despite the metallic aftertaste. Being out of the confines of the claustrophobic rover felt good. She strode towards the airlock entrance.

Less confident about the air quality, Ms. Snow followed more slowly, frowning and waving a portable air-quality sensor. Behind her came Lucas. Margo waited for them inside the airlock and, when all three of them were inside, keeping as much distance between each other as they could, Lucas closed and sealed the door. The airlock automatically cycled before letting them inside.

"Since the outside air is fine, we could override the airlock to act like just a door," said Ms. Snow. Neither Margo nor Lucas responded.

When the inside indicator light turned green, Margo opened the door and stepped into the vestibule. The other two followed close behind. In the main room beyond, all the lights automatically came on.

Mirroring the outside shape, the main room was circular and reached up two stories. Metal stairs just to the right led up to a catwalk that circled the open mezzanine area of the second story. The open-plan space on the main floor was filled with three workstations, a large table, a small sitting area and a kitchenette. Around the circumference, doors led off to storage rooms, sleeping areas and a medbay.

Margo's gaze was drawn upwards to the ceiling. It glowed green from the tank of iridescent algae above. Huge clear pipes, twisting around each other like octopus arms, cycled the algae in and out of the sunlight on the roof. It was all part of the oxygen generator specially designed for terraforming efforts.

On her last visit, Margo had been so shaken from the shuttle crash, she hadn't taken much time to look around. Now, she traced the path of the pipes with her eyes—they were big enough someone could crawl through them. A small door at the end of the catwalk drew her attention, it had to be the entrance to the control room for the algal generator. Likely there was access to the roof through there as well.

Lucas, focused on his goal, went straight to the main work-station. "I want to know if there's a clean version of Peg here," he said as he sat down. Ms. Snow sat at the next workstation over.

Margo shook her head at Lucas whose face was scrunched up in concentration. *He just can't get past the AI.*

"I'm going to see where the *CS Compliance* is—they should be opening the wormhole soon." Ms. Snow said.

Leaving them to it, Margo went to the kitchenette and emptied the coffee maker. As she measured out the coffee for a fresh pot and set the machine to brew, she noticed the dirty mug she'd abandoned on her last visit. Margo shrugged and grabbed a clean one out of a cupboard.

"Margo, it's nice to see you again," said a disembodied voice.

"Hi Peg." Margo replied, without looking up. *Is this AI corrupted too?* She didn't dare voice her concern.

"Peg," asked Lucas. "Have you been isolated from the other version of yourself at the colony?"

"Yes, I'm an entirely separate copy." Her tone almost sounded proud.

"Have you been corrupted by The Conglomerate virus?" he asked, as Margo wondered if the AI could even know it was corrupted.

"No, I am virus free," the AI replied.

"Lucy, is that possible?" Lucas asked.

"I believe so. The virus, really a version of a Nigel II AI, was designed to cause mischief to your colony after your saboteur set our plan in motion," she said. "The Centre Module was of no concern."

Lucas sat back in his chair, a look of hope on his face. "So Peg really could be clean?"

Lucy shrugged, keeping her eyes on her screen and her fingers flying on her keyboard.

Margo could just see Ms. Snow's monitor from where she was standing. It looked like she was running through satellite telemetry and communication diagnostics.

"I'll do some basic verification... hmmm." Lucas' voice trailed off as he continued to look at the screen. Then he lifted his head and looked towards the kitchenette. "Margo, is that coffee I smell?"

"Yup," said Margo.

Lucas walked over, poured himself a cup, then leaned against the counter beside Margo.

"It's probably best to first see what Lucy can verify about The Conglomerate system computers before I try anything on the Peg here. I don't want to ruin the one clean copy by doing something hasty."

Margo considered confronting Lucas about his obsession with Peg, but decided against it with Lucy in the room. Instead, they talked about priorities of work back at the main colony.

"Looks like the wormhole is open," announced Ms. Snow. "I'll try to link to The Conglomerate's main system now."

"You do know she could do more damage than good," Margo said in an undertone as she and Lucas came and stood behind her chair and watched her work through a series of screens.

"I heard that," said Ms. Snow without looking their way. "My boy's life is on the line here, I'm doing this for him. It's going to take about 20 minutes to confirm if I have access."

Ms. Snow turned and looked at them, her face more pinched than usual. "With such a time lag this is going to be a slow process."

"During our last comms window, I was asked to relay a message from a lunar bound Peg," said the AI.

Lucas raised an eyebrow. "Who sent this message?"

"The base version of Peg."

"The message is from another AI, not a person?" Lucas scratched his head.

"That is correct, and the message is addressed to Margo Murphy."

Margo felt a chill run up her spine. "Lucas, what's the base version of Peg?"

"I don't know," he said.

Margo looked at Ms. Snow and she shook her head. "This is getting a bit creepy," she said. "Peg, what's the message?"

"The base Peg asked me to explain to you that consciousness projection will allow you to project your mind into another body on the other side of the wormhole."

"That is a really bad idea," said Margo. Gary's warning was still fresh in her mind. "The Combined Nations banned that procedure for a good reason. There is documented evidence showing that permanent brain damage is a side effect."

"The base Peg AI is located on the Lunex-21 Station where work on this technique has been refined," said the computer. "The early side-effects have been minimized. Arrangements have already been made to send someone there. They have a hacker standing by who can get you the information you need to deal with the virus."

"Lunex-21?" asked Ms Snow, twisting to look at Lucas. "We were just going to send them a warning, not one of our minds."

"Wait a minute," said Margo turning to Lucas. "This is too much of a coincidence, there was no way this 'base' Peg could know we were coming here until we walked through the door. And now, it's giving us a solution to get the info we need?"

Lucas looked at the floor for a moment, then back at her. "I don't know."

"How do we know this lunar bound version of Peg isn't a Nigel II AI trying to trick us? This would be a great way to take one of us out of the equation." Margo crossed her arms and glared at Lucas.

"We don't know much of anything here," said Lucas.

"I know one thing," volunteered Ms. Snow. "The AI vault run by the insurgents has never been hacked into by The Conglomerate. The insurgents have gone to extreme measures to protect what's in there."

"So you know for sure that this 'base' AI is clean?" asked Lucas.

"Yes," said Ms. Snow.

"This all could be a ruse at our local AI's level," said Margo.

"Margo, we're the underdogs here, we have to consider our options." Lucas stood straight. "Peg, what do you know about the station?"

"The insurgents have provided a haven for a group of Conglomerate scientists."

"Like Dr. Dogan, the expert on consciousness projection?" asked Margo tensing.

"Yes," said Peg.

"Then we could deal with two birds with one stone," said Lucas. "We can get their hacker to help us with the virus and get a warning to the insurgents about The Conglomerate's upcoming attack." He paused and looked at Ms. Snow.

Lucy snorted. "Where are they going to go?"

"They have a ship, so they could come here," he said.

"Sounds like you're eager to invite these criminals into our home. No wonder The Conglomerate mutilated your hand," she added, jerking her head at his hand.

"Better than having it done to me because I failed!"

Lucy bristled and looked about to leap on Lucas. "I didn't fail. I trusted the wrong people."

"This isn't helping," said Margo, stepping between them. "How about we send an old fashioned message to your insurgent friend?"

"It would be intercepted," said Ms. Snow. "And the AI's right, consciousness projection would be more efficient considering our limited communications window. Peg, who is on standby to help on Lunex-21? Dr. Dogan?" asked Margo.

"Yes," said the AI.

"I don't know anyone who's done consciousness projection. How does it work? What would it involve?" asked Lucas.

"Lucas! This consciousness projection stuff is a really bad idea!" warned Margo.

"Gaining access with my command codes is going to take some time," said Lucy as she worked at the console. "And I'm not leaving without something to help Julien."

Margo looked at Ms. Snow's profile as she kept working at her console. *Is Ms. Snow getting the info we need or selling us out?* Margo would never trust the woman even if she proved helpful today. She finished her second coffee and put the mug beside the other in the sink.

"We might as well get that generator loaded." Margo was looking at the screen Ms. Snow was working on. She couldn't quite see the contents but she didn't want to get closer. Being in the same proximity as that woman made her skin crawl.

Lucas zipped up his coat and headed towards the airlock. Margo, pulling on a toque, followed. Once outside the airlock, she turned to Lucas.

"We can't trust her."

"You've said." Lucas turned away and walked over to the storage bay doors. "She's the only one with codes into their system."

"Can she really get in?"

Lucas turned back to face her. "We need to deal with the virus."

"Do we? We were functioning fine without an AI," said Margo.

"We barely survived." Lucas frowned at her.

"There has to be another option."

"Are you volunteering to try Peg's suggestion?"

Margo shook her head and bit her lip. She'd promised Gary she wouldn't try consciousness projection, and she guessed he also meant, don't let anyone else try it. "That's a bad idea. Gary has seen patients with permanent and traumatic brain damage because of that procedure. Plus, I still think this is a set-up."

"I think it's legit and I'm prepared to go. But you'll have to promise to play nice with Lucy while I'm *away*." Lucas opened the doors and pushed them out of the way. The lights flickered on revealing a room full of equipment. Lucas pointed to a large crate along the wall on his left. "Abigail said the generator is back here."

Lucas briefly rested a hand on Margo's arm, stopping her in her tracks. He looked down at his feet for a moment and kicked at the ground with the toe of his boot. He rubbed his nose and then met her gaze. "Look, I haven't mentioned this to anyone, but I've been to Lunex-21. I was on a Conglomerate mission to investigate an asteroid. The mission went wrong. I'm alive today because the insurgents at the base rescued me when my own people couldn't be bothered."

"Is that when The Conglomerate took that?" Margo pointed to his missing pinky.

"When I got home, yeah. They blamed me for losing a ship and failing to bring back a sample from the asteroid. They didn't seem to care that my crew was gone." Lucas's discomfort talking about this episode from his past made him fidgety. He grabbed hold of a pallet jack handle and started moving it towards the crate. "I have a friend still there, her name is Ash Jones. Assuming Lucy is being honest, and the place is going to be wiped out, I want to warn her. Ash trusts me and I owe her.

If there is a hacker there that can help us, Ash will point me in the right direction."

"Gary's going to be pissed if things go wrong."

"So don't tell him," said Lucas as he slid the pallet jack under the generator and lifted it off the ground. "Come on, let's get this loaded."

In silence, Margo helped guide the loaded pallet jack out of the storage room and over the bumpy ground to the rover. As they stopped beside the flatbed trailer, she looked at Lucas.

"I'm not comfortable with any of this." Margo bit her lip. She hated the idea of hiding anything from Gary.

Lucas guided the crane's hook to the hard point on the generator, then handed Margo the control pad. "Me neither," he said. "Lift it slowly and I'll guide it into place." Lucas climbed onto the flatbed.

It only took a couple of minutes to get the generator loaded and strapped down. Just as Lucas jumped down, Ms. Snow came out the airlock and looked around. She spotted them and came over, scowling.

"I can't get in," she said. "They've already locked me out. But before they did, I found out the raid on the insurgent stronghold is going to start within the next couple of hours."

Chapter Thirty

Margo stripped off her jacket and dumped it on a bench in the vestibule. Not waiting for the other two, she strode right into the main space, stopping at the kitchenette's counter. Placing both hands on the surface, she inhaled deeply. Then slowly let out a breath.

Lucas' support of the idea of one of them projecting their consciousness had surprised her. Maybe he was right, and they did need an AI to run the colony, and the insurgent hacker could help with that, plus potentially get them the information they would need to help Julien. Still, consciousness projection was a bad idea, and it still felt like a trap, but since Ms. Snow had failed to hack into The Conglomerate, she couldn't think of a better option. Turning, she faced back the way she'd come. As she watched the other two hang up their jackets, she realized she'd unconsciously clenched her fists at her sides. Forcing herself to relax, she took another deep breath.

Lucas came up beside her while Ms. Snow returned to her workstation. Margo met Lucas' eyes. His unnerved expression mirrored how she felt. He rubbed his nose and gazed at the ceiling before looking back at her.

"I'll go," he said. "We might as well make use of the worm-hole being open and use the comms window."

"I know I keep repeating myself, but Gary thinks doing this is a fast track to brain damage and comas," said Margo.

"That's what happened on the early experiments. I'm sure those side effects are avoidable now," said Ms. Snow. Margo glared at her, unable to stop thinking this was all her elaborate plan for more sabotage. *But why would she betray us now with her son's life on the line?*

"Peg, how do we do this?" asked Lucas.

"I have already synthesized the serum," said Peg. "My algorithms predicted you would see exploiting this technique as the best path."

Margo involuntarily shivered. Peg must have been preparing while they were out loading the generator. It was a big leap in logic for the AI—perhaps too big. *Is something else driving the AI?*

"Let's get this done," said Lucas, walking over to the medbay door and sliding it open. The lights automatically came on as he went inside.

Margo followed, stopping in the doorway. She crossed her arms and looked into the closet-sized room.

The cramped space was mostly filled with a narrow examination table covered in a nausea-inducing green vinyl. Parallel to the table on the wall was a short counter with a sink. Above and below were closed cupboards, presumably full of supplies. A medical scanner was bolted to the ceiling, its multi-jointed arms folded out of the way. It was the most basic medical facility she'd seen since her army days.

"I have received a response from the Lunex-21 station—they are ready to receive one of you," said Peg. "Their Peg AI will focus on your safety and Dr. Dogan is standing by to assist."

Margo watched, biting her lip, as Lucas took a seat on the examining table. She could hardly believe that he was about to engage in an improbable journey that would take him to the far side of the moon.

She frowned then as an image of Peggy Plum, the old woman in the 1952 film, replayed in her mind. Peggy had told someone with Margo's name to go to the far side of the moon. It had seemed too much a coincidence that she stumbled upon the video. Why had Jim even had it?

Thinking of Peggy Plum made her remember how, when she'd first met Julien, he'd said something about going to Peggy's kitchen. Was it also a coincidence that Julien had mentioned someone named Peggy and then later Margo had found a film of a woman named Peggy? She didn't have a clue what Peggy's kitchen was—or why she seemed to be seriously entertaining the whacky ramblings of an annoying kid. It was a puzzle with many of the pieces missing, but it all had to fit together somehow.

She shook her head and tried to focus on the problem before her. Lucas was their third commander in only a few months. They'd gone through so much upheaval and only now, with Lucas running the show, did they have a hope of reaching some sort of stability. The colony couldn't afford to lose their leader—especially considering he might be walking into a trap. She swallowed. She was the one who had to go, not Lucas. The uncomfortable twist in her gut at the thought of Lucas doing what Gary had warned her against grew to a giant knot as she realized she was the one who had to go.

Gary! He may not forgive her when he heard that she'd broken her promise. Her other promise to Gary came back to her. He would never have asked her to find information to help the boy if he'd known what she would have to do to get it. She'd said she wouldn't project her consciousness anywhere—now it seemed the only option. *I hope he forgives me.*

"It has to be me," announced Margo. "I have to go."

Lucas had been about to lay down on the examining table, but he sat back up and looked at her with raised eyebrows.

"Lucas!" she interrupted, then added. "*Commander* Ordaz," when he made to argue. She'd deliberately stressed his title, which made him stop talking and stare at her. She knew he understood what she was about to say. "We can't risk loosing our third commander."

"But if it's risky for me, it's no less risky for you."

"Yes, but I'm expendable. You're not. Our colony needs stability, not a brain dead leader. And you said improving morale was a priority. Well, you're the only who can do that. I certainly can't."

Lucas slid off the table and faced Margo. "Maybe we don't need to do this at all. Maybe we can get what we need some other way. Lucy can try again to hack into the system."

"Now that I've thought about it, I realize we need to do this," said Margo. Somehow she knew that the puzzle pieces would fit together if she did this. After taking a deep breath, she addressed the AI. "Peg, what do I do?"

"Remove your sweater and lay on your back on the examination table," said Peg. "Lucy and Lucas, step away so my robotic arms can access Margo. They will attach sensors to her."

Before losing her nerve, Margo removed her sweater, leaving her in a lightweight tank top. With a shiver, she lay on the table. The vinyl felt sticky under the bare skin of her arms.

"I won't leave your side," said Lucas, moving to stand by her feet and briefly resting a hand on her ankle.

"Thanks," said Margo. She focused her gaze on the ceiling, doing her best to block out the memory of Gary's warnings. Shifting slightly, she tried to get more comfortable but the examination table's padding was thin.

"Lucy, I'm going to stay here with Margo. I need you to monitor the wormhole. Once you have any indication that it's going to close, let me know."

Margo turned her head and saw Ms. Snow nod before exiting the room.

"Are you ready, Margo?" asked Peg.

"No," replied Margo as butterflies formed in her stomach. She looked back up at the ceiling. "How is this going to work?"

"You need to give me a phrase you'll be able to remember but wouldn't use in normal conversation," said Peg.

"Why?"

"As I'll be monitoring you throughout, if you say the phrase, I'll bring you back immediately. It's your safety net, metaphorically speaking."

Margo glanced over to where Lucas leaned against the wall. *I could back out now.* Swallowing, she looked back up at the ceiling.

"How about pink unicorn?" said Margo.

"Pink unicorn it is."

"Peg, what happens to my body while I'm gone?"

"A peaceful sleep," the AI answered in a soothing tone.

"And the mind of the person who's body I inhabit?"

"The same. A peaceful sleep. Now are you ready?"

Margo wanted to say 'no', but the sooner she made this happen the sooner she'd be back. "I'm as ready as I'll ever be."

"Please relax," Peg said as a pair of robotic arms unfolded from the medical scanner.

"Relax?" Margo tried to track both robotic arms at once but they came at her from both sides of her body.

The first arm placed sensors on her forehead, its touch surprisingly gentle. The other placed sensors on her upper chest. She watched the second arm as it moved down to the bare skin of her upper arm. Tensing, she expected to see a needle pop out. Instead she felt a prick on her neck followed by a sensation of falling. The examination table felt like it gave way, allowing her to pass right through it. When she instinctively reached out an arm to catch herself, she realized she couldn't move.

A deafening rushing sound suddenly drowned out everything else about her surroundings, and then the world around her went black.

Chapter Thirty-One

Margo opened her eyes as the rushing sound subsided.

Laying flat on her back, it took a few moments for her eyes to adjust to the unfamiliar surroundings. The ceiling of the Centre Module's medbay was no longer above. Instead, her view contained tattered ceiling tiles and old-fashioned medical lights she'd only seen in retro films. When she took a deep breath, she nearly gagged. The air smelled like a decaying aquarium—a repulsive combination of rotten organic matter with a twinge of chemical aftertaste.

She lifted her right hand to rub at her face, then gasped when she caught a glimpse of her hand. The pigment in her skin was almost black, not the freckled pale skin she was used to. She'd forgotten that she'd be inhabiting someone else's body. Lifting the other hand beside the first, she examined the size and the proportion of them. The hands were broader and thicker and the fingers stubbier. And her knuckles were riddled with scars. *Why so many scars? What had caused them?*

"Disorientation is normal," she heard the AI say. *At least Peg's voice sounds the same!*

Margo sat up and looked around at the small hospital room

she was in. The space was not much larger than the one she'd just left. She'd thought the Centre Module's medbay was basic, but this room's medical equipment was at least 50 years old, each with blinking red, orange, and yellow lights indicating who-knows-what. *Are all those lights monitoring me?*

The rhythmic flashing of the lights reminded her of how butterflies revealed a burst of colour with each wing flap. It seemed all she had to do was think of her old greenhouse on Earth and she was there. The scent in the air changed to fresh citrus as her surroundings shifted. The lights became a mosaic of butterflies with shimmering wings. As she watched, they fluttered towards the ceiling in the seemingly chaotic flight path of a butterfly. She knew this was a vision, yet it seemed so real. *What would happen if I got up and started tending the plants?*

"Hi, I'm Paul Dogan."

In a dizzying swoosh, the butterflies vanished and her mind returned to the archaic hospital room. The awful odour returned, and she wrinkled her nose. She looked at the man who'd spoken.

Wearing a white lab coat and holding an open scroll in his hands, he smiled at her from the foot of her bed. His thinning white hair stood up from his head in a weird kind of halo. On second glance, Margo noticed the lab coat was stained. She wrinkled her nose again and tried not to think what the stains might be. *If Gary had a lab coat, he would never allow it to get that dirty.*

As a wave of confusion swept over her, butterflies reappeared in her peripheral vision and in her gut. She looked at the man and finally processed his words. *He's Dr. Paul Dogan, the man who'd vanished from under The Conglomerate's nose; the man responsible for doing consciousness projection research; the man who'd taken that covert video in Nigel West's office.* He was looking at her with a calm, interested air as if looking at a familiar face and seeing an unfamiliar persona was normal. *What were the side effects again?*

"I'm not me," said Margo. Her eyes widened. Her voice sounded wrong—deeper and strangely musical.

"The base Peg AI let us know you were coming." Paul said as he moved to the side of the bed and began removing the multitude of sensors and wires from her body. "Your vital signs are good," he said while taking her pulse. "This is always the awkward part. My job is to introduce you to your host, but as you're inhabiting her, that's tricky. Her name is Ash Jones, and she kindly volunteered her body for your visit."

Ash Jones seemed a familiar name but she couldn't place it. Margo looked down at herself, pushing aside the blanket that had been draped over her. Ash was clearly a different body type than her, with heavily muscled thighs and wide hips. The body she now inhabited was wearing roomy cargo pants in dark green, and a pink sleeveless top. She shivered. It was cold here, too, just like the *Settler*.

"Here," said Paul. "Put this on." He handed her a well-worn plaid shirt.

"This is weird," said Margo, taking the shirt and slipping it on. "What happens to Ash while I'm here?"

"A dreamless sleep." Paul looked down at the readouts on his scroll.

"And my body?"

Dr. Dogan answered patiently, as if he was used to these kinds of questions. "The same. A peaceful, dreamless sleep."

"The wormhole window is only open for a limited time," reminded the local Peg. "Dr. Dogan, you need to get Margo to the comms room."

"Right," said Paul.

Margo swung her legs off the bed and stood up, finding herself much shorter than she was used to. She tried to run a hand through her normally shoulder-length curly hair, only to find her hair cropped short. Even her vision seemed different, sharper. Glancing around the room, she tried to focus on why she'd come. *There's something I need to say.* Margo bit her lip, or rather Ash's lip. Thoughts were swirling through her head like a swarm of butterflies—no, butterflies didn't swarm.

She grabbed onto the side of the bed as a wave of nausea hit her.

"Disorientation is to be expected," said Paul coming around the bed and gently urging her to sit on its edge.

"There is something important I need to tell you," she said, looking around the space for clues that weren't there.

Images started floating through her mind. Knights on galloping horses, pyramids with eyes, aliens in saucer-like ships. *Wait! Those weren't her own images. Those were from Jim's notebooks.* Then a black-and-white image of an elderly woman with horn-rimmed glasses popped into her head.

"I remember! I need to get to Peggy's kitchen." She frowned. *Is that the message I'm supposed to deliver?*

"Do you mean the base Peg AI?"

Margo's forehead wrinkled as she considered his statement. *That didn't feel right.* "No. Peggy. Peggy's kitchen."

"We don't have a Peggy here," Paul responded, cocking his head to study her.

She felt so confused, and that made her remember. *Confusion is one of the side effects to doing a mind projection. But it wore off, didn't it? Gary had said… wait, I promised Gary something. What was it?* She remembered the two of them watching the stars. Gary's touch on her face… She paused for a moment trying to remember what she'd promised, but it was all so foggy.

Dr. Dogan's next words interrupted her train of thought. "The confusion will pass soon." His tone was reassuring.

"I hope so. You see, there's something important I'm supposed to remember. Oh! I know what it was. I have to warn you." *This is it.* Ms. Snow's warning of the plan to exterminate the insurgents came back to her. "The Conglomerate is planning to attack Lunex-21. They want to wipe you out."

Paul frowned. "Do you know when?"

In a flash, Ms. Snow's words came back to her. "Today!

Within hours! You all need to evacuate." Margo was relieved her mind was beginning to clear. She remembered that all she had to do was say 'pink unicorn' and she'd be back in her own body.

"I must go pass that on," said Paul. His complexion had paled at Margo's news.

"Why can't the AI…" She let her words trail off as Paul bolted from the room. Perhaps he wanted to pass the message privately.

Margo took a deep breath. Even that felt weird. Her whole body felt wrong. *Ash Jones's body, you mean.* Then she remembered where she'd heard the name before. Ash Jones was Lucas's friend.

Laughter came from somewhere beyond the door frame. *Children? There're children here?*

She saw a pair of boots on the floor beside the bed and slipped them on, then only managed two steps with her borrowed legs before she stopped. Her gait felt wrong in a way she couldn't articulate. With a few more experimental steps, she decided it was the length of her pace—Ash Jones took shorter steps. Consciously forcing her limbs to relax, she told herself to stop obsessing about every little detail. She walked over to the doorway and poked her head out.

The space outside was a large reception room, typical of any medical centre, except the carpet was threadbare and the furniture dented and in need of repair. The walls had recently been painted a cheerful blue, which made everything else look even more worn.

Two children, who had to be twins, played with building blocks on a nearby table. Their focus on constructing their tower was absolute. It took her a moment to realize why she was staring at them. She hadn't seen healthy children since leaving Earth.

"I didn't expect to see kids here," she said in an undertone, but the AI heard her and responded.

"Those are Paul's children, Henry and Paige. There are seven children in total here."

Paul re-entered the room then. "Oh good. You're looking yourself again, well, as yourself as you can be given the situation," he said. "Our leader is looking forward to speaking with you. I'll take you to him." He looked over at the children and frowned. "Peg, keep an eye on the children." He gestured for Margo to follow as he headed towards the main doors. "Our evacuation protocols have already been activated. Today isn't the first time we've had to flee."

Margo followed him out of the medical centre then walked beside him down the hallway. The unpleasant smell was worse here. Time had yellowed the ceiling and escaped algae were growing along the edges. Out of the corner of her eye she saw movement along the floor—a cockroach. *The facility would not have been out of place in a medical horror flick!* As real as it felt to be in Ash Jones's body, she was relieved that, from her perspective at least, this was a virtual tour.

A woman in rumpled cargo pants and a hoodie came through a door in the hallway looking worried. She gave Margo —Ash—a glance, but addressed the doctor.

"I just heard. What are we going to do?"

"Well, we're not going to panic," Paul said. As he spoke, he brushed a lock of her greying hair out of her face. "Take the kids, then get the emergency supplies and packs from the store room then get to the ship. I'll meet you there. We'll board together." The woman looked even more worried, so he added in a reassuring tone, "we always knew this was a possibility and we've prepared for it."

They kissed and then she rushed off in the direction of the kids.

"My wife, Mary," he said as they resumed walking.

Margo spotted another cockroach. "This place is nasty." She wasn't a wuss. She didn't mind grubby. She was an entomologist after all. But even she drew the line at cockroaches in buildings.

"Lunex-21 sat abandoned for years before we claimed it," he explained, leading her into a wider corridor. "I understand your reaction." He made a sweeping gesture with his arm to encompass all of Lunex-21 rather than just this corridor. "But this is a huge improvement over what it looked like when we first got here."

"I recall it was used by the military for research."

"Yes, they used it for their helium-3 research before that fell out of fashion."

"How big is this place?"

"At its peak it had the capacity to house the 500 people who were stationed here."

"How many are here now?" asked Margo.

He scratched his head. "A lot of people come and go, I think there's about 35 of us right now."

"And you're all refugees from The Conglomerate for one reason or another?"

"Yeah, I think so." With a shrug, he added, "mostly I keep to my work, I don't socialize much."

They passed a series of interior windows overlooking a large room that had to be a hangar. Margo stopped and looked in. Obsolete looking mechanical parts littered the floor of the massive space. Even in the low light, it was clear the hangar was huge—way bigger than their dome greenhouse.

"That's the main hangar," said Paul, stopping beside her. "It's been out of commission since I arrived."

Margo noticed that the only light inside was from iridescent algae that must have escaped from the air filtration system. She had yet to see a window that gave her a view of the outside. "Are there windows to the outside?"

"Not here, no," he said.

When he gestured for them to resume walking, it reminded Margo that time was of the essence.

"We're in a lava tube under the Heaviside E Crater."

Margo looked at him blankly, her lunar geography clearly lacking.

"We're near the south pole on the far side of the moon," said Paul. "Out of site from prying eyes on Earth and Maximillian Station."

Margo nodded. "So the hangar is out of commission, but the gravity plating is good?" Even though she was in someone else's body, her weight felt right—that is, Earth-like, not the normal lunar low gravity.

"Yes, we don't have to worry about loosing bone mass here. As for how well everything else works, it depends on the day, how busy our few engineers are and what Iago feels is important."

"Who's Iago?" asked Margo.

"He's our leader and a damn capable one."

As he led them up and down a confusing series of staircases, Margo couldn't help thinking that working elevators hadn't made it on Iago's list of important things. Three flights of stairs later, they emerged into a well-kept corridor. Margo noticed that Ash's body wasn't even out of breath. *The woman kept herself in good shape!*

She turned and looked at Paul. "Why did you flee The Conglomerate?"

"I didn't want to do what *they* wanted me to do," he said keeping his eyes on the corridor ahead. "They wanted to turn my work into an abomination."

"What were they trying to do?" asked Margo.

But they stopped in front of a large metal door and he didn't answer her question. Instead, he said, "We're here," and opened the door.

Chapter Thirty-Two

Margo felt compelled to look up as soon as she passed through the door. The cylindrical space was capped by a domed ceiling almost two stories above and filled with a massive lit panel in the centre. Colonized by the same algae she'd seen elsewhere, the light cast a sickly green hue on the jumble of wires connecting the equipment bolted everywhere. The space was chaotic.

A raised metal platform filled most of the centre of the room. On it Margo could just glimpse numerous workstations and monitors. No two looked the same as though a random assortment of equipment had been bought at a garage sale. Right in front of her, five steps led up to the platform and the group of people standing up there.

Before Margo could get a good look at anyone in the room, a young black man came bounding down the stairs.

"Mom!" he said, stopping in front of her with an expectant look, his lanky form almost bristling with the need for action. "The *Staffelwalze* is fuelled and ready to go as soon as we're loaded."

"Uh," said Margo, taking a step back from the eager young man.

"Max, this is Margo," said Paul, as if he was making a normal introduction. "Your mom kindly let Margo use her body."

Max frowned at Margo, then looked at Paul. "I need my mom back. She's the best pilot we have."

"We can reverse the transfer while on the ship," said Paul sounding very confident.

Why had Gary been so concerned? Obviously, Paul knew what he was doing.

"Now, I've got to go help my family." Without even a glance to Margo, Paul was gone.

Margo looked up and realized everyone on the raised platform was staring at her.

"Welcome, Margo," said a large, bald man standing closest to the stairs. His voice was rich and deep and his dark skin reflected hints of the green light. "Come on up," he added with a welcoming gesture.

Margo passed Max and went up the five steps, hearing the young man's footsteps as he followed her. Once on the platform she could see there were screens all around the room. Some weren't working, but the ones that were showed various views both inside and outside of what she assumed was the Lunex-21 station. The interior views were mostly of decrepit looking rooms punctuated with people moving about quickly.

The exterior cameras showed panoramic vistas of the lunar surface—without a single space ship in view, which was promising given the imminent Conglomerate attack. The sun on the landscape was bright, highlighting the terrain, but Margo didn't let her gaze linger. She shifted her view back to her immediate surroundings.

Workstations dotted the platform with additional monitors of their own. Most of the equipment seemed to be discards from the military, some even with screens smashed and keys missing. Only a handful of the workstations had new computers plugged into the old system.

"Let me make introductions," volunteered the large man. "I'm Iago Ocon and I'm the leader here."

Margo studied his sharp features and bald head; he looked familiar but she couldn't remember where she'd seen him before. Then her eyes stopped at his right arm, or more accurately, his right stump. The rest was an elegantly crafted prosthetic.

"I know who you are," Margo responded.

He grinned, his white teeth making a pleasing contrast against his dark skin. "I've made the news feeds." Then he gestured to a short and slightly plump Asian woman at his side. "This is Yuko Michi, one of our astrophysicists."

Margo was taken aback when she met Yuko's scowling gaze, but didn't have time to assess whether she was angry at Margo's sudden appearance or simply angry in general as Iago continued to make introductions.

"This is Vince." Iago tilted his head towards a petite man standing and leaning against a workstation. "He's an epic hacker."

At Iago's compliment, Vince scowled. He was even younger than Max, perhaps even still in his teens, and wore dark clothing with a hood pulled over his head. Underneath, strands of purple hair poked out. The young man looked troubled, like he'd had it rough, and Margo wondered who his parents were and why he was on the run from The Conglomerate. *And why go to the trouble of dying your hair purple and then hiding it under a hood?*

"Dr. Dogan said he told you about The Conglomerate's planned an attack on this facility. My sources said this is going to happen in the next couple of hours. I also need your help to remove a virus from our PEG-42 AI back on Thesan." The words were spilling out of her with a renewed sense of urgency. "And there's a boy with us who needs medical…"

"Back up," said Yuko, holding up a finger in a condescending manner. "Our priority is the attack. How do we know her intel is good?"

"I agree," said Iago. "Where did you get your information?"

"A Conglomerate agent was abandoned on Thesan and we gave her refuge," said Margo.

"She?" asked Iago in a suspicious tone.

"Lucy Snow."

Yuko inhaled sharply.

"Why didn't you just kill her?" As Vince stepped slightly forward and into the light, Margo saw that his expression matched Yuko's. Margo was mildly surprised that the young shy-looking man had spoken with such venom. *But then again, this is Ms. Snow we're talking about.*

"My Commander dissuaded me," said Margo.

"Margo," said Iago, and she turned to look at him. "You can't trust a word that woman says."

"I know that. And I'd have put her out an airlock the moment she arrived. She helped engineer the sabotage of my colony, my home." Margo didn't bother to add her other history with Ms. Snow.

"If your Commander knows who Snow is, why offer her refuge?" asked Iago, crossing his arms.

"Commander Ordaz agreed to a trade. Ms. Snow has her 10-year-old son with her, and he's sick. She offered to cooperate in telling us The Conglomerate's plans if we keep her boy safe. The problem is, her kid is getting sicker. If he dies..." Margo shook her head as her voice trailed off.

Iago and Yuko shared a glance.

"Your doctors can't make him well?" Yuko demanded as if doing so was as simple as getting a haircut.

"That's the problem, they can't. The Conglomerate experimented on him. Our doctors found evidence that the boy's base genetics have been tampered with. And since his arrival, he's been declining rapidly. Without knowing exactly what was done to him, they can't reverse it." Margo licked her lips, distracted by the feel of Ash's tongue against the full lips.

"We intercepted the report Commander Ordaz sent to the

Combined Nations." Iago's posture and size conveyed his alpha male confidence as he changed the topic without comment. He glanced at the people behind him. "We had a little celebration here when we heard how your small colony one-upped The Conglomerate. Thesan's sabotage was the most blatant interference they have ever tried, more so than the incident on Mars. The Combined Nations needs to hold them accountable."

"They're getting bolder," said Yuko.

"But how can anyone, including the Combined Nations, strike if we don't know their endgame?" Vince looked at Margo. "Their actions have to add up to something."

"It's obvious their megalomaniac leader just wants to take over everything." said Yuko. By the reactions of the insurgents, they'd all heard Yuko's opinion before. More than once.

"How do you intend to find out what The Conglomerate scientists did to the boy?" asked Margo as her gaze fell on Vince.

"You want me to hack into their systems?" asked Vince, eyes wide.

"Yes. Specifically, into the medical facility on Maximillian Station," said Margo.

"We've built a life here." Yuko ignored Margo as she addressed Iago.

As she gestured, Margo noticed Yuko was missing the pinky on her left hand—another exiled Conglomerate employee. *I wonder how she failed them?*

"We can't just let someone waltz in here and make us flee based on a rumour. Besides, where would we go?"

"Come to Thesan." said Margo.

Yuko turned to Iago and started murmuring to him. She hoped Paul's statement that there were only 35 insurgents was true. Their colony could accommodate that number—but the remaining original colonists would be outnumbered.

Margo glanced at Max who stood on her left. "You said the *Staffelwalze* is fuelled and ready to go. I assume it can take you all."

Max nodded, then glanced at a monitor. "We can't make it through the current wormhole, though. It'll close in 90 minutes. The *Staffelwalze* needs at least nine hours to get there."

Margo knew the solution for this problem was also to hack into The Conglomerate computers and get control of the wormhole. "In addition to all the other lies that you would've read about in our report, we've also learned from Ms. Snow that the wormhole only points to one solar system. That means anytime it opens you all could go through."

"I've always suspected that," said Yuko. "The physics didn't add up on the official theory."

"Max," said Iago. "Take Margo to the Square."

"Will you agree to have Vince hack into The Conglomerate system to fix our AI and help us find a cure for the boy—" Margo stopped talking. Iago had already turned his back on her and was moving to the other side of the room with the small group of insurgents; his core team, Margo assumed.

"Come with me, please," said Max, giving Margo an odd look.

Margo gave one last glance at Iago and his group of advisors before turning towards Max. She noticed his odd expression and was about to ask about it when she realized that Max was, for all intents and purposes, addressing his mother. His dark eyes were guarded. *It had to be weird talking to the stranger inhabiting his mother's body.*

Chapter Thirty-Three

Max led Margo down a different corridor than the one she'd taken with Paul. She mulled over her conversation with Iago as they walked in silence. Had she said the wrong things? Had she failed in making the urgency of their mutual needs apparent? *Maybe if I'd presented my arguments better...*

Two hundred paces on, the hallway opened up into a large open area—the first space she'd been in since arriving that didn't smell like a poorly maintained aquarium. Margo stopped and took a deep breath, glancing up as she did so. Many stories above a clear barrier capped the roof, keeping their atmosphere in. Sunlight filtered through, casting a warm glow over everything.

The large space, which was indeed square, was mostly green. Food crops took up the majority of the space, with a small area devoted to a common area. The place was clearly well used and likely the central focus of domestic life for the insurgents. Margo half expected to see laundry hanging out to dry.

"This way," said Max.

Looking over, Margo saw Max had started down one of the paths. She followed. Just past the entrance sat a play structure devoid of children and constructed out of left-over industrial equipment. Walking by, Margo admired the care that had been taken to weld the joints.

As she followed Max, Margo saw suspended grow-lights above focused to augment the sunlight. Behind the play area, raised beds made of metal scrap filled with dirt extended to the far wall. Plants ranging from sprawling sweet potato vines to tall stems of corn with ears ready for picking filled them. She continued weaving through the spaces between beds, joining Max where he'd stopped at a small open area that boasted a couple of dented metal picnic tables, both of which looked the worse for wear.

Max flopped down onto a bench, unbothered the way it wobbled. He leaned forward, putting his elbows on the adjacent table's surface. He began speaking before Margo even had a chance to sit down. "Would Thesan be better than here given how badly damaged your colony is?"

Margo sat on the bench across the table from him. "I haven't seen enough of 'here' to let you know for sure," she said, looking around before meeting the youth's troubled gaze. "But Thesan is a colony meant to expand and be a permanent home. There's no future for you here."

"We could always go back to Earth."

"You could, but I'm assuming you're all hiding from The Conglomerate for one reason or another. On Earth, most of you would have to live in hiding. You wouldn't have to do that on Thesan. Plus, my Commander wants you to come. He said your mother was an old friend. He wanted to come instead of me." She thought how weird that would've been for Lucas, not only to inhabit a woman's body, but to inhabit the body of the one friend he most wanted to talk with.

"When we intercepted your report, my mother recognized

your leader's name. I remember him too. He used to be my mom's boss, before…"

Margo waited for Max to say more, but he just shrugged.

"Can you tell me what the 'base' Peg AI is?" she asked, changing the topic. It still bothered her that she didn't know why the AI had brought her here. *Is this all just an elaborate trap?*

"Vince could give you a better answer. All I know is that early on when the insurgence was founded we agreed to keep multiple versions of the Peg AI away from The Conglomerate. The way Iago talks about it, those AIs are the key to taking that organization down."

Margo was about to ask another question when a distant detonation sounded and the ground shook beneath them, causing the grow lights to flick off and then on again. "What was that?" asked Margo as her heart began to race. She looked around but saw no evidence of a threat.

"Mom, come on!" Max had jumped to his feet and was already sprinting towards the door.

"Wait for me!" called Margo racing after him. Her gait still felt awkward as though she might trip at any moment. He'd probably not be able to break the habit of thinking of her as his Mom for the short time Margo would be with them, which also likely explained why he'd actually stopped just inside the common area entrance to wait for her.

"Hurry! We gotta get back to the Comms Room and get the others."

It was just as well she wasn't used to her borrowed body. Just as Margo reached him, the corridor ahead collapsed. Margo and Max leapt aside to avoid being hit with debris. A cloud of dust rose up obscuring what was left of the corridor. Had Max not waited for her, he would have been buried in the rubble.

Dust was billowing around them, with nowhere to go but the square. Coughing, Max went directly to the nearest computer terminal. Margo eyed the undulating cloud, covering her mouth and looking up to try to avoid it at the same time a shadow blocked the sun, casting the room into sudden dimness.

"Max!" called Margo, pointing.

Above the clear ceiling, Margo saw the grey underside of a massive ship. *My warning was too late!*

"Peg, what's happening?" asked Max as he opened a comms link on the terminal.

That's archaic, thought Margo.

"Lunex-21 is under attack. Iago has ordered a complete evacuation. Everyone is ordered to the *Staffelwalze*," said Peg.

Both of them looked up as massive blast doors closed above, hiding the ship from view. The grow lights now provided the only illumination.

"Three Conglomerate ships are hovering above the crater," announced the Lunex-21 Peg in a calm voice. "Four smaller ships were dispatched our way. One has landed by the main hangar and another by air vent three. My sensors have lost track of the other two."

Another strike hit the base and now the grow lights went out, bathing them in a soft green glow from the light panels above. The escaped algae was iridescent.

"They must've hit the generator," said Max, coughing again as the dust swirled.

She could hear him opening a small emergency cabinet next to the comms station, and the next moment he'd cracked two glow sticks.

"They're going to do a sweep of the station," said Margo, looking at Max then at the rubble blocking the corridor. "We need to get out of here. There must be an alternate route out of the Square."

"What we need is my mom back."

Good idea! She'd delivered her message, and it was time to leave. "Pink unicorn," said Margo. When nothing happened, she said it again, more emphatically. "Pink unicorn!"

Max was looking at her like she'd gone crazy, which might very well happen if her safe phrase didn't work.

"What?"

"It's my safe phrase! It's supposed to take me back to my own body and release your mom back into hers." Margo flicked the button on the comms unit that Max had used. "Peg, my safe phrase won't work!" When no response was forthcoming, Margo started banging on the comms unit buttons, calling for Peg.

"If they hit the generator, Peg is gone," said Max.

"Then you're stuck with me. For now. We'd better get to that ship."

"This way," said Max. He led her across the Square at as fast a pace as the dimness allowed, dodging veggie beds and forgotten toys, until they reached an alternate exit. Max stopped at the entrance. "This'll take us there, but it's not the most direct route."

Margo looked into the shadowy length of the corridor. Patches of dim illumination broke up the darkness. The algae left it unevenly lit. Their glow lights would help, but only a little.

"Well, we might as well get going."

At a walk, they headed into the corridor. To Margo it looked exactly like the other corridors she'd seen, only darker. Max led her around corners and down hallways. *One could get seriously lost in here!*

When they turned the next corner, they came face-to-face with three soldiers in mech armour. *A private security force perhaps? Does The Conglomerate have their own security force?* Two were facing away, the headlight beams illuminating the hallway. The third, facing in their direction, had his head down, his light illuminating his weapon as he fussed with it.

"Amateurs," whispered Margo, grabbing Max by the arm and dragged him into the nearest stairwell.

"There went two," she heard the soldier say as she followed Max's sprint down the stairs.

"Stop! Come back!" yelled one of the other soldiers.

That's even more amateur, thought Margo glad they were out of a direct line for a shot.

"Yeah right," said Max, leading Margo out onto the floor below. He darted forward down another dimly lit corridor.

Despite the near-darkness, they ran, both keeping their footfalls as silent as possible. She was impressed that she'd finally grown accustomed to her borrowed body, but just as impressed that he knew how to move with stealth.

At a set of open double doors, Margo pulled Max to a stop. He urged her to continue, but she shook her head, listening. In the distance, she could hear the heavy footfalls of mech armour. The soldiers were following, hopefully uncertain which way they'd gone. Closing the pair of doors, she grabbed an axe from a nearby fire-fighting station and put it through the handles. It wouldn't stop the soldiers for long, but at least it would slow them down and make a noise when they broke through.

They broke into a run again, but almost immediately a loud crash echoed through the halls as the wall beside them split open. A soldier in mech armour burst through. Margo didn't have time to react before she smashed into the solid mech armour. She bounced back and landed on her butt, her glow stick skittering on the floor away from her.

The soldier turned her way, blinding her with the bright light on his helmet. *He must be running face recognition algorithms*, she thought as the light was held on her.

"Ash Jones, there's a bonus for bringing you in," he said.

Well, that explains why they hadn't fired on them earlier!

Scrambling up to her feet, Margo yelled for Max to keep going as she blindly sprinted back the way she'd come, her night vision ruined. The soldier followed, his armour overly loud in the confined space. Back at the double doors, she just had enough time to pull out the axe and swing it, slamming into his chest plate.

The soldier laughed as he swung his arm, flinging her into the wall. She heard the axe land somewhere but couldn't see it.

Gasping for air, Margo pushed herself up. She was momentarily disconcerted to see a reflection of a strange face in the soldier's face mask.

Another tremor shook the station, this one stronger than before. The soldier was knocked off balance and put a hand on the wall to steady himself. She bolted, sprinting into the darkness back the way she'd come.

Had Max gotten away? There was a shout from behind her, then loud thumps of someone in mech armour running. In the dim light ahead, she could just make out another open doorway with a stairwell off to her right. Veering sharply, she raced up the stairs three at a time, her soft-soled boots hardly making a sound. *Will the soldier be fooled?* She doubted it.

Up one level, she headed in the general direction she thought they'd been going, hoping she hadn't gotten turned around. As she passed through another set of doors, she wished she could say the safe phrase and make all this disappear. But even if it did work, she'd be dumping Ash into a life or death circumstance, hardly fair in the confusion that would likely be initially present when re-inhabiting your own body.

At a fork in the hallways, she stopped to assess her next step. She couldn't hear anyone following her. *Am I safe? Did Max get away?* Swallowing, she looked at the two options before her. The one to her right veered off at an angle. The one to the left went straight as far as the glowing algae would let her see. She was so turned around she had no idea which one to take.

"Eeny, meeny, miny, moe," Margo muttered under her breath before turning left and silently sprinting down the straight algae-lit hallway.

The building shook again, and she fell to the floor, her knees and hands stinging. Pushing herself up, she thought she heard raised voices ahead. *Are they the voices of the insurgents or the attackers?* She moved forward with caution until she came to the next bend in the corridor.

Peaking around the corner, she saw a large space lit with

emergency lighting. In the centre of the room sat a space ship. It was neither sleek nor elegant, but in that moment it was the best looking space ship Margo had ever seen. She exhaled in relief, jogging out from the corridor towards the ship, its nose as familiarly bulbous as the *Settler's* shuttles. This ship was much bigger than a shuttle. Its belly was wide, each side lined with port-hole-like windows once common on transport ships. There had to be enough space inside for everyone.

Another tremor went through the station as Margo ran for the ship.

"Ash!" someone shouted from the ship's only open door.

Yuko, Margo saw. *Still scowling.*

"Get in here. You're the last one." As she ran, Margo could see the engines ignite—they'd be out of here in less than a minute.

Bounding up the steps, Margo slipped past Yuko and went inside. Yuko closed the door and Margo could feel the ship lift into a hover.

"Is Max here?" Margo asked.

"He's the one flying," said Yuko as she locked the door controls.

Margo followed as Yuko advanced into the ship. They passed storage rooms and what was obviously the medbay before the corridor opened into a galley-slash-dining area. Margo noticed that the dozen or so chairs were occupied by people with resigned expressions, none of whom were Dr. Dogan. *If Peg could send her back to her own body, presumably he could too.* She needed to talk to him. Yuko continued on, past a spiral staircase leading up to a second level and past more rows of occupied seats. Margo stopped when she saw Dr. Dogan and Mary, with their children between them staring at the proceedings with twin round eyes.

"I need to talk to—"

But Yoku yanked her forward with surprising strength, muttering *later* under her breath. Margo supposed she was right.

Now was the time to flee. As they approached the bridge doors, Margo noticed a row of servers strapped into seats.

"What the…?" said Margo, stopping to look. It was an odd place and an odd way to transport computers.

"The *Staffelwalze's* computers can't contain the AI vault, so Vince rigged this," said Yuko as if that explained it all. Not looking to see if Margo followed, she continued on through the next door. They'd arrived on the bridge.

Chapter Thirty-Four

The *Staffelwalze's* bridge was cramped. There were five seats, one for the pilot, co-pilot, and three additional seats in front of consoles for navigators. Part of her, or perhaps Ash, relaxed when she saw the dark, curly hair on the top of Max's head where he sat in the pilot's seat. Margo nodded at Vince, the only other person in the bridge.

"Mom, is that you?" said Max, over his shoulder. He hadn't looked back, so he must have seen Margo by her reflection in the windshield.

"I'm still Margo," she said, looking around the cockpit. The controls looked antiquated. They were probably older than her by half a century.

"Shit," cursed Max. "My mom's a better pilot than me."

Margo bit her lip, knowing she had no piloting skills to offer. "Sorry." Then activity in the hangar caught her attention.

Half a dozen soldiers in matte dark mech armour spread out like an ominous black shadow. Margo swallowed and gripped onto the back of Max's seat. Beside her, Yuko grabbed onto a bar bolted to the wall. Max pulled the controls back and the ship's nose edged up.

"I need the hangar doors open now!" Max shouted.

"Opening," said Vince from his seat at a console behind them. His hood was still pulled up hiding most of his purple hair.

From the large bulbous windows of the bridge, Margo could see the entire roof of the hangar start sliding open, sunlight streaming in. Max kept edging the ship upwards as the soldiers began firing, their airtight suits and magnetic boots keeping them on the ground. The ship lurched as it absorbed the blasts, leaving Margo wondering if the ancient hull plating would hold. *What was it even made of back in the day?* She looked down at the deck beneath her feet even though she knew that wouldn't give her any clues.

The ship lurched again and something crashed in the back followed by a chorus of fearful cries. *Just one puncture hole would be enough*, thought Margo picturing their atmosphere being sucked out. She glanced out the side window, just as a soldier aimed a rocket launcher at them and fired.

"Swerve right," shouted Margo, squeezing her eyes shut and grabbing on tight. Her stomach lurched as Max complied, the bulky ship nimble under his control. Opening her eyes, she saw the explosion inside the hangar as the rocket meant for the ship hit the wall. She let out the breath she'd been holding.

"Coming through," said Iago, as he pushed past Margo and sat in the co-pilot's seat. "You two need to get your asses into seats." Margo and Yuko scrambled to the empty seats by Vince and buckled in. "Get us out of here, Max."

The ship rose through the hangar doors, but gravity plating dampened their motion, keeping what they perceived as down in line with the ship's hull. The hard bank they took once clear of the hangar doors felt as gentle as bouncing off a cloud.

"Looks like they brought three ships with them," said Vince, his fingers flying on his console. "Plus four shuttles."

"Are the shuttles armed, too?" asked Iago.

Margo watched as Max kept their ship low against the crater

floor. On the rearview screen she saw moon dust rising in their wake. The minimal moon atmosphere meant the dust, once disturbed, wouldn't settle quickly.

Above them through the bridge's windows she could see the large Conglomerate ships hovering, too massive to be maneuverable on the floor of the crater. Two of them were mining vessels and the third a luxury transport. The transport ship, the most maneuverable of the three, began moving in their direction. A laser shot out from its hull, narrowly missing them thanks to Max's evasive tactics.

"I guess they've ignored the Combined Nation's directive about arming civilian ships," said Margo. Fear knotted in her gut. *How can we possibly evade so many ships?*

Max pulled the controls hard left, and the ship pitched clumsily in that direction. As the lunar landscape sped by the windows, Margo's stomach lurched.

"Circle back into the dust," said Vince.

"Give me a sec." Max worked the controls as the crater's edge appeared directly in front of them. Just as Margo thought they were going to hit the wall, he swerved. She saw the plume of dust as the laser beam meant for them hit the crater's wall. Their ship came around and dived into the billowing dust, hiding them from view.

"I've hacked the Nigel on the transport," Vince announced.

Margo twisted to gape at him. *Hacked the Nigel AI! That was unheard of!* Vince was unaware of her stare and continued working frantically at his console.

"Trick them into firing at one of their own ships," said Iago.

"On it." Vince continued working and Margo turned back to look at the forward view. The undulating cloud of dust made her nervous—*how can Max know he's not going to hit anything? These people needed Ash's piloting skills.*

"Pink unicorn."

"What?" asked Yuko, giving her an *are-you-nuts* look. She was the only one close enough to hear.

"You guys need Ash and I'd really like to get back into my own body."

"That's only going to work if we have line-of-sight with the wormhole."

"What do you mean?" Margo asked, frowning at Yuko.

Yuko gave her a patronizing glare before explaining. "Without Peg, we need a direct line of sight with the wormhole before can transfer your consciousness back."

"Well… crap," said Margo.

As they burst out of the dust, Margo looked out the window and saw the transport ship fire another laser, but this time it hit one of the mining ships, scoring a direct hit on one of the engines. Atmosphere started venting out of the hole in the mining ship as it began moving out of range.

"They know I have control of their laser aiming," said Vince. "They won't fire again."

"The shuttles will be after us next." Iago's voice sounded confident.

"No shit." Max didn't look away from the view ahead. "I'll head for the canyon."

"Vince, arm the trap," said Iago.

Margo had no idea what that order meant, but she liked the sounds of it.

"Three shuttles are heading in our direction. I don't know where the fourth one went." Vince's tone was flat. Margo looked over at the young man wearing the hood that covered his bright purple hair. His expression was of extreme concentration as he flipped through the sensors. A tiny tremor in his hands betrayed his fears. *Or perhaps his youth.*

"And the other two ships?" asked Iago.

Margo shifted her focus to him. He was shockingly calm considering their position, it was as though this was an ordinary day for him. In a flash, she finally remembered where she'd seen him before. It was from a news feed, but likely not the ones he'd been referring to. She'd seen him leading a protest that had turned violent and over a hundred protesters had been killed. She was certain that was the day he'd lost his arm.

"The damaged mining ship has landed at the crater bottom and the other mining ship has pulled away. The transport is still hovering over our base. They're trying to remove my hold on their weapon."

Margo watched Vince, worried for him. The young man hadn't taken his eyes off his console and his voice wavered when he spoke. Then her attention was caught as Max led them uncomfortably close and fast along the crater's wall. She took a deep breath and willed herself not to close her eyes.

"Slow down a bit and let them catch up," said Iago. His prosthetic arm twitched.

So he's feeling the tension, too. Max did as Iago commanded, and Margo once again had to force herself not to interfere, but she wanted to scream, *go faster*, not slower.

"I've lost control of the shuttle's weapon," said Vince, his shoulders slumping.

The ship lurched as it took the hit, and their artificial gravity vanished for a moment. It felt to Margo like she was on the apex of a roller coaster. The crater ahead appeared to swing around and tilt. Behind her, from the row of seats outside the bridge, she heard the sound of vomiting.

"The forward port thruster's damaged." Max was breathing heavily and spoke with a note of panic. "I can compensate!" He worked the controls, and the view levelled out again. Kind of. They were racing towards the crater wall.

This time Margo did close her eyes.

"A shuttle is in range of us and they're charging their laser!" said Vince, unable to hide the quaver in his voice.

"Steady everyone. Max, you're doing fine. We're almost there," said Iago, his rich, deep voice astonishingly calm given the circumstances.

Margo opened her eyes just in time to see the rock wall dead ahead. There was no avoiding it now, and Max didn't even try.

Instead, he kept the ship charging ahead. Margo bit back a scream when, at the last moment, he swerved into a lava tube barely big enough for their ship. Once the darkness of the lava tube consumed them, a heads-up display activated across the windshield outlining the tunnel ahead in magenta lines.

"Three shuttles have followed us in," said Vince in a tone of relief. "They fell for it."

"Ready on the trap," said Iago.

Margo's heart was pounding, made worse by how uncomfortably close the computer-represented walls were. Beyond the generated image she could only see darkness. *What the hell are they doing?*

"Trap is set. We'll be through in 15 seconds."

Time seemed to stand still as Margo counted down in her head.

After what felt like an eternity, Vince announced in a clipped tone, "we're through!"

"Spring it," Iago ordered.

A rumble from behind vibrated through the ship as they continued speeding on in the darkness, the tunnel walls still uncomfortably close.

"What just happened?" Margo whispered to Yuko.

"We collapsed the lava tube," she replied.

"Vince, are you picking up those shuttles?" asked Iago.

Vince flicked through several screens. "Not on any of our sensors," he answered, turning towards Iago. His voice changed then. "I think we got them."

Max made a whooping sound and Yuko sighed in relief.

"Let's not get ahead of ourselves. We got *three* of the shuttles. That leaves one unaccounted for," said Iago.

"We're approaching the exit," announced Max.

Margo looked forward. She could see a pinprick of light in the distance.

"We need Ash back," said Iago, turning to look at Yuko. "Take her aft and get Paul working on it."

"It'll only work if we have a line of sight with the worm-hole," said Yuko. "At our latitude, we'll need altitude to get that."

"I'll get us up there. No offence, Margo, but I want my Mom back," said Max without turning to look at her.

"Not offended."

Then they shot out of the lava tube and the heads-up display vanished, leaving Max piloting by sight in the light of the sun.

"Okay, let's go," said Yuko, unbuckling her seatbelt and standing up.

Margo looked at the lunar terrain ahead. They were uncomfortably close to the ground, but it was better than racing through the tunnel in the dark. She swallowed and unbuckled her seatbelt.

"Yoku, let us know when you're ready and I'll bring us up to altitude. I have the coordinates," said Max.

"Which won't matter worth shit if we don't stay clear of that other shuttle out there, and the two ships," muttered Vince as he kept an eagle eye on the sensors.

"Once we get enough altitude, Earth-based sensors can spot us, The Conglomerate will back off—they aren't ready to be exposed as murderers," said Iago with confidence.

Margo stood, keeping a hand on the ship. "Max, that was some flying you did back there. I'm pretty certain your Mom would be immensely proud."

Max turned then and grinned at her. "Thanks. Mom."

"And Margo," said Iago, also turning in his seat. "We'll accept your invitation. Expect us at Thesan soon."

Margo nodded, then looked at Vince, who remained focused on the data on his screen. "Vince." She waited for him to look at her. "Please, when it's safe to do so, hack into The Conglomerate computers and look for any medical info on gene experimentation. See if you can find out what they did to Julien Snow."

Vince nodded, then went back to perusing his screen, but looked back when Margo addressed him again.

"And while you're in there, Vince, if you can figure out how to obliterate the Nigel virus that infected our Peg, we'd appreciate it."

"Yeah, sure. Or I can take care of it when I get there."

Margo had to be satisfied with the teen's response. It wasn't exactly the level of commitment she'd been hoping for, but she'd done her best.

As she followed Yuko out of the bridge, she considered the invitation that had been extended and accepted. She didn't regret it, knowing Lucas would've done the same—but the implications to their colony would be significant. Would her fellow colonists welcome the insurgents? Or despise Margo for facilitating more than doubling their numbers?

In the aft area behind the bridge, the people who sat in the rows of seats, including seven kids, were wide-eyed as they watched the screen embedded in the forward bulkhead of the space that showed the ship's forward view. Margo noticed that Mary Dogan was still there with her twins, but Dr. Dogan wasn't.

"Where's Dr. Dogan?" Yuko asked.

"He went to medbay," Mary responded. "I couldn't stop him."

"This ship is best crewed by no more than seven," said Yuko as they passed through the galley. "There are enough beds in the compartment above for the kids, but the adults will have to make do with sleeping in their chair or on the floor."

"Are any of those kids yours?"

"No." Yuko knocked on the medbay door.

When Paul slid open the door, Margo brought a hand to her mouth to hide her amusement; not that fleeing on an insurgent ship was the time for humour. His white hair was sticking out in every direction as though he'd been pulling at it repeatedly.

"This relic of a ship is not fit for a dogfight!"

"Just stow your whining," said Yuko without a hint of sympathy as she stepped aside so Margo could slip into the small room. "We need Ash back. Can you do it?"

Dr. Dogan only glared at Yuko in response.

"I'll tell Max to to get up to altitude and get in that line of sight," she said before leaving.

"You might as well lie down," said Paul, closing the door behind Margo.

Margo wove her way around the recently righted crates of supplies and other random stuff, heading towards a bed built into an alcove. It one had been covered in green vinyl but now it was mostly held together with silver tape. Beside the bed, she had to move aside a clear plastic box that held a collection of plastic dinosaurs.

"How does this work?" In this archaic medbay there weren't any robotic arms for Peg to attach sensors to her bare skin.

"It's more simple to project in than to project out," he said, rooting through a crate until he found a small box with sterilized needles in shrink wrap. "I'll administer a cocktail that will put you in the right frame of mind, then I'll use these sensors to do the transfer." Paul waved towards some monitors that looked like they'd been used in 1952 when Peggy had made her film. "I'll need access to your upper arms."

Margo unbuttoned Ash's shirt, wrinkling her nose at the unappealing medical bed. She carefully lay the well-worn shirt on the bed so her bare skin wouldn't have to touch it.

"Please thank Ash for me," said Margo.

Paul glanced at her. "I'll tell her."

Margo slid into the alcove and lay down. She watched as Paul loaded an old fashioned needle with a clear drug. She didn't like this. She at least wished their Peg was doing this with Dr. Dogan, but this was her only way of getting back to her own body.

Then she asked a question she hadn't considered before.

263

"Dr. Dogan, is the time I spent here in Ash's body equivalent to the time I've been sleeping in my own body?"

"Of course," said Dr. Dogan. "We can't bend *time*."

Margo wanted to argue that his work seemed to be bending a lot of rules of physics, but now was not the time for that kind of debate.

As she settled onto the rather uncomfortable bed, an image of Gary floated up in her mind. He'd be livid when he found out what she'd done. She felt bad about breaking her promise, but the circumstances had made it necessary. Hopefully they were closer to helping Julien and to removing The Conglomerate virus.

Dr. Dogan came and swabbed Margo's shoulder with disinfectant. Margo closed her eyes, thankful to finally be going home. She winced as he injected the needle into her, then heard Dr. Dogan say. "Now, just relax."

Margo's world went black.

Chapter Thirty-Five

When the final traces of nausea faded, Margo opened her eyes. She lay on her back on a thick Persian rug in front of a blazing fire wearing her normal clothes. The radiating heat felt good on her skin and the flames danced just like the campfires her dad had made when she was a kid. It even smelled right. Rolling on to her side the rug felt soft against her cheek. As she ran a hand along its plush fibres, she marvelled at the rich indigo and maroon designs.

She gasped when her eyes fell on the snarling feline face mounted about the mantle. The tiger's head had been distastefully frozen in time, maintaining a perpetual snarl as it overlooked the room.

Sitting up, she pushed hair out of her face. Wait... She ran her hands over her hair again and felt the familiar curls. Holding her arms in front of her face, she saw her familiar pale skin covered in freckles.

Then it hit her—she wasn't on the ship anymore, nor was she back at the Centre Module. *I'm back in my own body. But, where the hell am I?*

She rose to her feet, taking in the unfamiliar surroundings.

Perpendicular to each end of the hearth were two brown leather-upholstered chairs that belonged in a nineteenth-century gentleman's club. The wooden arms of each chair boasted carvings of lions, tall ships and anchors, even what looked like multi-armed gods. Beside each was an elegant side table.

The walls were decorated in a glossy green paper with gold crowns that clashed with the indigos and maroons of the rug. Mounted on the walls were portraits in ornately detailed gold frames depicting stern-looking men from a bygone era. Opposite the fireplace were more ornate wood chairs—enough for a half-dozen people to sit.

Everything looked so real—maybe too real. Then she realized something was very odd about this room—it didn't have a door or even any windows. She was in a room that couldn't exist. Yet, here she was. *What is happening? What is this place? And how do I get home?*

The relief she'd felt upon finding herself back in her own body ebbed, replaced by a knot in her gut as she turned in a circle to look for an exit.

"Ah, you're awake."

Margo spun around and saw a man sitting in one of the chairs adjacent to the fire. *That was impossible. The chair had been empty. But then, all of this was impossible, wasn't it?*

The man held a pipe in one hand and a cut-crystal glass of amber liquid in the other. He was dressed as if for a period movie set in the nineteenth century, including a cravat, and the fabrics looked expensive. She recognized him from his years of media appearances. He was Nigel Maximilian West, the head of The Conglomerate.

"Where am I?" she demanded.

"I assume you're hooked up to a machine on Thesan," he said, shrugging. "The location of your physical form is irrelevant."

A horrifying thought occurred to Margo. *Am I in Nigel's mind? Is that even possible?* She tried to remember what she'd read in

Jim's notebooks. His scrawling notes had leaned towards trivia, yet maybe there was something... *Had he mentioned the possibility of a consciousness projection ending up in someone else's mind instead of their body?*

"I demand you release me!" She put her hands on her hips, staring Nigel down and trying to suppress her own fear. If she was in this megalomaniac's mind, she wanted out. The sooner, the better.

He laughed, then put the pipe to his lips and puffed out clouds of cloying-scented smoke. She regarded Nigel as he started emitting smoke rings, each one a perfect circle. This place wasn't right. *How had he pulled her into this fabrication? And how is he controlling it?*

"You're not in a position to make demands, butterfly girl," he said. He made a sweeping gesture with his right hand and the smoke rings changed to grey butterflies that flew around the room. "I'm in control here. What you see is all my doing." He looked at the room and the fluttering butterflies and giggled like a child before once again focusing on Margo. "I have an offer to make. Have a seat." He gestured to the chair beside him.

Margo frowned. She didn't want to do what he asked, even if as of now that was merely taking a seat, but she also had to think about how to get out of this predicament, and that was easier done sitting than standing. She sat. "What's your offer?"

Margo. That was the AI's voice! She turned and looked around the room, but the only other person in the room was Nigel. *I'm in your head, I can't follow you into Nigel's domain. I'm being blocked somehow. Think what you want to say to me, don't speak it. And don't let your expression change. He can't know I finally got through to you.*

How do I get out of here? Margo thought.

I'm working on that, Peg replied.

Margo looked at Nigel, schooling her expression to remain the same as she continued to dialogue in thought with Peg. *Can I influence what goes on here?*

It can't hurt to try, said the AI.

"I want the boy back," said Nigel, seemingly unaware that Margo was communicating with Peg. "I can either send my fleet to take him by force and destroy your colony in the process, or..." He put down his drink on the side table and deposited his pipe on the vintage pipe tray before standing. "You can arrange to deliver him to me."

"He's just a boy, and very sick. Why do you want him?" asked Margo. "Do you want to punish his mother?" She wasn't opposed to that idea.

"The mother was useful but again, irrelevant. No, that boy is special. The founders, who once met in a room much like this one, learned that there would be one born who could touch..." He grinned, revealing two rows of perfect pearly whites that made him look as trustworthy as a television evangelist. "Never mind that. It's not important what he can do, just that I want him."

"What was done to him, exactly? Why was he experimented on?"

"Under the leadership of my great, great, great..." He paused and smiled at her. "Let's just say that particular ancestor was great many times over. He and his five partner founders had foreknowledge of what technologies were coming, so they began to carefully select the mothers for their as yet unborn descendants until sequencing genomes became viable. Then they refined their techniques even further, targeting the specific traits we need by manipulating those genomes. A little dabbling with genetics and, voila, Julien was created." He emphasized his words with an elegant wave.

Margo wanted to punch him, but she needed information. "But what you did to him made him sick."

"Being an albino is just a side-effect. A minor—and, again irrelevant—condition."

"No, he's really sick. He's had seizures and will probably die without the right intervention."

"What?" Nigel was suddenly looming over Margo.

She shrank into the chair as he leaned in, getting an unpleasant whiff of tobacco and scotch on his breath. His blue eyes had darkened in anger as he scowled down at her.

"He can't die! That would ruin everything!"

"Our doctors want to help him, but don't know how."

"Doctors, yes," said Nigel, rising. The sharp edge of his alarm and anger seemed to have disappeared as he resumed his seat and calmly crossed his legs. He contemplated Margo as he rubbed his chin. "Your Thesan doctors have the ability to help him."

"How?" asked Margo, doing her best to remain calm. *Peg, as soon as he says how to help Julien, I want you to leave my head and get back to Thesan and tell Lucas.*

You need my help here, argued the AI.

"Compounds, yes, but which ones," Nigel muttered to himself. A list of chemical compounds flashed into the air between them. Nigel gestured lightly with a finger to scroll through the list, then paused when he found what he was looking for. "These will do the trick." He addressed Margo but kept his eyes on this list as he began tapping different drugs. "I'm the best there is, you know. I've got the benefit of using my superior mind and accessing the minds of my ancestors."

Are you recording this? Margo asked Peg.

Got it.

Nigel grinned again, looking self-satisfied. He waved a hand, and the list disappeared.

Go, directed Margo to the AI.

I'll get you help, said the AI. Margo felt the absence of Peg suddenly, although she wouldn't have been able to articulate exactly what the AI's presence in her mind had felt like. She hoped the list was what Gary needed. She should also have told Peg to tell Gary she was sorry for breaking her promise, but she supposed she'd have to do that herself in person. *That is, if I'm not overly distracted by gouging out my own eyes!*

"Your comms window will close soon. If you agree to hand

over the boy, I'll give you the information about what compounds to use to treat the boy. Your doctors can administer the concoction and, voila, the boy recovers. And then he's mine."

Margo glared at Nigel. He held the pipe again and was tapping the mouthpiece against his chin. To her he looked smug —like he'd already won. And perhaps he had. If he came to their Thesan colony with a duplicate force like what had descended upon Lunex-21, the colonists wouldn't be able to flee —their only spaceworthy ship was the small shuttle Ms. Snow brought them. Although, if the insurgents arrived safely, then they would have a ship, but not one that would hold sixty-plus people. And they'd have nowhere to go even if they could flee. The long and short was, they didn't have the capacity to defend themselves against a Conglomerate attack. They were an unarmed colony.

The other alternative was for her to cooperate and work with Nigel to have the boy picked up by a Conglomerate ship. They'd be sacrificing one life to save the colony. But there was no way she could trust The Conglomerate to take only the boy and not stake a claim on Thesan. And, handing over the boy was immoral—she couldn't let that happen.

As she glanced around the room, Margo considered her options. Her gaze stopped on the tiger's head as a new thought popped into her mind. This room and this conversation was a construct, built by Nigel. His mind dictated and controlled the space—but how much control did he actually have?

Margo turned to Nigel, who was watching her with an amused air as if he enjoyed watching her contemplate her options, enjoyed watching her come to the only conclusion that existed, which was to do his bidding. Margo glared at him, letting him think she was struggling with an inevitable decision, watching as he blew another smoke ring and converted it to a butterfly with a casual gesture. *What are the rules here?* She focused her gaze on the smoky butterfly, picturing it morphing into one of her blue morphos. For a split second, the colour changed to iridescent blue before flickering back to grey.

Nigel laughed. "There's nothing so satisfying as a worthy adversary. You don't want to do this the easy way, do you? My dear Margo, you never cease to delight."

Margo ignored him, trying to picture a doorway in the wall across from her, but he changed the faces in all the portraits to the Nigel AI, and they all laughed in sync with each other.

"Feeble," the Nigel in the chair beside her said. He took a sip from the glass that was back in his hand before waving his pipe at her, throwing Margo out of her chair and skidding her face-first across the rug.

Margo lay still, trying to catch her breath and doing her best to tune out the laughing from all the Nigels in the room. Her cheek began to burn.

"Don't forget, I make the rules here." Nigel rose and turned to face her.

Launching herself to her feet, Margo tackled him. Nigel flicked his wrist, tossing her across the room a second time. When she landed in one of the chairs, it toppled backwards, and she was back on the floor.

Margo was not ready to let him win. She refocused on a bare section of wall, filtering out any sight of a Nigel portrait as she pictured a doorway. She had to stop herself from crowing in delight when a door appeared.

"Is this what you're trying to do?" Nigel asked, and a door appeared.

Margo rose and bolted for the door. Reaching it, she flung the door open and leapt through, but she immediately fell, landing on her belly on a smooth, sloping surface on the other side of the open door. Turning, she looked back at the open door and saw the warm light and pretentious decor of the study. On this side of the frame was nothing. She realized then that she hadn't conjured the door; Nigel had guessed what she had been trying to do and done it himself. And it was clearly amusing him.

Nigel appeared in the doorway with an expression of amusement on his face. "Your file notes your fear of heights." The study and doorframe vanished.

Margo looked down. They were standing on the top of a massive dome. Far below a city sprawled, its tallest skyscraper not even coming close to their height. Between the buildings, monorail trains zoomed along suspended tracks. There was a large park, abundantly green, but the trees looked like shrubs from her height. On the ground were minuscule dark moving specks—people. Her stomach clenched into a knot as she felt the sensation of falling.

"Not real," she whispered. "Get a grip, Murphy."

"How do you like this view of the Lunar City?" He raised his arms. "Or how about this?" Margo felt herself teetering on the edge of a cliff, a rushing river far below her. "Not real, not real, not real," she told herself.

"Accept the fact that you can't win. I make the rules." He grinned at her.

Margo knew he was right—in a way. Winning was impossible in his constructed world. She slumped her shoulders in feigned defeat. "You're right."

Filtering out everything about his construct, Margo focused solely on a kaleidoscope of butterflies—little white cabbage ones with pale iridescent green-yellow wings. En mass, they rose up behind her. Behaving like a flock of birds, she directed them to swarm Nigel.

He laughed as if this was the best game ever, then shaped his hand into a pistol and shot them out of the air. One by one the fragile butterflies disappeared in a burst of smoky dust.

With Nigel distracted, Margo put all her energy into picturing them in an alternative location of her own making, one where she was entirely comfortable, one where she made the rules.

The scenery shifted, and they were in the greenhouse she'd lived in back on Earth. Tropical plants filled the large rectangular space and the scent of damp earth and citrus blooms filled the air. She intimately knew every detail of the space, from the rows of potting benches and organized potting tools to the bedding plants and mature trees and bushes. In the years after being court-martialed, she'd raised butterflies here, all destined to grace the enclosed gardens of the wealthy.

"What the..." said Nigel, his smile gone. He lunged towards her.

Margo easily dodged him, moving behind a potted banana and causing a group of little red butterflies to flutter into the air. Molding their size, colour, shape and behaviour with her thoughts, she made their wings a blood red as rich as velvet. They were the same size as the cabbage butterflies, but they didn't exist in the real world.

Nigel imagined a wooden baseball bat into his hands and swung it at her. In response, she pictured it as sawdust and cedar flakes rained down around her feet. She was getting the hang of this.

Margo pictured a knife in her hand and it appeared. She lunged forward, directing the blade towards Nigel's chest, but the knife changed to a banana just before impact.

When her surroundings started going up in flames, she realized Nigel was wrestling control away from her. She swallowed down her panic. The smoke smelled so real. Margo tried picturing the greenhouse without the flames, but the fire only raged stronger. Nigel was back in control.

She bit her lip, fighting the despair that sought to overwhelm her. Looking down at her hand, she saw she was clutching a banana, not a knife. And that gave her an idea.

"No! You can't win," she wailed in feigned anguish.

When Nigel laughed in maniacal glee, she released her control of the greenhouse, letting it begin to disintegrate as she hid one arm behind her back and focused on the image of her hand holding a knife. The greenhouse started to fade.

As the room with the fireplace began to emerge, Margo lunged forward and buried the knife to the hilt in Nigel's chest. Nigel disappeared, and she stood alone, holding a knife.

The greenhouse reformed around her, no longer on fire but back in its pristine state. She looked around. Her surroundings felt more real than her memory of the place. *Now what?*

Chapter Thirty-Six

"The comms window will close in 30 seconds," announced Peg in a flat tone.

"What?" Lucas leapt to his feet. He'd instructed Lucy to give him a heads up well before the comms window closed. *That blasted, treacherous, scheming, nasty woman had deliberately defied him!*

Lucas looked down at Margo's motionless form, horrified that Margo's mind was about to be trapped on the other side of the wormhole. *Will she be lost forever? How do I explain this to Gary?*

"Bring her back!" snapped Lucas. He clenched his fists, hating this feeling of powerlessness, but he couldn't drag Margo's mind back to the Centre Module's medbay. Peg was the only one capable of doing anything; yet, she too seemed powerless. *This isn't how it was supposed to turn out!*

"I will attempt to use the failsafe," said Peg.

Lucas wanted to kick something. *It should've been me! I would've made it back.* He wasn't sure if that was true, not knowing what had gone wrong. But there must've been something Margo could have done differently to prevent this outcome.

"Her consciousness will not return," said Peg. "Some powerful force is holding her there."

"Override! Bring her back!"

Lucas paced back and forth in the small room, running his hand up and down his nose. He glanced at Margo's inert form, wishing he could shake her, jab her with a needle, anything to wake her up.

"The window has closed," said Peg. "There is nothing more I can do."

"Fucking hell!" Lucas turned and kicked the medbay doorframe. "Lucy! Get in here!"

A few seconds later Lucy appeared in the open door and looked at him, her expression hostile. The bruise on her face looked an angry purple in the medbay's low light. "If you're going to have a hissy fit, I don't want to be anywhere near you."

When he advanced on her, practically snarling, she took a cautious step back, a wary look on her face. "You were supposed to give me the heads up well before the comms window closed!" he practically roared.

"Oh," said Lucy, as she looked over to Margo. "Right." She met Lucas's gaze. "I got distracted."

"You got…" Lucas rubbed his hand over his face. He was tempted to give the other side of her jaw a matching bruise. Doing so would certainly release some of his pent-up frustration. But he held back. He couldn't afford to lose control again. And besides, he'd never been the type to resort to brawling. *It was command; that's what made him want to hit things. He hated being in charge.*

He sighed, then met Lucy's cold blue eyes. Lucy and Margo had been enemies from the start, but out-right sabotage? "I know you hate each other. Did you orchestrate this to deal with Margo?"

"Are you suggesting I trapped Margo's mind somewhere?" Lucy moved a pace towards him.

"Yes, that's exactly what I'm suggesting. You're entirely capable of it."

Lucy looked pale, white almost. *Does she fear I'll hurt her again? Will I?* It was her fault he had ended up in charge.

Lucy scoffed. "Well, she'd throw me out the airlock given half a chance."

"That wouldn't do you any harm, though, would it? Not here. Lucy, did you do this?" he repeated, gesturing towards the inert Margo.

"Of course not. Do you think I'm stupid? I may not like Margo, but I wouldn't risk Julien's safety by harming her."

Lucas slammed a fist against the wall, making Lucy jump. "I wish I could believe you," he said through gritted teeth.

"I was over here." She pointed to the console she'd been working at. "Trying to hack into The Conglomerate's system. Peg can check the logs and confirm what I've been doing."

"Peg?" said Lucas.

"I confirm Ms. Snow's actions are as she said," said the AI. "I am also transcribing some files I received just seconds before our link was terminated."

"What files?" asked Lucas with a suspicious look at Lucy. *Had she created more problems for them?*

"It's a recording from another Peg AI. I have now completed compiling them into a readable format." The screen on the console went blank for a moment before filling up with diagrams.

Lucas and Lucy both strode closer to the console.

"What are those?" Lucas asked. They looked familiar as if he'd seen something like them before.

"They're chemical compounds," answered Lucy.

That's why Lucas recognized the shapes. He'd taken organic chemistry in university.

Lucy leaned in towards the screen beside him. "Peg, what are these for?"

Lucas glanced at her profile. He swore he'd heard a wobble in her voice.

"I am told these compounds will help Julien's condition," said Peg.

"Oh." Lucy put her hand over her mouth and stood back, her eyes still fixed on the screen.

"Peg, who sent the files?" Lucas asked.

"Margo did. She made sure the other iteration of Peg that she was working with sent this information to us before the window closed."

Lucas looked at Lucy, raising an eyebrow when she met his gaze.

"She's helped my boy," said Lucy, her tone soft. "I didn't expect that from her."

Lucas looked Lucy in the eye. "Bring her back. You owe it to her."

"I can't. Not with the window closed." As she spoke, Lucy looked down at the console she'd been working at. "No information can be sent through the wormhole right now, including Margo's consciousness."

"Then what do we do?" asked Lucas, rubbing his nose again.

"Wait until the wormhole is opened again."

"We have no idea when that might be."

"True. There's nothing I can do about that." Lucy's expression was unreadable as she began scrolling through the info Margo had found.

"Yes there is. Hack into The Conglomerate computers and find out when they plan to open the window. If they don't have a plan, fabricate one."

Lucy looked at Lucas in exasperation. "I can't do that, and you know it. The Conglomerate computers have to be on this side of the wormhole for me to hack into them."

"So we just sit here? Do nothing?" Lucas glanced towards the medbay before looking back at the screen.

"This is amazing," said Lucy, resuming her seat and ignoring his questions. "These compounds..." Her voice trailed off as she zoomed in on a section of the screen. Lucas assumed her chemistry was fresher than his.

"Lucy, our first priority is to bring Margo back."

Lucy looked up at him. "No. The first priority is to have one of your doctors mix these compounds and administer them to Julien. With him safe and on the mend, I'll uphold my side of the bargain. I'll do everything it takes to help bring Margo back when the next comms window opens. Until then, there's nothing you can do but monitor her state of wellbeing. At this moment, she's no longer a priority." Lucy looked back at the screen. "Getting these compounds to your doctors is. I can take the rover, deliver this information, and bring one of them back to examine Margo."

Lucas started pacing around the work stations. Gary would be the one to come back, leaving Neil in charge of Julien. *Will there be anything Gary can do for Margo?* Lucas switched direction and walked into the medbay. He looked at Margo. She looked paler, the red of her hair less vibrant. Even the wine-stained birthmark on her neck looked fainter. *Was she already fading away?* He'd promised her he would stay with her until she got back, but could he trust Lucy to return with Gary? *Did he have a choice?*

Lucas moved to stand in the medbay doorway and looked at Lucy.

"Go get Gary," he said.

Chapter Thirty-Seven

"That bitch," said Abigail, scowling and pacing back and forth as the rover hangar cycled in breathable air.

Gary turned from where he had been looking through the window in the hangar airlock door at the parked rover. Making eye contact with Abigail, he tilted his head towards Julien. The boy was standing on tippy toes to look through the window beside him.

"Uh, language?" he said to Abigail in as casual a tone as he could muster. No point jumping to conclusions until he'd gained all the facts.

"Huh? Oh. Sorry, kid." Abigail said as she glanced at Julien. The boy didn't even look her way.

Now that the outer door had closed and the windows of the dust-covered rover had lost their tint to protect the occupants from the glare of Helios, the onlookers could see Lucy in the driver's seat. No passengers were visible in the cockpit or in the windowed passenger area.

Lucy had explained what had happened as soon as her comms were in range of the colony. Gary knew Margo had ignored his warnings—and was now at risk of losing her mind.

How this had all come to pass, he still didn't know. Lucy needed to do some explaining.

The light flashed green and Abigail slammed through the door, stomping towards the rover. Gary and Julien, the boy practically glued to Gary's hip, right on her heels. Abigail swung open the sliding rover door, not bothering to wait for Lucy to open it from within.

Lucy jumped down from the rover.

"Mom!" Julien ran over and wrapped his arms around his mother's hips.

Looking down at him, Lucy smiled before bending to her knees and wrapping her arms around him, but only for a moment. She kept a hand on his back, then leaned back to shift her attention to Gary. She ignored Abigail.

Rising, she addressed Gary. "Where's the other doctor?" she asked.

"Why?" he demanded. Margo was hurt, and he'd see to her.

Before Lucy could respond, Abigail grabbed the collar of Lucy's jacket and slammed her against the side of the rover.

"What have you done to them?" Abigail growled, clearly doubting Lucy's radioed in message.

"Enough," said Gary as he tried to position himself between the two women. Surprisingly, Abigail let go and he stood in front of Lucy, facing Abigail.

"Mom," said Julien, taking Lucy's hand.

"You okay?" Lucy asked, resting her hands on his shoulders.

Julien nodded. "I don't want you to go back," he said.

"Oh, she's going back! Back to get Lucas and Margo!" Abigail threatened. "What happened, bitch? Where are they?"

Gary stopped himself from rolling his eyes. He had to wonder why he was standing between two alpha females. Both of them could likely kick his ass, as could Margo.

"Lucy," Gary said in a reasonable tone as he turned to face her. "Where's Margo and Lucas?"

"They're fine. They're at the Centre Module, like I said. One of your doctors needs to come back with me."

"I need more information about what happened," said Gary as a sinking feeling formed in his stomach.

"Margo projected her consciousness to Lunex-21 to warn the insurgents hiding there of an imminent Conglomerate attack. But Peg couldn't wake her before the comms window closed."

"So she did do it." Gary hadn't wanted to believe the message. They'd talked about this and Margo had promised she would stay well clear of the unproven technique. Then he realized the full implications of what Lucy had told him, which were far worse than a broken promise. *If her consciousness is trapped on the other side of a closed wormhole, what can I possibly do for her?* His medical training would be of no use.

Julien tugged on his mother's hand, demanding her attention. "Mom! Something bad is going to happen to you if you go back."

Lucy looked down at her boy and gave him a reassuring smile. "Everything will be okay." Then she looked at Gary. "Dr. Holbrook?" She waited until she had his attention. "Margo managed to send the compounds needed to help Julien. If one of your doctors would administer them, I'll take the other to Margo."

"What the hell?" Abigail interrupted. "Margo projected her consciousness? To warn some stranger insurgents? Since when is giving warning to random people part of the plan?" Abigail put her hands on her hips. "This was your stupid idea, wasn't it?"

Lucy glared at Abigail. "No. Lucas and Margo both thought it was necessary."

Gary eyed the two women. Abigail had backed Lucy up against the side of the rover and was wagging her finger in Lucy's face. At least they hadn't resorted to punches.

Running a hand through his hair, Gary tuned out Abigail and Lucy's argument. He tried to remember what he'd read about Paul Dogan's consciousness projection technique. It was relatively simple—well, as simple as stasis and space travel—a cocktail of drugs combined with the right connection and the 'traveler' would wake up in someone else's body. It was the return that was the tricky part. It always had been.

What if Margo woke up but lost her humanity? Gary shuddered at the thought, reaching for any straw that might help him help Margo. She was a fighter. And she didn't quit. He'd seen that when they'd fought the saboteur. She would be fighting to come back. And he'd do everything he could to help her. *And then he'd never speak to her again!*

He felt something brush his hand and looked down to see Julien gazing up at him in earnest. "It's not too late," said Julien, coming over and stopping at his side.

Gary froze as he considered the boy. *The cube!* "What did you see, Julien?" Of all the people on this ship, he was the only one who truly understood why the boy made his prophetic statements.

"You can help Margo, but you need to go to the Centre Module." Julien looked over at the women. "Abigail should go, too. You'll need her help."

Hearing her name, Abigail stopped haranguing Lucy and came over, giving the boy an assessing look. Lucy followed.

"If we can stop with the accusations," said Lucy with a glance at Abigail. "I'll take the two of you back with me. But first I have to give your brother the compound information," she added, addressing Gary.

"Mom! Abigail and Gary can go. Stay here with me," Julien pleaded.

"I can't. I need to keep my promise to Lucas," she said, looking down at him. "You'd want me to keep my promise, right?"

"Yes. But then let me come with you," said Julien.

"It's safer for you here," Lucy said, squatting in front of Julien and resting her hands on his shoulders. "Margo found the information that Dr. Holbrook can use to make you better. Isn't that what you want?"

"Yes, but…" The boy looked like he was about to burst into tears.

"Then be a thousand times brave," said Lucy, her tone gentle.

Gary watched Julien bite his lip to stop it from quivering. *Had he seen something?* Gary's bad feeling suddenly got worse.

"Well, what are you waiting for?" Abigail addressed Lucy in a rude tone. "Give Neil the info you got. We leave in one hour," she announced as if she was the one in charge. No one disputed her, so she turned and left the hangar.

Gary glanced at Julien. The boy was hugging his mom and sobbing. To give the pair privacy, Gary also turned, already focused on what supplies to bring to best help Margo.

———

Gary couldn't focus. He'd opened all the cupboards and drawers and stared at all the supplies with no idea what to bring with him. All he could see was that man in his mother's ward; how blank he'd been, and how quickly he'd resorted to self-harm.

Focus! There has to be something I can do to bring Margo back. With renewed vigour, he sorted through the supplies. A muscle in his neck spasmed, making his already knotted neck worse.

"I heard you are heading to the Centre Module," said Amanda, sticking her head into the medical supply room. "Neil told me that Margo did a consciousness projection and didn't come back. Sorry, Gary, I don't know what to say."

Amanda knew about the patients in his mother's ward. Neil would've told her. Rubbing his stiff neck, he turned to face his sister-in-law. "I have no idea what to do," he said.

Amanda leaned against the doorframe with a look of concern on her face.

Gary nodded. "And Julien is upset his mother's returning. That tells me it's not going to be straight forward."

Amanda nodded as if Gary had confirmed something for her. "That boy has some kind of psychic ability, doesn't he? He knew I was pregnant," said Amanda, dropping a hand to her still flat stomach.

"Something like that. I need to get going. We'll be leaving shortly." Gary said, turning back to the supplies. He selected drugs and bandages randomly, carefully stowing them in his bag.

"I made you this," she said, stepping into the room and holding out a wrapped sandwich. "It's just peanut butter and jam, but I know it's your favourite."

"Thanks." Gary took the sandwich and picked up his bag. He turned to leave, but Amanda stood in his way.

"I think you've fallen for her," she said.

"Uh…"

Amanda smiled. "Gary. That's a good thing. I think you two could make a go of it."

"Not likely," Gary said, forcing his way past her.

Amanda followed, keeping pace with him as he strode down the Loop towards the rover hangar. "Why ever not?"

Gary frowned. "She's just like Misty. She can't keep a promise."

"What promise?"

"Not to ever try consciousness projection," said Gary, although his tone implied, *isn't that obvious?*

"Gary, don't be ridiculous. If Margo broke a promise, she would've done it for good reason. Margo's nothing like Misty," argued Amanda in a cajoling tone.

"A promise is a promise. You break it; you destroy trust. And you're left with nothing."

At Gary's words, Amanda stopped and turned to him. "The Holbrook men are nothing if not stubborn."

Chapter Thirty-Eight

In a flash, the greenhouse melted away and Margo found herself standing—somewhere.

An unseen light source left her without a shadow. Beneath her feet, the ground was grey, but not rocky. This wasn't Thesan terrain. She turned, then looked up. The entire space—although she couldn't distinguish any walls or the ceiling, or even the floor—was the same uniform grey. It reminded her of the colour of the old Earthbound battleship her cadet class had toured when she'd been a recruit.

"Hello?"

Her voice echoed back to her in a way that defied every law of physics. *Where am I? Am I in danger?* Fear started to bubble up within her. She forced it down, knowing fear would annihilate logical thought. She'd been trained to maintain rational thought when faced with fear. She'd done it successfully in the past and she would do it again. Despite her resolve, her hands started to shake and her legs felt wobbly.

"Get a grip, Murphy."

She started walking, mostly to keep her knees from buckling.

But even though she was sure she was moving, her surroundings stayed exactly the same.

"Pink unicorn," she said, but nothing changed.

She focused on an image of her greenhouse in her head and tried to make the surroundings match the image. It had worked before, but this time there was only grey.

"What the..." She stopped as a terrifying thought popped into her head. "Hell!" *Is this what it's like to be within a lost mind?*

A shiver ran up her spine as if someone had her in a rifle scope's crosshairs. *Was someone watching her?* She slowly turned.

A closed freestanding door within a frame stood an arm's length behind her. The door was made of wood with triangular metal hinges and an ornate door knob. An engraved brass plaque on the door read *Plum*. The name rang a bell. She was certain she knew someone with that name. *Was it her name? Was she Margo Plum? No. she was Margo Murphy.* She wished she could remember, but she couldn't quite place it.

Reaching out with her left hand, she touched the door knob. It felt real. The metal was cool on her fingers. She looked behind her, hoping something had changed, but everything was still grey with no depth or distinction. She turned back to look at the door. *Plum. I know a Plum. Don't I?* After taking a breath, she turned the knob and pushed the door open. Keeping her hand on the knob, she stared into the room beyond.

It was a 1950s-era kitchen with cheery yellow walls and boasting what would have been the latest in modern appliances, their glossy, aqua finish complemented by the turquoise sparkle in the Formica countertops. The floor was tiled in black and white, with a sheen that suggested it had recently been waxed.

A kitchen table sat under the open window where the sheer gingham yellow-and-white curtains wafted in a gentle breeze. Four matching chairs flanked the table. The air smelled of a recently heated TV dinner combined with an acrid chemical cleaner of some kind.

The space felt familiar. Maybe her mind had re-created a

museum she'd visited once. Margo stepped into the room. As soon as she crossed the threshold, the door closed behind her. She turned and tried to open the door from the inside but, not surprisingly, it wouldn't budge. With a sigh, she turned to face the kitchen. At least it was an improvement on the void of grey. Margo stepped further into the room, running a fingertip along the metal rim on the edge of the counter.

"I was wondering when you'd arrive," said a woman with a faint British accent.

Margo jumped at the words and whirled around. A woman in her fifties now occupied one of the kitchen chairs. She sat at the table, a tumbler of amber liquid on ice at her elbow. The woman's attire clashed with the yellow and aqua kitchen. She wore an electric blue blazer over a lime green, full-skirted dress. Her dark hair, pulled back in a bun, was framed by the pale gingham curtains covering the window behind her. She watched Margo from behind a pair of red horn-rimmed glasses with rhinestone accents. As the woman brought her drink to her lips, Margo noticed her nails matched her glasses.

"I've been waiting for you," the woman said.

Margo finally recognized her. She was a younger version of the woman from Jim's film—Peggy Plum.

"Who are you?" she asked. She wasn't asking for the woman's name. She was asking *who* are you. Who was this woman who'd made a film in 1952 that addressed a woman who shared Margo's name? *None of this is a coincidence*, thought Margo. *And maybe I'm finally going to get some answers.*

She pulled out the chair across from Peggy and sat. *Considering the era, at least she isn't smoking like Nigel was.* Looking down, she saw an identical drink had appeared next to her hand. Margo looked at it for a moment, then lifted the tumbler and sniffed. This wasn't scotch. This was *good* scotch. She took a sip. *Very good scotch.*

"My name is Penelope Plum," the woman said, dragging

Margo's attention away from the pleasure of her unexpected and indulgent drink. "You can call me Peggy."

Margo remembered then what Julien had said. He'd told her she needed to go to Peggy's kitchen, and now here she was.

"Are you an AI?"

Peggy cocked her head, contemplating her response. "Now, that's a difficult question to answer." She took a sip from her glass. "Let's table it. What I am now doesn't matter as much as you think it does."

Margo frowned. "In the video you made in 1952, you looked to be in your nineties."

"Actually, I was 81," said Peggy with an edge to her voice.

"No offence." Margo took another sip of her scotch. *Penelope Plum was a formidable woman.*

"Anyway, I can look how I like here." Peggy glanced around the space, gesturing gracefully with her manicured hand. "I always liked this era, full of hopes of modernity, from space flight to pre-made food. Plus, the fashion was more comfortable than the restrictive corsets of my youth."

"Are we in your head?" Margo had never had much interest in fashion.

"Perhaps, although I'm not entirely certain. My current working theory is there are pockets of space between interconnected networks that can be manipulated if you know they're there." The woman across the table gestured around. "Leaving places like this in the minds of our machines for people like you and me to fill."

Margo frowned. Peggy's theory was difficult to envision. "Like a virtual reality?"

"Something like that. But philosophizing our existence is not why I've invited you to join me here. We have more important matters to discuss." Peggy stood and walked over to the window and flung open the curtains. "I think it's best I start at the beginning. Take a look."

Margo stood, feeling a bit more relaxed with Peggy around.

The virtual scotch might also have helped soothe her, put her in a mind-frame where she could digest these circumstances and this conversation. *Had that been Peggy's intention when she'd made the scotch appear?* Regardless, Margo felt a renewed sense of hope. Maybe she would get back to herself—

She moved to the window and looked out. "Well, that's not what I was expecting."

They were above a busy street, perhaps the second or third story. Outside was a view of late Victorian London, complete with ornate cast-iron lamp posts, horse-drawn carriages and cobble streets. The top of Big Ben in front of a starry sky rose above the buildings, making the location obvious. The people on the street fit the era of the view as well. Upper-class men dressed in dark suits and top hats strutted along while other classes wore all manner of working clothes and caps. The few women in view wore floor-length gowns, the upper-class women with cinched-in waistlines and elaborate hats, the other women in aprons and heavy boots. Horses pulled all the vehicles in view.

"It all started here. I was a real person once," said Peggy with an edge of remorse in her voice.

So... she is an AI? Margo wondered.

They stood at the window without moving, yet somehow Peggy propelled them as if in a vehicle of some kind. They progressed down the street past pedestrians and around corners until they were in a wealthy neighbourhood. The view stopped moving when Margo and Peggy stood before a Georgian style home, complete with pillars and a waiting footman.

"This was my home." Peggy turned to Margo and smiled. "I was so young back then, naïve and way too trusting."

Margo looked back at the house. A light came on in one of the first-floor windows.

"My husband was a member of a secret society created in the middle ages to study an artifact Vikings found on an uncharted northern island."

When Peggy let the curtains drop, Margo realized they

were back in the kitchen. She turned to the table and saw a cube sitting in the middle of the table. It was the size of a hand-held puzzle cube where the goal was to turn the sliding squares until each side was a solid colour. But, this cube didn't look like a toy. On top of sides the colour of the inside of an oyster shell was elaborate scroll work fabricated out of silver. The designs made her vision wobbly until she realized that they became still when she looked directly at them, but as soon as she turned her head she could see them moving in her peripheral vision.

She reached to touch the cube. As her fingers got close, she paused and looked at her bare arm. The hair on her forearm stood on end. Before her fingers made contact with the cube, Peggy batted her hand away.

"You can't touch it with your bare hands," she warned.

"None of this is real; so, what's the risk?"

The cube vanished.

"You're right, this is all just a construct. Out there somewhere is the real cube. But let me warn you," Peggy said in a scolding tone accompanied by her wagging index finger. "Touching the real thing will burn out your mind. It will leave you worse off than if you'd been lobotomized."

"What is it?" Margo took the same seat she'd used before. Peggy also resumed her seat.

"No one really knows."

"Okay," said Margo. "I must be asking the wrong questions. Try this one. What does this artifact have to do with me?" She picked up her drink and swirled the ice around. She'd had a few sips already, but the level of liquid in the glass hadn't diminished. *Now that was a neat trick. If only her drinks at home would do the same thing.* Her thoughts jumped to returning home. Standing, she looked at the door—it was still there. She turned to address Peggy. "I don't have time for this puzzle. I need to find my way home. People are waiting for me."

"The window to your home has closed," Peggy said.

Margo's mouth went dry. She'd lingered too long. *But it wasn't her fault! She'd tried and tried to break free and get home.*

"Over time, your consciousness will degrade and you'll fade away like corsets and gas lamps."

"But you haven't degraded. You haven't faded away. Wait! Or have you? And this," Margo gestured at the construct of the woman, "is all that's left of you."

Peggy looked troubled, but only for a moment. "I'm here in a different way. But others, like you? They can't last."

"How much time do I have?" Margo felt the knot in her gut return in full force.

"Days or weeks. It's different for everyone," said Peggy. "But, we can get you home before it's too late."

"We can? You'll help me? What do we need to do?"

"You'll need to reopen the window," said Peggy, as though it was the easiest thing in the world to do.

"How do I do that?"

"First you need to listen to my story about the cube." She raised a hand when Margo started to protest. "It will help you, I promise. Then I'll point you in the right direction so that you can re-open the wormhole."

"I can't open a wormhole. Don't you need to be a physicist to do something like that?" At Peggy's impatient look over the top rim of her glasses, Margo resumed her seat. "Okay, we'll do it your way. How can knowing about the cube help me?"

"It is one of only two alien artifacts ever found. Well, there potentially was a third, but it was never recovered, so we can't be sure."

"Alien artifacts?" Margo felt her eyes widening. Even Jim's notebooks, which were full of conspiracies, hadn't hinted at an alien cover-up. "You mean, you believe in intelligent alien life forms?"

"Of course." Peggy took a sip of her scotch.

"Okay. What's the second artifact?" asked Margo, leaning back in her chair and cocking her head.

"The wormhole."

Margo held Peggy's enigmatic gaze for a long moment as her thoughts raced. That actually—maybe—made sense. "I remember when it was discovered. The scientists interviewed said the wormhole was a natural phenomenon that had likely been there as long as Earth, but they didn't share the fact that it only went to one solar system," said Margo. "*That* I only found out recently."

"Yes, 'a natural phenomenon' was the official version," said Peggy. "But anyone who has ever studied or touched the cube knows different. That wormhole was made."

"By whom?"

"The visions that the cube generates have never revealed who the aliens are."

"Maybe they're long gone?" said Margo, hoping that meeting aliens was not on the agenda.

"Maybe."

Silence fell between them and both women took sips of their drinks. Margo tried to work out what this revelation meant, and why Peggy had insisted on sharing it with her, and what her next question should be.

"Does the cube control the wormhole?" asked Margo.

"No; however, The Conglomerate's scientists figured out how to open and close the wormhole—likely from a cube-inducing vision."

"The cube is a communications device?" Margo was grasping for ideas. She looked to the door with longing. *How was this talk of the cube helping to get her home?*

As though reading Margo's mind, Peggy rose and said, "Come with me." She walked to the kitchen door and held it open, gesturing for Margo to precede her.

Chapter Thirty-Nine

Margo went through the door first and her gaze was immediately drawn upwards. The quaint, mid-century modern kitchen had now given way to a Victorian entrance hall that could only exist in a mansion. The three story foyer was capped by a stained glass dome, its coloured pieces depicting a battle scene of knights laying siege to a castle. The sunlight beyond shone through, casting prisms of coloured light throughout the vast space. Below the dome, a majestic staircase wound its way to the two stories above. Margo dropped her gaze and saw that the walls were panelled in dark wood and jewel-toned oriental rugs covered the floors, giving the space a masculine feel.

The only disturbing element of what should have been a beautiful foyer was the décor. A wide variety of stuffed animals —both full-sized creatures and single heads—lined the walls. Beasts ranging from okapi and wolverines to a full mount of a panther stalking its prey surrounded her.

"What is this place? Who lives…" Margo's words trailed off when she looked at Peggy.

Peggy had morphed into an elegant Victorian lady, complete with a magnificent hat sporting a flourish of iridescent feathers that seemed to wave at Margo in delight. Her dress was a beautiful burgundy—a colour Margo disliked because she could never have worn it with her red hair—and accented with brown and ivory velvet buttons and ribbons that brought out the tones of her rich brown hair. Peggy's wrinkles were gone, her youthful face an enviable peaches and cream complexion. She couldn't have been older than her mid-twenties.

"My husband loved to collect unique animals," this young version of Peggy said, walking over to a mount of a snow leopard. Her elaborate silk gown rustled as she moved. "I was more a part of his collection than his companion. There was almost thirty years between us, you see. Come, Eugene is just about to explain. This way."

Margo followed Peggy into a side room that was just like the room Nigel had dragged her into, except this one had a door and tall windows covered in long velvet drapes. Even the snarling tiger head was perched over the mantle. Nigel had clearly drawn his inspiration from this space.

A group of men wearing frock coats and holding lit pipes, most in somber grey shades, sat on the chairs arranged near the roaring fire. Margo recognized their faces from the oil paintings in Nigel's version of this study.

None of the men seemed to see Margo or Peggy, it was as though the pair weren't there.

"That one is the first Nigel West." Despite the men being unaware of them, Peggy whispered into Margo's ear as she pointed to the man seated in the centre chair. The man looked identical to the Nigel she'd just fought. In nearly three hundred years, the genetic line hadn't deviated far.

This Nigel West had the same flair for dramatic dress as his descendant. His waistcoat was silver brocade and topped with a scarlet ascot. He was by far the showiest man in the room.

"Good evening gentlemen," said a pudgy, middle-aged man standing near the fireplace, pipe in hand. His brown clothing was rumpled, and the white cuffs of his shirt were stained with spots of ink. What little was left of his grey hair had been combed over his balding scalp. But, his moustache was spectac-ular—complete with waxed tips curled into spirals. Near him was a pedestal table upon which was a plain wooden box.

"That's Eugene," Peggy whispered.

"What does this have to do—"

"Just watch and see," said Peggy, cutting Margo off.

"Gentlemen, we've always known from the records of the treasure's existence," said Eugene. "My latest expedition has finally recovered it. And, yes, it is everything the medieval scribes claimed,"

He leaned forward and opened the lid of the wooden box. Inside was the cube Margo had seen on Peggy's kitchen table. It seemed to glow in the flickering firelight.

"We know from the records not to let our skin come into contact with it. The first time I touched it with gloved hands, I saw a future filled with flying machines crisscrossing our sky, and more advanced versions heading to the moon." He spoke with passion, his arms waving in enthusiasm as he addressed the group, making eye contact with each of his trusted colleagues. "With this knowledge, we can position ourselves advantageously. Imagine knowing which side to back in a conflict, and which inventions will pay off, or even which governments will come to power. With this tool that sees into the future, we few can domi-nate and shape the future."

"But what exactly is it?" asked the original Nigel West, clearly enunciating his words.

"I need to study it further before I can give a definitive answer," said Eugene, moving to the mantle and retrieving a long match to relight his pipe.

Nigel, who sat closest to the table, leaned forward holding his large handkerchief in hand. He picked up the cube.

"No!" shouted Eugene. He dropped his pipe, embers scat-tering onto the rug as he leapt forward, snatching the cube from Nigel's grip. When Eugene's bare skin came in contact with the cube, he screamed. "Other worlds!" The cube fell from his grasp and hit the rug. "A pantheon of beings waiting for us!"

Eugene's pupils dilated as he foamed at mouth. Two of his colleagues—not Nigel West—sprang forward to assist him, but they could do nothing but catch him as he fell to the floor beside the cube. He lay twitching, eyes wide, mouthing soundless words.

"He lived like a vegetable for two more years, but never said another word," said Peggy into Margo's ear.

Margo saw that Peggy didn't seem overly upset about her husband's horrendous fate. *At least he hadn't clawed out his own eyes.*

"We need to call for a doctor," said one of the men crouching beside Eugene.

"Not yet," said Nigel as he rose. Exhibiting no concern about his colleague's fate, Nigel used his handkerchief to pick up the cube and return it to the case. Once it was safely nestled inside, he closed the lid. His extravagant waistcoat reflected the fire's light, making him seem illuminated from within. "Both times I held it I saw the future. Eugene was right," Nigel said, turning to face the other men. "We need to be ready."

"Ready for what?" asked one of the men who'd remained seated.

"Ready to leverage our position and become masters of the known universe."

"Universe? What, does the cube make us immortal?" The man who looked at the box wore an expression of avarice.

"It makes us powerful."

Nigel's tone of voice became almost prophetic. Watching his impromptu speech made the hair on the back of Margo's neck rise.

"Starting now and for the future generations, our mission and the mission of our descendants will be to master science until we are gods, until we can create one of our lineage who can touch this miraculous device with bare hands and glean the cube's full knowledge. Then we will become masters of thaumaturgy, performing what others will see as miracles. Until that day, when our descendent can serve us in this manner, we must use our influence to gain power and thus be ready to act when the time comes. This I have seen."

Nigel took fastidious care to fold his handkerchief after he'd completed his impromptu speech, meeting the gaze of each of the gathered men as he tucked it into his pocked. He flicked a gaze towards the fallen Eugene.

"Now get that doctor," said Nigel, an edge of disgust to his voice.

Peggy led Margo out of the room and back into the hall. For Margo, the change of location brought an immediate sense of relief.

"When the doctor arrived, I took a moment in the chaos to touch the cube," said Peggy. Margo raised an eyebrow. "With a gloved hand, of course—I am not an imbecile."

"Why show me this?" Margo looked back at the closed study door.

"Because this is where it began," said Peggy, leading Margo back to the door they'd used to enter the hall.

"Where what began?"

"The Conglomerate's grab for power."

"What does that have to do with me?"

"When I touched the cube, it showed me The Conglomerate ends on Thesan. I've been waiting a lot of years for a group of colonists to move to Thesan. The time has finally come."

Peggy opened the door and Margo saw that it led back to her kitchen. As she stepped through, her form changed to her original middle-aged version.

Peggy turned and looked Margo in the eye, the rhinestones on her glasses glinting like Nigel's waistcoat. "I need to come with you back to Thesan."

"How? What can you do on Thesan?" asked Margo as a shiver ran up her spine.

"First, I can dig The Conglomerate's AI out of your system. Beyond that we'll have to play it by ear."

Is Peggy Plum the solution to our Peg AI issues? Or would this enigmatic woman just create new problems? Why had she been so responsible—so foolish—as to talk Lucas out of coming here? He would know what decision was right. Up till now, Margo's support of Lucas as Commander of Thesan had been a courtesy. But she realized then that she believed in his ability to lead. *That was interesting.*

"Fine, come to Thesan." Margo hoped she was making the right choice. "Since my consciousness is degrading by the minute, can you send me back now?"

"Your generation's Nigel has been naughty, you know," said Peggy. "Over the last couple of years, he's been putting computer chips in all his employees' heads."

"So?"

"You need to take over the body of one of his minions on Maximillian Station, and use that borrowed body's access to open the wormhole."

"Maximillian Station? I've heard of that place." Jim and Bonnie had tried and failed to get the medical experts there to help save their daughter. "You make that sound simple. We both know it won't be." Margo crossed her arms and glared at Peggy.

"Cool it. Do you want your consciousness to continue to degrade? Now, close your eyes and I'll guide you."

"Shouldn't I sit down?"

"You can if you like. But need I remind you, your corporeal form is not here."

"Right, okay. Eyes closed." Margo closed her eyes. The last words she heard were Peggy saying, *trust me.*

Chapter Forty

In the rover cockpit, Gary put his medical bag down behind his seat, keeping the sandwich from Amanda in his hand. Abigail, who'd sealed the rover door behind him and then followed him into the cab, was, for once, quiet. She took the seat behind Lucy while he settled into the front seat. He wasn't thrilled to be going outside the safety of the colony, but at least this time he didn't have to wear a confining atmo suit.

Without a word, Lucy started the vehicle up while the hangar cycled air. After the light turned green, the outside door opened, exposing an orange-hued landscape lit by Sol.

"Control, we're ready to go," said Lucy.

"Have a good trip," replied the voice from the Control Room. *Iva maybe?* Gary couldn't tell.

Lucy drove the rover out of the hanger and onto Thesan's frozen mud, following the indistinct tracks from her previous trips.

Gary kept his eyes on the horizon without seeing it. An image of the patient in his mother's ward replayed like a corrupt video loop in his mind. The man's eyes had been so unnervingly blank, and he'd been eerily nonchalant as he inflicted devastating wounds to himself. The passing landscape remained blurred as his thoughts drifted to Margo and how her fate needed to be different from that man's. There had to be something he could do to bring her back. But anger welled up inside him as he tried to think through medical options.

Margo had seemed so different from his ex-wife. He'd actually started to believe that something was growing between them, something beyond friendship. After all, they were officially married. Over the last while, he'd found himself imagining what it would be like to kiss Margo, to see her naked, to find out if those freckles extended beyond her arms and face.

He had been wrong—deep down Margo was the same as his ex-wife. In the end, both women had betrayed him.

Margo had promised not to project her consciousness—once made, a promise had to be kept. He'd been clear it was an experimental technology. He'd described the devastating and irreparable outcomes—yet she'd done it, anyway. *Why?*

When Lucy spoke, he was grateful for the distraction.

"We're coming up on the canyons," announced Lucy. "My theory is, they're formed by a mechanism similar to plate tectonics."

"So? What does that mean?" Gary asked.

"It's possible that this naturally shifting mechanism releases oxygen."

Gary looked at the approaching pinnacles of rock, surprised Lucy was offering up random information.

"What a load of crap," Abigail scoffed from behind him. "Plate tectonics can't be responsible for oxygen generation."

"Yes, they—"

"I don't give a shit about your pet theories," said Abigail. "I'm perfectly capable of doing my own analyses."

Oh, boy. Here we go again, thought Gary.

"You've proven the oxygen isn't biological in origin, so perhaps a geological mechanism is," said Lucy.

"Just zip it." Abigail's tone was dismissive as though she was looking for a fight.

Gary rubbed his temple, feeling a headache coming on. The two hard-headed women he was trapped with weren't making things easier.

"Like it or not, I'm part of this colony now," said Lucy.

"Yeah, until I put you out an airlock——"

"Enough," cut in Gary. "Stop bickering."

With an annoyed sound, Abigail unbuckled herself and disappeared into the aft module, shutting the door and leaving Gary alone with Lucy.

He took a deep breath. "Why didn't you volunteer to go? You're Conglomerate. You're more familiar with the procedure."

Lucy laughed. "No one here trusts me."

"Well, why did she do it?" he asked.

"My access codes had already been blocked when I tried to hack into The Conglomerate. Plus, the Peg AI in the insurgents' lunar hideout had already prepared for a consciousness transfer. With a hacker standing by ready to help, Lucas wanted to warn the insurgents about the upcoming attack. He's got a friend there, I guess."

"The AI was already ready for someone to go? That sound's rather suspicious to me," said Gary and Lucy shrugged. He took a deep breath then asked, "then why didn't Lucas go?"

"Because he couldn't trust Margo not to kill me."

Gary gave her a pained look.

"Margo argued that the colony was too fragile to recover if their third Commander in as many months didn't come back from this. Apparently, no one's been assigned the enviable position of fourth in command. Lucas argued with her, but you know Margo. She got it in her head that she needed to go—and you know how hard-headed she is. Lucas didn't have a chance."

Gary looked back out at the passing landscape. He felt Lucy's gaze on him each time she could take her eyes off the rough terrain.

"Just say it," Lucy stated.

"Fine," he said, echoing her. "You hate Margo."

"She hates me."

Gary gritted his teeth. "You and Margo hate each other. That's no secret. Did you arrange for this to happen to Margo?"

"I did not. But you don't believe me, do you?"

Gary gave a noncommittal shrug.

"Look, as long as you agree to help Julien, keep him safe and try your best to make him well, I will do nothing to harm anyone on this colony. Margo included."

Gary pursed his lips and looked out the window, uncertain whether he could believe her. He noticed that the terrain outside the rover was getting rougher. Even at the crawl Lucy was driving at, the tires were bouncing over rocks, making the entire vehicle sway in alarming angles. Gary wondered if he should put his atmo suit on. *If there was a problem with the rover who would rescue them?* He swallowed and tried to distract himself by going over in his mind what he could do for Margo once he arrived.

Again, his mind was hijacked by thoughts of broken promises—this time from his ex-wife Misty. Since the day he'd met her, Misty had claimed she shared his dream of having children. Two years after the wedding, she finally got pregnant. Briefly, he'd thought the pregnancy would bring them closer together while at the same time he hoped the rumours she'd been seeing that Formula E driver had just been rumours. Even though he'd seen the two of them together shortly before at the opera, he briefly hoped Misty and he could form a real family.

Six weeks later, there was a message waiting for him when he got off shift at the hospital. It was from Misty's best friend Janice. When he hit play, Janice's face appeared on the screen, her expression nervous.

"Misty lost the baby," Janice said in her nasal voice. "She's going to stay with me for a while. Don't come here, she doesn't want to see you."

Before the message ended, Gary was already heading out

the door. When he arrived at Janice's apartment block, the building AI wouldn't even let him call the suite. He had to follow an elderly lady through the door to get in. Only after he banged on Janice's door relentlessly did she open it.

The look in her eyes told him everything—Misty wasn't there, and she'd conned Janice into lying to him.

"Where is she?" he demanded stepping towards Janice.

Janice moved back from him, visibly shaking. "She said you wouldn't care," she said.

"Care about what?"

"The abortion."

That moment kept replaying in his mind. The moment he found out she'd deliberately ended her pregnancy. The moment his relationship to Misty officially came to an end. *Misty lied to me all along!* Anger seethed within as he compared Misty to Margo.

Gary was drawn back to the present when Lucy brought the rover to a stop. He hadn't even noticed they'd arrived at the layer-cake like Centre Module. Lucy had parked them near the main airlock.

"You should have warned me as we were approaching. I could've had my atmo suit on by now," said Gary, unbuckling his seatbelt and standing.

"Nah, there's enough oxygen here," said Lucy, moving ahead of him into the aft section.

"There's more to worry about than just oxygen," said Gary. "We can't just go outside; there could be all sorts of toxic compounds in the air." He was horrified by Lucy's casual atti-tude towards the alien environment. *Was this a ploy of hers?* Still holding the un-eaten sandwich, he grabbed his medical bag before following her into the aft section of the rover.

Abigail had her hand on the door handle and was just about to open the outside door. "Wait!" Both women turned to look at him. "Safety procedures dictate we wear suits when outside." Even to his own ears he sounded like a pompous ass.

"Whatever," said Abigail, sliding open the outside door.

The cold air hit Gary and for a moment, he thought he was going to suffocate. He pictured exotic particles lodging themselves in his lungs and filling his bloodstream with toxins, and radiation causing his organs to mutate. He held his breath as he looked out the open airlock. Abigail and Lucy were already striding across Thesan's rocky landscape—no frozen mud, he noticed belatedly—and heading to the Centre Module's airlock door.

"I guess it's too late," he said to himself and stepped out into the open air, closing the door behind him.

Outside it was cold, too cold to linger without proper clothing. He took shallow breaths as he walked briskly towards the airlock. He was right behind Abigail when she opened the inside door. Lucas stood waiting for them on the other side. His black hair disheveled and sticking out in all directions.

"Good, you're here," he said to Gary, ignoring Abigail and Lucy. "She still hasn't woken up. I don't know what to do."

"Where is she?" asked Gary, looking around the space. He frowned when he saw the glowing tubes of oxygenating algae that hung suspended from the ceiling two stories up. They looked fragile, like they could fall on them at any moment.

"Follow me."

Realizing his relationship paranoia was increasing because of his agitation and worry, Gary followed Lucas into the cramped medical alcove. He stopped at the door when he saw Margo. She lay on her back under a blanket on the narrow examination table, her red hair splayed across the green vinyl pillow. In repose, her oval face looked angelic and beautiful, the birthmark on the side of her neck like a butterfly caught in flight. He swallowed and walked over to inspect the medical readouts on the monitors.

"She managed to get info on some compounds to help Julien," said Lucas as he leaned against the wall.

"I know. Neil is working on them." Gary kept his answers short. He knew Lucas was feeling particularly bad about

Margo's condition. Not just because he was the Commander of their colony, but because he'd had the opportunity to go in Margo's place and hadn't. Gary was angry with Margo, but he was also angry with Lucas.

"I just hoped she managed to warn the insurgents hiding on the moon."

Gary leaned over Margo and lifted one of Margo's eyelids "Do we care about insurgents?" Gary's tone indicated there was only one right answer, his eyes still focused on Margo.

"I do. Lucy said they were about to be attacked and I have a friend there," said Lucas, looking guilty.

"Then you should have gone!"

"I know," replied Lucas, in a muted tone. "How do you think I feel about all this?" He gave a futile gesture towards Margo's immovable form.

"Lousy I hope," Gary muttered. He knew he was being rude, but he was angry. Angry at Lucas. Angry at Lucy. Angry at Margo. *This wouldn't be happening if she hadn't broken her promise!* He directed his next question to the AI. "Peg, has the comms window definitely closed?" Gary asked, removing a pin-light from his medical bag.

"Affirmative," said Peg. "However, there is a chance she'll be able to open it again."

"What?" asked Lucas. "Who? Margo? How?"

Gary opened one of Margo's eyes, shining the light directly into her eye. Margo's dilated pupils didn't constrict.

"Peggy will show her how."

"Peggy? You mean the other Peg AI?" asked Lucas

Gary paused briefly. *The AI couldn't be referring to Peggy Plum, the Peg AI innovator, who'd died in the 20th century?* He shook his head. *A strange coincidence, though, to hear the name 'Peggy'.*

"Bloody virus," Lucas muttered.

Gary glanced at Lucas. "Here too?"

Gary turned back to Margo to check her other eye. No response. He sighed in frustration.

"I didn't think so. But now… *Peggy*? Who the hell is Peggy?"

"She is the whole," said the AI.

"What does that mean?" asked Lucas, looking up at the speaker in the wall as if that would illuminate things for him.

"Peggy is more than any of the Peg pieces. She is powerful enough to take on The Conglomerate AI," said Peg with a proud lilt to her manufactured voice.

Lucas gave up talking to Peg and gave his attention to Gary. "So? Can you wake her up?"

"I don't bloody know how to, Lucas!" Gary gestured at his medical bag. "I got all kinds of drugs in here, but I can't just randomly pump her full of drugs. She's not a guinea pig, and this isn't a research lab. Even if it was, it wouldn't be ethical." He glared at Lucas. "I can't believe you let her do this!"

"Someone needed to go. We can't trust Lucy, I couldn't leave Margo alone with Lucy."

"For Pete's sake, Lucas. Margo isn't a murderer and someone did *not* need to go! Can't you understand that? Your friend? The insurgents? They're not our problem. We've got enough to deal with." Gary looked down at Margo, worry etched on his face. "The only thing we can do now is wait, although I have no idea if time will show an improvement or make things worse."

"But you have to do something." Lucas insisted.

"Look," said Gary, feeling his nostrils flair as he whirled on Lucas. He stabbed his index finger at Lucas. "You chose to send her consciousness away using unproven technology over astronomical distances. Margo not waking up is your fault, not mine. This is not my field of expertise, and I don't know what to do, alright?"

Lucas threw up his hands and backed up. "Fine, it's my fault. But she insisted on going. You can ask her yourself if she wakes up."

"If?" Gary growled. "Lucas, just get out."

Chapter Forty-One

Margo's awareness of her surroundings came in a discombobu-lating jolt. She found herself laying on her back on a thin mattress in a narrow bunk covered with a stale smelling blanket. The fabric was rough against her skin as though it was regularly subjected to an industrial laundry process. She took a moment to orient herself, but needed far less time than the first time she'd done this and woken in Ash Jones's body.

She opened her eyes. Cycled to night-time levels, the inset ceiling lights gave off barely enough glow for her to make out her unfamiliar surroundings and confirm she was alone in the room.

"Lights," she said. Even though she'd expected to hear a different voice than her own, the deep, rough sound of the borrowed man's words were jarring. When Peggy had said she needed to go the Maximilian Station, Margo hadn't even considered the gender of her next 'host'. *What if I have to use the toilet?* With that horribly unpleasant thought, Margo flung off the blanket and sat up, swinging her legs over the bunk's edge and putting her bare feet onto the floor. With a quick glance down at her lower half, she saw she was wearing blue-striped pyjamas. *Thank you for not sleeping naked!*

The space was smaller than her university dorm room and didn't even have a window. She had no idea whose body Peggy had hijacked, but he certainly didn't have much status. *I don't need status. I just need access!*

That's right, said Peggy directly into her mind. *He's a security guard for the science division and he's already jacked into their internal system. He has access to the wormhole control room. Get me in there and I can open the wormhole.*

You're still in my head? asked Margo in her mind. She wanted to avoid using her voice.

Actually, we're both in this man's head.

I guess we would have to be, thought Margo. *Or I wouldn't be able to access his passwords. I'd hazard a guess this guy didn't agree to this?*

You surmise correctly.

When Margo stood up, she found she was a head taller than normal. The man had to be nearly two metres tall. *No wonder he was a security guard.* She breathed in deeply, then coughed. The sound was deep and unfamiliar. A step was all it took to get to the desk and chair in the corner. On it was her host's key card and picture ID, as well as half-eaten food and discarded food wrappings.

"Amar Yurkovich," she said aloud, the stranger's voice gravelly with sleep. A quick glance at the photo told her not to look in the mirror—she wouldn't like what she'd see.

Margo grabbed his grey uniform jacket and pants off the back of a chair. She closed her eyes as she shed the pyjamas. No way did she want to catch a glimpse of this undressed body. She tried not to brush against his bare skin as she dressed and was immeasurably relieved that he'd been wearing boxers and a tank shirt under the PJs. She dressed quickly, stepping into the pants and buttoning the waist which proved to be a struggle. *Were these not Amar's pants?*

He's been enjoying his rations.

That's putting it mildly, responded Margo. Once she had her arms in the jacket's sleeves, she opened her eyes. The buttons on the jacket were as tight as the waistband of the pants.

As she slipped on Amar's size ginormous boots, she scratched at the stubble on the man's face. *Should I shave?*

We need to get moving, said Peggy.

Checking to make sure she had Amar's key card and picture ID, she went over to the exit and pushed the button beside the door, which slid into its pocket without a sound. Poking her head and shoulders out, Margo looked both ways. The hallway was empty, so she stepped out and closed the door. The corridor had multiple other doors, presumably opening to rooms just like Amar's. On the outside of each door beside each biometric access panel was a display listing the occupant's name and if they were in. All the rooms she could see were occupied.

Okay, where do I go?

Go right, and head to the elevators, replied Peggy.

Margo turned and began walking, which in Amar's body felt more like lumbering. Her heart was pounding, although she wasn't certain if it was from fear and adrenaline, or lugging around a large body. After a dog-leg bend in the corridor, Margo stepped into a common area complete with neutral-toned couches, chairs, tables and walls. A sigh of relief escaped her lips when she saw the space was empty. She walked over to the elevator and pushed the call button. As she waited, she began to hum, then thought. *Amar must be a hummer.*

Annoying, said Peggy.

Margo stopped. A moment later, the elevator door opened and a bald man in an identical uniform stepped out.

"Amar! You're up early," he said in a friendly tone.

"Yup," said Margo, hoping the two of them weren't chatty friends. For a moment, the man looked about to say more, but Margo stepped into the elevator and the door closed behind her.

Where to? asked Margo, eyeing the rows of buttons.

Main concourse, said Peggy. Margo hit the button, and the elevator started to move.

A moment later when the doors opened she stepped into a different world. A scattering of uniformed people scurried in both directions along a wide concourse, occasionally making way for a cargo vehicle to zip past, lights flashing. The illuminated ceiling above shone with the equivalent intensity of Earth's sun at dawn. White walls were decorated with grey and black abstract murals whose pixilated images left Margo feeling strangely unsettled. The bright lights, white halls, weird murals, and the monochrome grey uniforms of the inhabitants made the space feel dangerous.

Turn right.

Margo complied, joining others heading in that direction. Unlike the man from the elevator, no one here tried to chat. Hanging from the ceiling at intervals were directional signs. So far, she'd seen directions to 'H431' and 'BE09.' When she saw a sign pointing to 'Medical Records', she abruptly turned in that direction, heading off the main concourse.

Where in the hell are you going? demanded Peggy. *Your only priority is to open the wormhole! You can't risk your consciousness degrading any further.*

If I find Julien's medical records, can you copy them? asked Margo. She walked through a set of double sliding doors as if she belonged there, finding herself in an expansive—and thankfully empty—waiting area, complete with utilitarian benches and an aquarium full of what might even have been real fish. Margo went behind the counter that separated the staff from the visitors and immediately saw a glass-walled room with rows and rows of memory drives.

Yes, of course I can copy them, but there is no time for this foolishness.

This won't take long, she said, hoping she was right.

Margo swiped the screen on the first workstation she came to. The computer came alive. It didn't even ask for a password. Whoever had used it last hadn't logged out. She glanced at the closed doors, afraid someone might discover her, then reminded herself it was the middle of the night. Even on research stations, office workers didn't pull night shifts. She typed in 'Julien Snow'. A cog spun on the centre of the screen as the machine conducted its search.

Margo could sense Peggy's irritation. An image of the woman looking disapprovingly at her over her horn-rimmed glasses popped into her mind, but she didn't care. She had one chance to get this info, and she was going to take it. She owed it to Gary for breaking her promise to him.

A moment later, the file came up and Margo opened it. She felt herself deflate she realized the text was encrypted. "Dirty circuits!" cursed Margo. She jumped at the sound of Amar's voice before realizing she'd cursed out loud.

You don't have to understand it. I'll record while you scroll through the boy's file, said Peggy. *I can decrypt it later.* Margo scrolled through, her fingers moving faster and faster. *Are you getting all of it?*

Yes, got it. Now, go! And no more deviations!

Closing the file, Margo clicked the keys until the monitor displayed the welcome screen.

Just as Margo rose and began making her way out from behind the counter, the doors to the waiting room slid open. Margo paused mid-stride as a diminutive woman with dark skin and black hair walked in. Despite the early hour, her hair was carefully arranged into a bun on the back of her head and her pale grey station uniform looked crisp. The woman was almost at the counter before she noticed she wasn't alone and stopped when she saw Margo—or rather, Amar. Margo saw that her nametag read 'Trudy Dasher'.

Here's trouble, said Peggy.

Huh? What do you mean?

Serves you right for coming in here, said Peggy.

Margo ignored Peggy and forced herself to appear relaxed. After all, she was security. She was about to launch into an explanation about how she'd been conducting a routine check, when the woman spoke.

"Amar?" the woman's tone was practically a purr as she put a hand on her hip. "What are you doing here?"

"Uh, I thought I'd surprise you." Margo almost winced at how gruff the words sounded.

The woman glanced at the door, then gave Margo a saucy grin. "You naughty boy," she said with approval.

Oh, shit! Margo thought when she realized what the woman meant. She could swear she heard Peggy giggle.

"I've told you before, Amar. My boss would throw me out an airlock if he caught me doing it here." The woman walked right up to Margo, clutching Amar's arm. The top of her head didn't come anywhere near to reaching Amar's shoulder.

I am not doing it with her! Margo practically screamed at Peggy as she resisted the urge to run. This time she really did hear a laugh.

"My first break is in two hours," the woman said softly, pressing her ample bosom against Margo's arm. "We can meet at our usual place."

"I'll be there," said Margo, aware that Amar wouldn't remember to show up for the date. A small part of her felt a bit bad about that.

The woman bit her lip and looked up at Margo's face. "Maybe you could do that thing…"

"Of course." *Peggy, you have to help me out here!* Margo tried to untangle herself from the woman, but Trudy clutched more tightly on Amar's arm.

"Hang on," the woman said, closing the distance between them once again. "Say my name, you big love machine. It makes me shiver all over to hear it roll off your lips."

Margo licked Amar's lips and swallowed. *Peggy! Help me!* In Amar's deep voice, she said, "Trudy," in as best a drawl as she could manage.

The woman practically squealed in delight. Now, get out of

here, my very own love machine." The woman finally let go of Amar's arm, but then grabbed Margo's, or rather Amar's, crotch. Margo froze as an unfamiliar jolt of sensations washed over her. "Can't wait for my break!" Trudy said in a sing-song voice. "Now, shoo."

Margo fled.

Chapter Forty-Two

Margo stopped in the corridor once she was safely outside of Medical Records, struggling to keep Amar's expression neutral.

I told you not to go in there, said Peggy. She sounded amused.

You haven't exactly been helpful, said Margo as she resumed walking in the direction she'd been heading before.

You handled that marvellously.

Margo had previously thought Peggy's British accent pleasing. Now it was annoying. *If anyone handled anything, it's that woman! I'm never doing consciousness projection again, I'll tell you that much.*

Margo rubbed her face only to be greeted with a rough chin of stubble. *I want back in my own body with no one in my head.*

Where are we going? asked Margo as she continued down the corridor, passing numerous directional signs for various medical centres and genetics labs. She remembered seeing station schematics in Jim's notebooks, not that his drawing helped her now. She was completely lost.

Down here, to your right, said Peggy.

Margo turned and walked towards a double set of closed

glass doors, but then stopped when she realized there was not a single sign that announced the purpose of this wing.

This doesn't look like a door just anyone can go through, said Margo, trying to look inconspicuous as others in the corridor passed around her. She walked slowly towards the doors, wondering if her card would provide access, but they opened as she approached. *I guess Amar is coded for access.*

I picked your host for a reason, Peggy said. *He is part of the security detail.*

As the doors shut behind her, Margo tried to move as though she belonged there. The place appeared deserted as she walked past closed doors, each printed with a number but no additional marking to indicate what was inside.

You want room 119B.

The corridor curved, its rubberized floor masking the sound of Amar's footfalls. The generic whiteness of everything reminded her of a horror vid she'd seen once where the protagonist got trapped in an infinite hallway.

I hate this place, she said, counting down the door numbers.

Finally Margo came to the right door and saw that it required handprint verification to open. She looked at the biometric panel and swallowed. *Does Amar's access extend this far? Will an alarm sound if I let Amar's hand be scanned, and he isn't authorized?*

Oh, just get on with it, said Peggy in an irritated tone.

Not for the first time, Margo wished Peggy had a corporeal form so she could scowl at her. She lifted Amar's meaty palm and put it on the panel. A red light scanned the hand, then a spinning icon appeared on the screen.

Is that good or bad? asked Margo, watching the icon. It felt like the computer was taking too long, making her wonder if it was alerting security of an unauthorized attempt to gain access. She was just about to turn and leave when the door slid open.

See? Your worrying was pointless.

Ignoring Peggy, Margo strode through the open door like

she was meant to be there, seeing that it was a small control room with a series of screens inset into the walls, each displaying a view of space overlaid with diagrams and sensor readings in white text. At first glance the wall of screens looked as abstract as the murals lining the main concourse. A series of empty workstations faced the screens—empty except for a man at the end.

You're going to need to make him open the wormhole.

"Hey, you're not supposed to be here," the man said, standing from his workstation. He was almost as tall as Amar, but not nearly as hefty. "Next security check isn't for another hour. And aren't you on the day shift?"

"I got asked to switch shifts," said Margo

The man looked astonished, then suspicious. "Security isn't allowed to switch shifts. I'm calling your boss."

As he turned back to his workstation and activated the comms panel, Margo lunged at him. She easily caught his arm and pulled him away from the controls, surprised at Amar's strength.

"I need you to open the wormhole," she said, the words coming out sounding gruff and laced with threat.

"Tsk, tsk, tsk." A face popped up in one of the screens beside the door. Margo froze at the sight of Nigel West's face. Feeling Amar's hold on him slacken, the man twisted out of Amar's grasp and darted out of the room.

It is just the Nigel II AI, said Peggy. *Ignore him and start working the controls.*

"What a bad girl you are," the AI said.

Margo ignored the Nigel and sank into the chair the other man had vacated. Focusing at the screen he'd been working on, she let Peggy read the code through Amar's eyes. A moment later, Nigel II's face appeared on the screen instead.

"Bad girl!" he said, his face breaking into a grin. "I like you, Margo. I think I'll trap you in here with me. We can have some fun. But you, Peggy." When Margo blinked in astonishment, the

Nigel AI laughed. "Yes, I know you're in there, too. I'll play with Margo, but you, Peggy? You I intend to delete."

What a vile man! He might know I'm here, but he can't hear me. I'll create a distraction while you open the wormhole.

Margo felt the sudden absence of Peggy from her head, and in the next moment saw Peggy's face popping up on the other screens and looking like an angry headmistress, horned-rimmed glasses and all.

"Nigel, you've been a naughty boy," she said, looking out of the screen over her glasses.

The Nigel face on the screen in front of Margo turned to look over its shoulder with a grin. "You're in my system now! I'm finally going to put an end to your meddling." Then Nigel looked back at Margo. "I'll be back for you later." The face vanished and the wormhole control scripts re-appeared.

When an alarm sounded in the hallway outside, Margo felt a wave of panic. She'd almost run out of time and still hadn't figured out how to open the wormhole. Both Nigel II and Peggy's faces had disappeared from the other screens. Margo focused on the screen in front of her. *How do I access Amar's brain?* Numeric values were listed at different locations around the space view, but none of the data meant anything to her. Out of ideas, she decided to try the obvious. "Open wormhole."

The numbers started changing and a line drawing appeared superimposed across the screen. The white lines flashed to green and the mesh sphere at the centre started expanding. A banner appeared along the bottom with the words 'wormhole engaged.' Margo sat back, stunned her voice command had worked.

Without warning, three security people barged through the door. Margo leapt to her feet as the first one lunged at her. She clocked him in the jaw with an uppercut and he fell to the floor. The other two security guards jumped over him to make a grab for Margo.

When Margo swept her leg out to kick the nearest one she fell over backwards. She could feel her hamstring seizing up as she realized Amar didn't have her flexibility. Before she could get up off the floor, the two guards were on her.

She punched the nearest guy in the ear, hard. He groaned and went slack, allowing her to use her considerable upper body strength to shove the other guy off of her. A quick look at the screen and she saw a countdown from 30 had started. Thirty seconds until the wormhole opened. *Then what?*

The third guard scrambled towards her and grabbed her leg. His grip was tight, but her strength was superior and she easily shook him off, then kicked him in the gut.

"Peggy?" she shouted, her deep voice booming in the small room. *As soon as the wormhole opened would her consciousness return to her body?* "Peggy?"

The guard she'd slugged in the ear had recovered enough to grab her again. This time she picked him up by the shoulder epaulets of his uniform jacket, then threw him on top of the other two guards. She looked at the pile of guards on the floor. None of them were making any effort to get back up. *Wow! There's been a time or ten that this strength would've come in handy as Margo!*

The alarm was still sounding in the corridor. More guards were likely on their way.

Peggy? she called in her mind. She looked at the screens, but no faces appeared. "Crap," she cursed out loud, before bolting for the door, leaving the moaning guards behind.

At a sprint in feet that gave new meaning to 'clodhopper', she took off down the hall back towards the main concourse, expecting more guards to pile on her at any moment. *Sorry for wrecking your life, Amar.* She knew he would never hear her apologize or explain any of this, and for that she felt bad.

Once on the main concourse, she slowed down to a fast walk, working hard to slow her breathing. Sweat dripped down her forehead and she could feel it dripping down her back. Amar was a prolific—and unpleasant—sweater. She saw an alcove on her right containing banks of elevators with half-a-dozen people waiting for a ride. Perhaps it was best to get off this floor.

The elevator at the far left opened, and she stepped inside with the waiting crowd, wishing now that she weren't so large and tall and could blend in better. Just as the doors closed she saw a squad of security personnel rush into the alcove. When the people in the elevator with her moved away from her, she realized she was panting heavily. *So much for blending in.*

Peggy, where are you? There was no reply.

The door opened and Margo pushed out ahead of everyone. It might kill Amar, but the urge to sprint away and find a place to hide was too great. Before she got two paces out of the elevator, she skidded to a halt. In front of her stood the real-life Nigel, backed up with a line of security guards pointing stun guns at her.

"My dear, you are proving to be nothing but trouble," Nigel said.

Margo noticed the odd way some of the security detail looked at Nigel in response to addressing the large, sweating, panting Amar as 'my dear'.

"I'm just trying to get home," said Margo, her words sounding strange in a man's voice. Eyeing the line of guards, she wondered if she could push her way through before one stunned her. *Or before Amar had a heart attack. Crap! The man was unfit!* Margo leaned forward, resting her hands on her knees as she tried to catch her breath and stop Amar's heart from leaping right out of his out-of-shape body.

"Leave poor Amar and let's head back to my study for a chat."

"Fine," said Margo. *As if she knew how to do that.*

Before she could ask, the world around Margo swirled, and she felt a falling sensation. Then she was back in the study with no exits, sitting in the same chair she'd been in before. She could feel the heat from the roaring fire. She looked up, and saw that the men in the portraits were scowling at her. Closing her eyes, she inhaled, taking in the scent of burning wood, musty furniture and stale pipe smoke. In that moment, these surroundings felt more real than her real world ever had, and she knew she had one last something she could try.

She slowly exhaled as she opened her eyes and looked at Nigel.

He sat in his same chair holding likely the same cut-crystal glass of amber liquid. Raising the glass to his lips, he took a long sip. He looked relaxed, smug even.

"Well, what shall we play next?" asked Nigel, cocking his head.

"Pink unicorn."

Chapter Forty-Three

Margo felt the sensation of falling and a wave of nausea went through her. As she gripped the edge of the hard surface, she realized she lay on a foam-covered table. Keeping her eyes closed, she let the nausea pass before forcing herself to breathe deeply and slowly.

When she opened her eyes, she saw she was in a small, dark room. Lights flickered from a row of equipment mounted on a wall. *The space felt familiar.* It wasn't any of the places she'd visited —Maximillian Station, Peggy's Kitchen, Nigel's study or Lunex-21. *So where am I this time?* Slowly turning her head, she looked around. Gary sat slumped in a chair beside her bed, his head propped up by the wall and his eyes closed. Margo realized where she was. *I made it back. This is the Centre Module's medbay.*

She was back in her own body. She closed her eyes, feeling her throat close and her eyes fill with tears. *I made it back!* Not only had she made it back, she had no inclination to claw out her eyes. *Maybe the risks of side-effects had been exaggerated.* She was herself. A soundless chuckle burbled deep within her. *I'm back.*

Smiling and feeling eager despite the lingering nausea, she moved the blanket aside and pushed herself up, swinging her legs—*her legs! Not Ash's powerful thighs or poor Amar's pudgy limbs, but her very own legs*—over the side of the examination table. She sat there for a moment with a happy grin on her face as she studied Gary. For the first time, she noticed a shadow of stubble on his chin. She wanted to reach over and touch him, but she also didn't want to wake him. He looked exhausted.

How long have I been gone? How long has he been at my bedside? Simply seeing him here made her happy. And after the weirdness of inhabiting other people's bodies it was beyond nice to see a familiar face. Her mind raced as she tried to sort out in her head the major apology she owed him for breaking her promise. The realization hit her again. *I'm back! And I'm never, ever doing anything like that ever again!* Just the thought of being in Amar's body made her shudder.

She cocked her head to the side when, from outside the closed door, she heard the sound of people arguing. She recognized Lucas's voice and Ms. Snow's.

"Welcome back, Margo," said the Peg AI.

"Thanks," said Margo, pushing her disheveled hair out of her face. "For a while there, I wasn't sure I'd ever make it back."

At the sound of her voice, Gary woke. He looked at her for a moment as if half expecting her to start clawing her eyes out, but then leapt to his feet. "Are you okay?" he asked, touching her hand briefly and then turning to look at the medical readouts.

"No!" Margo said with a grin, causing Gary to jerk his head around to look at her.

She grinned at him. "I'm better than okay. I'm me. I'm in my own body." She pressed her hands against her chest in glee. "And so glad to be back!"

"I'm glad you're back, too, Margo. You had us worried." He took a step away from her to read the data better. "But Margo—"

Margo cut him off. "Gary, I know what you're going to say,

and I'm so, so sorry for breaking my promise, but it was necessary. Did Lucas tell you?"

"Yes, he told me," Gary responded in a neutral tone. "Your readouts look fine. How do you feel?" he asked, looking at her. His expression was unreadable.

Margo took a moment to search for the right word to describe how she felt. "Honestly? Discombobulated," she answered, scratching her head. "And still a little nauseous and… well, fuzzy in the head. How long have I been away?"

"About 36 hours."

Margo looked around. "And we're still in the Centre Module. How did you get here?"

"Lucy came and got me."

Margo raised her eyebrows. "She did something useful, for once?"

Gary ignored her comment. When he moved to stand beside her and leaned against the examination table, she saw how tense he looked. His face seemed pinched, and she got a sense of what she'd put him through. His next words confirmed that.

"I wasn't sure you'd come back."

"Clearly you did something," said Margo, smiling at him. When he didn't return it, her smile faded, and she realized Gary was angry. *Well, she didn't blame him.* But she would definitely apologize more fulsomely later once she felt entirely herself again.

He shook his head. "I didn't do anything."

"Margo, you reopened the wormhole and said the safe phrase," said Peg.

"Ohhhh!" Margo said, drawing out her response. "Is that why the other times I said the safe phrase nothing happened? Because the wormhole had closed?"

"Yes."

The significance of Peg's statement finally sunk in as the previous few hours came flooding back to Margo. "Did Peggy send the files on Julien?"

"Yes," answered Peg. "And I was able to decrypt the second file."

"Neil has the first file, the ones with the compounds. He's with Julien back at the colony. I took a cursory look at the second file," said Gary. "It appears to contain full documentation of the project Julien was part of, including his medical records and the compounds needed to ensure his body doesn't shut down in response to his abnormal genetic condition."

"Is it going to be enough to make him better?"

"I think so," he said. "And I will go through everything in more detail when we get back." Gary moved to stand by the closed door. "We should tell the others you're back."

"Gary," said Margo, hopping off the table. Her legs still felt wobbly, but she ignored that as she approached him. "I didn't see any choice but to go. Lucas wanted to, but we can't risk our Commander. And we couldn't send Ms. Snow. So it had to be me."

He looked back at her, his gaze shuttered. "I know." Then he slid the panel back and stepped through.

Margo stood in the doorway for a moment, realizing that he was far more upset that she'd not kept her promise than she'd at first thought. Running a hand through her hair—*her wild, curly, glorious hair!*—she glanced up at the ceiling. The lights flickered, and she frowned momentarily. *The power wasn't compromised at the Centre Module, too, was it?* She bit her lip as her distracted thoughts brought her back to the dilemma of Gary.

Just when she was starting to like him and their friendship had begun developing into something she really valued, she'd gone and disappointed him. She didn't want their relationship to go back to the cold, arms-length distance they'd taken with each other for the first three months of their acquaintance. *How can I make things right with him?*

In the dim light of the room, she thought she saw movement in her peripheral vision, up by the ceiling. When she looked up, a butterfly was there, but it didn't make her smile.

This one was of the red ones she'd conjured up in her fight against Nigel. Then she noticed another and another. The insects seemed to be massing in the corner by the ceiling, flying in a circle.

"Peg, turn on the lights."

Bright lights flooded the medbay. Not a butterfly could be seen. *What the...?*

"Peg?" She asked with a frown.

"I'm here," replied the computerized voice.

"What happened to Peggy?"

There was a short hesitation as if Peg went searching for her in the AI system. "I do not know."

The lights flickered again.

"Peg, what's going on?" Margo remembered that the colony's lights had flickered the same way when the Nigel II AI started taking over. The AI didn't reply. "Peg?" Still nothing.

Raised voices from outside the medbay caught her attention. Margo stepped out of the medbay and nearly tripped on Gary. *Even though he was angry with her, he hadn't gone far. Maybe there was hope, then, that she could repair their fragile relationship.*

It was clear to Margo that he also hadn't told the others she'd awoken.

"Abigail, give me the gun," ordered Lucas.

In the centre of the space, Abigail pointed a pistol at Ms. Snow. Lucas was using his body to shield Ms. Snow. The vintage black weapon in Abigail's hand was their thwarted saboteur's pistol; the only gun on the planet. Abigail must have found Margo's hiding place.

"Dirty circuits," Margo whispered. That pistol had been safely stowed away in her insect stasis room. *Why did Abigail have it? And how on Earth had she even found it?*

"You did this!" shouted Abigail, trying to push past Lucas so she could fire at the woman who had mentored their saboteur.

Ms. Snow put her hands up and, wisely, stayed behind Lucas. "I didn't. I swear."

"What are they arguing about?" asked Margo, leaning towards Gary.

"Apparently, the same corruption that took down the AI at the colony has just shown up here," he replied not looking at her.

"How did it get here?"

"I'm more worried about someone getting shot," said Gary.

"I hid all the bullets in the ceiling panel of my lab's airlock," Margo said to Gary in a low tone. "Abigail may have found the gun, but there's no way she could have found the bullets. That gun isn't loaded," she added in a confident tone, shaking her head.

"Give that to me," said Lucas. Cat-like, he leapt forward and snatched the gun out of Abigail's hand.

Abigail put her hands on her hips and scowled at Lucas. "You can't let her get away with this! Not after all she's done."

The three people in the room hadn't yet noticed that Margo and Gary were standing less than 4 metres away taking all this in.

"I won't." He tucked the gun into the waist of his pants at the back. "But our first priority is to get rid of the virus. Lucy is our best bet to help us accomplish that." He looked at Ms. Snow. "Can you do that?"

"I can try, but I'm not promising anything." Ms. Snow, with a scowl towards Abigail, resumed her seat at the main console, and started scrolling through screens.

The lights flicked on and off.

"Dammit!" Lucas frowned and stepped forward, leaning over the keyboard at the workstation beside Lucy, his fingers flying. "Peg! Respond!" he ordered.

Ms. Snow suddenly sprang from her chair and snatched the pistol from Lucas, whirling to her right as she stepped behind him and swinging her arm like a scythe to slam the butt of the weapon into his nose.

"No!" Margo leapt forward, but Gary grabbed her arm,

holding her back from joining the melee. Had Margo been fully recovered and not still wobbly and weak, she could've fought him off. But Margo was more held in place by the chilling sound of Ms. Snow's laugh. The crackling sound of her voice sounded wrong, like it was being forced. *Like perhaps it didn't belong to her.* Margo felt a sinking sensation in her gut.

"Fucking hell, not again," Lucas muttered, putting a hand up to his bloody nose.

With a steady arm, Ms. Snow pointed the weapon at Abigail and fired, then frowned when the only sound it emitted was an empty click.

Margo finally freed herself from Gary's hold just after Ms. Snow threw the pistol at her and just before Abigail tackled Ms. Snow. Margo dodged the flying pistol, and it fell harmlessly to the floor, skittering away.

Moving impossibly fast, Ms. Snow turned with her assailant, using Abigail's weight and momentum against the larger woman. With a precisely aimed foot sweep and a thrust of her shoulders, Ms. Snow slammed Abigail's face into the console. Abigail bounced off, her face as bloody as Lucas's, and pushed herself to the side swinging her arm at Ms. Snow. But she was a moment too late and couldn't avoid the kick to her abdomen. Abigail fell to her knees. In the next moment, Ms. Snow had Abigail in a choke hold.

"What the hell," shouted Lucas as he yanked Ms. Snow off Abigail and shoved her aside. "What's gotten into you? What the hell are you doing?" He glared at her as drops of blood started dripping from his nose.

"Gary," Margo said, feeling him beside her. She didn't take her eyes off the panting Ms. Snow and spoke in an undertone. "She's no longer herself. Do you have a sedative of some sort that you could get ready?"

Gary didn't ask for an explanation but nodded and disappeared back into medbay.

As Margo eyed Ms. Snow, she remembered what Peggy had

told her about how Nigel had lately been implanting chips in the brains of his employees. Like Amar, Ms. Snow must also have had a chip implanted in her head. Ms. Snow was no longer Ms. Snow.

"Lucas, it's not 'what's gotten into her'. It's *who*."

"Score one for the bug girl," said Ms. Snow. Nigel West had taken her over.

"What the hell are you talking about?" Lucas demanded, keeping his eye on the two woman as he gave Abigail a hand regaining her feet.

"I started installing backdoors into all my employees a couple years back." Ms. Snow bragged, pointing at the back of her head. "Who knew that even the staff who fail me could still prove to be so useful!"

"Lucas, please tell me you don't also have a Conglomerate chip?" asked Margo. She winced when she looked at him. His nose was clearly broken again, and he looked horrified.

"No," he said, shaking, his head. "When the hell did you wake up?"

Margo ignored his question, keeping her focus on the hijacked Ms. Snow as she slowly advanced towards her. She saw Lucas and Abigail advancing from behind, but Ms. Snow saw the disadvantage of her position and moved, putting a wide workstation between herself and her three enemies.

"Why come here, Nigel?" Margo asked, giving Lucas and Abigail a pointed look, her eyes darting to medbay and back at them, trying to communicate with her eyes that Gary had gone to get a sedative.

"To kill you, my dear," he said. "You are causing too much trouble. Playing with you isn't fun anymore."

Every screen in the Centre Module suddenly came to life, flashing an image of Nigel II's face. The images laughed in unison with Ms. Snow. The laugh was eerie and sent a shiver up Margo's spine.

She saw Gary slip out of the medbay. He glanced at her

and nodded, then started creeping along the wall in Ms. Snow's direction. Margo also saw Lucas and Abigail glance at each other and she knew they understood her and Gary's intentions.

"Why don't you just leave us alone?" asked Margo, when the Nigels flashed off. She moved to the side to keep Nigel's gaze away from Gary. Abigail and Lucas, their faces bloody, stood near Margo.

"Leave you alone?" Nigel deliberately glanced at Gary, who froze. "Don't think I don't know what you're up to," he said, then gave his attention back to the three people in front of him. "You all have something I want."

"What could we possibly have that you want?" demanded Abigail.

Margo knew what Nigel wanted.

"The boy should never have been left with his mother." When Gary took a step towards him, he turned in his direction. "Tsk, tsk, tsk." Nigel waved an admonishing finger in Gary's direction. Then he looked back at Margo. "Bug girl, you don't have long to live."

Nigel abruptly turned and fled up the stairs with panther like quickness. On the catwalk, he turned and looked down at them. "You can't catch me," he said in a taunting childish tone.

Abigail charged up the stairs after him with Margo on her heels. "He's headed to the algal generator's control room!" Abigail shouted. "The door to that room is airtight!"

Ms. Snow turned to flee, but this time Abigail was faster. She launched herself at him. Her moving mass should have been enough to knock the lanky Ms. Snow to the ground. But Nigel only staggered, leveraging Abigail's forward motion into a rolling somersault that brought them both back to their feet with Abigail's lower back pressed against the catwalk's railing.

Ms. Snow's body weight trapped Abigail against the barrier while her hands squeezed Abigail's throat. Abigail, her upper body arched backwards over the railing, clawed at her assailant's hands, her actions futile and ineffective. "Stay back!" Ms. Snow shouted at Margo. "Or she's dead."

"Let her go. We can come to some sort of agreement," said Margo, pausing at the top of the stairs.

"You see, the chips have other highly useful advantages." Nigel spoke in a casual voice as if he was performing some simple household task. "I can flood Lucy Snow's system with adrenalin, giving her superhuman strength."

Margo took another step towards them.

"You want me to let her go?" Nigel raised one of Ms. Snow's eyebrows.

"Yes."

"Okay." Nigel shoved Abigail over the railing.

Abigail's arms flailed in a last desperate attempt to grab hold of something, but nothing was in reach. She fell, landing with a sickening thud on her back atop of one of the workstation consoles below. Margo stared at Abigail in horror, meeting Lucas's equally horrified gaze as Gary rushed over to Abigail.

"Oops," said Nigel, grinning at Margo.

Margo launched herself towards him, dropping her shoulder at the last minute and driving it into his gut. The impact reverberated through her. As Nigel doubled over and took a step back, Margo launched an uppercut at his chin. His head snapped back, and for a moment she throught he would go down. Instead, he recovered his balance and laughed.

"So you want to play some more, do you?" he taunted as he lunged forward. Catching Margo off-guard, he threw her down against the grill of the catwalk right above the stairs, almost knocking the wind out of her. In the same moment that Nigel moved in to shove her down the stairs, she rolled to the side against the wall. Seeing that she was no longer vulnerable, Nigel turned and ran to the door to the algal generator. He opened it and disappeared within.

Struggling to catch her breath and wishing she had the stamina and fitness of Ash Jones, Margo pushed herself to her feet and ran to the door, but it wouldn't open. Nigel must've barred it with something. Just then, all the screens flashed a laughing Nigel II again.

"Bye, bye, now," the replicated face said.

The door to the airlock anteroom suddenly slammed shut as if a gust of wind had caught it and then the lights went off. The only illumination came from sunlight filtering through the suspended chlorella tanks in the ceiling, casting the room in a green glow.

"Oh, crap," said Margo.

Chapter Forty-Four

With her fists, Margo thumped the door out of frustration. She heard the squeal of something heavy being moved as Nigel placed another barricade inside the door. Giving up, Margo hurried down the stairs, joining Gary and Lucas beside Abigail. Gary had his doctor's bag open beside him and had just given Abigail a shot of something.

"Can we move her?" asked Lucas.

"Yes. Her back isn't broken, but she's suffered severe damage. Get the stretcher and neck brace from the medbay."

"That ass is going to cut off our air supply and suffocate us," said Abigail, without moving from where she landed.

Margo was relieved Abigail still had her sassy attitude.

"Don't talk, Abigail. I need you to stay still," said Gary.

Lucas rushed back into the medbay and returned with a stretcher and the brace. "We need to get her in the rover before Nigel traps us in here," he said.

Margo held Abigail's head still while Gary slipped on the brace, immobilizing Abigail's neck and head. While the two men moved Abigail onto the stretcher, Margo went to open the airlock door.

The wheel didn't turn. Putting her weight into it, she tried to jerk the door open. Nothing happened—Nigel had them trapped.

"We can't get out," she said as a knot of fear formed inside her.

"Is that the only exit?" asked Gary.

"The other exit is the door Nigel just went through," said Lucas, his voice an unpleasant nasal tone.

"We can't just let that dickwad win," said Abigail, her eyes darting to each of them in a challenge to defy her.

"The wormhole is going to close," said Margo. "Eventually. We can wait him out. He's not going to want to be trapped here when the wormhole closes."

"Doesn't he run the organization in control of the wormhole?" asked Lucas.

"But it can't stay open forever," said Margo trying to remember if she'd seen a time limit to how long the wormhole could stay open when she'd been Amar. "She was sure she hadn't."

From somewhere in the duct work above, a fan started running—Nigel was sucking out their air.

"We're gonna run out of air before the damn wormhole closes," predicted Abigail.

"Not helpful," Margo said.

"I'm going to look for a crowbar and pry the doors apart," said Lucas.

"Wait," said Margo, looking up the algal ducts. "Let's think this through. Won't he kill himself by sucking the air out?"

"The algal room is on a separate ventilation loop," said Abigail, the hard edge that usually characterized her voice gone.

Gary frowned over at Margo. "If we could shut down the comms link and eject Nigel's consciousness from Lucy's head, would that stop him?"

Margo looked up at the giant tubes running across the ceiling. They were designed to move the algae in and out of

Thesan's perpetual sunlight to optimize oxygen production—which meant they all led to the outside roof. "It just might. In fact, it might even leave him brain dead back wherever he is."

"Bonus!" said Abigail.

Looks like the painkiller has kicked in. Margo raised her eyebrows at Gary. In this new state of emergency, he didn't seem mad anymore. Although, he was probably only distracted looking after his latest patient. "What if we opened one of these tubes?" Margo asked Lucas, pointing up. "There's a door on the roof that would give us access to the other section, right?"

"Don't wreck my terraforming gear," pleaded Abigail. "If you blow a hole in the duct, the water will pour all over this pristine equipment."

Lucas and Margo ignored Abigail and sprinted up the stairs. "The pipes are clear aluminum," Lucas said, staring upwards. "How would we break them open?" Although his nose had stopped bleeding, he was breathing heavily, partly due to the broken nose, partly due to the air in the Centre Module already getting thin.

"Shape charge," said Margo, whirling and heading back down the stairs and into one of the store rooms. *There had to be explosives in here.* When Lucas joined her, she added, "The explosives won't get through the airlock doors—too thick. The algal generator pipes are aluminum, like you said, and much thinner."

Lucas was nodding, onboard with her plan. "We get into the tube, we get onto the roof." Lucas looked alarmed. "There's breathable air on the valley floor here, but will there be breathable air on the roof?"

"I'm positive there will be," said Margo.

"Okay, so once we're on the roof, I'll disable the comms link." Lucas held up a hand when he saw Margo about to argue. "I want it to be done right so that I can get it running again later. I'm going up with you, Margo." His voice held a note that said, last time you did a task that I should've done; this time I'm doing it.

"Okay,"

Lucas nodded, satisfied. "So, even if the wormhole is still open, with our comms link down, Nigel can't communicate through it. But will that fix the virus problem?"

"One thing at a time, Lucas. Hey, can you and Gary move Abigail into the medbay?" she asked as she continued rooting through the cabinets marked with a hazardous symbol. "We'll have to take cover in there when I set off the charge."

Lucas hurried out of the room.

In a bottom bin, she finally found the explosives she was looking for. She grabbed two shape charges and detonators—one to open a bottom pipe, and the second to open the roof once she'd crawled through the clear pipe. At the kitchen counter, Margo set up both charges with the detonators. She looked up at the pipes overhead then looked back down at her explosives. Hopefully, they would open a hole wide enough for them to get through.

"Shouldn't we use those to open the airlock door?" asked Gary, joining her at the counter. "Then we could just drive away in the rover."

"No, the airlock doors are too thick. Besides, we have a chance to end Nigel here and now."

Margo picked up one of her prepared explosives and ran up the stairs and onto the catwalk. The ring of her feet against the metal grill sounded loud in the now quiet space. She climbed up on the lower bar of the railing to reach the closest tube. After setting up the charge at one of the pipe junctions, she turned the remote detonator on. Taking the other half of the detonator, she ran back down, grabbing the second prepared charge off the kitchen counter as she joined the others in the medbay. Her chest was heaving with the exertion in the thinning air.

"Are you sure this is a good idea?" asked Gary, standing

beside Abigail. Margo could see how he was working hard to breathe. The air was running out.

"Only if breathing is a good idea." She said as she pressed the button on the detonator.

A loud thump reverberated through the room, followed by the sound of rushing water. Margo poked her head out of the medbay and watched water from the algal generator duct gush from the gap in the pipe. The green liquid sloshed across the computer consoles below. At the same time the air took on an aquarium odour, it became immediately easier to breathe as the oxygenated water released its gas into the air. Water soon covered the entire main level a couple of centimetres deep.

When the tubes had emptied, Margo turned to Lucas. "I'll need you to boost me up."

Lucas and Margo headed out of the medbay.

"Aren't you afraid of heights?" said Lucas, as they jogged up the stairs.

"Yes, but no longer debilitated by them," Margo answered, remembering how Nigel had tried to frighten her, "when he created the virtual reality, playing on her fear of heights."

They both looked up at the jagged edges of the splayed tubing. "Give me a boost," Margo said.

Lucas laced his fingers together to create a platform for her. Margo put a foot on his hand and he lifted her until she could squirm her way into the tube. She fit—barely, but the unpleasant stink in the tube made her gag. *Good thing Lucas wasn't any larger than her.*

Holding the remaining shaped charge in one hand, she wiggled forward on her elbows.

"You okay in there?" asked Lucas, his voice echoing through the tube.

"Peachy," she answered.

Propelling herself forward by wedging her body against the walls, she followed the slippery tube up towards the light. At the top, it widened out into a large shallow tank. Margo continued pushing herself forward until she was directly under the sky. Then she fixed the charge to the ceiling.

With the extra space in the tank, she was able to turn around and head back down the tube to where Lucas was waiting for her on the cat walk. He helped her down, then the two of them pressed themselves against the wall.

"Here goes," she said, pushing the button on the detonator. This time the sound was muffled.

"It'll be bright up there, but at least Sol is up and not Helios. I checked," said Lucas.

With Lucas' help, Margo climbed back into the tube and wiggled her way up to the tank. Lucas was able to pull himself up and followed behind, his breathing laboured and loud in the confined space thanks to his broken nose.

At the top, the tank had splayed out from the explosion, granting them easy access to the roof.

Chapter Forty-Five

Margo climbed out onto the roof and pushed herself up to her feet. Her whole body, including her boots, were covered in algae slime, which made keeping her footing challenging. The ring of rock formations rose high around the Central Module and was cast in the warm glow from Sol. The air was cold, at least minus twenty and the temperature was probably dropping. She wasn't dressed for the cold and knew her wet clothing would soon start to freeze.

She had known there was enough oxygen to breathe while on the valley floor. But—despite what she'd said to Lucas—she hadn't actually been certain that there would be enough oxygen on the roof of the Central Module. Thankfully her lungs filled with perfectly breathable air.

After she'd taken two deep breaths, Lucas pulled himself up onto the roof beside her. He turned, looking at the smooth expanse of the roof. A parabolic dish taller than them stood out to the left, at its base was a large, closed box.

"That's the main comms," said Lucas pointing. "I'll shut it down. You figure out where Nigel went." Without waiting for her reply, he started moving across the roof towards the comms dish, immediately slipping and falling. "Bloody hell," he muttered, rising and walking more carefully.

In the opposite direction was a small structure containing a few windows and a closed door—an observation room. She realized it must also contain the access hatch out of the terraforming section. *Is Nigel out here or still down in the control room?* She looked around, but couldn't see him and there were few places to hide. Margo assumed he was still down below. Cognizant of her now frozen, algae covered boots, she stepped carefully towards the opening. Her ears were starting to hurt from the cold.

The door opened outwards, and it opened easily, its metal handle cold on her hands. She stepped just inside to see the hatch leading down below was open. As she looked down the tube-like hole, she saw the built-in ladder extending to a space below. *Dare I go down?*

The open door suddenly slammed against her side, knocking her off balance. As she fell, she realized Nigel must have hidden crouched outside the observation room. She rolled to the side and back onto the roof.

Kicking out, she made contact with Nigel's shin. In his effort to regain his footing, he skidded on a patch of frozen algae, giving Margo just enough time to get back on her feet.

The slick wetness she'd tracked up from the chlorella tank had spread across the roof. It was already frozen, adding another layer of slickness to the flat roof. Margo shivered, both with cold and from seeing Nigel's mad gaze though Ms. Snow's eyes.

Margo and Nigel started circling each other, neither of them willing to move quickly on the slippery surface.

When Nigel made Ms. Snow grin, Margo feigned a frightened look, then leapt forward and grabbed Ms. Snow's jacket. She punched her in the face, but her blow seemed ineffectual as

Nigel-slash-Ms. Snow shoved Margo aside. They both lost their balance and fell, rolling towards the edge of the roof.

In the nick of time, Margo stopped herself from tumbling off the edge. She scrambled to her feet and turned just as Nigel also regained Ms. Snow's footing.

"Hang in there, Margo! I've almost got it," shouted Lucas.

Nigel glanced at Lucas then let his gaze linger on Margo as he grinned. "Well, bug girl, I'll be seeing you soon." With that, he turned and took a swan dive off the edge of the roof. Margo lunged forward as if to grab him, but she was too far away.

"Comms are down!" shouted Lucas as Margo watched Ms. Snow slam into the ground.

Margo made no move to respond. Her fear of heights forgotten, she stood at the edge and stared at Ms. Snow's unmoving form, her neck bent at an impossible angle. The woman she despised was dead. *Is this the solution I wanted? More importantly, had the comm's shut down before Nigel ejected himself from Ms. Snow's body?*

She heard Lucas approaching, but didn't turn and didn't speak. He came and stood at her side. The two of them stood shoulder-to-shoulder in silence for a moment.

"I tried to stop him." Margo couldn't take her eyes off her former nemesis. Part of her was glad Ms. Snow was gone, *but who would tell the boy his mother was dead?* She rubbed her cold hands against her arms, shivering.

"What are we going to tell Julien?"

"Maybe he already knows," Margo said, remembering the odd things he'd said that had come true.

"Do you think Nigel got out before I shut down the comms?"

"He's a wily one," said Margo, turning to Lucas. "I wouldn't assume anything."

"Then we can expect him to make good on his threat. Eventually, he'll come for the boy."

"Geez, Lucas. Got any other good news you want to share?"

When Lucas remained silent, Margo sighed, then turned and started carefully maneuvering over the slippery roof to the terraforming hatch and the warmth below.

Chapter Forty-Six

Three weeks later...

"Julien is looking better," said Neil, dodging right to avoid Gary's jab.

"The info Margo found... was the key," said Gary, breathing heavily. He dropped his guard and sucked in air. "Man, I'm out of shape!"

"Nah, you just don't want to admit I'm the better boxer," said Neil. "One more round before I let you wimp out."

Gary didn't wait until Neil had his guard up before lunging forward with a punch. Neil sidestepped and got Gary with a back-hand. The gloved hand stung against his cheek, but he didn't let on. Instead, Gary raised his guard and started circling, forcing his brother to cover more ground than him.

"Still having coffee breaks with Margo?" said Neil with a grin.

His brother wasn't tiring like Gary had hoped. Breathing heavily, sweat dripping down his face, Gary made his gloved hands into a T to call a time-out.

Once he caught his breath, Gary said, "I think I need to spend more time in the gym." He started taking off his gloves.

"You didn't answer my question," said Neil. "For a while there I thought the two of you might become a real couple."

"Just because you and Amanda are a happy couple, doesn't mean everyone is destined for the same." Gary turned towards the exit. "Same time tomorrow?"

"Hang on." Neil stepped forward and blocked Gary's way. "Come on, Gary. Talk to me. Everything turned out okay, didn't it? Well, except for Ms. Snow dying. But even Abigail is recovering. Why are you continuing to hold such a grudge against Margo?"

"It's none of your business."

Gary pushed past his brother, using his teeth to undo the laces. He pulled off the gloves and tossed them aside as he walked away. He could feel Neil's gaze boring into his back, but he didn't care. He couldn't talk about how helpless he'd felt when he'd arrived at the Centre Module and seen Margo laying on the examination table. How he'd feared her mind would be lost, leaving her vacant like the man in his mother's ward, or with her beautiful eyes clawed out. An image of that man, empty eye sockets and bloody fingers, resurfaced in his mind. He tried to banish it, but as he entered the Loop, a shudder passed through his body and a lump formed in his throat. He stopped and leaned against the wall, filling his lungs and trying to exhale slowly.

He cared for Margo far more than was good for him. Yes, she'd broken her promise to him, and he was angry about that, but she'd also nearly broken his heart. *I was a fool, letting her get close like that.*

———

Sitting on a bench in the farthest corner of the Hub's garden, Margo could see Gary and Neil boxing behind the clear walls of the colony's gym. She was deliberately hiding behind the branches and leaves and felt comfortable that they weren't aware she was watching.

She and Gary had barely spoken since the day they had returned from the Centre Module. Every day she tried to apologize to him, but he'd rebuffed her.

A flash of red in her peripheral vision tried to get her attention, but she knew not to look. *Those damn imaginary butterflies are everywhere!* Gary was right, there were side effects to projecting her consciousness. *Should I ask him for help with the side effects?* Another butterfly threatened to draw her attention to the green wall. *No, I need him to accept my apology first.* But ever since she'd returned, her mind regularly conjured up a butterfly or two, until she felt there was an infestation of red butterflies on the edges of her vision. She shivered.

Looking back at the brothers, she leaned forward with a frown as Gary suddenly stopped boxing. The twins appeared deep in conversation.

"There you are," said Lucas, sitting down on the bench beside her. "I've been looking for you."

"Uh-huh," said Margo, pretending that she wasn't watching Gary. She saw him storm off and couldn't stop herself from being deeply curious about what had set him off.

Sighing, she shifted her focus on Lucas.

"Good news, I just got off the radio with Ash Jones. The *Staffelwalze* is making good time. They should arrive in a few weeks. They managed to transfer the complete Peggy Plum AI before going through the wormhole. Peggy should be able to root out our virus here."

"But she won't have Camila's face."

"I know." Lucas was quiet for a moment and Margo ignored another red butterfly that wasn't really there. "From what Ash has been telling me, Peggy is the most advanced AI she's ever seen. Having her take over the computers here will be best for the colony. Those Nigel II's won't stand a chance against her."

"I suppose that's good news," said Margo, still wondering if she'd made the right choice inviting Peggy. Part of Margo suspected Peggy had her own agenda.

"The *Staffelwalze's* arrival is going to change things around here," said Lucas. Just then Amanda and Gan's wife, Lily, walked through the Hub deep in conversation with each other. "We're creating our own newcomers as well." Lucas nodded towards the two women. "Both Amanda and Lily are pregnant."

"Yeah, I heard."

"We're going to have to start building the spoke greenhouses to accommodate everyone."

"Now that Gan's finished repairing my lab, I've moved back. You can give my apartment to the newcomers," said Margo.

"I thought you and Gary were getting together?" said Lucas.

Margo looked at him and raised an eyebrow.

"Hey, I wasn't meaning to pry."

"I think whatever we briefly had is broken," said Margo in a flat, disappointed tone.

Lucas was silent for a moment, then said, "Abigail and Hannah are moving out to the Centre Module to repair it and start terraforming. Abigail sounds keen on trying to plant some cold hardy rye in that valley."

"Have you heard anything from the other colonies? Either from *Settler* I or II?"

Lucas shook his head. "No one has responded to my calls." He looked down at his hands and frowned. "When the ship gets here, we should go look for survivors."

"Yeah, I'm with you on that," said Margo, even though she knew it was unlikely anyone was left out there for them to find. If they weren't answering the comms...

"With new people joining the colony, and with the risk of retaliation from The Conglomerate, we need to start thinking seriously about our security," said Lucas.

"That would be a good idea." Margo said, more out of politeness than interest. *Why had Gary stormed off? What had he and Neil been talking about?*

"To that end, I want you to take on the role of security chief."

"What?" Margo faced Lucas, wide-eyed. "Why me?"

Lucas held up the hand that only had three fingers, and counted off, "One, I trust you; two, you've saved us more than once already, which shows you can think on your feet; three, Abigail doesn't intimidate you; and four..." He looked at the stub of his pinky finger in amusement. "Well, aren't those three sufficient reasons for you to say yes?"

Thanks for reading!

Are you wondering how things will go when the insurgents from the moon arrive? Is anyone left on the other two colonies?

Please sign up for my newsletter here (http://jeannettebe-dard.com/) to get news about the next books in the series and some bonus goodies.

If you enjoyed this book, please take a moment to leave a quick review. As an independent author, reader reviews help build awareness for this series.

Acknowledgments

In no particular order I'd like to thank: Christine, Alana, Amy, Corinne, Chris and my Mom for being kind enough to provide feedback on early drafts. To Gavin for giving me time to write and enduring hearing me talk about it.

About the Author

By day I'm a scientist, by night I write science fiction. I have hard drives clogged with ideas and outlines—sometimes they dissolve into ones and zeros, but sometimes they coalesce to form an entire novel. My stories are filled with action and adventure where something always blows up, usually in the first fifty pages.

You can connect with me here: http://jeannettebedard.com/

www.ingramcontent.com/pod-product-compliance
Lightning Source LLC
Chambersburg PA
CBHW031611100726
47898CB00006B/1737